PRAISE FOR
THE ALCHEMIST'S CODE

"The even more intriguing sequel to *The Alchemist's Apprentice* (2007) is a mystery solved by the clairvoyant and sage Nostradamus and his apprentice, Alfeo Zeno . . . Duncan's alternate late-Renaissance Venice is wonderfully drawn and quite believable."   —*Booklist*

PRAISE FOR
THE ALCHEMIST'S APPRENTICE

"Brimming with wit and low-key charms; neither aficionados nor newcomers will be disappointed."
                              —*Kirkus Reviews* (starred review)

"The occult is a grace note in this cynical whodunit, juicy with period detail."   —*Entertainment Weekly*

"This book is fun . . . There's humor and adventure, mystery and magic, all rolled up in one package . . . *The Alchemist's Apprentice* can be enjoyed by both mystery lovers and fantasy fans."   —*SFRevu*

"Duncan mingles arch fantasy and a whodunit plot in this alternate version of old Venice . . . Nostradamus and Alfeo's adventures provide more amusement than chills in this charming farce, which comments lightly on class prejudice, political chicanery, and occult tomfoolery."   —*Publishers Weekly*

"Dave Duncan's wit shows a distinctive intelligence, a clear-eyed vision that's both irreverent and astute."   —*Locus*

"Duncan's latest novel launches a new series set in an alternate Venice and filled with the author's customary touches of humor, light satire, and fast-paced action. [Duncan] shows his mastery of both storytelling and character building."
                                              —*Library Journal*

continued . . .

ACCLAIM FOR DAVE DUNCAN AND HIS PREVIOUS WORK

"Dave Duncan knows how to spin a ripping good yarn."
—SF Reviews.net

"Duncan is an exceedingly finished stylist and a master of world building and characterizations." —*Booklist*

"Dave Duncan is one of the best writers in the fantasy world today. His writing is clear, vibrant, and full of energy. His action scenes are breathtaking, and his skill at characterization is excellent." —*Writers Write*

"Duncan excels at old-fashioned swashbuckling fantasy, maintaining a delicate balance between breathtaking excitement, romance, and high camp in a genre that is easy to overdo." —*Romantic Times*

"Duncan can swashbuckle with the best, but his characters feel more deeply and think more clearly than most, making his novels . . . suitable for a particularly wide readership."
—*Publishers Weekly* (starred review)

"An enormously clever and impressive reshuffle, whether you regard the final twist as a brilliantly contrived sleight or an outrageous swindle: for panache, style, and sheer storytelling audacity, Duncan has few peers."
—*Kirkus Reviews* (starred review)

THE
ALCHEMIST'S
PURSUIT

DAVE DUNCAN

ACE BOOKS, NEW YORK

THE BERKLEY PUBLISHING GROUP
Published by the Penguin Group
Penguin Group (USA) Inc.
375 Hudson Street, New York, New York 10014, USA
Penguin Group (Canada), 90 Eglinton Avenue East, Suite 700, Toronto, Ontario M4P 2Y3, Canada
(a division of Pearson Penguin Canada Inc.)
Penguin Books Ltd., 80 Strand, London WC2R 0RL, England
Penguin Group Ireland, 25 St. Stephen's Green, Dublin 2, Ireland (a division of Penguin Books Ltd.)
Penguin Group (Australia), 250 Camberwell Road, Camberwell, Victoria 3124, Australia
(a division of Pearson Australia Group Pty. Ltd.)
Penguin Books India Pvt. Ltd., 11 Community Centre, Panchsheel Park, New Delhi—110 017, India
Penguin Group (NZ), 67 Apollo Drive, Rosedale, North Shore 0632, New Zealand
(a division of Pearson New Zealand Ltd.)
Penguin Books (South Africa) (Pty.) Ltd., 24 Sturdee Avenue, Rosebank, Johannesburg 2196,
South Africa

Penguin Books Ltd., Registered Offices: 80 Strand, London WC2R 0RL, England

This is an original publication of The Berkley Publishing Group.

This is a work of fiction. Names, characters, places, and incidents either are the product of the author's imagination or are used fictitiously, and any resemblance to actual persons, living or dead, business establishments, events, or locales is entirely coincidental. The publisher does not have any control over and does not assume any responsibility for author or third-party websites or their content.

Copyright © 2009 by Dave Duncan.
Cover art by Jim Griffin.
Cover design by Judith Lagerman.

PRINTING HISTORY
Ace trade paperback edition / March 2009

Library of Congress Cataloging-in-Publication Data

Duncan, Dave, 1933–
    The alchemist's pursuit / Dave Duncan.—1st ed.
        p. cm.
    ISBN 978-0-441-01678-5
    1. Nostradamus, 1503–1566—Fiction. 2. Alchemists—Fiction. 3. Astrologers—Fiction.
4. Courtesans—Crimes against—Fiction. 5. Murder—Investigation—Fiction. 6. Venice
(Italy)—Fiction. I. Title.

PR9199.3.D847A8 2009
813'.54—dc22   2008049489

PRINTED IN THE UNITED STATES OF AMERICA

10 9 8 7 6 5 4 3 2 1

THE
ALCHEMIST'S
PURSUIT

1

"This doesn't make any sense," I said. "What use is it?" I saw at once that I had asked a bad question. My master was glaring at me.

He had spent all morning instructing me in numerology—gematria, isopsephy, and similar thrilling pastimes. He had quoted from the Kabbalah, Pythagoras, Johannes Trithemius of Sponheim, Hermes Trismegistus, Heinrich Cornelius Agrippa, Saint John the Divine, and his own celebrated uncle, the late Michel de Nostredame, marking critical passages that I was now required to memorize. He had set me a dozen problems to work out in my free time, if I ever got any.

And I had just implied that he had been wasting his time and mine.

I never know from one hour to the next what he will tell me to do: cast horoscopes, run errands, blend potions, help him with patients, rescue damsels, memorize pages of ancient mumbo jumbo, cast spells, decrypt letters, massage the doge's lumbosacral musculature, or fight for my life—all in the day's work. Apprentices do as they are told; they never ask why.

Yesterday it had been sortilege. Today it was numerology. The real problem was the excess of rheum in his hips, which the current February weather had aggravated until now he was barely able to walk. He had needed help from Bruno, our porter, just to make it out of bed and across the *salone* to his favorite chair in the atelier. There he had refused any breakfast and set out to stuff me with fifteen hundred years of numerology before noon as a way of taking his mind off hurting and growing old. I had run back and forth at his bidding, doing calculations at the desk, fetching musty tomes from the great wall of books, squatting alongside his chair while we went over the texts, word by incomprehensible word. I admit that he never complains of his infirmities, but when they trouble him he complains massively about everything else. I had never known him crabbier than that morning. It was past noon, dinnertime.

"Sense?" he snarled. "Sense? You mean it does not appear to make sense to *you*! Do you claim more intelligence than San Zorzi or Pythagoras? Can you concede that smarter or better informed persons might make *sense* of it?"

"Of course, master."

"For instance, suppose you explain to me how the doge is elected?"

Doge? So far as I knew, our prince was still in reasonable health for his age. I had updated his horoscope just a month ago, and it had shown no need to elect Pietro Moro's successor for several years yet. The way Venice chooses its head of state is certainly madder than any numerology, but I felt the Maestro was playing unfairly by throwing it in my face.

"The patricians of the Great Council, but only those over thirty years of—"

Thunk . . . thunk . . .

Saved! Seldom have I been happier to hear our front door knocker. I rose, relieved to straighten my knees. The Maestro scowled, but greeting visitors is another of my jobs. I went out into the *salone* and opened the big door.

The visitor was unfamiliar, wearing a gondolier's jerkin

and baggy trousers in house colors I did not recognize, but his sullen, resentful expression was all too typical of his trade. He was taller, wider, and older than I.

"For Doctor Nostradamus," he said, thrusting a letter at me. That was the name written on the paper, but he wouldn't know it unless he had been told.

"I'll give it to him directly. Wait for the reply." I shut the door on him and went back into the atelier.

"Read it," the Maestro growled impatiently. He is old and shrunken, but that day he seemed more wizened than ever, huddled in his black physician's robe, clutching a cane in one hand, with another lying nearby, balanced on a column of books. Normally he walks with the aid of a long and elaborately decorated staff, but lately he had been forced into using two canes. He dyes his goatee brown and days of neglect had turned the roots to the same bright silver as the wisps of hair dangling from under his bonnet.

I broke the wax and unfolded the parchment. "It's from the manservant of *sier* Giovanni Gradenigo, written in an appalling scrawl and signed 'Battista' in the same hand. He begs you to attend his master in haste because other doctors have given up hope of his recovery."

The Maestro winced at the thought of going anywhere. "He's no patient of mine."

"No, master. *Sier* Lorenzo Gradenigo commissioned a horoscope from you four years ago, but he belongs to another branch of—"

"I know that! Tell him to call Modestus."

"The letter is from the Palazzo Gradenigo. Those Gradenigos are richer than the Pharaohs ever were."

The Maestro winced again, this time at the thought of the fee he was losing. Where money is concerned, if he can't take it with him he's not going. His medical practice has dwindled to a few very wealthy or important persons and he rarely gets called out any more, but this attack had him so crippled that he would be unable even to stand at a patient's bedside. "Do as I say!"

"Yes, master."

I went over to the desk and penned a quick note, recommending Isaia Modestus of the Ghetto Nuovo as the second-best doctor in Venice. I signed the Maestro's name to it, sealed it with his signet, and took it out to Surly, who scowled at the *soldo* I offered him.

"It's as much as I ever get," I told him cheerfully.

"I can see why." With that parting sneer, he took the coin and slouched off down the marble staircase. He ought to know by now that the grander a palace is, the worse the chance of a decent tip.

I locked the door behind him, but I paused outside the atelier because I saw Mama Angeli rolling along the *salone* toward me without a glance at all the magnificent Titian and Tintoretto paintings, the giant statues, and the shining Murano mirrors she was passing. She carried a burping baby on her shoulder, while a squalling toddler staggered in her wake. She has lots more that came from where those came from— and a flourishing herd of grandchildren besides—but she is the finest cook in Venice, and when I say "rolling" I am not exaggerating much.

She glowered at me, chins raised in anger. "My *Filetti di San Pietro in Salsa d'Arencia* will be ruined."

I groaned and rumbled simultaneously. "The Ten could use you. None of their torturers can touch you for pure sadism. I'll see what I can do."

That wasn't much. I got no further than the first syllable of Mama's name.

"Sit!" The Maestro jabbed a gnarled finger at the floor by his chair.

"Yes, master." Instead of sitting on the floor as suggested, I planted myself on one of the piles of books that stood around his chair. I wasn't seriously worried that otherwise he might order me to roll over so he could scratch my tummy, but the thought did occur to me. I would probably have to re-shelve every one of the books before I got any dinner, if I ever did get any dinner. Nostradamus forgets all about food at times. He could outfast a camel.

"Now," he said, screwing up his face in a truly hideous grimace, "explain to an ignorant foreign-born how the Venetians elect their doges."

"The Great Council starts by drawing lots," I said. "That's called sortilege." Probably almost all the twelve hundred or so eligible patricians will attend for a ducal election, because they happen rarely. "Each one draws a ball out of the pot and thirty of those bear a secret mark." The Maestro must have been told all this sometime and he never forgets anything. I couldn't see what it had to do with numerology. Or my dinner.

"Then they draw lots to reduce the thirty to nine." I had been hoping to eat quickly and pay a brief but possibly rewarding visit to my adored Violetta, who lives in the house next door, Number 96. She works nights and I work days, so the noon break is our best chance to be together. I had not seen her for three days and was missing her sorely. "Then the nine elect forty. The forty are reduced by lot to—"

Thunk . . . Thunk . . . Thunk . . .

I smiled woodenly and went out to see.

And gape. Poised like an alighting angel on the landing outside was the most breathtakingly gorgeous exciting ravishing woman in the entire world. The perfection of her face, the lightning speed of her wit, and the enslaving madness provoked by her peerless body inspire men to pay hundreds of ducats for a night with her. Sometimes more than that. She was, of course, Violetta herself, my beloved, the finest courtesan in Venice.

Violetta will sometimes provide the Maestro with strategic advice on the wealthy, for it is among them that she spends her evenings and finds her patrons. I visit her whenever I can; she *never* comes calling on me.

"I'm busy," I whispered. Whatever his other frailties, the Maestro has ears like a bat. I rolled my eyes in the direction of the atelier.

"It is wonderful to see you again, Alfeo." Violetta sighed a low-pitched, heart-stopping sigh. She had automatically slid into her Helen-of-Troy persona, which meant that she wanted something; no man can resist Helen. Her voice thrilled like a low note on a cello, and eyelashes fluttered over deep-set eyes promising all the joys of the Prophet's paradise. "But you mustn't try to distract me, you lovely man. Later I'll have lots of time for whatever it is you want. I came to consult Maestro Nostradamus."

"Consult? If you need your horoscope cast, I'll be more than—"

"No. I want him to find somebody for me." She extended a hand, and I perforce offered my arm, for she was wearing her platform soles, which make her considerably taller then I am. In February her hair lacked the glorious auburn glow that it gains from summer sunshine, but it was coifed, scented, and bejeweled as if for a state banquet. A pearl necklace and low-cut scarlet gown shone through the open front of a floor-length miniver robe. Altogether, dressing her would have cost a duke's ransom and taken at least a couple of hours; she rarely opens her eyes before noon.

I locked the door behind her and escorted her into the atelier. The Maestro was scowling again. There are few people whose company he enjoys at all and he hates to be interrupted, so he ranks unexpected visitors with lice and vipers, even if they bring money with them. Violetta can be an exception because in her Minerva mode she is at least as brilliant as he is, and the idea of an educated woman fascinates him. I hoped she would be a welcome distraction for him in his present mood; his expression suggested that he thought I had sent for her.

"Donna Violetta Vitale, master."

"I can see that. Send her home and you come right back here."

It was my turn to sigh. I had never known him quite this bad.

"I trust I find you well, Doctor?" Violetta said, advancing toward him. But that silvery, flutelike voice belonged to Aspasia, her political and cultural mode, and if anyone could outmaneuver Nostradamus, it was she. She bobbed him a curtsey, then made herself comfortable on one of the two green chairs on the far side of the fireplace. I beat a strategic retreat to the desk in the window, where I was out of the Maestro's sight and could adore Violetta at my leisure. Her eyes are the deep blue of the sea when she is Aspasia. I don't know how she makes these transformations and neither does she; she claims it is not a conscious choice.

"I do not recall inviting you to be seated, woman. Who is this person you want me to find?"

The city regards Nostradamus as an oracle. All sorts of people come asking *Who? Where? When? What?* and sometimes even *How?* or *Why?* questions. Amazingly often, he can answer them, for a price.

"A murderer."

His mouth shrank to a pinhole and his eyes to slits. "You think I'm a common *sbirro?* Any time I have exposed a murderer it has been because I needed to know his identity for some other, more worthy reason." Not true at all, but he likes to think that unmasking criminals is beneath a philosopher's dignity. "Talk to the *Signori di Notte.* Or go directly to the Ten." He dropped his gaze to the book on his lap, believing that he had just ended the conversation.

Violette lobbed a sympathetic glance across at me, who

must live with this. "You have a wonderful wit, *lustrissimo*, or do you really think that the Lords of the Night can catch anything more serious than head colds? This matter will not interest the Council of Ten."

After a moment Nostradamus looked up, frowning. According to what it would have you believe, the Most Serene Republic is governed by the nobility of the Great Council, who elect one another to dozens of courts, councils, and committees, whose mandates overlap so much that every magistrate has some other magistrate watching over him. Our head of state, the doge, is a mere figurehead who can do nothing without the support of his six counselors. This grotesque muddle is justified as necessary for the preservation of freedom and prevention of tyranny.

In practice, the real government is the Council of Ten, whose official mandate is to guard the security of the state, but which meddles in anything it fancies—permissible wages and prices, what clothes may be worn, the way banks operate, so on and on. The Ten certainly include murder within their jurisdiction.

The Maestro eyed his visitor angrily. "The name of the victim?"

"Lucia da Bergamo."

"Your relationship to the deceased?"

Violetta's smiles normally brighten the room, but this one brought enough pathos to make a songbird weep. "She was my mentor."

"She was a . . . courtesan?" That he did not choose one of the word's many vulgar synonyms I found mildly encouraging.

"She was."

"Dying is a hazard of your trade. Women who earn their bread in bed are always at risk. Why should this one be any different?"

I spread my hands and shrugged hugely to tell Violetta

that the case was hopeless. In his present mood, the Maestro would not shift himself to investigate a murdered pope, let alone a courtesan.

She raised a perfectly shaped eyebrow. "She still had all her clothes on, and also her jewels."

That was certainly unusual, and the Maestro took a moment to respond.

"When and where did she die?"

"She was last seen three weeks ago, January fourteenth. Her body was found floating in the lagoon about a week later."

"Bah! What the fish left of her body, you mean. It is impossible! No witnesses, of course? No clues or leads? Has her last customer been identified?"

Stony-faced, Violetta said, "I did not hear the news until three days ago, and some of it only this morning. No to all of your questions."

"Impossible. Ask the recording angel on Judgment Day." He bent to his book again.

"You are the greatest clairvoyant in Europe."

He did not reply.

"Clairvoyance only reveals the future," I said softly. "Not the past."

Violetta ignored my remark. "Lucia left me everything she had, and I will gladly pay it as a reward for the capture and execution of her killer."

The Maestro raised his head like a hound that has scented its quarry. "And how much is that?"

Violetta-Aspasia looked close to tears. "Depending on how much the house sells for, the notary told me he thought it would amount to about 1,470 ducats."

Nostradamus painfully twisted around to stare at me, no doubt wondering if I had stage-managed this conversation. I had no difficulty in looking suitably startled. A courtesan with such a fortune was almost as amazing as another one offering to give it all away. Giorgio, our gondolier, would need a century to earn that much, because his wages are limited by law to his board and fifteen ducats a year.

Obviously Lucia had been a *cortigiana onesta* like Violetta, an honored courtesan, one who entertains men with her wit and culture. Sex is not the least of her attractions, but it is far from the only one and not necessarily the greatest. Men are drawn to Venice from all over Europe by the beauty and skill of our courtesans. The state permits them to ply their trade and then taxes them exorbitantly.

"Alfeo!" Nostradamus snapped.

"Master?"

"Warn Mama that we have a guest for dinner and tell Bruno I need him." Although he rarely displays it, Nostradamus does have a sense of humor; sometimes he can even laugh at himself.

2

The dining room on the upper floor of Ca' Barbolano can seat fifty. The Maestro and I dine there in splendor every day, with silver tableware on damask tablecloths under grandiose Burano chandeliers. I dine, he nibbles. The palace belongs to *sier* Alvise Barbolano, who is richer than Midas and a similar age. The old man lets the Maestro stay on the top floor rent free in return for some trifling services, including business astrological advice, trading clairvoyance, and effective roach poison. The Barbolanos live below us, on the *piano nobile*. Below that are two mezzanine apartments, occupied by the Marciana brothers and their respective families; they are of the citizen class, partners with *sier* Barbolano in an import-export business.

I once suggested to the Maestro that he obtain a chair on wheels, but he does not need it while he has Bruno, who is a mute, a little larger than Michelangelo's *David*. He happily lifted Nostradamus, chair and all, and carried him through to the dining room. He loves to be useful.

And Mama Angeli loves to cook. St. Peter's fish comes from the deep sea especially to bathe in her orange sauce and I marvel that the holy man himself does not descend to sample the result. Even the Maestro ate industriously for several minutes. Violetta has dined with royalty, but she raved about the food and discussed with me the two magnificent Paolo Veronese paintings on the wall. She was still Aspasia, her political mode.

I asked her about Carnival, which had been running since immediately after Christmas, and she began describing some of the better masques and banquets she had attended. Her escorts at such affairs would have paid many ducats for the privilege, whereas I can only take her to the free street shows, and rarely get the chance, because she is so much in demand. Her closets are packed with such a multitude of exotic Carnival costumes that I have never seen her in the same one twice.

Nostradamus quickly grew bored, laid down his fork, and leaned back.

"Tell us about the victim, madonna."

It was criminal to spoil a good meal with such a topic, but Aspasia would never be so crude as to reject her host's conversational lead.

"Lucia was about forty. She retired two years ago and turned her house into a home for street girls anxious to reform. Nuns from Santa Spirito supervised, so that there could be no scandal. The last time she was seen was when she went off in a gondola with a masked man. She had said that they were going to the Piazza to dance."

I decided that I agreed with my master; the case was impossible. It had probably been impossible right from the beginning and after three weeks the trail was ice-cold.

"How did she die?" he asked.

"The notary did not know. He hinted that she was probably a suicide but the *shirri* were calling it murder so she could be buried in hallowed ground."

Who could tell, after the body had spent a week in the lagoon?

"Who found the corpse?" Nostradamus snapped. "Who identified it after so long in the water? Are you completely certain that the dead woman is who you think she was? If she was dragged under by the weight of her clothes she would surface when distension of the corpse buoyed it up, but putrefaction would be well along by then."

Violetta understandably laid down her fork. "I recognized the jewelry when it was shown to me."

"That it was returned at all makes me highly suspicious," the Maestro said angrily. "The first instinct of any Venetian recovering a body is to strip it of valuables. Fishermen, I assume? Bah! They're all rogues. Even the *shirri* would not pass up such an opportunity. Who found the body, and where? Who delivered it to the authorities? How did they locate you to identify the jewels?"

"I do not know, *lustrissimo*. These are things Alfeo could find out for you."

"I have more important things for him to do. Your friend committed suicide. Or she was drunk and fell into a canal."

"Not Lucia."

Nostradamus snorted. "Alfeo, call Bruno. I am going to lie down. See your friend home and come right back. You have work to do." He had been sleeping so badly the last few nights, that he had started taking to his bed in the middle of the day, not his normal practice.

Before I could rise, Violetta turned to look at me and I was startled to see a golden glint in her eyes.

"I become so nervous when I think of this terrible act," she said. "Many ladies in my profession feel the need of a strong, full-time defender. I do believe I shall have to hire a reliable bodyguard."

I said nothing. What she was hinting was the worst of nightmares for me, my greatest fear. I know how to use a sword and if my beloved ever decides that she needs a guardian, I shall be lost. Loving a courtesan is one thing, living off her earnings is another, but I can refuse Violetta nothing. If she wants me as her bravo, then her bravo I must become. Then the Grand Council will order my name struck from the Golden Book, a noble house that has endured for centuries will end, and scores of ancestral ghosts will wail in shame.

The Maestro knew exactly what she meant and scowled at her furiously. Those gold serpent eyes had warned me that he was now dealing with Delilah, who is as deadly as a spiderweb, but he does not know her as well as I do. Delilah can lie like sand on a beach.

"Rubbish. Alfeo, you can have the rest of the afternoon off. Investigate all you want, but be back by curfew."

"I may borrow Giorgio?"

"Yes, yes. Now get me Bruno."

A murder so old, with the corpse half rotted and already buried, with no known motive or witnesses, was a totally impossible assignment, and a wonderful excuse to spend some hours with Violetta. It wasn't quite impossible enough for me to suggest that we just give up and go to her house for a glass or two of wine and a few cantos of the *Divine Comedy*.

Giorgio Angeli is Mama's husband and our gondolier. Since the boat had not been used yet that day, we emerged from the apartment with Giorgio carrying his oar and Corrado, one of his sons, laden with the cushions. The surly boatman in the Gradenigo colors was plodding up the stairs toward us. The look he gave Violetta almost made me draw my rapier to start improving his face.

He handed me another letter, this time addressed to *sier* Alfeo Zeno. I broke the seal.

"Hey! That's for *messer* Zeno!" Surly barked.

"That's me," I said, scanning the text. Normally I dress as an apprentice, which I am. I had changed into something a little fancier so I could wear my sword, but I was still leagues away from what a young noble should wear—a black, floor-length robe if he is already a member of the Grand Council. If he is not, then he is expected to deck himself out in illegal grandeur, far beyond what the sumptuary laws allow. Drab as I appear, I am of noble blood and born in wedlock, the equal of any nobleman in Venice. I just happen to be poor enough to beg alms off seagulls.

"Yes he is," Corrado said, smirking.

The note was brief and written in a very precise and disciplined hand.

Sier *Giovanni Gradenigo is not long for this world and urgently wishes to speak with you. Come at once to Palazzo Gradenigo.*

Fr. Fedele

I do not swear in the presence of ladies, women, or even courtesans. I was tempted to. The first note had not meant what I thought.

"Go," I told the boatman, "and tell Friar Fedele that I am on my way. Giorgio, please hurry."

As men and boy ran off down the stairs, I followed, holding Violetta's arm to steady her.

"Change of plan?" she inquired sweetly.

"Unless you believe in extraordinary coincidences it is," I said. "This must take precedence." I explained about the other note, giving her the wording verbatim.

"Then that wasn't your fault!" she declared. "It was ambiguous and perhaps Battista himself did not understand that his master just wanted to tell Nostradamus something, not consult him as a doctor. The wonder is that a servant can write at all, not that he is unskilled at writing letters."

We passed the great doors to the *piano nobile* and started down the next flight.

"It shouldn't take long," I said. "We can start work on the murder right after."

She smiled—oh, how she can smile! "I must change, anyway. I can't go exploring with you in these clothes. Drop me at my door and pick me up as soon as you have paid your respects to *sier* Giovanni."

By the time we reached the watergate, Giorgio was ready for us and the Gradenigo boat had already gone. I handed Violetta out through the arches and then joined her aboard. It may seem strange to take a boat to go to the house next door, but there is no pedestrian *fondamenta* on our side of the Rio San Remo. There is a narrow ledge, though, along which an agile young man can work his way to the *calle* dividing the two buildings and then on to 96's watergate. Corrado was already well on his way along it, so that he could hand Violetta ashore when she arrived. At his age even a touch of such a woman's fingers is enough to remember, and in his case to brag about to his twin.

It took us only a few minutes to arrive at the Gradenigo palace, which is so large and sumptuous as to make even Ca' Barbolano look so-so. There were at least a dozen gondolas outside the watergate, and about twice as many gondoliers waiting in the loggia, gossiping in threes and fours. Only the rich use two boatmen to a boat, so I did not need the livery and insignia to tell me that a widespread family was gathering for the deathwatch. I noted a couple of boats pulling away, though, and assumed that they were now carrying the news to more distant, or less wealthy, relations.

I was too late.

At the exact moment I stepped ashore, the bell of Santa Maria Gloriosa dei Frari began to toll a few streets away. The bored boatmen made the sign of the cross and then carried on with their talk. They had already been informed of the death.

Had the dying man shared his urgent message with someone else? I had no need to knock, for the door stood open, and an elderly manservant waited there holding a piece of paper. I thought of San Pietro at the Gates greeting Giovanni Gradenigo.

"I am Alfeo Zeno. Friar Fedele sent for me. I have come too late?"

He bowed a smallish bow, frowning at my garb, then glanced down at his list. "Indeed you have, *clarissimo*." He looked behind him, into the grandiose hall. "The friar is coming now."

I walked into the great hall and wished I had time to admire the enormous splendor of marble, glass, and gilt—about a week would do. It all seemed like a monument to human folly in the presence of death, but Gradenigo would have seen it as evidence that he had preserved, and doubtless expanded, the family fortune. They would be reluctant to admit it, but the Venetian aristocracy admires rapacity above all.

Several people were standing around or moving about their business with suitable gravity, but I went straight for the priest, who was obviously leaving. We met halfway between door and staircase; I bowed.

Bareheaded and barefoot, Friar Fedele wore the gray habit of the Order of Friars Minor, with the belt cord dangling at his side tied in the required three knots, representing his vows of poverty, obedience, and chastity. Obedience is an old Venetian virtue that the Great Council enthusiastically preaches to the commonality, but poverty and chastity are rarely popular at any level.

The fringe around his tonsure was brown but his beard was closer to red. He seemed about thirty or so, with a weatherbeaten ascetic face, humorless and arrogant, a face chiseled out of granite, more suited to a Dominican than a Franciscan. Personally I like my clergy to be New Testament, warm and forgiving. One glance at Friar Fedele told you right away that he was straight out of the Book of Judges, all blood, blame, and brimstone. He looked me over, his gaze lingering for a moment on my rapier and dagger.

I held up the letter with his name on it. "I am Zeno, Brother. I fear I have arrived too late."

He nodded. "Do not grieve unduly, Alfeo. He was much confused at the end. I wrote that letter because he insisted and we must humor the dying, but I don't think you would have heard anything of importance. He might not have known you."

"I am sure he would not, because we never met. I assume that he wanted to confide something to my master, Doctor Nostradamus, and asked for me because I am the doctor's aide?"

He gave me the same answer any other slab of granite would—silence.

"Do you know what *messer* Gradenigo wanted to tell my master?"

Fedele shrugged. "I cannot say. He was babbling much of the time."

"He was elderly, I believe."

"He had passed his allotted span, yes."

"But a good man, from all accounts." I believe in being charitable to the dead, lest they come back and haunt me.

"He was a fine Christian, a devoted husband and father, and he served the Republic well. He went peacefully to his reward." Fedele raised his hand to bless me.

I doffed my bonnet. Then I stood up and watched him stride away with his habit swirling around his ankles, bare feet making no sound on the terrazzo. *I cannot say.* Fedele had not said that he did not know. It was an odds-on bet that he knew perfectly well but had been told under the seal of the confessional. I glanced around the hall and decided that now was definitely not the time to pry. Whatever the dead man's problem had been, if anyone knew it, it would keep.

I went back out to the bustling landing stage and had to wait a few minutes before Giorgio was able to slip his boat in close enough for me to board. His oar stroked the water and we were on our way. The Frari bell was still tolling.

"Too late?"

"Too late," I agreed. "The dying man wanted to tell the Maestro something, but he's never been a patient or a client. Why the Maestro? Odd."

"He was a good man, they say." By "they" he meant the other boatmen, who often know more than most people know they know. "He did things for the poor."

Being one of those, I said a prayer for his soul.

Back at Number 96, I disembarked. "The lady said she would be ready when we returned, but don't count on it."

Giorgio grinned and rubbed his trim beard with the back of a hand. He is a small man for a gondolier, stronger than he looks. "It is you I distrust, Alfeo."

"Not today," I said. "Or at least, not yet." I unlocked the bawdy house door and went in. Violetta's apartment is one floor up, and that part of the house is not bawdy, just voluptuous.

3

So where do we start?" she asked as we descended the stairs. She no longer teetered on ten-inch soles. Paint and silks had gone, and she was enveloped in the neck-to-shoe brown dress of a domestic servant. Her magnificent hair was hidden under a shawl that hung to about where her calves must be. Even so, she would catch every male eye within eyeshot.

"With the puzzle, of course," I said.

"Which puzzle?"

"Why her body was not looted of valuables. Which were?"

"Pearl earrings, a gold ring, and a gold brooch with an amber pebble enclosing an insect. That's not to my taste, but worth a lot as a curiosity. Her gown was . . ." She shuddered and tightened her grip on my hand. "I suppose the sea will have ruined it. And she wore a string of pearls worth at least a hundred ducats."

"You are joking!"

"No, I am not! They once belonged to Dogaressa Zilia Dandolo, the wife of Doge Lorenzo Priuli."

I whistled. A murderer leaving such riches on a body made no sense at all.

"She wore all that to go dancing in the Piazza?"

"I wondered that," my love admitted. "I spoke with her maids and the nuns, and they agreed that she seemed quite excited. An old friend was coming for her, she said, but she didn't say who. I know the gown she wore, and it was one that was very special to her. Her client arrived at dusk in a gondola, and he stayed aboard, in the *felze*, so only one of the maids caught as much as a glimpse of him, and all she could say was that he was wearing a mask. Lucia boarded and off they went."

Never to be seen again. Everyone wears a mask at Carnival.

I said, "Perhaps she was murdered on a *fondamenta* somewhere and fell into the canal before the murderer could strip her finery. Where was she found, and where did the finder take her? Or did he just inform the *sbirri* somewhere to go and collect her?"

"The only answer I know is that the morticians were summoned to the *sbirri* office in Castello."

Castello is the eastern end of the city. It gets more than its fair share of floating bodies because they tend to be carried seaward by the tide and found by fishermen.

We found Giorgio sitting in the gondola trading barbs with a group of Marciana lads unloading a boat outside Ca' Barbolano. They were threatening to tell Mama that her husband was waiting for the brothel to open. He seemed to be holding his own quite well, but Giorgio has a prudish streak and would be happy to escape. We boarded and set off to Castello.

Our way led along the little Rio San Remo and then out into the Grand Canal, which was magnificent that fine afternoon, with just enough of a wind to ruffle the blue water. The trading fleets were due to leave soon, so many lighters were heading to the basin to load them, sweeping past us, borne onward by sails or many oars. The scene was lovely, but Violetta was lovelier. I rolled down the blinds on the *felze* so we could do a little preliminary cuddling. Regrettably, her mind was still elsewhere. I wanted Helen and she was hazel-eyed Niobe, the one who mourns.

"He was a good man," she said, "Gradenigo, I mean."

"Not a client?"

"You know I never discuss my patrons. Besides, he was before my time. It will be a huge funeral." Her finger idly drew patterns on my knee. "You didn't discover what he wanted to tell the Maestro?"

"No, but I can try to find out later. Good man how?"

"He gave much to charity. He was a member of the Scuola Grande di San Giovanni Evangelista, and he paid to rebuild one of the chapels in the Frari."

"I don't recall him ever holding office." No one can keep track of all the noblemen in the Great Council, but I try to stay up to date on the inner circle, the fifty or sixty old men who actually run the Republic, rotating the senior offices among themselves.

"He did," my love said sadly. "He was a senator—maybe even one of the Ten—but he withdrew from politics years ago. As I recall, he suffered some bad health and never returned to the *broglio*."

I had never seen her be so morose before, but having a close friend murdered will upset anyone. Like the Maestro, I found it hard to believe that Lucia had been murdered if her finery had not been stolen.

Investigating a mystery with Violetta was almost absurdly easy. *Sbirri* are mostly ignorant, rough men, and if they have ever heard of Nostradamus, they at once suspect black magic. They hassle apprentices on principle. Another reason I stay away from *sbirri* as much as I can is that their offices tend to be dark and smelly places, reeking of centuries of prisoners. Castello's was no different, but we strolled in and

I presented my servant, the dead woman's niece, who was seeking more information about her aunt's sad end.

Violetta-Delilah was emphatically not a male apprentice. She was spring sunshine and very soon had the duty captain almost drooling, with his pupils dilated like water buckets. He was a hulking lunk who kept scratching; the vermin inhabiting jails may have any number of legs.

He insisted on taking down Violetta's name and address, although I noted that the paper went into a pocket in his cloak, which didn't matter because the information she had given did not refer to anyone in particular. He would be happy to tell madonna what he knew, he murmured, leering. He did not need to look up the records, he sighed. He had not been there himself, he whispered, but he had heard it from the other constables. Besides, how could anyone forget a murder victim being delivered by a *senator*?

Violetta clasped her hands to her mouth. "A senator?"

"Senator Marco Avonal. A fine nobleman, to trouble himself with a body."

"And what happened then? She was buried right away?"

He shrugged with an oily don't-trouble-your-pretty-head smile. "The Board of Health insists, madonna. If the body is not recognizable, then we note anything that might help it be identified and call in the morticians. She was laid to rest on the Isola before sunset, and may the Lord have mercy on her soul."

Isola di San Michele is the cemetery island. It would have taken me an hour and an extortionate bribe to have learned as much as Delilah had discovered already.

She stifled a sob. "Amen! So you kept her jewelry to identify her?"

The captain shook his head regretfully. "His Excellency took them and gave us a receipt. You will have to ask him for them."

"They have already been returned to the lady's estate," I said. "Could your comrades tell how she had died?"

He looked at me as if he had forgotten I was there, his pupils contracting sharply. In his opinion, I was exceedingly redundant. "It was very gruesome, because the crabs and the fish had been busy. But, just between us, Captain di Comin is a very clever man, and he noticed that the gristle of the dead woman's windpipe had been crushed. Some of the remaining flesh around her throat—"

Violetta cried out and faked a dizzy spell, so I could whisk her out into the fresh sea breeze. I had assumed she was pretending, but even out on the *fondamenta* she was unusually subdued. That was Niobe showing; as Medea she could have torn the captain apart with a smile on her face.

"You want to know any more?" I asked.

She shivered. "No. It's too horrible to think about. You?"

"No. Now we know how her jewels survived, and that's progress. Let's go and call on the noble gentleman."

"Where to?" Giorgio asked as we boarded.

"We need to locate a Senator Marco Avonal."

"Rio di San Nicolò," Violetta said. "I'll direct you when we get there."

Aha! When we had made ourselves comfortable in the *felze*, I said, "You are acquainted with His Excellency?"

She bit her lip and nodded.

If Avonal was rich enough to be a friend of Violetta's he might also have known an ex-courtesan who had been worth 1,470 ducats. I decided to wait a while before asking questions. We were passing through the Basino di San Marco, but I lowered the curtains, sacrificing the view of the fleet at anchor in the hope of a cuddle with Helen. Alas, my companion was currently Minerva.

"Discovering a body is easier if you know where you left it?"

Minerva is the clever one, but even I had seen that much.

I said, "I always find it so."

"But why would a murderer turn in the body himself, whether he found it by chance or simply fetched it from where he put it?"

"I don't know." I was fairly sure I could think of a reason or two when I did not have to meet the withering gaze of those brilliant gray eyes. "Will you come in with me to see Avonal, if he's home?"

"No."

Chilly silence.

"Dearest, if you want the Maestro's help, or even mine, you will have to be open with us."

She pouted. Aspasia or Medea would still have refused, but Minerva could understand. "Very well. We met when a patron took me to a musical soirée at Avonal's house. I was asked to play the lute, and did. Evidently I impressed him, because a couple of days later he sent a note, asking me for an evening . . . oh, it must be about two years ago. He was not a senator then, just an official in the Salt Office. He took me to a dance in the Palazzo Corner Spinelli. He left early and took me home."

"And stayed the night."

"Of course. He was a skilled and considerate lover. He asked me again, about a month later . . . That time he just wanted sex. I agreed, although lovemaking should be the crowning episode of an enchanting evening, not a scheduled commercial transaction like a haircut. There are plenty of prostitutes for that. He was quite different!"

"Different how?" I asked. I was finding the conversation stressful. The woman I love was telling me about other men in her bed.

"Weird! He was rough and aggressive, almost a different person." She, who is all women by turns, did not seem to notice the irony. "I had to ring the bell."

"What bell?"

She smiled sphinxly. "I have a hidden bellpull by the bed. Antonio came. Avonal drew on him. Antonio disarmed him, snapped his sword over his knee, and threw him out. No, not into the canal. But I shall not come in with you to see His Excellency."

Antonio is the senior bouncer at 96. He is nowhere near as big as Bruno, the Maestro's porter, but a sight more blood-curdling, with a forked beard and the scarred face of a life-long fighter.

"Was Avonal one of Lucia's patrons also?"

"I don't know. He could have been. She had retired, but that doesn't mean . . . Maybe not completely retired. If she was asked nicely." At that point, Minerva inexplicably yielded place to Helen, threw her arms around me, and kissed me until my hair smoked.

"Mm . . ." I said when I was allowed a chance to breathe. "I do think this case is insoluble. The best thing we can do is go home and discuss it."

"Later." She smiled a promise and cuddled a little closer.

"I love you," I said. "You rule my heart as *la Serenissima* rules the seas."

"Oh, really? That would have been a much better compliment a hundred years ago."

And so on. Banter was very enjoyable but did not help me plan a strategy for calling on Senator Avonal. I knew nothing about him except that his name was uncommon and nobles from small clans rarely win election to senior offices. He must be personally impressive or extremely rich or both. Violetta was not much better informed, unable to tell me what other posts he had held, or what allies had helped him win his seat in the Senate.

The Senate meets three or four afternoons a week, but I had not heard the *dei Pregadi* bell in the Piazza ring to summon it, so he might be home. Or not. Having no official standing, I cannot command an audience with anyone, and

Avonal was neither a patient of Nostradamus's nor a client for astrological counsel. If he were not home I should have to leave my name; if he were home he might refuse to see me, and either way I might never get a chance to speak with him at all. Proper procedure would be for me to go home and pen an effusive letter begging a few moments of His Excellency's valuable time at some date and hour he would select, for some reason I must invent. Normally I would have played safe and done so, but that day I was making inquiries on Violetta's behalf, not my master's, and tomorrow he might remind me that my time is his time and tell me to stop wasting it. I would have to risk the direct approach.

Violetta directed us to a watergate opening directly onto the Rio di San Nicolò—no grandiose frontage or loggia, just an unprepossessing doorway in a plain brick wall.

"Announce me," I told Giorgio.

He crooked his eyebrows. "To call upon Senator Avonal?"

"The villain himself."

"One floor up," Violetta said. "The door to your left."

Giorgio brought the boat in and moored it with the stern nearest the steps, so he could disembark. Then he adjusted his bonnet, stepped ashore, and vanished into the dark corridor.

I had to ask, "You are absolutely convinced that Lucia did not commit suicide or just fall into a canal in her party clothes?"

"Absolutely." But her eyes gleamed gold.

"Not you, Delilah. I want to hear it from Aspasia."

"Oh, Alfeo, you idiot! I wish you would stop this silly game of giving me different names." But then she spoke in Aspasia's voice. "Lucia was a very hardheaded and sensible woman. A merely pretty woman can amass a fortune, but only a very clever one can hang on to it."

"Thank you." I kissed her.

At last Giorgio reappeared and nodded to me—His Excellency would be graciously pleased to receive me. Now it was my turn to climb the stairs. The relevant door was closed and I was left to enjoy the customary urinal fragrance of a communal corridor for several minutes before it opened. A manservant confirmed my name and bowed me in.

The hallway was tiny by Ca' Barbolano standards, and niggardly for a senator, even one setting an example of frugality in the ever-cramped city. Four doors led off it, all closed, and several works of art cried out to be inspected, if not necessarily admired, but I had no time to study them or the furniture because my host was standing in the center of the room, arms akimbo, studying me. He had the windows at his back.

I bowed very low, as nobles do to one another. The minimum age for election to the Senate is forty and I would have judged Avonal at less than that, still a *giovane* in political terms. He was big, but broad more than tall, with a heavy face supporting a thick sandy beard and a grim expression. Part of his size came from the scarlet robes of a senator, but the nobility do not wear their robes at home, so he had put his on especially for me, either to honor me or impress me.

My first thought was that this man had bedded Violetta once and frightened her another time and I had a sword and he did not. I suppressed bloodthirsty instincts.

"I am more honored, Your Excellency—"

"Just state your business." Avonal had an oddly squeaky voice for such a monolith. I had expected a boom.

"I am doing a favor for my servant Maria da Bergamo," I said. "Two weeks ago you retrieved the body of a woman from the lagoon and delivered it to the authorities, a most Christian act. The unfortunate woman has since been identified as Maria's aunt. She wishes me to convey her deepest thanks and appreciation. Of course I add my own, *clarissimo*. Now she has recovered from her initial shock, she is dearly anxious to know more about this terrible affair. So far I have learned no more than your name, Excellency, and I presume to inquire what other details you can supply to put the child's mind at rest?"

He paused, as if debating whether to throw me out at once or bid me *buona sera* first and then throw me out.

"I was on my way to the Lido to ride my horse, which I stable there. Riding is an uncommon pastime in Venice, but not an illegal one. We saw the body floating, so I had my boatmen lift it aboard and we delivered it to the *sbirri* in Castello for Christian burial. I took possession of the valuables still visible on the corpse, because I knew what would happen to them otherwise. The next day I handed them to my attorney and told him to have them identified and see that they were returned to the dead woman's family."

I opened my mouth but he forestalled me.

"Before you ask, I will add that the corpse had obviously been in the water for some days and I spent the previous three weeks in Milan. I was part of a senatorial delegation to the duke; we returned the previous day, so there is no possibility that I killed her. Furthermore, yes I did recognize the amber brooch. I saw it four or five years ago, on a woman whose name I do not recall and have no wish to be informed of now."

His beard bristled aggressively. His squeak rose a fifth. "She was a whore and I have no doubt your so-called servant is another. If you are truly a *nobile homo*, then I suggest you spend more money on clothes and less on servant girls. Go back to San Barnaba and stop pestering your betters."

San Barnaba is indeed the parish of my birth, but his remark was only a taunt, not a spectacular guess, because it is also home to many of the impoverished nobility, the *barnabotti*.

I bowed low. "I thank you for a very succinct statement, Your Excellency."

The manservant still stood by the door. He opened it and I left.

As I trotted downstairs, I mused that what a successful politician in Venice needs, apart from the accident of noble bloodlines, is oceans of money, a large family, and a strong speaking voice, in that order. Avonal seemed to have none of those and yet he was already in the Senate. He seemed to be an honest man, but I doubted that this was the secret of his success.

4

I insisted then that we let Giorgio go home to his brood and Violetta and I celebrate Carnival, for dusk was falling. If the Maestro's orders to be back by curfew had been intended seriously, he should have known better.

Donning masks, we went off to celebrate Carnival, dancing and drinking, laughing and eating by the light of bonfires. We cheered the fireworks and booed at a bullbaiting, while all around us swirled bishops and abbesses, duchesses and clowns. It was an enchanting evening, and the crowning episode, as provided by Helen, was beyond compare. It was well after midnight before I hammered Ca' Barbolano's door knocker to waken Luigi, the archaic night watchman.

When I let myself into the apartment I saw light under the Maestro's door, so I peeked in. He was leaning back on a pile of pillows, reading—and still awake, which was not surprising for he sleeps little at the best of times and even less lately. He reads so much by artificial light that I cannot understand why he hasn't long since gone totally blind. Scowl and nightcap, sheets and book, together formed a puddle of lamplight in the darkness as if an apprentice artist had been practicing chiaroscuro.

"Need anything?" I inquired helpfully.

"No. Learn anything?"

"I met an honest senator."

"Incredible!"

"We thought so." I summarized our afternoon. "Lucia was expecting an old friend and went off in a public gondola with an unidentified man. I did not talk with the women who last saw her, because Violetta had already done that. A week later her body turned up in the lagoon. It took a couple more weeks to establish her identity and inform her friends, and if she hadn't been found by an unusually public-spirited person, no one would ever have known what happened to her. I agree that the case seems hopeless."

Nostradamus nodded with satisfaction that the minor mystery of the valuables had been disposed of and the murder case looked so impossible that he need not be tempted by the reward. Then I told him about the second summons and my visit to Palazzo Gradenigo. His face darkened. He loves all mysteries except those he cannot hope to solve and Giovanni Gradenigo might have taken his secret to the grave.

"I could hardly push myself into a house of mourning when the old man was still warm," I concluded. "But first thing tomorrow, I go to find Battista."

"Not first thing. It will wait. I have letters to be encrypted."

"His master has died. He may well be out of a job and gone. He may be gone already."

The sage had not thought of that, so I won that round.

Normally I snap awake just before the *marangona* bell in the Piazza announces sunrise. That day I heard it as I was walking—or possibly sleepwalking—across the Campo San Polo, heading for the Palazzo Gradenigo. I had not bothered to disturb Giorgio, hoping that some exercise would clear my sleep-deprived wits. Already workers were hurrying to work, many darting into the churches for a hasty prayer. It was a fine day for early February, promising a timely spring.

At that dewitching hour I did not expect to run into any of the Gradenigo family and even their senior servants might snatch a little extra time on the pillow. A manservant should be an early riser, though, and perhaps an unemployed manservant facing the need to find a new employer would have worried himself awake. I found the rear entrance, a gate into the yard, and to my delight it was already unlocked. Routine in the palazzo was still in disarray, or seemed to be so, for no one argued when I appeared at the servants' door and announced that it was urgent that I speak to Battista—I did not even have to invent some tale about being sent by the morticians or the attorneys. I made myself as comfortable as possible on a stone bench in the yard and shivered in patient silence.

In a few minutes a man emerged from the house and hurried over to tell me that he was Battista da Schio. Servants rarely possess family names, and normally have no need of them, anyway. They are often immigrants from the mainland, and for legal purposes are then identified by their birthplace. He was around fifty, a brown-gray sort of person smaller than me, looking as if he might have been chosen for timidity and mousiness.

"Sit down," I said cheerfully, which he did distrustfully. "I'm Alfeo, assistant to Doctor Nostradamus."

To my surprise, he turned chalk white. His fright was so obvious that I could not ignore it.

"There's no need to be alarmed. I apologize . . . The doctor apologizes for misunderstanding your message and not sending me over right away. As I wrote . . . You did receive the reply I sent?"

Battista shook his head and seemed to grow smaller still. I began to understand.

"Did *sier* Giovanni tell you to write to Nostradamus?"

Shake again. The man had lost his tongue.

"Then tell me why you did, please. I will keep your secret if you have one, I promise."

His tongue returned and played with his lips for a moment. "The master kept asking for . . ." His voice was very soft and hesitant. ". . . for someone to send for Nostradamus. He was a kind master and he was dying and no one was doing what he said." Taking encouragement from my nods, he went on, a little more sure of himself. "I was attending him all the time. He needed . . . a lot . . ."

"How did he die?"

"He bled to death, kept vomiting blood. It started about four days ago and was getting worse. The doctors . . . He sent the doctors away."

"Wise of him." Hematemesis is not the worst way to die, but not the best or most dignified, either. The most likely cause was a tumor in the stomach. "Was he in much pain?"

"He never said he was, not to me. But I never remember him complaining about anything."

"So you were attending him, cleaning up, changing sheets. Horrible job! I hope they paid you extra?"

He shook his head and avoided my eye.

"So who else was there?"

"Friends, family. They'd been coming to say good-bye ever since the doctors told him to send for a priest."

I could imagine the scene: The dying man struggling to say his farewells to all the visitors, fighting against nausea, probably also pain and the gross indignity of puking out his own lifeblood. And Battista creeping around like an ant between all the grandees.

"But you managed to slip away and write for Nostradamus to come?"

"Er . . . yes."

I had not got it quite right, but I had a trump to play. We

get good luck and we get bad luck, and there is no sin in taking advantage of the good. As it happened, at my Monday evening fencing class my good friend Fulgentio had grumbled that it was impossible to keep good servants and his man had just left him, after less than a month. Every gentleman in Venice has his own manservant, of course, so I'm told.

"What will you do now that *messer* Gradenigo has been called to the Lord, Battista?"

"Look for another job, *lustrissimo*."

"I'm not a *lustrissimo*, but I know one. A good friend of mine, who has more money than the king of Spain. He's looking for a manservant. I swear as I hope for salvation that that is the truth, or it was true four days ago. Tell me the story properly and I'll take you to him and introduce you to him in person if he's home, or to his steward if he's not. Now talk, because this bench is freezing my ass."

Battista very nearly smiled at that. He spoke up more confidently.

"When the friar came back . . . He'd given the master the last rites the day before, but he came back. And the master kept saying that he needed Doctor Nostradamus, and everyone thought he was rambling, because the other doctors had given up on him. At last the priest, Brother Fedele, said he would write a note and went out of the room. I thought right away he just said that to keep him quiet and he came back so soon that I was suspicious and I went downstairs and asked Giacomo—he's the chief gondolier—and he said that no message had gone out to any Nostradamus. He asked the boys, and a couple of them knew where Doctor Nostradamus lived. So I wrote a note and Giacomo charged me a ducat to send a boatman with it. I paid him out of my savings."

I said, "Giacomo sounds like a first class sewer rat, but at least it did get delivered. And when my reply came back, who got it?"

Battista scowled at the ground. "The friar."

Now the fog had blown away. "He denounced you to . . . ?"

"Donna Tonina."

"*Sier* Giovanni's daughter?"

"His daughter-in-law, Tonina Bembo, wife of *sier* Marino."

"And so you are out of a job?"

Battista might have been going to lose his job anyway, but a priest's anger would carry much weight. Why had the two notes arrived in the wrong order? Either the friar had written his version first but had waited to send it until he knew it was too late to do any good, or else he had written his only after he knew that Battista's had been sent and rejected. Why the delay? And if Fedele had written just to humor a dying man's delusions, why had he sent the note anyway? In case questions were asked later? Comforting a dying man with little white lies is not a mortal sin. Why involve a total stranger if the dying man is raving and out of his senses? It made no sense.

"Have you any idea what your master wanted to tell mine?"

Battista shook his head, but not vigorously enough to convince me, so I waited. Eventually he squirmed and said, "I think I heard him say that Nostradamus could find people, sir."

"Ah! Yes, he often can. He has been asked to find missing people many times. Who did *sier* Giovanni want found, do you know? A missing heir?"

Good servants do not gossip to strangers, and Battista mumbled and muttered. Then he drew a deep breath and said, "A killer, *lustrissimo*."

I recalled my offhand remark to Violetta about absurd coincidences and dismissed it. "That could be. Even the Council of Ten has consulted Nostradamus sometimes. Go on."

Seeing that I was taking him seriously, he said, "My master was troubled about a woman, someone he had known when he was younger. One of his visitors had told him. He mentioned it a lot. She had been found murdered. She had been so beautiful, he said, that Titian had put her in one of his paintings, he said."

Not too much of a coincidence, I decided. Everyone in the city would know about Lucia's brutal killing very shortly, if not already. But why should a dying patrician worry about a murdered prostitute? The social gulf between them had been wider than the Adriatic Sea.

"A courtesan?"

Battista nodded, looking so astonished that I felt ashamed of myself.

"And her name was Lucia?"

"No, *lustrissimo*, it was Caterina."

That made a big difference.

5

I marched Battista out of the yard and took him back with
me to Ca' Barbolano, where I presented him to Mama with
orders to feed him until he popped. Then I sent Corrado and
Christoforo off to tell Fulgentio that I had a potential servant
for him to interview. The twins love running errands to Ca'
Trau, because they are often tipped two or even three *soldi*
apiece there.

The Maestro had not yet emerged from his room and I
needed my hunch confirmed before I stuck my neck too far
out, so I slipped into my room and locked the door behind
me. Three of the iron bars on the central window are loose
enough to lift out and the *calle* between Ca' Barbolano and
Number 96 is so narrow that I can jump it easily going there
and almost as easily coming back. This saves me a lot of stairs
at the trifling risk of a very messy death.

In moments I was climbing over the railing around the
altana on 96's roof. I unlocked the trap and clambered down
the steep stairway.

What had been a late night for me had been an early one
for Violetta and I hoped I would find her awake. She wasn't,

but Milana was, cleaning the kitchen. Milana is the most consistently cheerful person I know, although she has a twisted back and is so tiny that she must often get jostled and bullied when she goes to the market. Being devoted to Violetta and totally in her confidence, she knew all about yesterday's events. Her expression when she saw me that morning told me right away that my guess had been correct. If anyone knew of a second murdered courtesan, it would be people in the trade.

"Caterina Someone?" I demanded.

Milana nodded. "Caterina Lotto. She was murdered on Sunday in her room in San Samuele. The *shirri* arrested her doorman, Matteo Surian."

Doorman is a polite way of saying bravo and pimp, but I knew the name. "Matteo the Butcher?"

Again Milana nodded.

"Saints! I wonder they didn't start a riot." Matteo had been my childhood hero. I'll get to him later.

"I think they very nearly did," Milana said with a fleeting grin. "He was released before nightfall. It was very sad about signora Lucia. I did not know signora Caterina, but I think my mistress will be unhappy when she hears this news."

"I am appalled. The Maestro will be, too. How did Caterina die, do they say?"

"She was strangled with a cord."

Memories of Lucia's crushed windpipe made me shiver. "Tell Violetta that I shall come back as soon as I can. Meanwhile, any more gossip you can collect, the better." I turned to go.

"*Sier* Alfeo?"

I turned back and said "?" with my eyebrows.

"There was a third," Milana said sadly, "about a week ago—Ruosa da Corone, in San Girolamo."

"How?"

"The same way."

Three courtesans, all strangled. Who could doubt that this was the work of one person?

"I'll be back as soon as I can," I said. "Bolt the door behind me."

I found Nostradamus in his favorite chair in the atelier with no cane or staff in sight, meaning that Bruno had carried him there. In front of him stood Battista—telling him to sit would have made him uncomfortable—answering a barrage of questions. I went quietly to the desk to listen.

The Maestro was trying to track down the news about Caterina Lotto, whom I had thought to be the second victim, but had apparently been the third. Who had told Giovanni Gradenigo the news? Who had thought an old dying nobleman would be interested in the death of a courtesan? The picture that Battista was painting was a dramatic one, a pageant of Gradenigo's life trooping past his deathbed to bid him farewell. There had been scores of family members, of course, including noblemen in their floor-length black gowns, with matching bonnets and the cloth strip known as a tippet draped over the left shoulder. There had been senators, wearing the same but in red. There had been sobbing grandchildren and great-grandchildren, servants, tenants, friends from all levels of Venetian society, and many tradesmen from the *scuola*.

The dying man had spoken with every single one of them, Battista reported, refusing to allow anyone to be turned away, interrupting the parade only when overcome by nausea or the need to bring up more blood. It was impossible to say who had told him of the courtesan's murder, just as it was impossible to know why the information had upset him so much and made him call for Nostradamus.

"Had he been one of her customers?"

"Oh no, *lustrissimo*!" Battista looked more horrified by that slur on his master's honor than he had when discussing his death. "I was with him for almost twenty years, *lustrissimo*, and never did I hear any hint of anything that . . . He was an upright Christian, very loving and faithful to his wife. No, no."

"What did he say about this Caterina, then? Anything special about her, anything odd, peculiar about her?"

"Just that she had been so beautiful that the great Titian had painted her."

Titian died twenty years ago. A courtesan can fall a long way in twenty years. She would not have been so beautiful at the end.

"Did he speak of her as if he had actually seen her beauty for himself?"

Battista thought for a moment and then nodded uncertainly.

Baffled, the Maestro tugged his beard. "His wife predeceased him?"

Nod. "Almost a year ago, poor lady. My master never quite recovered from the loss."

Nostradamus has an incredible instinct for finding the germane in a jungle of irrelevance. "Then, if *sier* Giovanni was such an upright, moral man, what was the connection . . . ? What was his attitude to courtesans in general?"

Battista squirmed. "I don't understand . . ."

"Did he despise them? Rant against their wickedness? Call them names, like 'she-devils' or 'vessels of evil'?"

"Oh, no, *lustrissimo*! He was a gentle, patient man. I never heard him speak of any sinner like that."

Silence. The dead man was starting to sound like a candidate for sainthood.

"Then did he ever try to help them, then? Courtesans, I mean, fallen women? Battista, I am trying to discover why your master's dying wish was to ask me something or tell me something, and you are the only one who can help me find out what it was that troubled him. I cannot honor his wish if you won't help me. Why should your master, facing the eternal, have worried about the death of a woman of the streets?"

The mousy little man seemed to cower even more. "I cannot recall . . . Well, maybe. I heard him say to one of his visitors, something about the terrible trouble they can cause. I think he meant the sort of women you mean, *lustrissimo*."

"Ah! That could be helpful. Do you remember who he said that to?"

Battista tried. He closed his eyes and stood for a moment, moving his lips as if praying, clenching and unclenching his fists. "It was one of the nobles, an older man. Yes, he wore the long sleeves of the Council of Ten. Don't know his name, there were so many . . . They were talking about the old days, when the master was on the Council, too."

I raised my eyebrows at that.

Nostradamus said, "He was in politics? I did not know that."

Not just in politics but very successfully so if he had risen as high as the Ten.

Now Battista was nodding vigorously, happy to have pleased, anxious to help. "There was talk once of him being elected a procurator of San Marco!"

That is the second-highest honor to which a nobleman can be elected, for the procurators are elected for life, like the doge, and there are only ever nine of them. Their duties are nominal, although they hold permanent seats on the Senate and can be elected to other posts also. The doge is almost always chosen from among the procurators, so they are potentially doges in waiting.

"When was that?" the Maestro asked.

"About seven or eight years ago. But then the master gave up politics. He started going to church more and spending his time on good deeds and his work for the *scuola*."

"A sudden conversion?" Nostradamus said wryly. "Like the blessed San Polo on the road to Damascus?"

Battista hesitated, then nodded. "It was a big surprise to us all, refusing election."

"Servants and family?"

The man nodded. Of course a patrician's household would follow his political career with interest. Battista must have dreamed of being valet to the doge, living in the palace. Very subtly, the Maestro probed, trying to find out without blurting out a direct question, if there could have been a connection between a dead courtesan and Gradenigo's sudden abandonment of politics, most likely a scandal. Battista sensed the way he was being led, though, and went back to denying that his master could ever have been involved with any courtesan.

Eventually the Maestro thanked him and told me to give him a lira for his trouble, which was an astonishing outburst of generosity. I hoped it meant that he was going to take up Violetta's challenge and track down this monstrous slayer of courtesans.

That morning had more surprises than the lagoon has fish. When I led Battista out to the *salone*, I found Fulgentio Trau out there, admiring Michelangelo's *David*. It is only a copy in chalk of the original in Florence, but it is actual size and always makes me wonder how big Goliath was.

I need not describe Fulgentio. As well as being the same age, we are the same size and build. You can tell us apart because he has the clothes and I have the looks. We attend the same fencing class and he is almost as good as I am—good enough to have earned him a post as one of the ducal equerries, whose duties include guarding the doge. Fulgentio is a citizen-by-birth, so his name is written in the Silver Book, not in the Golden, like mine. The main difference between us, though, is that he is rich beyond measure, having three older brothers who are bankers. Under Venetian law, brothers inheriting property from their father automatically hold it as a *fraterna*, a financial and legal partnership, so Fulgentio has an equal share in the family wealth although he has no interest in banking as a profession. His brothers could negotiate a separation but seem content not to. Possibly he has agreed never to marry, so that any children he may sire cannot dilute the family fortune; one can't ask even the closest of friends such questions. Some people suspect that his part of the bargain is to bring home secrets he has overheard in the palace, but I could never believe that he would stoop to spying. Fulgentio, in short, is very rich and perfectly happy.

We bowed to each other in a parody of courtly etiquette.

"Pardon the rags," he remarked, indicating his ducal livery. "But then I couldn't wear anything really good when grubbing around in such a slum."

"Oh, I know," I retorted. "I keep applying for a transfer to the galleys."

He chuckled. "I just dropped in on my way to the palace. Is this the man you mentioned?"

"This is Battista, who is in need of a position because his employer of many years has just died."

While Battista was bowing, I gave Fulgentio a private thumbs-up sign to show that I approved of my candidate, which I did even more after listening to his interview with the Maestro. Then I excused myself and left them to talk while I went back into the atelier.

Nostradamus was scowling ferociously, of course, because he had failed to solve the mystery of the deathbed summons and almost certainly never would.

"The man was delirious."

"Yes, master."

"And the deaths of two courtesans in less than a month is pure coincidence, so don't—"

"Three, master."

"What?"

"There was a third, a Ruosa da Corone. Lucia was last seen on January fourteenth. Caterina was murdered last Sunday and Ruosa about a week ago. Only the Caterina date is firm."

"Sit down." He waved at the two green chairs on the other side of the fireplace. "And talk."

I am rarely honored with one of those chairs, but this time I could provide no more information to justify my favored status.

"It's hopeless!" he growled. "The Council of Ten may not care about a strumpet here or there, but it will certainly not ignore a massacre like this. The Ten have their *sbirri* and Lord knows how many informers throughout the city. They will dig out all the information. You seriously expect me to solve a jungle bloodbath like that while sitting here in my atelier?"

"No, master."

"No what?"

"No, I do not expect you to. I only brought the man back with me because Fulgentio is looking for a valet and Battista impressed me. I realize you cannot perform miracles, and clairvoyance only works forward, not back. And whatever Gradenigo wanted to tell you is gone forever."

He scowled even harder at me, as if he suspected me of taunting him into taking the case. Which I probably was, although I was mostly worried about Violetta's safety.

"The monster may very well strike again!"

"Yes, master."

He waved a hand.

"Write, then!"

Surprised, I rose and headed for my side of the big double desk.

"And none of that fancy fandangle calligraphy of yours. Just honest, legible italic. Good linen parchment."

I selected paper and a quill and opened my inkwell. I said, "Ready," because he had his back to me.

"A contract between me and that harlot of yours. One hundred ducats nonrefundable for expenses . . ."

I grunted to show that he was going too fast. He almost never asks for money in advance, only on results. That way he cannot be charged with fraud.

". . . the balance of 1,370 ducats payable upon the apprehension and conviction of a man responsible for the murder or attempted murder of at least one courtesan in Venice within one month before or after this day's date."

I spattered blots all over the text and swore like a galley slave. *"You are contracting to catch a murderer who hasn't even killed his victim yet?"*

Despite the pain in his hips, he had managed to lever himself around to smirk at me. "Why not? Clairvoyance works forward, doesn't it? All I have to do is foresee the next victim, and all you have to do is be standing behind the closet door."

6

Fifteen minutes later I was back in Number 96, finishing Violetta's breakfast while she scanned the contract. She wore another simple housemaid's dress, which I gathered Milana had sewn for her overnight. It was plain, but few senators' wives would boast of anything better made. I had come by the sea-level road because I was wearing my rapier; swords and acrobatics do not mix.

"Just what sort of expense is Nostradamus planning to spend my hundred ducats on?" my darling demanded.

"I have no idea," I admitted. "But I expect he does."

"I want him to catch the man who killed Lucia da Bergamo."

"He can't. No witnesses, no evidence—the strangler's scot-free on that one. But obviously the same man killed all three victims. And obviously he may kill again."

She nodded reluctantly, a tiny frown marring the perfection of her forehead. "You think I'm in danger?"

I brought out my tarot deck. "I can find out, if you wish."

"Will it really tell?" Minerva's big, luminous gray eyes studied me. "You believe in the cards that much?"

I nodded. "Tarot has limitations, but even the Maestro

admits I am good with it. But I'm not a fairground fortune-teller, love. I won't babble pap about being lucky in love or old friends re-entering your life. If the news is bad, I'll tell you. I might desensitize my deck if I misquoted it."

"Let's do it, then." At once she began clearing a space on the table, which is very small, an intimate place to be shared by two.

I shuffled the deck and gave it to her. "Hold it for a moment in both hands. Now cut it and deal off the new top card. This will represent you or the question you want answered."

She turned over the queen of coins.

"Excellent!" I said. "The highest-paid courtesan in Venice, who else?"

She laughed. "How did you do that?"

"I didn't! I told you this is serious, not make-believe. This deck is almost two hundred years old. It's had many owners and enough time to absorb every dream and fear that mortals know." I took it back and dealt four more cards, facedown, forming a cross around the first one. "Now the one closest to you is the problem. Turn it over—sideways."

She did and then gave me a sharp look, for it was XIII of the major arcana—Death.

"But it's reversed!" I said quickly. "That's good! Lay it down that way."

"What does Death reversed mean?"

"That the problem is to avoid Death, I think. Now turn this one, the helper or path." This time she found trump X, which on my deck shows a lion. "This stands for Strength, although some decks call it Fortitude, and other artists may use other pictures."

"Should I perhaps hire Bruno to protect me?" she inquired teasingly.

"I wish you wouldn't joke about this!"

"Sorry. Now what?" She was amused, not sorry. Although Violetta has great esteem for the Maestro's clairvoyant

abilities, familiarity breeds disrespect and she is too aware of
my faults and weaknesses to hold me in similar reverence.

"The opposite one, the snare to be avoided."

She turned over II, the Popess, reversed, and looked inquiringly at me.

"That is the most cryptic card in the arcana," I admitted.
There never was a Pope Joan. In my deck she is shown on a
throne, wearing robes and a papal miter, holding a book on
her lap. "I need to think about it. Let's see the last one, the
goal or solution."

She turned the top card and it was the knight of cups reversed. Now I knew I must do some fast talking, because I
could recall few layouts more perplexing. With three cards
reversed and only two trumps, it was certain to be ambiguous. "The queen of coins means that it is your reading, and
Death reversed means that the problem is to keep you alive.
Strength or Fortitude may mean that you will have to be
brave. The knight of cups baffles me, I admit. The jack of
cups usually means me, the alchemist's apprentice, but I don't
think I've ever appeared as a knight in any suit. Besides, I
don't want to be reversed! And the Popess reversed has me
totally befuddled."

"And here I thought I was consulting an expert!"

"It's a very unusual spread. I'll consult Nostradamus. I
suspect it refers to some people we haven't met yet."

Violetta's eyes had darkened, but they were twinkling
with amusement. "What use is a prediction that can't be understood until it has come to pass?"

"Ask Apollo. That was how he did it at Delphi. Trust
me. All will be revealed in time."

"As long as Death stays reversed," she retorted.

"Let's get Giorgio to row us over to San Samuele so we
can visit with my old hero, Matteo the Butcher."

* * *

The rest of the world admires and envies Venice for many things: our wealth, our republican form of government, our skilled and luscious courtesans, our glittering state processions, the beauty of our jeweled city on its hundred islands, smug and safe and well fed in its fish-rich lagoon. Another of our unique features that is almost as famous and perhaps not as envied—although travelers come from far and wide to view it—is the War of Fists.

Its needs are simple. We have more than four hundred stone bridges ready to hand in Venice, almost all of them narrow, humpbacked, and lacking parapets or railings of any kind. Moreover, they almost always mark the boundary between two parishes. Line up a few hundred enraged, combative young men on either side and you can resume the War of Fists. It happens spontaneously quite often in the fall, between summer and the start of Carnival, and the Council of Ten thunders against it. The greatest battles, though, are planned weeks in advance, enlisting the best fighters from all over the city, and there is not a great deal that the Ten can do to prevent those encounters. Indeed, the government has been known to organize them to entertain important visitors, such as one I remember about ten years ago for delegates from some place called Japan, which is said to be near Cathay, at the other end of the world, but I doubt that the visitors had come all that distance just to watch armies of carpenters and fishermen trying to pound their opponents into submission or submersion.

The contesting teams are always the Nicolotti and the Castellani. Whatever began the age-old dispute between the two factions is now lost in mists of myth, but the hatred between them is virulent, leading sometimes to outright murder. The dividing line between the factions winds across the city roughly southwest to northeast, and it makes a particularly large curve around my birth parish of San Barnaba, which lies on the eastern, Castellani, side of it. Being of patrician birth, I cannot participate in such plebeian pastimes except as a supporter, although I did once manage to steal a very minor role in one great battle, as I shall explain.

Now San Barnaba is fairly central in the city, flanking the outside of the more southerly of the two great bends of the Grand Canal. It is also frontier territory, abutting Nicolotti parishes on two sides, and it boasts a very visible and accessible bridge, so favored for battles that it is known as the Ponte dei Pugni, the Bridge of Fists. When a battle is scheduled, the inhabitants throw up rickety bleachers to rent to spectators, and those lucky enough to have windows or roofs overlooking the scene can charge enormous fees to the rich and great. You can understand, then, that I was always a staunch Castellani supporter because it would have been more than my juvenile life was worth to utter one good word about the despicable Nicolotti scum. San Remo parish fervently supports those glorious Nicolotti heroes, so I shall never be completely trusted there and must guard my tongue when anything concerning the War of Fists creeps into conversations.

The opposing forces are not mere rabble. Many parishes or other groups in the city pride themselves on sending semimilitary companies of fifty or more young men, marching in step, wearing the same uniform. Both sides have their various leaders, known as *padrini*, who provide some sort of order and plan strategy, and of course every one of these is a great fighter who has earned respect and reputation in a hundred previous clashes. By the time the battle is due to begin, thousands of pugnacious young men have worked themselves up into fighting fury, every vantage point in sight is packed with spectators, and the canal is paved solid with boats. Abuse is hurled, blood froths, and skilled *padrini* have concealed reserve forces in nearby warehouses, so they can throw in fresh troops at a critical moment.

The main part of the engagement is the general assault on the bridge, with the objective of taking it and driving one's opponents back down the far side or off into the water. It is a rough sport, with injuries and sometimes even deaths, and the fortunes of battle may swing back and forth many times during an afternoon. Prior to the assault, though, the finest fighters like to show off their prowess in one-on-one matches, either challenging particular opponents or taking on all comers. The *padrini* organize these and umpire them. Very often a *padrino* himself will fight a bout, to show he has not lost his skills, and great is the excitement as the champions come forth on the crest of the bridge to bellow their challenges. The boxing is not especially brutal, for the match ends as soon as one man draws blood or sends his opponent to the canal below.

In my youth, one of the Castellani's great fighters and *padrini* was Matteo Surian of San Samuele, who was a butcher by trade and therefore chose the Butcher as his nom de guerre. I was present on the day he fought his last fight, when he went up against the despicable, garbage-eating, dog-spawned "Mankiller." Mankiller had killed a man in a bout once and had never been forgiven for it, although the death had been a drowning and undoubtedly an accident. That wonderful battle ended when Matteo punched Mankiller clean into the canal. Matteo gave up fighting after that, the day of his greatest triumph. But that most glorious, golden day, he let Alfeo Zeno hold his shirt while he was out there fighting.

I decided then that I would have an account of that honor engraved on my tombstone.

7

San Samuele, the parish where Caterina Lotto had died, lies directly across the Grand Canal from San Barnaba, but I know it well because there is a *traghetto* crossing there, and when traffic is light the boatmen will sometimes let penniless boys ride for free. Giorgio rowed us there and promised to return at noon. It is far from being the best area in the city, and Caterina must have gone down in the world, but that is normal in her profession.

Finding the great Matteo Surian, Matteo the Butcher, proved more difficult than I expected. True, he had retired from the War of Fists years ago and if he was a courtesan's doorman he might have retired from his official trade also, but he was still a legend. He had just been arrested and released for a murder that must be the talk of the parish. Despite all that, the first three pairs of ears I asked had never heard of him. The last pair belonged to a burly youth dressed as a porter and Violetta intervened.

"Oh, please help us. I would be so-o-o grateful!" She accompanied the words with a smile that suggested she wanted to rip all his clothes off and her own as well and rape him, right there in the *campo*.

He turned brick red and said, "Try the *magazzen*, madonna."

Every parish has a *magazzen*, where cheap wine is available around the clock, and San Samuele's is larger than most, perhaps because so many of the cheaper prostitutes live in that area and bring in trade. It was not a place I would willingly take a beautiful girl, but I dared not suggest that my companion wait outside.

Even on that workday morning a surprising number of customers were sitting around in the dim, rank-smelling place, all of them male. Right away I spotted the man we wanted, slumped at a tiny table in the farthest corner with his back to us, a huge hunched shape, paradigm of abject drunken misery. No one else could be that big or that unhappy.

"There he is," I said and took two steps.

My way was blocked by a competent-looking young bravo with one hand resting on his sword hilt. "Sit there," he said, nodding to a table well away from Matteo.

Keeping my hands in full view, I said, "Hello, Ugo. Been a long time—Alfeo Zeno."

Ugo lowered his guard half a hairsbreadth. "You're on the wrong side of the canal."

"Viva Castellani! But you remember that I was a friend of Matteo's? I held his shirt back in '82, remember? I'm here to help him."

"Come back in a month. He can't be helped right now."

I was afraid of that. Matteo had been a proud fighter all his life, a man other men either feared or greatly respected. Multitudes had cheered him. To have his woman murdered and then be accused of killing her must have been a thunderous shock to his self-esteem, even if his relationship with Caterina had been purely business, which was highly improbable.

"We can try," Violetta said in Helen's seductive tones. "I was a friend of Caterina's."

Ugo glanced at her, expanded the glance into studied

appreciation, and reluctantly stepped aside. "If he doesn't want you, you're out." Since everyone else in the room except Matteo himself was watching our encounter, that seemed very likely.

"Is it true the *shirri* arrested him?" she asked.

Ugo nodded. "Idiots. About forty of us marched on the jail."

That was worrisome news. The Ten might pay little heed to the death of a prostitute or two, but the slightest hint of civil insurrection will always trigger repression. Nevertheless, I just said, "Thanks," and escorted Violetta over to the fallen hero.

Matteo's great fists, resting on the table in front of him, were battered wrecks but his features, although too coarse to have ever been handsome, had suffered no damage during his pugilistic career. His clothes were of a style and quality that he had never worn as an honest tradesman, but they were stained and rumpled as if he had been in them since Sunday. His graying beard was matted with grease.

While I fetched a stool for me, Violetta sat down on the one opposite him. He raised his gaze from the wineglass to regard her with eyes like gory stab wounds.

"I'm Violetta. Caterina are I were friends in her great days. She was a wonderful person. I've seen the picture Titian painted with her as the Goddess Juno."

Those awful eyes turned to me.

"Alfeo Zeno. I held your shirt on the Ponte dei Pugni on All Saints' Day in 1582. Proudest day of my life."

He let the information soak in like the slow flow of a tide, but eventually he nodded slightly and reached for the wine flagon. The waiter rushed over with two more glasses, and I could almost hear the tension in the shop snap.

Matteo took a longer look at Violetta, then me again. "You her doorman?"

I grinned and nodded, which was a lie, but a lie in a good

cause and one that might suddenly become an unwelcome truth if the unknown strangler continued his rampage. *Yes, we're all pimps together.*

"You done good. Lucky man."

"None luckier," I said. "Matteo, I also work for Doctor Nostradamus. You know of him?"

But Matteo was studying the empty glass in front of Violetta, over which the neck of the flagon wavered unsteadily in his grasp. I beckoned the waiter and told him to bring a bottle of his best. I would take the cost out of Violetta's hundred ducats.

Matteo set the empty flagon down heavily. "She can still stiffen a man right up with one glance," he mumbled. "Even now. Could, I mean . . . before."

The waiter brought a dusty bottle and poured three glasses. It wasn't bad. Even the drunken pimp looked pleased when he took a swallow.

"They threw me in jail," he said.

I said, "Nostradamus sent me. You've heard of him?"

"They thought I done it."

"You do want the murderer caught, don't you? You want to watch his head being chopped off?"

"What had she ever done to deserve that?"

"Did you see who—"

"I *loved* her! It was my house. She paid me rent, but that was all."

Trying to hold a conversation with him was like trying to catch fish in the middle of the Piazza. Violetta and I took turns casting nets, but always hauled them in empty. I was ready to give up when suddenly something silvery flapped in our web.

"He the wizard?" Matteo mumbled.

"Nostradamus is not a wizard," I protested quickly. "He's a wise man and a seer. He's very clever and he wants to catch the strangler. It would help if you could answer some questions."

He scowled at me. "The *sbirri* send you?"

"No."

He belched. "The Ten?"

"No." The buzz of talk had resumed in the *magazzen* now and I didn't think anyone could overhear our conversation, but I would have bet my liver that at least one person in that room would be reporting to the Ten before nightfall. "If you can tell us what you know about him, it would help Nostradamus to find the Strangler." Somehow the killer's description had become his name in my mind.

"Didn't get a good look at him." The giant pushed down on the table to straighten himself. Amazingly, he even seemed to sober up a little also. "He came early, 'bout sunset. Boy brought a note, see, and she sent back word that she would be ready then. And he came, but I didn't see his face much."

"What did you see of him? Was he big? Small?"

"All men are small," Matteo said deadpan. He had probably been making that same joke for forty years. It was a reflex. "Dressed like a friar. All I could see inside his hood was beard."

"Dressed like a friar?" Violetta said. "But you think he wasn't a friar?"

"Didn't *smell* like a friar."

That was not conclusive evidence. Vows of poverty do rule out spare linen and luxuries like soap, but many laymen in Venice cannot afford them either.

"Masked?" I asked.

"This's Carnival, isn' it?"

"But did you see anything of his face at all?"

"Beard. Gray beard."

"Did you see what he was wearing on his feet?" I asked, not expecting an answer.

"Bare feet. Saw them when he came down. Had bare feet."

I glanced at Violetta and saw my own doubts mirrored in her. It takes a lifetime to become accustomed to walking the streets with bare feet. Even genuine friars often wear sandals. Our murderer had taken his disguise very seriously.

It took a lot of questions and repetition, but gradually a picture emerged. The former hero had sunk to being a harlot's doorkeeper. He lived in a room at street level. Anyone entering from the *calle* faced a staircase going up, with Matteo's door at the bottom standing open during business hours. The big man let visitors in; more important, he would see them leave, so no one could get away without paying. There were two rooms upstairs. The other one was occupied by someone named Lena, who was out of town. He did not say that she had gone off to the mainland to have an abortion, because that would make him accessory to murder, but that was what I suspected.

Caterina's had been a grim life for a woman who was once the toast of the Republic and had sat for the great Titian. She had still been able to insist on appointments, apparently. Had she lived another five years or so she would have been sitting in the window, bare-breasted, trying to haul the drunks in off the street.

Matteo had seen the Strangler and told him to go up— "Door on the right."

Then he had heard some bumping—"Very fast worker, I thought."

After that nothing until the second customer of the evening had plied the door knocker.

Matteo had offered him a seat, planning to go up and tap on the bedroom door, but the friar was already coming down, silent on his bare feet. The friar had handed him the agreed fee of one lira and left. The second man had been directed to the door on the right, had gone up, and had run down again, screaming. By that time the friar had vanished into the dark and the fog.

Caterina had been lying on the floor, fully dressed, with a purple groove around her neck where the rope had dug into the flesh.

There had been no sex, no robbery, just death.

No, Caterina had not had an alarm bell like Violetta's. She had sometimes banged on the floor, and then Matteo would go up and thump the john a few times before throwing him out. Evidently the friar had overpowered her before she could signal properly and all Matteo had heard had been her death throes.

Violetta was Medea, eyes blazing green in the gloom, ready to go and inflict a few death throes herself the moment she knew the target.

"That leaves one big question," I said. "I'm sure the *shirri* asked you already, but I must. Did you hear the man's name?" Matteo would not have read the note.

"No," the big man growled. "But I know the name he gave her. She laughed, see, and told me an old friend was coming to see her at sunset."

"Did you see the note?" I asked eagerly. "Did you give it to the *shirri?*"

No, he mumbled. He'd looked but couldn't find it. The *shirri* thought the friar must have found it and taken it.

"But she did tell you the name of this surprise caller?"

Matteo reached for the wine bottle, tilted it up, and drained it. If he had been drinking like this all week, it was amazing he hadn't killed himself yet.

"She did. *Shirri* wouldn't believe me. You won't."

"Try me. Nostradamus has taught me to believe all kinds of unbelievable things."

"Gattamelata." Matteo's eyes burned with a challenge to call him a liar.

I would never be so stupid as to do that, but Gattamelata means "Honeycat." I looked at Violetta, whose mouth framed a perfect O of surprise.

So now we had a name for the Strangler, except that Gattamelata had been dead for a hundred and fifty years.

8

Giorgio was waiting for us when the noon bells rang. As we were rowed swiftly along the Grand Canal, Violetta and I chewed over the Honeycat problem. That nom de guerre was made famous by Erasmo of Narni, one of the greatest of the condottieri who ravaged Italy in the intercity wars of the quattrocento. Toward the end of his career Erasmo led the armies of Venice with some success, although he is mostly remembered for being honest, a rarity in his profession. After his death in Padua, the Republic commissioned an incredible equestrian statue of him by Donatello to stand in that city. Bronze statues do not go around strangling women.

"It must be a nickname," I declared profoundly.

Minerva gave me a pitying look. "Did you work that out all by yourself, darling, or did Matteo drop you a hint? But not just an idle pet name, I think. Caterina knew it at once and called him an old friend. That sounds as if it was generally used. Other people might have known him by that name also."

"You're jumping to conclusions," I protested. "The other victims may have had completely different names for him.

You need to find someone else who knew him as Honeycat before you can make such assumptions."

"Me," she said, frowning in annoyance. "I remember stories about a man called Honeycat. He was reputed to be very generous and quite dashing. It was a long time ago, though, when I was just starting out, and I don't know his real name."

I was encouraged. "We can find out what it was, though! Lucia and Caterina were both, um, mature women. You have a long-ago memory. Now *that* could be a pattern!" And Battista had said that Giovanni Gradenigo had known Caterina Lotto "years ago."

Minerva nodded impatiently, as if she had seen that ages ago. "I'll ask Alessa."

Alessa is one of her business partners, part owner of Number 96. Alessa still supervises the brothel, but has retired from active male entertainment. She is a very shrewd woman, who had the sense to get out while she still had her health and money. I like her, and she would still be worth a serious cuddle.

I swung opened the door of the apartment for Violetta and followed her in. To my pleased surprise, the Maestro was halfway along the *salone*, just about to enter the dining room. He was leaning on his two canes, but at least he was mobile again. He waited for us, leering a welcome.

"Did you sign the contract, madonna?"

"I did. Send Alfeo around to collect the expense money."

"I will. Did you learn anything?" he asked me.

"We have a name for the killer, the nickname Caterina knew him by."

"Excellent, that will help. Now let's have dinner."

He began to tap his way painfully forward. I exchanged surprised glances with Violetta, for only very rarely does he express any interest in food. I was even more surprised when

I followed her in and saw the guest waiting there—Alessa, no less. I had never known her to visit Ca' Barbolano before.

I suppose he really is a wizard.

We all sat down and Mama Angeli came bustling in with loaded platters of her superb *Tagliolini ai Calamaretti*.

"We found Matteo—" I began.

"No talking business at table!" Nostradamus decreed.

Either he was just being perverse, because he loves to talk business at table, or he did not want Alessa to know what we had been doing. Either way, I was quite happy to start eating. I got one mouthful of octopus down before he started in on me.

"Alfeo, yesterday you began explaining to me how the Venetians elect their doge. I am still anxious to hear more about this fascinating procedure."

Everyone in Venice knows this. Alessa and Violetta smiled politely to hide bewilderment. Talking and eating at the same time is a skill I have yet to master, but I get a lot of practice when the Maestro is in that sort of mood. I detest cold food, though.

"The Grand Council chooses thirty members by lot," I said. "The thirty then reduce their number to nine, again by lot. The nine elect a committee of forty, and the forty are reduced to twelve. Twelve elect twenty-five, reduced to nine; the nine elect forty-five, reduced to eleven; the eleven elect forty-one. And the forty-one elect the doge." Quickly I scooped a loaded forkful into my mouth.

"We were discussing things that make or do not make sense at the time, I recall. You can explain the *sense* of all that Byzantine tomfoolery?"

"What I have always assumed," Alessa announced bravely—and in a slow, deliberate tone to give me time to chew—"is that the wise ancestral fathers of the Republic wished to avoid the dangers of faction. How terrible it would be if the Grand Council split into two or three contesting groups! That is what would happen, or might happen, if they merely relied on election. And likewise, if the choice were made solely by lot, then we might find ourselves with some incompetent idiot as head of state."

We have done that a few times anyway, but it would be criminal sedition to say so.

"It must go further than that," Violetta said in Aspasia's dry, calculating tones. "Not factions, I suspect, but a matter of the 'ins' and the 'outs.' The inner circle, the handful that like to think of themselves as 'the First Ones,' are certain to have matters arranged so that the next doge will always be chosen from among their own number. All this electing-then-reducing rigmarole allows them several chances to take hold of the process. Once they have a majority on any of the electing committees, they can make certain that only 'sound' people are chosen in the next round. From then on they have the election under their control."

I nodded to show that her analysis made sense, but I noticed the Maestro smirking as if he had another explanation for what is certainly a bizarre procedure. I was sure he wouldn't tell me if I asked, and Alessa changed the subject.

"The food is admirable," she said, "and the ambience quite commendable. I shall marry Alfeo so I can come and live here."

I choked on a throatful of octopus.

The Maestro soon tired of the idle chat and began to fidget, because he really did want to talk business. It may be that the three of us dragged the meal out a little just to turn the tables on him, but eventually we finished our dolce. Mama brought in cups of the newfangled and expensive drink called *khave*, and we leaned back in our chairs.

I was ordered to report, so I did.

When I had finished, Alessa was visibly tense.

"Madonna?" the Maestro inquired waspishly. "Did you know any of these wretched women?"

Alessa's plump fingers kept playing with her pearls. "All of them slightly, none of them well."

"All about your own age?"

"One must never ask a woman her age, Doctor, especially a courtesan." Even she could not smile at her joke.

"You have nothing more to say?"

"No, Doctor." She shook her head vigorously. "Except the obvious one, that this is a very horrible affair."

Nostradamus bristled. "Paraphrasis!"

"What?"

"Double-talk! I invited you to dine, madonna, because I knew from donna Vitale that the murdered woman Lucia da Bergamo had retired from her profession. Information from a man I questioned this morning suggested that Caterina Lotto may have had some undetermined interaction with a prominent patrician politician eight years ago, and I knew that she was living in San Samuele, an area favored by second- or even third-class prostitutes. In other words, I had reason to believe that two of the three victims that we know about were of roughly your generation. I ask you again, madonna, have you ever met, or heard of, a man known as Honeycat?"

Stony-faced, Alessa shook her head.

"Can you think of any man—a wealthy man, clearly— who patronized courtesans about eight years ago, who might have decided to start murdering them off? Or any reason why he should?"

Again she shook her head. Violetta caught my eye, hinting that Alessa was lying.

"If you know Honeycat, you are in very grave danger," the Maestro said.

Alessa rose, towering and statuesque on platform soles. "I thank you for the splendid meal, Doctor. If you would be so kind as to ask your boatman . . ."

I went and fetched Giorgio to take her home to the house next door. I steadied her arm as we descended the stairs.

"Is it normal for clients to hide their identity behind nicknames?" I asked.

"Clients?" Alessa shot me an amused glance. "Johns, you mean. Johns will try almost anything, Alfeo my dear, and can always find prostitutes willing to cooperate. Courtesans are different. Wealthy Venetian men provide little education for their daughters and keep their wives housebound—some don't get out more than two or three times a year. They have no friends, no recreations. Then the men wonder why their womenfolk are so dull! They patronize courtesans at least as much for entertainment as for sex, probably more. They pay enormous sums for the best of us, and wealth gives us power. We are not hungry or desperate. To answer your question, yes, I have had patrons who wished to remain anonymous. I almost always knew who they were before they asked, and if I didn't I made it my business to find out."

"But no Honeycat?"

"No Honeycat. Hercules, Don Juan, Squirrel, Jupiter, but no Honeycat."

We had reached the watergate, and I held her hand as she embarked in the gondola.

"Be careful, Alessa," I said.

I ran back up the forty-eight steps, but found Violetta and the Maestro where I had left them.

"Did you believe her?" he demanded.

"No," I said. "She knows. She may be too frightened to tell us."

"Leave her to me," Violetta said. "Meanwhile, the Maestro and I think we should see what we can discover about Ruosa da Corone. I have a friend in San Girolamo who'll know where she lives. Lived, I mean."

I looked for permission to the Maestro, who nodded disagreeably. "It's all a waste of time. Go if you must, but the Ten will have your Honeycat safely locked up somewhere by now."

I was inclined to agree, but I would not pass up the excuse to go adventuring with my lady. It seemed that the Maestro was not going to rise from his dining room chair until I had removed Violetta, so I did that. Smirking like an adolescent, I offered my arm and escorted her to the stairs.

"My master makes me work so hard!"

She was in a serious mood. "I don't see why you have to do all this asking of questions. The *shirri* can do that. Why can't he just peer into his crystal ball?"

"Looking for what? He needs something to hunt for." I did not mention that the Maestro might have to try foreseeing the next victim, but even for that he would still need some sort of a pattern to start from. "You didn't know Ruosa?"

"Only slightly—we met at parties sometimes. She wrote some quite bearable poetry and was a wonderful dancer; in her middle twenties, I'd think."

That meant she had been in her prime as a sex toy when Giovanni Gradenigo had met Caterina Lotto about eight years ago. Venice is unusually tolerant in such matters, but a political career can still be destroyed by a scandal if it is scandalous enough. Three women, all real people, all cruelly destroyed. What baffled me was the motive. Not a sexual crime, so far as I could see. Not robbery. One murder might be explicable, but three in as many weeks suggested a campaign—for what reason?

San Girolamo parish is in the north of the city, in Cannaregio, and Violetta's friend, Franceschina, was yet another courtesan beauty, probably even younger and very nearly as divine. She had a magnificent home, two female servants, and had just finished what would be her first meal of the day. Indeed, she was not even properly dressed yet, just swathed in a misty silk robe that caused me to start running a high fever. She greeted Violetta with chirrups of joy and an embrace that would have been worth a hundred ducats to any man on the Rialto. She smiled politely at me, assuming I was the "doorman" protector, which was what I was beginning to feel like.

"You sit there, love," Violetta said, waving me to the most distant chair in the room. "You don't happen to have a blindfold handy, do you, darling?"

Franceschina tinkled laughter. "No but his eyeballs are going to explode any minute, and then it won't matter. He's very cute. Wherever did you find him, dear? Would you trade him for my current gorilla?"

One of the maids brought in glasses of sickly sweet wine. The women settled together on a silken divan, holding hands and smiling at each other so skillfully that I couldn't tell if they were bosom friends or mortal foes. I sat cross-legged on the floor in front of them to adore. More of Medea showed in Violetta's eyes every time she glanced in my direction, but I was entranced. I had never seen two such beauties together before, and the way Franceschina's robe had slid apart to expose her leg was a once-in-a-lifetime experience—not to mention the glow of nipples through silk. Fascinating! She portrayed a silly, brainless child very well and I could put up with a lot of giggles in a good cause, but if she were as shallow as she was pretending, Violetta would never have described her as a friend.

Violetta's explanation of why we had come was very terse, as if she were anxious to finish our business and leave. Even Franceschina could not maintain her bubbly twittering when talking about strangulation, so she switched to high drama. Three murders were terrible, unthinkable, nightmares from the pits of Hades. She was shrill, yet she made me want to sweep her into my arms and comfort her. It was a masterly performance and reminded me that I had never watched Violetta display her skills professionally, because I am her recreation. Franceschina was either just reacting to a man in her house from habit or stoking my fires to annoy Violetta; or both. It was so well done that I didn't care why it was being done. I was getting a free demonstration of a hundred-ducat performance.

With many asides, endearments, and irrelevancies, she said that Ruosa da Corone had done very well for herself—she had retired from the trade, having acquired a husband, one of the rich and important Valier clan. "Of course it was only a church marriage, not a legal one, because his name would be struck from the Golden Book if he officially married a courtesan, and I expect the brothers agreed ages ago which one of them will produce the legal heirs. That's how it's usually done, but it was a true love match, and at least her children . . . her son, I mean, will be citizen class. Valier set her up in the most gorgeous apartment, with *two* servants and a *very* generous allowance and a room in the same building for her mother! So generous! And now this! So tragic!"

"But how did it happen?"

"Well nobody knows, darling! It was exactly a week ago, the Feast of the Purification of the Virgin. She sent the boy off with his nurse and the maid so that he could watch the parade, you know?"

Of course we knew, and I as a boy watched the great processions of Venice innumerable times. There are ten of them a year, and the one she referred to parades every February 2 from San Marco's to San Maria Formosa—which is not very far—to commemorate the valor of the men of that parish back in 943, when they rescued a company of brides kidnapped by a band of pirates. I don't go so often now, but I had watched that particular parade last week to see if I could cheer loud enough to catch Fulgentio's eye as he went by and make him blush. It is one of the full-blown "triumph" parades, and very grand, beginning with eight standard bearers, then six buglers blowing silver trumpets, fifty minor officials in ceremonial robes, then the city band and drummers in red, stunningly loud in the narrow streets. Right on their heels come the equerries in gowns of black velvet (Fulgentio looked very sweet), then some priests, more officials and secretaries in crimson velvet, the chancellors including the grand chancellor, who ranks second to the doge, and the doge himself in the ermine that only he may wear, followed by his umbrella holder, the papal legate, ambassadors, the ducal counselors, the procurators of San Marco, the three chiefs of the *Quarantia*, the three chiefs of the Council of Ten, the two censors, the Senate in their red robes, and I have left out some of the minor participants.

When the doge arrives at San Maria Formosa, he is presented with two hats and two flagons of malmsey wine.

The parade is a wonderful excuse for a woman to send off her child and servants so she can be alone to receive a lover.

Just in case we were stupid, Franceschina added, "Valier's on the mainland on business and she'd probably felt lonely. When the maid came back, there she was, dead!"

"Had she received any messages that day?"

Franceschina's eyes grew even larger. "But yes, she had! However did you guess that, darling? No one knows what it said, except maybe the . . ." She dropped her voice to a whisper. ". . . Ten, you know?"

Rumor, which she happily passed on, said that there had been no signs of robbery or sexual violence. "But the boy's with his grandmother. Why don't you go and see her, dear? She'll be able to tell you much more."

Violetta tossed back her wine and said that in that case she must rush because she had to be home before sunset.

"The music salon at Ca' Grimini?" Franceschina chirped. "Will you be there, too? Oh, I am *so* looking forward to hearing that Milanese castrato, Whatsisname! They say he's an angel, absolutely *divine*!"

"I've heard him," Violetta said. "He sounds like a canary with severe constipation."

The weather was changing, just to remind us that it was still February, there were few people in sight, and Giorgio had taken shelter from the wind in a nearby loggia. He hastened to meet us.

"Another call to make," I said. "Close enough to walk to. We'll be as quick as we can."

Violetta and I paraded along the *fondamenta* to the *calle* Batello, down that about three houses, into a wide arched doorway—where stood Filiberto Vasco, the *vizio*, with his feet planted, his arms crossed, and a big smirk on his face.

"Go away, Alfeo," he said. "There's a good boy. No admittance."

As deputy to *Missier Grande*, the chief of police, Vasco would never post himself as a sentry on a chilly February corner. He thinks he is much too grand for that. He must have known that we were coming and had braved a few minutes' exposure just for the satisfaction of yanking my leash personally. He and I have been keeping score for several years, ever since a rich uncle bought him a job for which he is hopelessly inadequate and far too young. He loves to frighten people by flaunting his red cloak and silver belt badge, and his greatest ambition is to see me hanged between the columns on the Piazzetta.

Violetta and I had halted, of course.

"Says who?" I demanded, just to remind him that his authority came from much higher levels. His even larger smirk told me at once what was coming.

"Why, the Council of Ten, of course. Are you going to cause me trouble, Alfeo?"

"Why should I? You've never caused me any."

Violetta gave my arm a warning squeeze.

"I was instructed to tell you, boy, that you are to stop meddling in things that do not concern you. And that goes for that mountebank, Nostradamus, also. Tell him so. Now go away. And behave yourself, or it will go hard with you."

Since he and I attended the same fencing class, I knew I was a better fencer than he was. I admit I felt a momentary temptation to prove it with my rapier, right then and there, which would have been a wonderful treat, but one leading to a quick appointment with the headsman's ax. I regretfully decided to behave myself.

"What things, specifically, *sbirro?*"

His smile was intended to show that my insults were childish and he would settle them later. "Don't pretend to be stupider than you really are, Alfeo."

"Oh, you mean the Ludovici robbery?" I asked, in the hope that he might mention some cases I hadn't heard about yet.

"I mean any criminal matter at all. The magistrates enforce the law, not you. Go. I shan't warn you again."

There was nothing more to say. No one can argue with the Ten. They never answer questions, never explain, and there is no appeal from their decisions. I turned and walked away with Violetta and all the dignity I could muster, trying not to trip over the tail between my legs. Vasco stalked along behind us to see us off, whistling a cheerful tune.

Giorgio emerged from his shelter, noticing my fury but keeping his face diplomatically inscrutable. It wasn't until he'd rowed us well out of the *vizio's* hearing that he spoke.

"Where to?"

"Home!" I said. "We have been forbidden to meddle."

"Does that mean they've caught the devil?"

I always warn him when whatever I'm up to may be dangerous, so he knew who we were after.

"No." I glanced at Violetta and she nodded agreement. "It means they're protecting him."

9

After dropping off Violetta at the watergate of Number 96, I found the Maestro in his favorite chair, comparing two manuscript copies of a work by al-Kindi, the ninth-century philosopher who may be better known to you as Abu Yusuf Ya'qub ibn Is-haq ibn as-Sabbah ibn 'omran ibn Ismail al-Kindi. This was a bad sign, because it probably meant that he had been taking his mind off his sore hips and the Strangler both.

I reported.

"Can't fight the Ten," he growled. He detests arbitrary authority. It often provokes him into mulish defiance, which would be grievous folly in this case.

"And since Matteo must have told the *shirri* about Honeycat," I said angrily, "and the Ten has records on everyone going back three hundred years, they must know who he is by now. He's a noble and they're protecting him!"

Nostradamus shrugged his narrow black-clad shoulders. "That depends how many people knew him by that name, but you are likely right. What matter if the Ten have forbidden us to investigate these murders? The state investigates crime, certainly, but it is every citizen's duty to prevent one.

The Ten cannot object if we seek to prevent a murder that hasn't happened yet." He sighed. "Pass me my canes."

"If you are serious about preventing a murder," I said, "you could summon a much more effective assistant than me."

He scowled. "Not yet. Later, if we must."

That made sense, because the second law of demonology warns that a demon will always try to cheat, betray, and deceive, no matter how securely it is bound according to the first law. Prevention of a murder would be an altruistic purpose and therefore permitted by the third law, but summoning can never be truly safe.

"What do I do next, then?" I demanded. I was as restless as a bluebottle. Catching a killer is serious work at any time, but catching one who is *going to* kill is much more stressful.

"Nothing. Now it is my turn."

Massively relieved that he was going to bring his powers to bear on the problem, I gave the Maestro his canes and helped him rise. He crept across to the slate-topped table where he keeps the big crystal ball. I removed the red velvet cover, lit a candle, put chalk where he could reach it, and went to close the shutters on the blustery twilight outside. On the way back I grabbed a sheet of paper and a crayon from the desk.

"Anything else, master?"

"Yes. Go and feed. If I find anything you may be in for some strenuous activity this evening."

Of course the Strangler might not be planning anything at all. He might have done all the killing he wanted, or still be tracking his next victim, or be languishing in the palace cells. Or not. I found that the Maestro's warning had left me with surprisingly little appetite and a strong desire for company— going one-on-one against a murderer always makes me feel lonely. One possibility was Vettor Angeli, Giorgio's eldest, who lives elsewhere and is a gondolier in his own right. Vettor's a good lad with a cudgel or fists, but to take him out against a vicious three-time murderer would not be fair. More appealing was the thought of Fulgentio. A ducal equerry from a wealthy family does have some status—not enough to deter the Ten from taking action against him, because nobody has that security, not even the doge himself—but enough to make them prefer not to. He had been on his way to the palace that morning, so he ought to have finished his watch now and be home or on his way there.

I scribbled a note to him, telling him to bring the foils and masks over, and his sword as well, just in case. That would be enough to fetch him. Having sealed the note with a scrap of wax I keep in my bedroom, I sent it off to Ca' Trau in the hot and grubby hand of thirteen-year-old Archangelo Angeli, much to his delight and the vexation of the twins, who would undoubtedly lie in wait to mug him for his reward when he returned. Only then did I stalk into the kitchen to see what Mama might have lying around uneaten.

An hour after I had left the Maestro, I peeked into the atelier. He was still staring into the crystal, which made strange lights dance on his face; his hand was moving jerkily, as if the chalk were directing it instead of the other way around. Normally he writes with his left hand, but in trances he uses his right and never remembers afterward what he has seen or has written. I went to fetch a bottle of wine and a glass. Tiptoing, I put them by the red chair and then departed as quietly as I could, although he was totally engrossed in what he was doing.

Fulgentio arrived a few minutes after that, burdened with two foils and his sword, followed by a grinning Archangelo carrying two fencing masks. Fulgentio and I practice together quite often, although only rarely at Ca' Barbolano. The Angeli pack gathered around excitedly and muttered in angry disappointment when I ushered him into my room and closed the door.

"Why my sword?" he demanded. "You feeling suicidal?"

"Three courtesans have been murdered in the last three weeks. Haven't you heard?"

He stared at me narrowly. He has backed me up a few times and knows what it is like to play for the top stakes. "It's the talk of the town. There's muttering about a fourth, but that's not confirmed. Nothing's confirmed." He grinned. "Blank looks all round. And don't waste your breath asking me if the Ten are looking into it. I'd assume so, but even *Missier Grande* may not know for sure."

"I know for sure." I savored his startled expression for a moment before explaining about the *vizio*'s message. "It sounds to me as if the Ten know who did it and are protecting him."

Fulgentio drew his sword and tossed it on the bed. "If you're planning to defy the Ten, my friend, you'll do it alone. They say the galleys are quite fun in summer, but when it snows—"

"The Maestro is trying to foresee the next murder."

That startled him. "And stop it? Tell you how to stop it? Can you stop a foreseeing?"

"Not if that would create a paradox. But if we were there to see it happen, we could make sure there would be no more. And if the Maestro foresees an *attempted* murder, then we could fulfill that prophecy." My turn to grin. "Don't get too excited. We have no special reason to think that tonight's the night. Let me go and see what the old devil has produced this time."

Another glance into the atelier revealed the Maestro slumped over the crystal, exhausted. Clairvoyance always smites him with a fearful headache. Between us, Fulgentio and I helped him to the chair by the fireplace. I poured him a glass of wine and he took it in shaky hands.

"What'd I see?" he demanded as he usually does.

"Haven't looked yet," I said.

I went to the slate table, where Fulgentio was already staring at the quatrain.

"This is meant to be writing?" he whispered.

"This one happens to be surprisingly legible and coherent," I said, "which is usually a sign that it deals with something imminent. Wait a moment."

In a minute or so I had it deciphered:

> *After what once was holy and is not now*
> *Three saints cannot foreclose blind vengeance.*
> *Where the holy in firelight is unholy in shadow*
> *The man of blood sees blood upon the grass again.*

"And what does all that mean?"

"Another murder, I think."

"Man of blood?"

"Honeycat, likely. But Honeycat is a strangler, so there's other violence involved." With luck it would be my rapier disabling the monster so that *Missier Grande* could come and cart him away to justice.

"Three saints?"

"That's a puzzler. Go ask Giorgio. He knows every brick and door in Venice."

Fulgentio strode out. The Maestro mumbled something. I went across and crouched, "What?"

"Tomorrow. 'When' is tomorrow."

"So it is! But where is 'where'?" No answer. "You want me to call Bruno?"

He grunted agreement, so I went and fetched our porter, who carried the old man to his room. Between us we put him to bed. This was the worst rheumatic attack I had known Nostradamus to suffer, and it raised the horrible prospect that he might soon be unable to walk at all.

By that time Fulgentio was giving Corrado a fencing lesson at the far end of the *salone*, to an accompaniment of massed jeering from the boy's assembled siblings. Mama was watching with eyebrows at half-mast, because the sword is the weapon of either the gentleman or the gutter bravo, and she does not want any of her sons to have anything to do with it. I edged around to Giorgio.

"Three saints?"

"It's a tough one." He scowled like a man caught out in his professional expertise. "Two saints are common enough. Or a gang of them hanging around on the outside of a church, fine. But exactly three—the church of San Trovaso is on the Rio San Gervaso e San Protasso. That's the best I can think of."

"Possible. Keep thinking." I couldn't recall any grass around San Trovaso.

I went back to the fencing lesson.

"Let me revenge your shame," I told Corrado, and took foil and mask from him. Then I went to guard against Fulgentio and got thoroughly whipped, suffering four hits in a row. My mind was on more serious things, you understand, and fortunately it came up with an answer in time to justify my inattention. I threw down my foil and tugged the mask off.

"The Piazza itself!" I told him. "The two columns on the Piazzetta? The saints on top are San Teodoro and San Marco, right? And the church of San Geminiano at the far end of the Piazza, facing the Basilica! That makes three."

Fulgentio was still protesting about grass as I dragged him and Giorgio downstairs. I had wrapped myself in my winter cloak and, needless to say, we wore our swords and daggers. We took an armful of torches, for the moon had already set behind the rooftops.

Venice is built like an ants' nest of narrow, twisting alleys and canals because of the wind—corners and turns slow down the gusts. But when we emerged onto the choppy Grand

Canal, we took the full brunt of the storm, and rain had begun. Huddled in the *felze* with Fulgentio, I explained my reading of the quatrain.

"It's really two statements. The first line tells you when, and that's after a day that was once holy and now isn't, at least not to us. Tomorrow is Saturday, which is the Jewish Sabbath. Our Christian holy day is Sunday, so we no longer keep Saturday as holy. Got that?"

"This's still Friday."

"I know. The Jews start their days at sunset, so their Sabbath has begun."

"And we look for a friar, who is holy in firelight but murders in shadow?"

"You're coming along nicely, lad. Yes. The second line tells us that three saints are watching where the man of blood will strike. May they help us!"

"Amen!" Fulgentio said. "But what's 'blind vengeance'? Does that mean that we kill the wrong man?"

I had no answer to that. "Let's start by finding three saints and grass."

Giorgio rowed us across the Grand Canal and into lesser but more sheltered ways. We disembarked behind the Old Procuratie, and I told him to go home and help Mama pigeonhole the children. Fulgentio and I walked through the arch to the north side of the Piazza. The smaller Piazzetta, abutting the Grand Canal, is normally closed in the evening for the nobles' *broglio*, but that night it was deserted. The great square itself was as bare, and the only lights came from torches. No one would dare light a bonfire on such a night, lest it burn down the Doges' Palace. Hawkers, pedlars, musicians had vanished and merrymakers were in short supply.

And so was grass. I had been hoping that some tableau might include turf, or there might be animal stalls with hay, for you can find almost anything in the Piazza during Carnival, but nothing came even close to being grass.

We soon decided that our cause was hopeless there, and so far neither of us had thought of an alternative to Giorgio's suggestion of San Trovaso, so we set off on foot. The walk warmed us, but we met with no more success. The only grass we located was behind the walls of the rich, and if the murder was to take place on private grounds, we could not hope to intervene. Fulgentio and I abandoned the hunt by mutual consent and set off at a brisk pace, back to San Remo.

We reached the Trau mansion first and he invited me in for a nightcap. I declined because I still had work to do and I knew that he must be up early to attend to his duties in the palace.

Leaving Ca' Trau, I crossed the *campo* and entered the *calle* that leads to the back door of Ca' Barbolano. After one house length it branches. The main branch continues with a single, minor jog, leading to the bridge over the Rio San Remo and the accompanying watersteps; the entrance to Number 96 is there, easily accessible from both land and water and well illuminated to attract customers.

I turned to the branch going off to my left, which is dark, narrow, and bends several times before reaching the courtyard gate to Ca' Barbolano, from which it continues somewhat uselessly to the canal. A stray puff of wind blew out my torch.

Torches don't do that. Wind makes them burn brighter.

The Word is a simple spell for creating fire—a morally neutral one, according to the Maestro, although the church may not agree with him—but even the Word requires the user to be able to see his target. Fortunately I could just make out a faint glow where the tip was still smoking, and no one could see what I was doing on that moonless, cloud-shrouded night. I transferred the torch to my right hand, made the required gesture with the left, and spoke the Word. Blue fire ran over the charred end and yellow flames followed it.

A voice ahead of me said, *"Arghrraw!"*

Low on the ground ahead of me, two eyes glowed golden.

Holding my torch high, back in my left hand again, I drew
my sword and inched closer.

"*Arghrraw . . .*"

Venice has several million cats, but they are usually not
as loud as that one. Lions and leopards are unknown. So why
was I standing around in the cold listening to a cat? It could
eat or fight or mate to its heart's content, so far as I cared. I
moved forward again.

"*Arghrraw . . .*"

Now I could see it better—tail up, back arched. Cats
rarely contract rabies, but they are especially vicious when
they do. A bite from a rabid cat must be one of the least pleasant ways of going to one's eternal reward, and I did not trust
my swordsmanship against feline reflexes.

"And a fine evening to you also, *sier* Felix," I said. "Sorry
to have disturbed you." I backed cautiously away and it did
not follow.

10

The wider *calle* brought me, of course, to the watersteps and Number 96, whose welcoming lantern still burned, for it was not yet midnight. The land door opens into the waterfront loggia, where half a dozen boatmen sat huddled around a brazier. Their gondolas nodded among the mooring posts outside the arches. Ripples slapped.

Violetta would not be back yet from the musical salon at Ca' Grimini, and she would not return alone anyway, so normally I would have gone right on by, walking to the far end of the gallery and then negotiating the ledge to the narrower *calle* and Ca' Barbolano. That would have required me to run the gauntlet of the boatmen's foul ribaldry, of course, but anyone who worries about gondoliers' manners should never visit Venice. What made me hesitate was not fear of ridicule but the thought of Alessa. Although she had refused to share information with us over dinner, she had now had many hours to reconsider. Ignoring several boatmen's offers to row me to much better establishments, I opened the door and went in.

The entrance is a cosy parlor, illuminated by numerous lamps and warmed in winter by a toasty fire, mainly for the benefit of skimpily dressed hostesses. The decor is heavy on red and gold and gilt-framed paintings of nudes that never saw the inside of Titian's studio. The air was weighty with wine and perfume, and sounds of drunken revelry were audible beyond the door at the back, which leads through to ground floor rooms for those who are short of either time or money and thus cannot afford to linger. The staircase in the corner leads to the owners' apartments on the *piano nobile* and then on up to a second commercial area, of higher delights and much higher prices.

Uttering cries of joy, two girls on duty jumped up to greet me. I rewarded them with a polite smile and headed to the stairs, where scar-faced Antonio perched awkwardly on a stool. On my admittedly rare visits to the brothel when it is open for business, I had never seen the chief guard displayed so prominently. Obviously security was tighter than usual at Number 96 and perhaps at every brothel in the city. Word gets around. Because of the temperature, he was stripped down to a shirt and breeches, which made him look even meaner than he does when respectably dressed, while the contrast with his two delectable companions emphasized his nightmare ugliness. He knows me, but he eyed me distrustfully on principle.

"She's still out?" I asked.

Antonio nodded.

"With someone known to you? Not masked, I hope."

"Of course," he growled. "Think I'm stupid? And we don't admit friars."

So many words had gotten around, and perhaps Honeycat would have to hunt outdoors from now on, as the Maestro's quatrain suggested.

"I need to speak with Alessa."

He frowned and then shrugged. Antonio's shrugs create drafts. "She's upstairs. I'll ask." He went, striding two treads at a time.

"You're Violetta's doorman aren't you?" asked the taller of the two seminudes. She advanced predatorily.

"You should try a little variety," the other suggested, starting a flanking maneuver.

"You're much too cute to waste on just her."

"Beware!" I cried, retreating into a corner. "Think what Violetta will do to you if you molest my innocence."

"On, now I have heard everything!"

"Shameless! Who's going to tell her?"

"I'm here on business!" I protested.

"So are we."

I was saved from an unmentionable fate by a blast of cold air from the outer door, wafting in a couple of drunken sailors, masked for Carnival and eager to open negotiations. While the girls were deftly removing the men's masks and boosting their ardor, Antonio came clattering down the stairs and beckoned me. I followed him up to where a second bravo guarded the door to the *piano nobile*.

Antonio introduced us while he fumbled for the key. "Luigi . . . Alfeo . . . Alfeo's all right. A friend." Once inside, he led the way along a dark corridor to Alessa's door, where he paused, as if suddenly uncertain. "She's not herself."

"What way not herself?"

"She's pretty drunk."

"Violetta would murder me."

The big man chuckled. "So she would." He stalked away.

A faint wedge of light showed under the door. As Venice sinks slowly into the mud of the lagoon, its doors and windows—even its walls—forswear right angles in favor of ideas of their own. I tried the handle and went in. Alessa lacks Violetta's flair for artistic arrangement and her apartment is overly cluttered with expensive knickknackery. I picked my way in near darkness through this forest of glass, ceramic, and plaster until I found her in an armchair in her *sa-*

lotto, huddled close to a dying fire and clad in a loose robe that no respectable lady would wear even when alone. Her hair was unbound, dangling everywhere, her face paint messed. Fortunately the single lamp on the mantel shed very little light on her shame, but the reek of wine confirmed what Antonio had told me. First Matteo and now Alessa—Honeycat was doing good things for the vintners of Venice.

With the poker and a couple of logs from the scuttle, I gave the fire new life. Then I pulled up a chair, laid my forearms on my knees, and looked across at Alessa. Her eyes had been following me, but so far she had not spoken a word.

"Well?" I said. "Violetta isn't here. You are ready to tell me Honeycat's name."

She shook her head and held out her goblet. I confirmed that the bottle on the floor beside her was empty, found another, opened it, poured her a drink, and returned to my post. "Well?" I said again.

"He didn't do it." She spoke with the fastidious care of the very drunk. "Not Honeycat I knew. Ish a common enough pet name." She turned her gaze on the fire and fell silent.

"Tell me about the Honeycat you knew." In vino veritas.

"He was lovely," she told the fire. "He was young and dishgush-tingly rich. He was fun. He was joy. Very few *giovani* we look forward to, Alfeo, but I adored Honeycat. We'd fight over him, us girls. Rich, noble, handsome. Knew his classics: Ovid, Plato, and all the rest. He was a lover. He lived to make love. Never tired. Mosht greedy men are rough—bang, bang, bang. Not Honeycat. Was patient, clever.

"He had a red birthmark. Down here . . . Looked like a cat, so 'course he wash known ash Honeycat. He'd arrive in his gondola at noon, take me to a dinner, then a ball. Senators, procurators, and their wives. Dance till midnight. Oh, he could dance! Then back here and row the boat till dawn. Over and over. Don't know how he did it. Felt I ought to be paying him, not him me. Sometimes we'd throw parties for him—two, three girls, and he'd go all night, never sleep. Always left a present, diamond ring, pearls . . ."

"Go on," I said. "I want to hear more about this prodigy." *His name! What was his name?*

"Getting old, Alfeo." She sighed. "Even the nights were bright back then. Did I ever tell you about the time the doge—"

"Tell me about Honeycat, Alessa."

"Ashk Violetta."

"She never met him."

"Lucia in'rodushed them."

"Yes?" I clamped my lips shut because they were trying to snarl. This was what I feared most.

"She was fifteen. Sweet as a rosebud." Silence. All this time Alessa had been speaking to the fire, not me.

"How old was he?"

"Mm? 'Bout nineteen."

Aha! Now I had a lead, because his birth would be recorded in the Golden Book.

"He lined her up right away," Alessa mumbled. "Violetta. Three days in the country at one of his family's places. Right after the funeral. Oh, I was jealous! She'd have come back hundreds of ducats richer after that." Laughter made Alessa's breasts gyrate like gypsy dancers. "Tired, but richer."

What funeral?

"She told me she didn't know Honeycat."

Again that earthquake laugh. "No. We never told. A girl had to discover the mark for herself."

"And Violetta didn't?"

"He never showed up for her. Was the day he ran."

"Ran?" I held myself back from physical assault with an effort. "Alessa, what was his name?"

She drained her glass. "Didn't kill anyone. He wouldn't. All Honeycat ever wanted was girls, girls, girls. Wouldn't've harmed a flea."

I slid to my knees beside her and ran a hand up her arm. "Tell me his name, Alessa. The Honeycat you knew? Not the killer, the one you knew?"

For a moment I thought she still wouldn't. Then she hurled the empty glass into the fire. "Michiel!" she said. "Zorzi Michiel!" She began to weep, great convulsive sobs.

Zorzi Michiel? Oh my God!

No wonder Vasco had warned me off.

I had what I had come for, and the implications were too staggering to think about right then. I stood up.

"Thank you, Alessa. Come along. I'll see you to bed."

She took my hands like a child, but I had to haul her upright. I put one of her arms around my neck and half walked, half carried her to her bedroom. As I said, she would still be worth a tumble, but in that condition she did not tempt me at all. I tucked her in, pecked a kiss on her forehead, and left.

Downstairs, I warned Antonio that Alessa's door was not locked; he said he would see to it. So I emerged into the loggia and the bleak night wind. There was no sign of the cat. Rather than risk the ledge, I paid one of the boatmen a couple of *soldi* to ferry me sixty feet or so back to Ca' Barbolano.

Zorzi Michiel, the patricide, the worst criminal in a hundred years! And I had been totally wrong about the Council of Ten.

11

By the time the Maestro appeared the following morning, I had done my daily housework. Like all apprentices I am required to keep my master's work area clean and tidy, and he won't let me do that when he is in there himself, which is almost always. That day I had dusted all the furniture along the southeast wall from the examination couch to the medical cupboard, and tidied the contents of that. I felt virtuous. I often feel virtuous, and with good cause.

I rarely speak to him in the morning before he speaks to me. That day I was quite prepared to break my rule, but did not have to, because he came hobbling in on his canes, and that alone would have justified congratulations. I rose when he entered, as a well-behaved apprentice should, and he gave me a good-morning scowl.

"Willow bark!" he said.

I had the draft ready, and all I had to do was stir it up again and bring it to him as he settled in his chair. He took a few mouthfuls, pulled a face, and then frowned up at me.

"You're looking abominably smug. You captured Honeycat last night after a brilliant display of swordsmanship?"

"No, master. That's tonight's program."

"Then you learned his name."

"Yes, master. Zorzi Michiel."

Nostradamus stopped the beaker short of his lips with his jaw hanging open. It was quite a satisfactory response. Finally he whispered, "Saints preserve us! Who told you that?"

Zorzi Michiel had blazed into infamy just over eight years earlier. I had no professional interest in such matters back then; I was apprenticed to a printer, typesetting six days a week and educating myself letter by letter. My greatest worry had been whether I should shave my upper lip or wait a month or so until the rest of the world could see what I could see growing on it, but I certainly heard about the Michiel trouble. Senator Gentile Michiel had been murdered as he was leaving the Basilica San Marco after late-night Mass. The cathedral of Venice is St. Peter's in Castello, which happens to keep the cardinal-patriarch about as far away from the center of the city as it is possible to be. Glorious St. Mark's is the private chapel of the doge, and Christmas Mass there is a very splendid state ceremony, attended only by the great. Murder in such a holy place and on such an occasion shocked the city to the marrow. The Basilica had to be reconsecrated and the Senate ordered a week of public penance and fasting. To make the crime even worse, it turned out that the murderer had been Gentile's youngest son, Zorzi, and the patricide fled from the Republic and its dominions just ahead of *Missier Grande* and his *shirri*.

"Donna Alessa told me. I caught her in a weak moment," I explained, without mentioning that my stroke of genius had been prompted by a near-dead cat. "She gave me an eyewitness description of his eponymous birthmark, a hemangioma of feline form in the genital area."

Nostradamus drank some more willow bark, grimacing at the bitter taste.

"Young Michiel was exiled," he said. "They put a price on his head."

"A thousand ducats, as I recall. But I misjudged the Ten yesterday. They're not trying to protect him. They know he's back and they want to catch him and do whatever horrible things they do to patricides." Also save the reward money, of course.

"Three brothers," the Maestro mumbled. "Gentile had three sons, Bernardo, Domenico, Zorzi. A couple of months after the crime, Bernardo tried to hire me to track down his brother."

"Oh!" I had not known that. "Did you?"

"Bah! You think I'm stupid, to get mixed up in a thing like that? If I'd thought I could find him, I would have gone after the reward myself. I just waited a few days and wrote back that the fugitive must have moved out of my range and I only charge when successful. Case closed. More willow bark."

He would give himself dyspepsia or even hematemesis if he used too much of it, but I do not presume to lecture him on physic. As I went back to the alchemy bench, I said, "So we abandon the case?" Had we ever *bandoned* it?

"No. Not now. The madman must be caught before he murders any more of his former playmates." Of course the Maestro now had a passable in-house swordsman to round up the quarry for him so he could pocket the reward, but we never mention such things.

"Why is he murdering them?" I asked.

There was a pause while Nostradamus considered his answer. "Because he is a madman? Because he thinks one of them betrayed him to the Ten? More important, why did at least two of the murdered women agree to receive such a monster?"

I should have wondered that. "Because he told them he was innocent? Had been pardoned? Was going to prove he hadn't done it?"

"Perhaps he didn't?" my master growled. "You say Alessa didn't believe he did."

I turned and stared across the room at him in rank disbelief.

"You plan to solve an eight-year-old murder and disprove the Council of Ten's judgment?" I had seen Nostradamus attempt and often perform miracles, but this seemed beyond even him. The entire resources of the state had pursued the killer of Gentile Michiel.

"Well, let's try a pass or two at it anyway." For the first time, he was showing some real interest in the problem Violetta had brought to him two days past. "Take a letter. Take two. Best paper."

I gave him the potion and returned to my desk. "Ready."

"The first to Bernardo Michiel. Wait. We don't know what office he may be holding now, so you'd better make a draft."

I reached in the drawer for a cheaper sheet. "Ready then."

"Usual greetings. *Your most esteemed and luminous Excellency*—or whatever he is at the moment—*will remember how some years ago, during a time of great pain and tragedy, Your Excellency*—or whatever—*did me the inestimable honor of asking my humble assistance upon a certain private and sorrowful matter but that, to my eternal regret, my talents were too meager to satisfy Your Excellency's gracious needs, so I was unable to oblige Your Excellency*—period—*I am newly apprised of some information that may pertain to the same subject and hence venture to advise Your Excellency of it in complete confidence and purely as a way of making amends for my earlier failure and without any thought whatsoever of seeking compensation other than Your Excellency's favor and the satisfaction of serving so eminent a noble*—period— *The bearer of this letter,* sier *Alfeo Zeno, has my complete trust and will recount the matter to you*—period—*I remain forever*—et cetera. Butter him up more if you think it needs it."

I hate it when he uses my title for his own ends, but that was the least of my worries by then.

"Master," I said grimly, "you expect me to walk into this man's home and tell him his baby brother, who murdered their father to the family's eternal shame and his own damnation, is back in town with a price on his head, slaughtering prostitutes?"

"What can he do except tell you to leave?"

"Have his boatmen beat me to a pulp."

"No he can't. This is Venice, not France. Nobles can't take justice into their own hands. That is certainly what the lawyers will tell you."

Who believes lawyers?

"And all I want you to do is apply your inestimable skill and experience at judging people to decide whether or not he already knows that his brother is back. They may be hiding him in that palace of theirs."

"In that case they'll cut my throat," I said glumly. "Or they may accuse me of attempted blackmail, after the Council of Ten has already warned me off once. Next letter?"

"Do it in good. To *sier* Carlo Celsi . . ."

That was better. I like old Carlo.

12

I went on foot because I needed the exercise. Jostling and dodging through the teeming alleyways of the city on a busy morning is a good all-over workout. Besides, if I had asked Giorgio to row me there, he would have wanted to wait for me and that might have cost him his whole morning. Sometimes Celsi has a room full of people waiting to see him, on other days he lacks company and will talk for hours. Celsi is the unofficial archivist of the city, constantly scribbling, filling tome after tome with accounts of all political and historical events, and even the major social ones. If anybody outside the inner circle of the nobility knew the truth about the Michiel scandal, it would be Celsi. He has never been one of the inner circle, for he is a blabbermouth and the First Ones prefer to act in silence, but he has ways of finding out what they have been up to. Even Violetta does not know as much about the doings of the nobility as Celsi does, so the Maestro consults him quite often. But Violetta can keep secrets and never expects any quids pro quos.

His living quarters are modest, shabby, smelling of ink, largely taken up with bookshelves. Vittore, his servant, knows me and always greets me with a cryptic smile, as if my arrival is no surprise. He offered me refreshment, which I declined, and assured me that the noble lord would be delighted to see me as soon as his present visitor departed. That might be hours yet, so I made myself comfortable and went back to puzzling over the Honeycat affair.

If Zorzi Michiel had not committed that horrible crime, then why had he fled? Had he perhaps been frolicking with one of his many courtesan friends at the time and later she had refused to give him an alibi? That might explain one courtesan death, but surely even Honeycat could not have been with three and all three given false witness? That stretched conjecture to fatuity, as the Maestro says. No, the obvious answer was that flight had been the only possible defense as soon as he realized he was under suspicion. The Ten allow no counsel, no open trial, no right to face accusers, no appeal. Prisoners may be found guilty without knowing their crimes and jailed without being told their sentences. Worse, like other states, Venice allows torture in serious criminal cases and none could be more serious than Zorzi's.

Of course the Strangler might not be Zorzi Michiel, merely someone using his name to gain access to his victims. Either way, I was still at a loss to imagine why he was killing courtesans.

After ten minutes or so, the inner door opened and out stalked a man I had met two days before, Senator Marco Avonal. Recognition was mutual. His face darkened; I smiled angelically—I practice that in a mirror. I sprang to my feet and bowed low.

"*Clarissimo!* An unexpected pleasure!" I straightened up just as the outer door banged shut behind him. Oh dear, what a shame . . .

"*Sier* Alfeo! I might have known," chirruped old Celsi. "Come in, come in, dear boy. Sit down, sit there."

He dragged me bodily into his sanctum, which might charitably be described as a box of four bookcases with a fireplace and two chairs. The window was partially blocked by a stand-up desk, on which lay a folio volume of blank sheets, ready to receive more news. He poured me a glass of red wine.

"You must try this ghastly French brew. So Nostradamus is dipping into the pot, is he? He's after the Strangler?"

Carlo Celsi is a year older than the Maestro, but still as spry as a mouse. He is very short—not reaching up to my shoulder—and rotund, sporting a mass of silver curls all over his lower face and out from under his hat. I have never seen him anything but pert, happy, and effusive.

"I brought his—"

"Does it say anything?" Celsi demanded, grabbing the proffered letter, "except that he wants you to pick my brains and tell me nothing in return?"

"No. That's it exactly."

"Good." My host dropped the letter in a wastebasket, unopened. "Sit, sit! You haven't changed your preferences since the last time you were here, have you, dear chap?"

"No, *clarissimo*." I always have to wade this river when I call on Celsi.

"What a tragedy! Well, drink up, and tell me why Nostradamus is interested in a few dead whores."

"Money, of course," I said. "And why is *sier* Carlo interested in Senator Marco Avonal? Because he discovered a body and turned in the jewelry, when he could have better pocketed it himself or given the proceeds to charity? Did he have some special reason for wanting the deceased identified?"

Celsi chuckled, leaned back in his chair, and took a sip of the wine, which I had already decided must be one of the most expensive vintages I had ever tasted. "He was here because I wrote and asked him to explain that. Of course he wants to be immortalized in the annals of the Republic, so he came in person to give me the entire story and make sure I spelled his name the way he likes it. What do you think of it, dear Alfeo?"

"I think he may be telling the truth."

The old man sighed. "So do I, unfortunately. No under-lying scandal at all! Some people are appallingly inconsider-ate."

"Was he in Milan?"

"Yes—and he returned with the others. I already checked."

"His Excellency puzzles me, though. He has a squeaky voice, belongs to a small and obscure house, lives with shameful thrift, and is barely adult by Venetian political standards, so how does he get elected to the Senate?"

Celsi sniggered affectedly as he does when he has a gem to impart. "The Contarini campaign, dear boy!"

"Which Contarini?" The Contarinis are a huge clan.

"The ambassador to Rome. The Great Council waxed very mad at him just before Christmas. It couldn't hurt him directly—only the Senate could recall him—but every time the Council had a vacancy of any sort to fill, it would nomi-nate three other Contarinis plus a nonentity, then elect the nonentity. When it put Avonal into the Senate itself, that was the last straw. The Senate recalled Contarini in self-defense." He chuckled. "They only sent Avonal along on the Milan jun-ket to get a respite from his efforts to make speeches. At the end of his term he will vanish back into well-deserved ob-scurity.

"So what is your master after this time?" He took a sip of wine to mask his appraising look at me. "He expects me to tell you who killed three harlots and what the Council of Ten is doing about it, mm?"

I couldn't resist that lead. "No. We know all that." My turn for a sip.

"You cherub! You do? You will swear to that? I have a reliquary somewhere with a holy toenail paring of Saint Theophilus of Bulgaria."

I backed down a little. "We know to a high degree of

probability. No, Nostradamus wonders if you would comment on the death of Gentile Michiel and his son's exile."

Celsi stared in amazement at bookshelves behind me and let out a long breath. "So-o-o? You think he's come back? *Strangling* the girls? That doesn't sound like young Zorzi. He used to hump them to death . . . I speak figuratively and with sinful envy. What do you want to know?"

"Everything, fair exchange."

"Nostradamus going soft in his old age? If he's willing to tell all, he can't know much. Well, let's see. Start with Gentile. Had a few uncles but no brothers, sisters, or cousins. A carefully husbanded tribe, the San Marco Michiels—they have always believed in keeping the family fortune intact. Gentile was publicly devout, straitlaced, sanctimonious. An obnoxious tyrannical prude, in fact."

"The sort who won't let his wife look out any window that overlooks a street?"

"Exactly. Gentile married Alina Orio—eccentric sort of woman. She lost five brothers to the plague, them and their families, extremely careless of her. That wiped out a whole branch of the Orio clan, so she ended up with all the property, very odd. Four sons and a daughter survived infancy."

"I heard three sons."

"Don't interrupt me when I'm gossiping. I might miss out a juicy bit. Bernardo was going to be the politician. Of course he wasn't even thirty then, but he'd already made a major speech in the Great Council, opposing a change in the salt tax that his father had supported in the Senate. Got a response from the doge himself, tremendous honor that, for a nipper! The patricide put the whole family in the lazaretto, of course, but Bernardo wouldn't give up; he kept on attending Great Council meetings. So they tried electing him to trivial offices and he accepted and worked hard at them. He's started making speeches again, and it looks as if they're about ready to forgive him. He's been nominated for several meaningful jobs lately, and come near to winning a couple of times. He won't want the old scandal dug up."

"What is he now?"

Celsi closed his eyes for a moment to think, then twinkled them at me. "Inspector of meats!" This was one minor politician he was recalling, out of hundreds, a fine feat of memory.

"Then, Domenico's the businessman. Doesn't attend the wind factory unless there's some critical vote coming up. He's a genius at buying up estates on the mainland, tidying them up, and selling them at a spanking profit. Dull, like all men who make money. Only those who make art or history are interesting, Alfeo dear. Dom's not the sort to hide a murderer— no profit in that. Has a couple of children by a long-term mistress.

"Next was Timoteo. He inherited his father's acid piety, but he seems to have meant it. He renounced his share and entered the cloister."

"He's a monk?" I spoke a little too eagerly.

Carlo Celsi has extremely sensitive antenna. He eyed me suspiciously.

"A friar. And a priest also, as I recall. Why?"

"Just wondered. The other brothers form a *fraterna*?" I asked, being as innocent as possible. I had caught a faint whiff of motive . . .

This time the old gossip missed my eagerness. "So far as I know. They have to go to law to disenfranchise, you know."

I nodded. "And the daughter?"

"Oh, they packed her off into a cloister years ago. That costs money too, but it's cheaper than providing a dowry. Did you hear the size of dowry old—"

I headed off his digression. "Which leaves only the infamous Zorzi."

"Correct."

"Obviously the last, since the rest had been named in alphabetical order. Or the sons had. What was the daughter's name?"

"Don't remember. Your brilliance is exceeded only by your personal charm. Zorzi! Oh, Zorzi was a hellion!" Celsi said admiringly. "If he hadn't been a nobleman's son he'd have been swept up by the Ten and banished for licentious living. Apollo he was, to look at, and he never seemed to be short of money. He and his father fought like cat and dog all the time, with the old man always threatening to disinherit him if he didn't reform his ways. That was why he came under suspicion, I think."

"Remind me about the murder."

"You were a teenager. Don't tell me you didn't lap up all the gory details!"

"Yes, but you always know more than anyone else."

Celsi snorted but looked pleased. "Christmas, a stormy night, and the Basilica atrium is black as tar at the best of times. Families reuniting as the women arrived from their section and the men from the nave, lamps being waved about . . . complete confusion. A lot of people even wondered if Gentile Michiel had been the wrong victim; he just didn't seem important enough for such a shocking crime. Right man or wrong, someone stuck a knife in his kidney. No one saw who it was. He was dead by the time they brought in a surgeon to try stitching him up, the killer long gone."

He shrugged. "A couple of days later Zorzi saw which way the wind was blowing and raised his sails in the nick of time. The Ten condemned him and put a price on his head. They did it with all the trimmings—placards posted at the Porta della Carta, the public crier marching around with his scarlet coat and his trumpeters. Now you're going to tell me Zorzi's come back and is slaughtering courtesans?"

"How much of a price?"

Celsi's curly silver beard twisted around a smile. "Trust Nostradamus! Old miser. A thousand ducats, no matter where he's caught. That's on top of the usual five hundred for handing in the head of an exile who sneaks back incognito. Has he come back? Truly?"

It was my turn to sing now, but I squeezed in one more question. "If the Mass was a formal state gathering, how did a kid like Zorzi ever get admitted? He couldn't have been a member of the Great Council at nineteen."

Celsi shrugged. "He could have, but he wasn't. I don't remember anybody asking how he got in. It would have been easy enough. It was dark, a melee. Gentile would be wearing his red senatorial robes, so his black ones would be stored in a chest at home somewhere, I expect." He scratched his beard. "I'm sure the Ten had good reason to declare the boy guilty. Probably witnesses recognized him. You really think he was *innocent*?"

"I don't. And if the Maestro does, he hasn't told me about it."

"What leads you to think he's come back?"

As I told him, I realized how weak our case still was. "Three demimonde have been killed in the last three weeks, all in the same way, all old enough to have been in the trade eight years ago. No signs of other violence, meaning rape, and no robbery, so the motive's a mystery. All of them seem to have been expecting an old friend, and at least one of those had claimed to be Honeycat, which was Zorzi's love name. He had a birthmark to justify it, in a confidential location."

"Pah! I wouldn't waste spittle on that evidence."

"And the Council of Ten has warned us to stop prying into the murders."

Celsi sniffed disapprovingly. "Better. That is odd, I grant you. I know how often the Three take credit that really belongs to Nostradamus—and to you, too, dear boy, of course. Why try to block you on this one, mm?"

"They want to take Zorzi Michiel themselves?"

"Perhaps. But three dead courtesans are a serious matter.

The state needs the taxes those women pay; the Ten can't want the trade shut down. It's a pity . . ."

He eyed one of his bookshelves, then heaved his portly frame upright and went to fetch a leather-bound ledger. He spread it on his lap, with the edge tucked under his paunch, and started thumbing through it. "My version of the Golden Book," he muttered. "I call it the Brass Book. You must be in here somewhere, everyone is. Yes, thought so. It's a pity the Devil finally took old Agostino Foscari. He would often drop a hint or two if I asked him nicely." He frowned at me. "Why're you looking like that?"

Because I had thought of something, and since I had not yet had time to report my idea to Nostradamus, I did not want or need to share it with Celsi. "Procurator Agostino Foscari? He died last fall, didn't he? Why him?"

Of course I couldn't deceive an expert. My host beamed like an antique cherub. "You still owe me a few secrets, dear boy. Out with it."

"You're saying that Foscari was one of the Three back then, back when Gentile Michiel was murdered?"

The Three are the state inquisitors. The Ten—who are actually seventeen, comprising ten elected members plus the doge and his six ducal counselors—do not have time to investigate criminal cases personally. They delegate that duty to the Three, a subcommittee of two elected members and one ducal counselor, known as the blacks and the red respectively from the color of their robes. The lips of the Council of Ten are notoriously sealed tighter than the Vatican's cash drawer, but Celsi was hinting that a case as old as the Michiel scandal was about due to spring a few leaks.

The old man smirked approvingly. "Yes, he was. Foscari was the red."

"And the blacks?"

"Just where is your nimble little mind running now, sonny?"

"Tell me the other two inquisitors who investigated Gentile's murder, and I'll give you a lovely, juicy morsel to make your day. I promise."

He pouted. "Or I shall claim a forfeit! The other two were Tommaso Pesaro, and Giovanni Gradenigo. He's gone too, now. Foscari in September, Gradenigo last Thursday, and you'll never get anything out of Pesaro. He won't tell the recording angel his middle initial. Now what's the big secret?"

"Nostradamus foresees another murder. We expect it this evening and we have a good idea of where it will happen." Or would have, when I had more time to think about it.

So I didn't have to discover what Celsi meant by a forfeit and we parted on good terms, with him rubbing his hands in glee at not being just on top of the news but actually ahead of it. I had put my master's reputation on the line, but it was worth it.

The one other question I had wanted to ask and hadn't was whether the young Timoteo Michiel, when he took his friar's vows, had taken the name of Fedele.

13

Back at Ca' Barbolano, I found a note from Violetta to say that she was going to a house party on the mainland and would be back on Sunday. It was addressed to me, but the Maestro had opened it and read it. He always does, so she knows not to include any lovers' secrets. For once I wished I knew where she was going and who was taking her.

I had just enough time before dinner to give the Maestro a quick summary of what I had learned. That left him to do most of the talking at table, which he normally does anyway. As we headed to the dining room, I was pleased to see that his lameness was less marked, his disposition was improving, and he was definitely caught up in the Honeycat case now. Which effect was the chicken, which the egg, and which the rooster, I do not speculate.

"So you think," he demanded, "that the dying Giovanni Gradenigo learned of the murdered Caterina Lotto and remembered that it was she who betrayed Zorzi Michiel to the inquisitors? That was all he wanted to tell me?"

While planning my response, I nibbled appreciatively on a mouthful of Mama Angeli's delicious *Taglierini* noodles. I had told Violetta that any connection between the death of her friend Lucia and the patrician's deathbed appeal had to be an impossible coincidence. Now it was starting to look like no more than close timing.

"Possibly, but I think he must have heard about the other murders too, at least one of them. One dead courtesan wouldn't mean much—that was your own reaction when Violetta told you about Lucia. It's hard to believe that three women all betrayed Zorzi," I hastened to add. "Which may mean that Honeycat doesn't know which of his lady friends shopped him and is going to avenge himself on all of them . . .

"Or," I added with sudden inspiration, "he wanted to kill that particular one without drawing attention to his own case, so he killed a couple of others as well." Too late I saw the trap I had fallen into.

"Bah! Rubbish! Why tell me? An antiquated, invalid retired doctor? Why wouldn't Gradenigo summon one of his Council of Ten friends, who could start a hunt for the returned exile?"

"I don't know," I said humbly. "But the fact that the old man was a state inquisitor right when Zorzi was exiled can hardly be pure coincidence."

"And just what is an impure coincidence?"

When I said that the Maestro's disposition was improving, I meant that it was returning to normal. I sidestepped the question.

"You want me to try Bernardo Michiel this afternoon, master?"

"You are not a court. I want you to try to get to talk with him. If he doesn't know where his murderous brother is hiding, then I don't know who else to ask."

"Domenico, perhaps," I said. "He's the one who buys and sells property, so he could give Zorzi sanctuary somewhere on the mainland. It would be easy enough to nip across from Mestre, commit the murders, and nip back again."

"By 'nip' you mean 'row'? Or 'swim'?"

"Sail or be rowed. And Bernardo was the one whose political career was swamped by his brother's patricide. I doubt if Domenico's real estate business would have been hurt much, so there may be less ill-feeling there."

One of Nostradamus's tiny fists thumped the table. "That is absurd speculation. Facts! You're job is to bring me facts, not guesswork. I do the guessing. You cannot predict the brothers' respective reactions to their father's death until you know them personally. Speak with Domenico if you get the chance by all means. And find out if the sanctified Timoteo is now going by the name of Fedele. *That* might be an impure coincidence."

Since Violetta was out of town, I abandoned thoughts of a siesta after dinner and trotted up to the archive boxes in the attic to find the Michiel file. It was thinner than a portrait painter in Constantinople, just a brief personal letter from Bernardo and the Maestro's even briefer response, dated the following week and written for him by my predecessor. I learned nothing I did not already know, such as that a nobleman writing on a topic that might interest the Council of Ten will do so in his own hand rather than trust a secretary.

Few of the Venetian nobility go back to work after their noon break and a meat inspector would find little to do by that time of day anyway. Confident that one or other of the Michiel brothers should be home, I copied out the Bernardo letter in an honest Roman hand and then created one to Domenico, giving myself the same glowing introduction without mentioning Bernardo's previous approach to the Maestro.

From the outside, the ancient Palazzo Michiel looks as if it is merely keeping its site warm until it can be demolished and replaced by something newer and grander. I was anxious to see inside it, though, for its art collection was reputed to be one of the finest in the city. Its location certainly is, just around the corner from the Doges' Palace, right on the Riva degli Schiavoni—the Croatians' shore—looking out over the basin where the fleets gather. I had Giorgio drop me off at the Molo and strolled the rest of the way, admiring the setting even while I huddled my cloak tight against a gray February bluster.

Three men were quietly freezing as they sat on a long bench in the loggia. One was clearly a porter; the other two were younger and probably apprentices. I wasn't going to put up with that treatment. I was armed and wearing my best outfit, wishing as always that the Maestro were logical enough to see that he should not try to exploit my title without dressing me to match it. I rapped the worn brass knocker hard.

The flunky who answered my signal recoiled slightly before my haughty aristocratic simper and I moved to step past him. He hesitated, but the sight of my sword convinced him, and he let me enter. I bestowed my *sier* Bernardo letter on him. He took it, asked if *messer* would be so kind as to wait, and vanished through an archway that offered no view beyond it except the wall of a corridor. In seconds a page emerged from wherever he had gone and hurried off across the *androne*, bearing the letter.

Indoors was probably no warmer than outside, but at least I was sheltered from the wind. By then I had observed another three men—well-dressed men waiting on well-upholstered benches—and had deciphered their clothing as that of a hungry young lawyer, an aging merchant with liver trouble, and a prosperous middle-aged Jew. The liver trouble I deduced from the color of the sufferer's eyes, of course.

I was more interested in the decor than a chance to rest my legs. The *androne* was large enough to revive the Battle of Agnadello, and the page was running up a quite admirable staircase. Obviously the palazzo had been heavily updated sometime in its latest century and I approved of the result, although it was going to start looking old-fashioned fairly soon. I presumed to wander around the big hall, admiring sculptures and wall paintings. Two of those I thought might be by Guariento. Nothing was new, but it was all fine quality.

An hour later I was sitting on a bench and starting to grow bored. The door knocker knocked, callers called, the flunky flunked. The visitors who had preceded me had been led off to attend to their business and been replaced by others. Other people wandered in and out unchallenged as if they belonged there, but nobody paid any attention to me at all. At the end of a second hour I was all alone and starting to suspect that I was not welcome. I have met such studied rudeness often enough that I can usually ignore it, but in this case I had reason to wonder if the Council of Ten had been informed of my presence there and we were waiting for *Missier Grande* to arrive and arrest me.

Finally a different flunky emerged from the cubbyhole, a spotty boy who was probably the most junior servant they could find in the entire palazzo. To his credit, he looked uncomfortable as he confirmed that I was who I am, and then informed me that *sier* Bernardo had no wish to meet with me.

"Then perhaps *sier* Domenico will? I have a letter—"

Alas, the second brother was not in residence at the moment. Would I like to speak with a secretary?

"No," I said, displaying admirable poise. "The matter is very confidential."

He escorted me to the great door and bowed me out. I refrained from tipping him for this service. I paused for a moment in the loggia while I wrapped my cloak tight about me. The *riva* was almost deserted now; the wind had risen and was whipping a fine spume off the waves of the basin, but it would be at my back as I walked to the *traghetto*. I had noticed that there was only one man left sitting on the bench, but paid him no heed until I started to move, for by then he had risen to accost me.

"*Sier* Alfeo Zeno?"

I nodded.

He bowed. "A lady wishes to receive you. Will you be so kind as to accompany me?"

"The kindness is yours," I retorted. "I trust I did not keep you waiting long?"

A polite but meaningless smile flashed across his face. "Much too long, but the blame does not rest on you, *messer*. This way, if you please."

He led me along the *riva* to the corner of the palazzo, then turned into a very narrow and inconspicuous *calle*. He puzzled me. He was stocky, with the breadth of a porter or stonemason, yet his dress was a vision in red and gold brocade, with osprey plumes in his hat and a ruff like a waterwheel, far too expensive for any servant, even a steward or secretary. His manner was genteel but lacked the *Stand Aside, Rabble!* arrogance of a young nobleman and he had not given me his name, as a gentleman would. I judged him to be about my age, but his beard was bushy and tightly curled, and beards can be deceptive. He could be some years younger or older.

Once around the corner and a dozen or so paces along the *calle*, he entered a shallow archway and paused to unlock a small but solidly built door, clearly a private entrance. Then he ushered me through, to a cramped, shadowy stairwell, and proceeded to relock the door. We began to climb.

14

The stairs were dusty and cobwebbed, a servants' access no longer used. At the top we emerged through another inconspicuous door, which my guide carefully locked behind us, although from the outside it looked to be of no importance, perhaps a closet. We had come to the sort of luxurious private quarters to be expected in so grand a palace. The decor was modern and I was hard put not to gape around me as my guide led me around a corridor and across an antechamber to a spacious reception room, presently occupied by three women.

I judged the one to my right to be a servant by her clothes, her shriveled, weathered features, and her occupation, for she was presently mending a child's britches. The one on my left was dressed as a lady of means, small and plump, somewhat mousy, aged perhaps thirty. She held a book. I had heard her reading aloud as I crossed the anteroom.

The one on the chair between their two stools was obviously the great person I had been brought to meet, donna Alina Orio, widow of the murdered Gentile Michiel and mother of his infamous killer. She held an embroidery hoop rather too far from her nose.

"*Sier* Alfeo Zeno, madonna," said my companion.

Skewered by eyes as sharp as the servant's darning needle, I bowed low. She was a tall, but not heavy woman, clad in fine velvet and lace, all in black, and carefully adorned with pearls and face paint. Palace life and ample servants and wet nurses had preserved her well; only the hollow cheeks caused by lost teeth acknowledged that she must be over fifty and had borne many children.

"Why is a messenger boy claiming to be a patrician?" she demanded.

"I am a patrician, madonna; my birth is listed in the Golden Book. I carried only a letter of introduction and bring a message in my head. I am apprenticed to Maestro Nostradamus, the astrologer and philosopher. Those are learned professions, permitted to the patriciate."

"So what is that precious message?"

My immediate fate balanced on a knife edge. If she had summoned me just to see what I looked like, she could now jettison me and carry on with her day.

"It was addressed to your noble son, madonna, but he chose not to hear it."

She considered that answer and decided it would pass muster.

"Leave us," she commanded, and the women rose in a rustle of taffeta. The maid curtseyed and hurried to open the door. The lady companion nodded with no comment and a completely expressionless face, although including her in the same command as the servant had to be a deliberate discourtesy.

"Be seated, *sier* Alfeo."

She handed the youth her embroidery to put away and clasped her hands together on her lap. They were more timeworn than her face, and the gesture revealed inner tensions that her expression never would.

I thought I had my guide identified by then as her

cavaliere servente, gentleman escort and general errand boy, who might, if he was lucky, also be her gigolo. There could be worse occupations, even if the woman was older by thirty years. I began to doubt my judgment when she did not invite him to take the other stool. Besides, donna Orio looked like the sort of grande dame who had conceived her children by prayer and never done anything so undignified as rollick naked with a man.

"Eight years ago next month, I told my oldest son to hire your precious Nostradamus to locate Zorzi for me. You are aware who Zorzi is?"

"Zorzi Michiel, your youngest son, who was sent into exile."

Her knuckles whitened. "Who *fled* into exile. He was condemned in absentia, the evidence that would have proved his innocence never considered. Nostradamus claimed he could not do what I ordered, but more likely he was playing safe and chose not to. Today the old fraud sends a boy with unspecified information. My son rightly decided to ignore you. Yet you waited two and a half hours and had to be sent packing like a beggar. Are you without shame, *sier* Alfeo?"

"There can be no shame in serving my master diligently."

She disliked my smart-aleck hint that the shame was her son's. Her mouth curled in an angry pout.

"Why does Nostradamus not deliver his own news?"

"Because he is frail and rarely leaves his residence now."

"Does your message concern Zorzi?"

That question posed a problem, but the Maestro expects me to make my own decisions and be prepared to defend them. He had said that if Bernardo was not hiding Honeycat then he did not know who else to ask. I did, now, but would she tell me anything? And if I told her anything, what would she do?

"Alas, madonna, I cannot reveal that to anyone except *sier* Bernardo."

That was the right answer and any other would have seen me tossed out a watergate without a gondola.

She sucked in her cheeks angrily, giving herself a monkey face. "Jacopo, where is Bernardo?"

"He is in conference with the bankers, I believe, madonna."

"Domenico?"

"Playing tennis." Jacopo seemed remarkably well-informed about the household's activities.

Alina pouted. "Will he do," she asked me, "or must it be Bernardo?"

"I was sent to *sier* Bernardo."

"Go and tell Bernardo I want him right away."

Jacopo departed. Bernardo was nominal head of Casa Michiel, but I was alone with the real head. I waited politely for her to name the topic of our conversation.

"My son was never guilty of his father's murder! He was the victim of a gross miscarriage of justice."

What else would a mother say?

"Alas, madonna, it is hard to contend with the Council of Ten when it does not reveal the basis for its decisions." It was also dangerous to accuse it of making mistakes.

"There was no evidence, no real evidence. There could not be. Yes, he quarreled with his father. He was wild and outspoken, but what boy of his age is not? His father sowed enough wild oats, even when he was old enough to know better. Zorzi was guilty of lack of respect, nothing more. He would never have hurt anyone deliberately."

"I have been told the same by others," I remarked.

Steely eyes glinted. "What others?"

"Persons who knew him." I did not add, *intimately*.

"You are too young to remember. You have been going around prying into those matters?" She ought not to scowl; it made her as ugly as a gargoyle.

"I was investigating other matters, madonna, and by accident ran into talk of your husband's death."

She kneaded her wizened lips together for a moment. "Nostradamus claims to foretell the future. Can he also envision the past?"

"Not as such, but I have seen him unravel old mysteries. Some of his methods are occult, but often he just uses the wisdom of a sage to cut away a web of lies and deceit that has concealed the truth."

Silence fell, as if I had dissolved and she were alone, staring at nothing. I was attracted by the painting on the far side of the room. "Is that portrait by Paris Bordone, madonna?"

She frowned as if only the rich should see art. "It is. You approve?"

"At his best he comes very close to the great Titian and I would judge that work to be one of his best. I cannot believe that it did justice to the subject, though." She had never been a beauty, but she had been young.

"Nostradamus teaches you flattery also?"

I laughed aloud. "Forgive me. If you had ever met him, you would understand my levity."

"Who painted that one behind you, *sier* Alfeo?"

Fortunately I was right again, and winter began to thaw into spring. Before summer arrived, her son did, with Jacopo in tow.

Bernardo Michiel was bulky, a meat inspector who brought his work home with him. Even in ordinary gentlemen's attire, without the imposing robes of a patrician, he was still a domineering presence. His beard was big, black, and bushy; his brows beetled.

I rose and bowed as little as possible without giving direct insult. Neither of us had a chance to speak before Alina Orio did.

"Here is my son, *messer* Zeno. Let us hear Nostradamus's message."

"Certainly, madonna. If he agrees?"

"Yes!" Bernardo barked. "Go on!"

"My master merely wishes to warn you, *clarissimo*, that there are rumors that your exiled brother may have returned to the city. Nostradamus advises you of this purely as a token of gratitude for your earlier interest in his work and seeks nothing in return."

The inspector of meats exchanged glances with his mother. "Rumors? You come here to repeat rumors? Neither facts nor evidence, merely scuttlebutt and tittle-tattle? I can gather a bellyful of that at any time from the sharks in the Ghetto Nuovo or the fish skinners of the Pescaria." His voice was the resonant trumpet of a trained orator and I was a public meeting.

I must now walk very close to the perilous edge of accusing the Michiel black sheep of three more murders. I drew comfort from the weight of my rapier at my belt, because I was fairly certain that either Bernardo or Jacopo could throw me out single-handedly, and they could call on unlimited assistance.

"I was instructed to mention two facts that may be relevant. First, a certain courtesan received a note purporting to be from a man she had known some years ago—not giving *sier* Zorzi's own name, I hasten to add, but a nickname by which he was known to her."

Bernardo's heavy features did not change by one eyebrow hair. "What nickname?"

"Honeycat. Based on a birthmark, I was told." Seeing no reaction to that, either, I continued. "Second, and perhaps more significant, the Council of Ten officially warned my master not to continue his current inquiries. So, of course, he will not."

It is very rare to mention the Ten without seeing some sort of response, but I saw none then.

"That's all? You have posited your premises, posed your paradoxes, and presented your peroration?"

"I have." I also scorn sarcasm and abhor alliteration, but did not say so.

"Then you have said all you wanted to say and may leave."

Jacopo moved forward to assist.

"Wait!" said the lady. "Thank you for coming, Bernardo. I have another matter to discuss with *sier* Alfeo." She waited until her son had stalked out in dudgeon and Jacopo had closed the door behind him before she continued. "Bring the casket."

Jacopo crossed the room and left by a second door, through which I glimpsed a bedchamber.

"Now, *sier* Alfeo, give me your opinion of that small painting above the escritoire over there."

I rose and went across to peer at the panel in question. My first reaction was repugnance, but after a moment it began to speak to me. I returned to my seat.

"Daring, but powerful. I have never heard of the artist, madonna. A Greek, from the signature, and his choice of forms and colors is unusual . . . At the risk of being presumptuous, I would guess that he is fairly young, searching for a personal style."

She raised eyebrows and pursed lips in guarded approval. "He was young when he painted that. "Doménicos Theotokópoulos, from our colony on Crete. He later went on to Spain, and I have been told he has met with success there. A very odd young man, he was. And the desk beneath it?"

Was hideous. "I claim no knowledge of furniture, madonna."

"It is made of ebony wood from the Spice Lands, very rare."

Very funereal. I praised a bronze cherub instead and she dismissed my opinion with a sniff.

"The escritoire belonged to my father. I should say that

ebony furniture *used* to be rare. I have seen examples in several great houses recently. I do hope it doesn't become a fad." Anything popular would be contemptible, obviously.

Jacopo returned with a shallow silver box, decorated with pseudoclassical figures in bas-relief. Donna Alina placed it on her lap and spread her papery hands on the lid possessively as if afraid it might float away.

"My dearest treasure," she said with a thin-lipped smile. "My son is not back in Venice. I can prove it. I know he did not murder my husband, *messer* Zeno. I know this as surely as I know the name of my Redeemer. I want Nostradamus to prove his innocence, by finding out who did slay my husband."

I had been expecting almost anything but that. I hoped my shock did not show as much as Jacopo's did. He looked at her as if she were raving. I pulled my wits together.

"Eight years is a long time, madonna. Memories fade, witnesses may no longer be available. Even my master may balk at such a challenge. Of course I will convey your wishes. And the Ten . . . I mean, he will have to consider whether the Ten's interdict covers that matter also." Even trying to overthrow the Ten's judgment on so notorious an affair might be judged subversive.

"I know things that the Ten do not," she declared confidently. "I know where my son is."

She opened the box without using a key, but I had recognized the words and gesture she used earlier to remove a warding spell. The same actions might or might not work for anyone else. She removed a slim book bound in brown leather, which she placed on her lap under the box, out of the way. Then she produced some loose papers.

"These are his letters. He does not write often, you will understand, because it is dangerous, but a few months after he fled he sent me his most solemn assurance, an oath sworn on his immortal soul, that he was nowhere near the Basilica when Gentile died." She took up the topmost paper and held it at arm's length. "This is the most recent. It is dated just after Epiphany." She squinted at the text. "Yes . . . *Maria now expects her confinement about Easter . . . after her difficulties with Gentile I try not to show her my concern . . .* And later he says, *Gentile is a very active little terror, and swims like a dolphin. I spend at least an hour every day with him . . .* You see, *sier* Alfeo? Would a man name his firstborn son after a father he had murdered?" She smirked triumphantly.

"I suppose not," I said. But why not?

"In one of his earlier letters he remarked how much he had enjoyed his father's attention in his own childhood and hoped to be as loved by his own children. He is engrossed with his family and concerned about his wife. He is in a far land which I shall not name, and *not* here in Venice writing letters to courtesans."

"Madonna, may I examine that letter you are holding and also the first one that you mentioned?"

"Certainly not!" She thrust the paper back in the box and put the book back on top of them. "It has his new address on it. There is still a price on his head, you stupid boy!"

"If Jacopo were to lay the paper on that escritoire," I said, "and cover the address with . . . with one of those books on the shelf, then I could see the rest of it. And the first letter is eight years old, so it can contain no secrets now."

She clutched the casket protectively in her talons. "Why? Why do you want to see my son's letters?"

"So I can assure my master that I have done so. I also want to compare the handwriting."

"Why?"

"Because my master has taught me much curious wisdom about handwriting. The first letter must have been written under great stress. The latest one sounds like the musings of a very happy man, even if he does have worries about his wife's lying-in. The writing should show that. Even at this distance I can perceive that he is left-handed."

"How do you know that?" she snapped, burning with suspicion.

"From the slant of the vertical strokes, madonna. Likely he was taught right-handed and tries not to use a reverse slant, but it shows here and there."

She hesitated, but then curiosity won out and she opened the box again. She gave Jacopo the top and bottom papers. He laid them on the ebony desk, covering part of one with a book, which he held firmly in place. Only then did I go over to join him and study the letters. The old one was much thumbed, almost falling apart, the second much fresher.

"Yes," I said. "I think *sier* Zorzi is not admitting how much he is worried about his wife—there is stress in those vertical strokes. But he obviously loves her very much, and his son also. And the first letter . . ."

I babbled on for much longer than it took me to memorize both pages, but my main interest was neither the text nor the handwriting. I thanked her. It was time for me to go. The day was drawing on toward evening and after dark I had a date, I hoped, with the Strangler.

"By your leave, madonna? Of course I will convey your wishes to my master. If he is willing to accept the challenge you have suggested, then I shall return on Monday with a contract for you to sign."

Donna Alina graciously allowed me to kiss her fingers, which were scented with rose water, and Jacopo escorted me out.

"That was neatly done," he remarked as we strode along the corridor. "I always thought one had to hold paper up to the light to see the watermark."

15

Some watermarks show through on a black surface," I admitted. "It was that hideous escritoire that gave me the idea."

"So I saw what you saw. The watermarks were different."

"As they should be, written in different lands, eight years apart. The handwriting is the same, as it should be. However, both watermarks are Venetian, so the letters are forged." Normally I do not reveal information like that to a witness, but Jacopo probably knew it anyway and I wanted to win his confidence.

He chuckled. "I am most grateful that you did not tell her so. Your mention of the Honeycat name was tactfully done, too. We were all terrified that you would tell the old bag about the murdered courtesans and throw her into convulsions."

I had concluded by that time that Jacopo was no true *cavaliere servente*, because he was no *cavaliere*. He was only a well-dressed lackey and younger than me. His present chattiness was an effort to seem better than he was. Who paid his tailors' bills?

"Does she have convulsions?"

"Not literally. She has a tongue like a skinner's knife, though."

"Who writes the letters, Bernardo?"

"Domenico." He laughed. "Bernardo may even believe in them."

I wondered if Jacopo had believed in them until he saw what I was doing with the ebony desk. He was leading me out by a different route, not the secret staircase. Now that Bernardo knew I had been allowed in, there was no further need for concealment.

"It is a harmless deception for a bereaved mother and widow," I said, "unless any genuine letters arrived from Zorzi and were suppressed."

"I know of none."

He wouldn't. They would have been burned by Zorzi's brothers, or turned over to the Ten, who would have read them first anyway. The Michiels' mail would certainly have been intercepted for a year or two after the outlaw's flight, and possibly still was.

I said, "The lady must have been very upset when her husband was murdered and her son blamed."

Jacopo said, "Much more upset about Zorzi than . . ." He shot me a quirky smile. "You are a sly bastard, Zeno!"

No, if he had been around back then, he was the bastard among us. I had Jacopo placed.

"I see a likeness to Bernardo," I said.

We were descending a magnificent staircase to the *androne*. The splendor of Palazzo Michiel belonged only to the legitimate heirs. By-blows would have no share in it.

"Well done," he said sourly. "Yes. Honor is indivisible. Half is nothing."

"And how old were you eight years ago?"

"I was just the cook's brat back then. Or a page, sometimes. I can remember Zorzi having screaming matches with our father and using me as evidence that the old tyrant was a hypocrite. Oh, how I loved that!"

"Your full name, in case I need to ask for you?"

"Jacopo Fauro, but just Jacopo will do." He stopped suddenly at a landing and looked me over. "You at least got your father's name, Zeno."

"I treasure it. But I got no money."

I was prying again and he knew it. He shrugged. "I got neither."

"You have another half-brother, a priest."

"Timoteo, now Brother Fedele of the Friars Minor. We are a versatile family—politician, financier, saint, patricide, and drudge. Anything else you need to know?"

"And a sister?"

"Sister Lucretzia."

"And who was the lady who was reading to donna Alina when I arrived?"

"Signora Isabetta Scorozini, Dom's wife."

I had detected no signs of overabundant love between her and her formidable mother-in-law. Scorozini is not a patrician name. While marriage with commoners is not forbidden, it requires the Grand Council's approval and I remembered Celsi's caustic comment on the Michiels' practice of limiting the number of heirs. He had mentioned a mistress. More likely Domenico's marriage had been blessed by the Church but not the Grand Council; it would be morganatic, so her children could not inherit.

We were almost at the bottom of the stairs; my sand was running out.

"How many children does Bernardo have?"

"None."

"Who gave Zorzi his nickname of Honeycat?"

Jacopo shrugged again, indifferent. "The family always called him that." His tone implied that he was not family enough to use nicknames.

We started across the *androne*, toward the main door. "I would offer you a ride home, but ordering boats is outside the limits of my authority."

"No offense taken," I said. I quite liked Jacopo. His bitterness was understandable. Nobility is passed on by the father and he had as much Michiel blood as the others, but he had grown up in *their* palace, destined to be *their* servant.

"Although perhaps your guardian angel is watching over you," he added, as we stepped out to the loggia and the *riva* beyond. His voice had changed and a slight sneer lurked under his beard. A man in the black robes and tippet of a noble was just about to embark in a gondola whose boatmen wore the family colors. He was clearly waiting for us, and Jacopo led me over to him between the passing porters and pedestrians. "*Sier* Alfeo—*sier* Domenico."

I exchanged bows with Brother Number Two. It was fairly easy to deduce that either his brother or his wife had informed him of the Nostradamus snake in the household grass. Donna Alina had taken care to proclaim the news of my presence, for some reason I did not yet know.

Jacopo played out the charade. "*Sier* Alfeo is just leaving and would no doubt appreciate a ride home, if it does not take you too far out of your way."

Domenico was in his thirties, a slighter, lighter Michiel, forged more in the tall, slender form of his mother than cast in the imposing mold of the Bernardo and Jacopo. He had a hook nose, a quiet voice, and a cryptic, sphingine smile.

"Of course. San Remo? It would be my pleasure."

"My honor and my debt," I said.

Rose water was not the only scent floating around the Palazzo Michiel. The place reeked also of conspiracy. I assumed that I would now be interrogated on what donna Alina had wanted and instructed on how she had misinformed me.

Domenico boarded first and handed me aboard, insisting I sit on the lefthand side of the *felze*, the place of honor, although that did not mean much in this case, because it is easier to direct the boat from that side when there are two boatmen, and I was the one who would name our stopping place. As we glided away from the watersteps, I murmured some platitude about kindness.

"Nonsense," Domenico said dryly. "I just wanted to have a word with you. Jacopo is not a very proficient thespian, is he?"

Set a trap and then expose it yourself? Domenico surprised me. There was something slithery about him, though.

"He is still young enough to learn from a good teacher," I said. "How may I assist you, *clarissimo*?"

He showed his lower teeth when he smiled, which is rare in a young man. "Tell me what you were up to with my mother, of course. Or rather what she wants from you. She is sometimes not very practical. My brother is worried . . . Let me start at the beginning. Our father's terrible death was a shattering experience for all of us, of course, but especially for Alina, for she was with him when it happened. The whole city cried out in horror when it heard the news, but she was there! Then, just days later, Zorzi's flight made it all doubly, triply worse. He had always been her favorite. She has never admitted that he was guilty."

"Was he?" I murmured.

"Who knows?" Domenico said, surprising me again. "Zorzi was taller than I am and she always insisted that the man who elbowed her aside was not tall. That was all she recalled of the killer—that he was no more than average height. But the Ten had to find a culprit quickly and Zorzi ran away. Run from hounds and they will chase you." Again that curious smile invited confidence.

"Is he still alive?"

"Of course not!"

That made three surprises and I was starting to feel outgunned. The family financier had let slip that he knew what parish I lived in, and therefore had most likely seen the letter I brought, but he was coming across as smarter than Bernardo, the family politician, or even the family flunky, who was sharp enough in spite of his lack of theatrical expertise. Perhaps Domenico's soft voice excluded him from politics, for it takes powerful lungs to be heard the whole length of the Great Council's chamber.

"The Ten put a price on his head," he said. "A thousand ducats? A fortune! Were I a gambling man, I should bet that it was less than a month before some bravo turned up at the palace with my brother's head pickled in wine or brine to claim the reward. The Ten never tell."

His face radiated sincerity as he said all this. The man was a master, and I was glad not to be buying real estate from him.

"Then the letters your mother receives are all fakes?"

He could not have known beforehand that I had been told about the letters, yet he never hesitated.

"Of course. She was still in shock from the murder when her son was convicted of patricide; we all feared she would go out of her mind and harm herself. Eventually my wife, Isabetta, and I concocted a letter to console her. We decided to risk this deception, knowing that if Alina saw through it, it would be taken as betrayal and make matters even worse. Zorzi and I had always had similar handwriting and my forgery turned out to be good enough. That letter saved my mother's sanity, *sier* Alfeo! Perhaps it was a reprehensible conspiracy, but I have no regrets. Ever since then we have supplied a new episode of the drama every few months. We led our phantom brother through several adventures. At present he is a senior aide to the Duke of Savoy, and anxiously awaiting the birth of his second child. Is this a sin?"

Who was I to be his spiritual advisor? "That may depend

on whether your brother is alive, *clarissimo*. Have any genuine letters turned up?"

Domenico studied me for a moment, as if adjusting his evaluation of a property. The roof is collapsing, but the stables are adequate . . .

"None that I know of. Would you really expect the Council of Ten to allow such a letter to arrive? The Ten watch every piece of mail entering the Republic. Their agents would backtrack it to its source. My brother Zorzi is long dead, *sier* Alfeo, may the Lord have mercy on his soul."

"Amen," I said. We were making fast time along the Grand Canal and would be at San Remo in a few moments. It was time to counterattack. "And now you and *sier* Bernardo are worried that donna Alina will fall into the hands of a charlatan clairvoyant, who will milk her of thousands of ducats by preying on her obsession to prove her son's innocence?"

He smiled, snakily. "You put it in starker terms than I would."

"Maestro Nostradamus is not a grifter," I said, even more cold-bloodedly, "but is aware of the dangers of being considered one. If he undertakes to prove your brother's innocence, *clarissimo*, then he will expect payment only after he has done so. If your brother was in fact guilty, then you will owe him nothing. Suppose he was innocent—then who did kill your father?"

Silence. The oars creaked in the oarlocks. Passing gondoliers yodeled their strange calls. We turned into Rio San Remo. My companion stared at our bow post, or perhaps the forward boatman's legs, saying nothing.

"*Messer?*" I queried eventually.

Domenico shook his head. "I have absolutely no idea, *sier* Alfeo. Nobody I know or can think of. My first thought when I heard the news was that Zorzi had committed that terrible, dreadful crime. I kept my opinion to myself, of course, but I never doubted that he was guilty, neither then nor later."

I said, "The next watergate on the right, boatman. I do thank you for the ride, *clarissimo*."

"It has been a great pleasure, *sier* Alfeo."

We smiled like fighters ending the first round of a long contest.

16

Dusk was falling, Carnival would soon resume in earnest. In Ca' Barbolano I ran up the forty-eight steps and let myself in. I found Fulgentio already there, coaching the twins in fencing under their mother's disapproving eye.

"Be with you in a moment," I shouted, and slipped into the atelier to report. The Maestro was at the desk, working on a horoscope that he would normally have me do, which was enough annoyance to justify his disagreeable scowl. He needed more light, but the fact that he had been moving around at all was encouraging.

"Progress!" I said as I hurried to the mantelpiece to fetch a couple of lamps. "The formidable donna Alina has been receiving letters from Zorzi for years, except that they're fakes done by Domenico. Bernardo may be in on the hoax, but I'm not sure of that. Timoteo is Friar Fedele, which confirms a tie between the Gradenigo mystery and Ca' Michiel."

I laid the lamps on the desk, backed off a couple of paces, and lit them both with the Word.

"There's another son, illegitimate, aged about nineteen or twenty, goes by the name of Jacopo Fauro and acts as stableboy to the lioness. Alina-the-terrible Orio wants to hire you to prove that Zorzi did not murder his father."

"So your afternoon was not completely wasted." Nostradamus had listened with one finger marking his place in the ephemeris and his pen poised in his other hand. Now he dipped the quill in the inkwell and went back to work. "Go and eat or do something useful."

"Will you take the lady's contract?"

"Of course," he muttered, scribbling a calculation on a sheet already almost entirely covered with hieroglyphics. "Unless you catch the Strangler tonight."

There are times I want to strangle him. "And where do I go to do that?"

He looked up furiously. "*Damnātio!* I told you! I told you he would kill again after the Sabbath and I told you where! Are you all idiots? You and that Trau boy and Giorgio— you're the natives. I'm foreign born. You eat my salt and pocket my gold. You work it out. Go and get him, preferably alive, but kill him if you must."

I left before I did strangle him. At the same time, I sympathized. If Fulgentio and I did not decipher the quatrain in time, tomorrow would bring word of another woman murdered somewhere and we should all curse ourselves, because the answer to the riddle would then be blindingly obvious.

I went to my room to fetch my sword and Fulgentio followed me in, closing the door. He tossed his foil and mask on my bed, to lie alongside a mysterious bundle. He was grinning like a child, as if we were going off to play hide-and-go-seek for sweetmeats instead of a woman's life. Fulgentio is smart—had he seen what I was missing in the quatrain?

"Had these made up," he announced, untying the cord around the bundle. "Secret-police costumes." He held up a pair of cloaks, white on one side and black on the other.

"Helps us find each other in the crowd and then sneak up on the Strangler."

"Sometimes I think you are crazy," I said, retrieving my sword from the top of the wardrobe, "and other times I know you are."

"Were I sane, friend, I would find a much more enjoyable companion for tonight." His amusement was as transmissible as always.

Masks are standard for Carnival, when servants and nobles can mingle on almost equal terms—the poor are still poor and the rich rich, of course—but masks and swords are an illegal combination, so we must keep our rapiers well hidden or risk being arrested by the *shirri*. Mama tried to drag me bodily into the kitchen to eat, but night was falling and I promised her I would buy something at one of the sausage stands. She shuddered and so did I. I warned her to lock up after us.

Clad in white like ghosts, Fulgentio and I left by the back door and the staircase down to the courtyard. I let us out the gate and locked it behind us. We were on a manhunt where we knew neither our quarry nor his range. It seemed hopeless to me—grass? three saints?

Fulgentio began recounting a complicated story that was making the rounds in the palace, all about the French ambassador's mistress. He kept it going until we reached our first real decision point, where the *calle* reached the *campo*. I hesitated.

He stopped to look at me, raising his torch high. "Not San Marco again, so where?"

I had it! "Of course San Marco!" I shouted. "Let's go!" Seized by a sudden urgency, I began to run.

"There is no grass in the Piazza!" he complained, running alongside.

"But there is grass in the *campo*!"

"Men have been strangled for much less provocation than . . . Saints preserve me! Of course!"

We came to the great bridge of the Rialto, which was packed with revelers, most of them heading in the same direction we were. A few wore grotesque costumes, but most were merely cloaked and masked. The night was full of torchlight, laughter, and singing, so it was hard to remember that we were on a trail of death. When we reached the far side, the mob split right or straight ahead, rivers of flame bound for the Piazza of San Marco.

We veered to the left and started to run again.

Campo San Zanipolo has the grass we sought, for it is one of the last large *campi* still unpaved. Also, it has the man of blood we sought. We had been concentrating too hard on Honeycat, Erasmo da Narni, and forgetting that there was another famous condottiere in Venetian history, Bartolomeo Colleoni, a greater warrior. My fencing instructor claims him as an ancestor. In his will, Colleoni left money for a statue of him to be set up on the *Piazza* San Marco, in front of the Basilica, but no statues have ever been allowed there. The Senate took the money but cheated and put the statue in front of the Scuola Grande di San Marco, calling that the Campo San Marco, but in fact it is the Campo Zanipolo, outside the Dominicans' church next door. The Republic did not skimp on the statue itself, though, a magnificent Verrocchio equestrian figure high on a plinth, and it is watched over by three saints, because San Zanipolo is actually two, John and Paul, smeared together in *Veneziano*. Grass, three saints, and a man of blood. Carnival was in full tilt when we arrived. Bonfires, music, dancing, drinking, horrible sausages, almost everyone masked, dancing, laughing. There were acrobats and jugglers and men on stilts. The *campo* was packed and somewhere in all that throng, the Strangler might be stalking his next victim.

"We'll never find him!" Fulgentio moaned. "Should we split up?"

I ran through the prophecy again in my mind. "Not yet. The man of blood *sees* blood, remember? The statue faces west."

We pushed our way through the throng, resisting anonymous hands trying to pull us into the dancing. Most of the action was around a raging bonfire to the east of the column. The smaller, quieter crowd on the west side was taking advantage of the relative privacy of the shadow to engage in kissing and other tender pastimes.

"In there!" I told my accomplice. "That's perfect for Honeycat. Nobody's paying any attention to anyone else."

"Provided he can recognize his victim. You watch this side. I'll go around the other."

"Look out for friars," I said as he hurried away.

That was easier said than done in the shadows, for many people wore hoods or head cloths, and almost everyone was masked. Prostitutes flaunted bare breasts; there were many of those, making me feel like a voyeur as I squirmed through between the couples. Fulgentio had wondered how the Strangler expected to recognize his prey. Were we wrong in our guess that he preyed only on women old enough to have known Zorzi Michiel? If any harlot would suffice, he would have no lack of choice here. And who said he had to dress as a friar?

A woman screamed. The sound came from in front of me, but there were about a dozen people between me and its source.

"*No!*" I yelled, and hurled myself forward. Had I been as big as Bruno I might have accomplished something conclusive, but I could make no speed as I clawed and ricocheted through the mob, most of whom were now heading in the opposite direction. I saw a friar's hood, but as I went to tackle him, I realized that he held a knife, so I tried to dodge at the last minute. We toppled into others and went down in a heap. My actions had been monumentally idiotic and I paid for my folly with a searing pain in my ribs.

But then the onlookers bellowed and responded, most taking flight with cries of shrill alarm, while the rest—mainly young men whose foreplay had been interrupted—sought redress. I was kicked, cursed, then kicked again. I was hauled up by the collar. I was bleeding, which probably saved me from worse injuries. Rage turned to shouts of alarm.

"Stop him! Catch him! Stop him!" I realized that I had been bellowing this for what felt like quite a while. "Is anyone else hurt?"

Yes there was, because another group had gathered around someone who was not standing. Women screamed in horror. My companions went to see and I fled.

I was armed, soaked in blood, and—so the *shirri* would claim—had created a disturbance to let my accomplice slit a purse or a throat. The least I could expect from them would be some ham-fisted barber sewing me up, a couple of nights in jail, and interrogation by the chiefs of the Ten on Monday. The fire in my ribs grew worse as I ran, but I must have taken a slash, not a stab, or I would be drowning in my own blood already. Superficial wounds can bleed more than punctures.

I crossed the bridge over the Rio dei Mendicanti and was faced with a dozen or so raucous, largely drunk, merrymakers filling the street from side to side. Many of them carried torches, and when I dodged through between them, they saw red all down my left side. Oh, how I cursed Fulgentio and his white cloaks! Fortunately nobody reacted fast enough to grab me, so I got safely past them, but then the shouting started and rapidly became a hue and cry.

Drunk or sober, they were fresh. I was winded and already feeling the loss of blood. I wasn't going to win a race and their shouts would alert any other group ahead of me. I needed a place to hide. The best Samaritans Venice possessed would not rescue a blood-soaked fugitive from the night without asking a lot of questions first.

"*Arghrraw . . .*"

A cat standing on its hind legs, scratching at a door? Sooner done than said. Some reactions are instantaneous, no matter how many words are needed to describe them later. Cats rarely condescend to be taught tricks, but will sometimes teach themselves, and this one must have learned that such antics would sooner or later persuade some friendly passerby to let it in. Probably the whole parish knew it and was proud of its cleverness. If that was the situation, the door was not kept locked. I was more than happy to let the cat in, follow it inside, and slam the door behind me.

I found a bolt and slid it. Then I slid myself—to the floor.

For a while I just sat there, leaning back against the planks and gasping. The cat had vanished into the darkness. Judging by the smell, the cat often did not go outside.

Evidently my pursuers had not been close enough to see how or where I managed my disappearing act, for no one hammered on the door. As soon as I had caught my breath, I stripped off my cloak, doublet, and shirt, all of them blood soaked. I wrapped the shirt tightly around myself to bandage the gash slanting across three ribs, and then dressed again, hoping I was putting the cloak dark side out. Maybe Fulgentio's invention did have some uses, but dark red would be more appropriate than black.

I stood up with care and the world did not spin or tilt at odd angles. There would be blood on the floor in the morning, but at least my exsanguinous corpse would not be there also. I whispered, "Thanks, cat," to the darkness. Rabid or otherwise, cats could be surprisingly useful. I opened the door and stepped out into the night with my head high, being as unfurtive as possible.

17

Since I had the big courtyard key with me, I let myself in the back way and did not terrify Luigi with my bloodstains. The stairs were even steeper than usual that night. Needless to say, the Maestro was not pleased to be wakened, but he could not refuse to sew his apprentice together. I put my garments to soak in a bucket, all except the cloak, which I burned in the kitchen fire. Only then was I free to go to bed.

Sunday, I decided, would be a day of rest.

I woke at dawn, as I always do. I rolled over and went back to sleep, which I never do.

When I did appear, the Maestro poked and prodded me and claimed that he detected no sign of the wound fever that kills more victims than wounds do. I knew that it was still too early to tell.

We said nothing more. We did not make eye contact until well after noon. I had failed him. He had foreseen when and where the Strangler would strike again and I had failed to block the attack. That was failure, the bitterest of tastes. The Maestro, for his part, had almost had to sign a receipt for one dead apprentice, and that was not part of the agreement either. Small wonder we had little to say to each other.

Most of the morning I spent reading and trying to memorize some of Ovid's *Metamorphoses* so I could be more worthy of my lady. He sat in his red chair with a copy of Paracelsus's *Paragranum*, but I noticed that he wasn't turning pages. He appeared to be staring at the slate table, doing absolutely nothing, which was another end-of-an-epoch landmark.

At one point I lowered my book because the print was a blur.

"He wasn't tall enough," I said.

Silence.

"Bulky," I said, "but not tall. Domenico said that Zorzi was tall. The Honeycat I caught wasn't tall."

"Honeycat uses a rope, not a dagger."

"A cord isn't fast enough in a crowd. He was forced back to using a knife because there were too many witnesses."

My master snorted. "Or because he wasn't Honeycat."

"But then . . ." But then had the Maestro's clairvoyance been distracted by a pending murder involving a different murderer?

"But what?" he snarled.

I thought it out as he has taught me. "He was Honeycat," I said. "Don't ask me why I think that, because I have no rational reason to, but I am positive that the man I grabbed as I fell was Honeycat. I know that isn't logical."

"But it may still be correct," he growled. "Stop thinking about it and eventually you will understand, even if you have to dream it."

The news had reached the parish and was distributed in the *campo* after Mass. There would have been no use my heading over to San Zanipolo to ask the residents what had happened there the previous night. I was an outsider and if the Virgin herself had returned to earth there to bless Carnival, even that would still be none of my business. The Council of Ten would have heard from its local spies, though, and I was half expecting *Missier Grande* to coming a-knocking at our door, or even send his *vizio* for me, which would be much more humiliating. Fortunately the Ten hesitate to invade the privacy of a noble's house and *sier* Alvise Barbolano is as noble as they come.

The Maestro lacks the Ten's resources, but he does have Giorgio and Mama Angeli. Both belong to enormous families, and there is hardly a parish in Venice that does not include some relative of theirs. In this case, as Giorgio explained when they all returned from church, one of his cousins' husband's brother Andreo lived in San Zanipolo where another poor woman had been murdered.

"I need to talk with him," the Maestro said. "Fetch him. Bring an eyewitness, too, if he can find one for you. Bring his entire family and feed them here if you want."

"He is not married," Giorgio replied without a flicker of a smile. "But he will eat enough to make up for that."

Finding a bachelor on a day of rest could have been tricky, but we were fortunate. Within twenty minutes a young man in his Sunday best was standing in front of the Maestro's chair, answering questions. Andreo was an apprentice carpenter and a juvenile version of Giorgio himself—short, heavy shouldered, and given to thinking before he spoke. He was as much of an eyewitness as we were likely to find, having been right there in the Campo San Zanipolo when the terrible thing happened. He had spoken with people who had seen the fight.

"They say she was attacked by two men, one of them dressed as a friar and the other wearing a white cloak."

"Tell me about the woman," Nostradamus said.

Andreo made the sign of the cross. "Marina Bortholuzzi was her name, *lustrissimo*."

"Stabbed where?"

"In the, um, chest, *lustrissimo*."

"What sort of woman?"

"The women claim she was a prostitute," Andreo said, carefully distancing himself from such knowledge—no man in the parish would now admit ever having heard of Marina Bortholuzzi. "They say she was past her best. Used to be very high and mighty and lately hasn't been paying her rent on time. So the women were saying."

The man in the white cloak had shouted and run away, drawing the crowd off so his accomplice could escape in the darkness. So Andreo said, and no doubt that was the popular account. It did not worry me overmuch, because the gash on my ribs was evidence as to what had really happened.

The Maestro sighed and thanked him. "Alfeo, a ducat for him."

He had done well. I had not. Lucia, Ruosa, Caterina, and now Marina.

Failure.

Soon after that we went into dinner, Nostradamus walking with the aid of his canes, although Bruno hovered anxiously in the *salone*, eager to assist.

We ate without exchanging a single word, the Maestro and I. I did not speak because I had nothing useful to offer. Zorzi had been tall. The false friar I had assaulted on Campo San Zanipolo had not been tall. Zorzi was almost certainly dead, his brother had said, murdered by a bounty hunter. Our evidence for identifying the killer as Zorzi Michiel was looking flimsier by the hour, and yet something nibbled and nagged away at the back of my mind, some thought that I could not get hold of.

The Maestro's silence was ominous. I kept hoping he would decide to try another foreseeing, but he didn't. Judging by past experience, I feared that he had dreamed up something else, some maneuver so exotic and dangerous that he was trying to find an alternative.

After dinner, when we returned to the atelier, he was hardly into his chair before he said, "You must go and see Carlo Celsi again."

"Sunday afternoon. He'll be attending the Great Council." And Fulgentio Trau would be on duty, which explained why he had not come to see me.

"This evening will suffice. Now a contract with donna Alina Orio. Better do a draft first."

"What terms?" I asked, reaching for a sheet of paper.

"Three hundred ducats to prove that Gentile Michiel was stabbed by someone other than his son, Zorzi."

I selected a quill and inspected its tip carefully. "You believe that?"

"Yes, but as yet the evidence is merely indicative, not indisputable."

Evidence? What evidence? He waited for a moment, no doubt hoping I would ask him so he could tell me to work it out for myself. When I didn't, he continued.

"The primary objective remains to track down this killer of courtesans, and I still believe that the two cases are connected. I want you to question every soul in that house who may, in your opinion, have any useful knowledge of either matter. The old lady can impose that on them, can't she?"

"Possibly not on Bernardo or Domenico, but I fancy everyone else is sufficiently terrified of her."

"Mm. Make that just two hundred ducats. I don't want to frighten her into changing her mind. And I shall need a week. If I haven't caught Honeycat by then, we shall have to try something else."

If he wanted me to go back to Carlo Celsi, he must already have something else in mind. He would have to tell me eventually, so I wasn't about to ask. I set to work on a draft, trying out a Carolingian minuscule hand that I had been studying. I was close to finished when someone rapped on the front door.

I rose eagerly, despite an angry reprimand from my stitches, because I hoped that the caller would be Violetta returned from her house party. As always, I left the atelier door ajar so that the Maestro could listen. I opened one flap of the big outer doors.

Many odd people come calling on the Maestro, but probably no couple I have ever found waiting out there at the top of the stairs has surprised me more. The woman was swathed from the ground up in the habit of a Benedictine nun, with only her fingers visible to show that there was a woman inside that menacing pillar of black. The man at her side, gray robed and tonsured, was the third Michiel son, the former Timoteo. I bowed to his austere, Old Testament stare.

"This is an unexpected honor, Brother."

"Unexpected no doubt, my son, but no honor." This was an attempt at humility, but it needed work. "Tell your master I wish to see him."

When necessary I can obstruct and obfuscate with the best of them, giving the Maestro time to escape by the secret door, but I was confident that Nostradamus would want to see this pair. I swung the atelier door wide.

"Brother Fedele and Sister Lucretzia, master."

Fedele shot me an angry glance, perhaps annoyed that I had been meddling enough in his family's affairs to know his sister's name, but he did not deny it. He strode in, gown swirling above bare feet, and paused to look around disapprovingly at the wall of books, the alchemy bench, the examination couch, and other curiosities. The nun followed him in and he pointed at one of the spare chairs we keep on hand for larger groups, one of two behind the door, near the great armillary sphere. She went to it without a word. Then the friar marched over to the Maestro, who smiled up at him.

"I am suffering from reminders of mortality today, Brother. Pray excuse my failure to rise, and do be seated."

Fedele perched straight-backed on the edge of one of the green chairs. "I am sorry to hear of your infirmity, Filippo. I shall keep my visit brief."

I crept back to the desk, turning my chair slightly so I could also keep a corner of an eye on the nun, sitting off to my right, but she was motionless as a statue. I wondered how much her eyes wandered behind her veil.

The Maestro was on his best behavior. "Your visit is welcome. May I offer you refreshment?"

"Thank you, no."

"Won't you present me to your honored sister?"

"No. I am escorting her back to Santa Giustina and dropped in here on the way. You sent your apprentice to see my mother yesterday."

"I sent him to see your brother Bernardo."

"Why?" No, Fedele was not Old Testament. He was a martyr, and his emaciated, anguished features belonged on a crucifix or a triptych from some gloomy, sin-obsessed medieval monastery. He looked as if he had been fasting since midsummer on an exercise regime of three flagellations a day.

"To give him a message."

"Why?"

The normal response would have been, *What message?* The Maestro hesitated a moment before speaking.

"Because I considered it my duty."

"Or to extract money from my family by preying on their sorrow?"

"No."

"But you will accept money if it is offered?"

The Maestro gingerly eased himself back in his chair and then put his fingertips together, five on five, which normally indicates the start of a lecture.

"Who wouldn't?"

That was almost a demand for a sermon, and the friar rose to the bait.

"You would be well advised to, Filippo. I look around at all this unseemly display and remember the words of our Lord about the camel failing to pass through the eye of a needle."

"Ah, an interesting metaphor. According to the revered Bishop Theophylact of Bulgaria, there was a gate in the wall of Jerusalem so narrow that in order to take a camel through, you would have to unload all its burdens and—"

"Let us talk about your burdens, my son."

The Maestro cackled one of his irritating cackles. "Brother, I believe we are talking at cross-purposes. You have asked five questions. Now let me have a turn, and then we may understand each other better. You were sixteen or seventeen when your father was murdered, may Our Lord rest his soul. You would not have been present in the Basilica, but you were old enough to comprehend. Describe the wound that killed him."

The green chairs face the window so that the Maestro has a better view of visitors than they do of him. So do I if I am at the desk. The priest must have found the question outrageous, but he hid his revulsion well.

"He was stabbed in the back with a dagger. The wound penetrated his tippet and his kidney. He lost consciousness almost at once and died before he could be moved out of the church."

"The dagger belonged to your family?"

The response was quiet but intense. *"Who told you that?"*

The Maestro chuckled again, evidently intending to enrage the priest even further—angry men make mistakes. "The Ten did. Not in so many words, you understand, but they must have had reasons to conclude that your brother was guilty and if the weapon had been readily available to members of the family, that would be a compelling one.

Right from the start I noted that as a plausible theory and your presence here reinforces my suspicion."

"What are you implying?" Fedele had lost color, which is more often a sign of anger than fear. Oh, what would San Francesco have said? And what was Sister Lucretzia thinking under her dreary draperies?

"I can understand," the Maestro said calmly, "that your family is reluctant to have old sorrows reawakened; I mean having your father's murder reexamined. Even so, I find your respective reactions excessive. *Sier* Domenico, a rich and no doubt busy nobleman, contrived to have a private discussion with my apprentice. *Sier* Bernardo, on the other hand, snubbed him in a way I would not treat a beggar. To-day they send you and your sister to call on me. Very curious behavior!"

"No one sent me," the friar said grimly. "I came in charity to warn you. I admit that our mother has never accepted Zorzi's guilt. She always took his side and defended his sinful ways. But the Council of Ten judged him guilty and my brothers have suffered enough for his fearful crime. They are noblemen of Venice. If you attempt to embezzle money from her by preying on her delusions, then they will complain to the Council of Ten, which will run you out of town at the very least."

"Alfeo, how far along are you with that draft?"

"As far as, '. . . permitted under the laws of Venice,' master."

"Let the good brother read it."

I took the paper over to our visitor. He did not comment on my penmanship, but merely read it slowly and carefully, like a lawyer. When he lowered it, he was frowning. I carried it back to my desk.

"No money in advance," the Maestro said. "No money at all unless I produce evidence acceptable in a court of law. Those are always my terms, Brother."

He did not explain that he was less concerned with the guilt or innocence of Zorzi Michiel than he was with finding the killer of the courtesans. To suggest that a noble family might be involved in that sordid affair would terminate the discussion instantly. We would be in jail before sunset.

Fedele shook his head sadly. "Filippo, Filippo! You are accusing the Council of Ten of convicting an innocent man. I urge you for your own safety not to let your words get back to them. Perhaps you should discuss the sin of pride with your confessor?"

"Perhaps." Nostradamus did not sound convinced. "I have two more questions, if I may beg your patience, Brother. Suppose for a moment that Zorzi, your brother, did *not* commit that terrible crime. And yet also suppose that, despite his innocence, before fleeing into exile he wrote out a confession and slipped it into one of the 'Lion's Mouth' drop boxes for the Council of Ten to read."

"Absurd. Suppose the lagoon turns to wine."

"But my question is, who—in your family, in the city, in the whole world—might Zorzi have loved enough to shield in this way?"

The priest studied him for a moment with the basilisk stare of an icon. "My brother was about as far from a saint as it is possible to be, Filippo. He lived for lechery and debauch. He loved only his own carnal pleasure."

Nostradamus sighed. "Then my last question. Why did Giovanni Gradenigo ask for me when he was dying?"

The friar glanced momentarily across at his sister, then back at the Maestro. "I cannot tell you. I can assure you that he was very confused near the end."

"But when you wrote, you addressed the message to Alfeo, not to me. How did you know to do that?"

Fedele smiled thinly. "Priests learn many strange things in the course of performing the Lord's work, Filippo. Do you remember Pietro Vercia?"

The Maestro nodded. "The forger?"

"A forger you exposed. The night before his execution, I heard his confession, but then I spent the rest of the night just listening to him talk. Condemned men tend to talk a lot as the noose approaches. He told me how you had never left your house, but you had sent your apprentice around asking questions, gathering the information you needed for your spells. So I knew you would send Zeno in your stead and I saved time by summoning him directly."

"Spells? That was why you delayed sending for me until it was too late?"

Fedele rose, tall and stark. "That was why. Giovanni had made his last confession and I could not allow him to taint his soul by contact with black magic. I do urge you to repent your ways, Filippo. Eternity is a long time to burn." He raised his hand to bless.

"Have you heard about Marina Bortholuzzi?" Nostradamus asked brightly.

"Who? No." The hand dropped.

"Another courtesan murdered. Last night in the Campo San Zanipolo."

"I shall pray for her," the friar said, and muttered a quick blessing.

He headed for the door. The nun rose. I rose. But then Fedele wheeled around as if he had reached a decision. His voice seemed to resonate with the baleful reproach of fearsome Old Testament prophets. "Murderers usually have some reason for killing their victims, Filippo, even if it is only to lift their purses. Have you discovered yet *why* our father was stabbed to death?"

"Not yet, Brother," the Maestro replied.

"Then I shall tell you before you make even more of a fool of yourself. This is not exactly a secret, just something unknown to the general public. Everyone in his family knew, and I know that the Council of Ten did. Two days before our father died, he announced that he was so disgusted by his youngest son's debauchery that he was going to disown and disinherit him. He would cut him out of his will and ask the Great Council to strike his name from the Golden Book for conduct unbecoming a nobleman. Now you know the motive for that terrible crime."

Without another word, the priest spun around and stalked out of the atelier. His sister followed. He unlocked the outer door for himself and departed. I bowed the nun out. She paused long enough to bob me a curtsey, and then floated away like a black ghost. I locked up behind her.

"Very interesting," the Maestro murmured as I returned. "So Zorzi had a motive and access to the weapon. Are you convinced now of his guilt?"

"No, master." Could any man learned in the classics have been so stupid as to kill his father only two days after that dramatic denunciation and with an identifiable weapon? Someone who wanted both Gentile *and* Zorzi removed could have done so, two birds with one stone. I could imagine the pious brother disapproving of the lecherous brother's lifestyle, but San Francesco would not approve of double homicide as a way of registering protest. *Cui bono?* as the lawyers say—"Who gains?" Well, the two older brothers had split the family fortune between them, hadn't they?

"As for motive," I said, "I told you what Celsi said: 'He and his father fought like cat and dog all the time, with the old man always threatening to disinherit him if he didn't reform his ways.' So what was special about the last time?"

"Why did you offer the paper to the friar with your left hand, apprentice?"

The sly old devil had noticed!

"So that it was directly in front of him, master. He took it with his right hand."

"And why did you want to know whether he was left- or right-handed?"

"Because the blade penetrated Gentile Michiel's tippet, which hangs over the left shoulder. That is why you think Zorzi did not kill him."

Nostradamus leered at me. "No bad at all! You are learning."

"Thank you, master."

Gentile had been stabbed in the back on his left side, possibly a misdirected attempt to find his heart in near darkness. An assassin in a crowd will try to position his own body to shield his actions from other people, which in this case suggested a left-handed killer getting directly behind his victim. Zorzi was left-handed, and that might well have been another factor that influenced the Ten in reaching their verdict. But Gentile had been reunited with his wife. He would not have been wearing a sword in church, but a man normally offers his left arm to his lady, the origin of that custom being to leave his sword arm free. Donna Alina had said she was pushed aside by a tall man, and even if she had dropped back a little as her husband forced their way through the crowd, the killer would not have pushed her with the hand that held his knife. More likely the killer had held the dagger in his *right* hand.

"It isn't proof, you understand!" Nostradamus said. "The Basilica was packed with people, so determining exactly where everyone was would have been impossible even then, let alone eight years later. But it is suggestive of a right-handed killer."

"Yes, master."

"Which hand did the fake friar use to slash you last night?"

"His right, master."

18

An hour or so later the knocker summoned me again, and this time it was Violetta, radiant as the sun clearing away fog. We shared a brief kiss while I was closing the outer door, and another as I ushered her across to the atelier. Nostradamus almost seemed pleased to see her. He did not rise, but he did apologize for not doing so, and he did invite her to sit in one of the green chairs. I, of course, went to the chair on my side of the desk.

"Alfeo," he said. "A report for my client, if you please." Polite preliminary chitchat is not one of his skills.

I said, "Yes, master," and reported, starting with the Maestro's foreseeing, my attempt with Fulgentio to block the killing, and our failure to do so. Violetta was in her Minerva persona, the brilliant one, and her gray eyes hung on every word I spoke, analyzing, remembering.

When I mentioned that I had called on Alessa and she had revealed the true name of Honeycat, she merely nodded, as if that were not news to her.

"You knew Zorzi Michiel, madonna?" the Maestro inquired softly.

She nodded again. "We met socially and then he invited

me to a spend a few days on the mainland. He was to come for me on the very day he fled from the city. Lucia vouched for Zorzi as very generous and excellent company, cultured and witty. I did not recognize the name earlier because nobody had told me he was the celebrated Honeycat."

"A birthmark," I said. "Only very *close* friends were in on the joke."

"Am I on his list now?" she asked. She was still under the shadow of the tarot's *Death reversed*.

"Who knows?" Nostradamus said. "We do not know the killer's motive for so many killings. You must be careful and Alessa even more so. Did Zorzi wear a beard?"

"No. Why?"

"Tell her why, Alfeo."

We had not discussed this, of course, but I knew the answer.

"Because the Basilica is the doge's private chapel and the Christmas service would be by invitation only. A nobleman in borrowed black robes might have bluffed his way in, but nobles are required to wear beards."

"It was dark," she said. "Beards are fairly easy to fake."

"True," the Maestro said, "and it may be that a fake beard turned up among his possessions. We absolutely must find out what evidence led the Ten to find him guilty. Go on, Alfeo."

So I described my visit to Palazzo Michiel and the death on Campo San Zanipolo that I failed to prevent. I finished with the warning from Friar Fedele and then waited to see what Minerva made of it all. So, significantly, did Nostradamus. She sat and frowned for a long minute.

"The lack of alibi makes no sense at all," she declared. "Zorzi was not the sort of boy to sit at home alone reading Dante. Surely someone could have testified that he had been elsewhere that night? Surely he was not stupid enough to use a dagger that could be traced back to him? Would the

Ten convict him on that alone? Who tipped him off that the Ten were going to arrest him? If he didn't kill his father, who did? And whether he committed patricide or not, who is going around killing courtesans now, eight years later? And why?"

"I regret," the Maestro said testily, "that as yet I can offer answers to none of those questions, madonna. But I am trained in the metaphysical, and so is Alfeo, although still to a limited extent. We are both convinced that the recent murders are connected to the death of Gentile Michiel, but we can produce no evidence except our intuition, which would not be accepted by a court."

Violetta smiled. "I have no legal training, but I may be able to offer a little assistance." Her eyes were bluer, her voice drier, and I recognized the political Aspasia. "I have been making inquiries among some of my fellow workers, both at the wedding yesterday and here in Venice. We compiled a list of those who belonged to what we called the Honeycat club, those in on the joke, as Alfeo puts it. As well as Alessa herself, my informants agreed that they included Lucia da Bergamo, Caterina Lotto, Marina Bortholuzzi, and probably Ruosa da Corone. We know of another six so far, although there must be many more. Our inquiries shall continue."

The Maestro sighed. "He was a busy lad."

"There are ten thousand prostitutes in Venice," Aspasia said. "But Honeycat could afford the cream, the *cortigiane oneste*. He was a skilled musician himself and wrote promising poetry. He demanded sex, certainly, and a lot of sex, but he expected much more. As Alessa puts it, nobody *slept* with Honeycat."

"How many hundred in total?"

"Several dozens," Aspasia said coldly. "But he did have favorites. We are spreading the word, and for the warning we have to thank you and Alfeo."

"I hope we can provide more than just that," the Maestro

said, now sounding quite snappish. He would naturally feel upstaged by a client who started her own investigation. "Yours is an excellent idea, madonna, but you did not go far enough. We need to know how *messer* Honeycat, if he has returned to the city after eight years, is finding his victims so easily. We know that Caterina Lotto had changed her place of residence at least once, but how many of the others had?"

He may have meant the question rhetorically, but Violetta answered. "Two. Lucia was still living in the same house as she had in his day. And Alessa is. We are also warning against any man who asks questions about specific courtesans and where they live now. Alessa or I will be notified right away."

Nostradamus grunted. "Alfeo?"

"Master?"

"Does the tax office in the palace keep a register of courtesans?"

"I expect so, master. It keeps records of everything else."

"Doctor," Violetta said, "you are taking a risk by even investigating this, are you not? The Ten have forbidden you to meddle."

He shrugged his narrow shoulders. "The Republic reserves the right to investigate crime, but it is every citizen's duty to prevent one, which is what I am seeking to do. I have not taken much risk so far, but I am afraid that the next step may be dangerous. And it could be much more costly than my normal investigations."

Violetta's eyes glinted gold. "You want another expense advance? How much?"

"I am not sure. Alfeo will try to learn that tonight."

"And what for?"

The Maestro chuckled. "To elect a doge. Alfeo told us how to do that at dinner on Friday, remember?"

"I fail to see the relevance," she said coldly.

So did I.

"You are happier that way, madonna," he said smugly.

"And now if you will excuse us, my apprentice and I have work to do. I know this is the Lord's day, but even my learned friend Isaia Modestus will break his Sabbath to save a life, and that is what we are attempting to do."

Toward sunset I set Archangelo Angeli on the balcony to watch the Rio San Remo, then went and gobbled an early supper in the kitchen. Giorgio was there, doing the same, having been warned that I would need him. Mama Angeli, who can smell trouble like a tigress scenting meat, knew right away that I was unhappy about what I was about to do that evening. She started asking questions that I would not have answered even if we were alone. As it was, her children were wandering in and out all the time. I told her that the Maestro was sending me to elect a doge. The youngsters laughed, but she was not amused. I was saved from her interrogation when Archangelo rushed in to say that he had seen two nobles going past in a gondola and a senator walking along the *fondamenta* on the far side. So the Great Council had adjourned. I nodded to Giorgio and we both rose.

We went downstairs, carrying his oar and the gondola cushions, and only when he pushed off from the loggia did I tell him I wanted to call on Carlo Celsi. He looked relieved, for there was nothing subversive about visiting a senior and respected patrician. It was the subject of our discussion that would be dangerous for me. By then the Maestro had explained his warped humor.

Twelve elect twenty-five, reduced by lot to nine; the nine elect forty-five, reduced to eleven . . . So on and so on. Why all that rigmarole to elect a doge? Alessa had said it was to prevent the Great Council dividing into factions. Violetta had suggested almost the opposite, that it was to keep the inner circle in power and the fringes out. The truth, as the Maestro saw it with his cynical eye, was closer to her view than

Alessa's, but he went further. It was much cheaper to bribe five or six nobles than hundreds, he said. Once a few "sound" men had won control of one of those tiny committees, their friends would hold a majority in all subsequent committees through to the final forty-one that made the actual choice. In other words, a doge was elected by bribery and that was what I was going to attempt that night.

My noble parentage and legitimate birth entitle me to take my seat in the Great Council when I reach the age of twenty-five. Many youngsters are admitted sooner, through various loopholes, but at twenty-five all I shall need to do is grow a beard, buy a gown, and turn up at the *broglio*. There I shall wait for some *nobile homo* to invite me in and introduce me to his companions, which should be no problem because so many of them already know me. That assumes that I behave myself until then and have enough money to buy the clothes. Manual labor would disqualify me; a serious scandal or conviction for a major crime like graft would. Graft is rife in the Great Council, but it is kept secret. I am especially vulnerable to a charge of corruption because I have no powerful family to back me and my apprenticeship to Nostradamus falls into a shady area on the edge of the permissible. Many narrow-minded patricians might welcome an excuse to strike my name from the Golden Book.

Nostradamus must know that, but he hadn't mentioned it when he told me what he wanted me to do. I might have refused but hadn't—I had failed Marina Bortholuzzi and couldn't bear the thought of more women being stabbed or strangled because I was too proud to get my hands dirty. I had spent the afternoon writing out two copies of the proposed contract with donna Alina Orio and then memorizing a long list of questions the Maestro wanted me to ask in the Palazzo Michiel if I got the chance. Now he was attempting more clairvoyance and I was going to dabble in the truly black art of subornation.

* * *

As always, Vittore greeted me with the cryptic smile that implied he had been expecting me. Celsi himself was standing at his desk, scribbling busily as he recorded the Council's decisions. He had not yet removed his patrician robes and bonnet; his tippet lay on a chair. He beamed gap-toothed.

"Alfeo! How wonderful to see you! How timely!"

"You are busy, *clarissimo*. I should wait upon you another day." I wanted an excuse to run all the way home and hide.

"Not at all, not at all. Wine, Vittore, wine, for my lovely friend. Sit, boy, and tell me all about your narrow escape last night."

"What narrow escape? Me?"

"Oh, it was all over the *broglio* this afternoon! Another woman murdered and there had been a scuffle. The killer escaped without anyone getting a glimpse of his face, but a young man was injured and ran away. 'That sounds just like my beloved Alfeo Zeno,' I thought to myself when I heard it. After all, you were the one who told us of Nostradamus's prediction . . ."

So he prattled. I settled in the chair, sipped more of his fine wine, and cursed myself for ever mentioning that foreseeing. It had done no harm to my master's reputation for omnipotence but it must have attracted the notice of the Council of Ten. It might even get us both convicted of murder—apprentice sent to fulfil prophecy.

"So what can I do for you tonight?" Celsi concluded, taking the other chair. He rubbed his hands. "Name it and it's yours."

"Two things, one little, one big. Why did *messer* Giovanni Gradenigo give up politics?"

For a few moments Celsi just stared at me like some puzzled gnome, but I was fairly sure that he was trying to work out why I was asking, rather than trying to answer my question.

"Why do you think that had anything to do with the Michiel case?"

Delighted to be right, I had no difficulty grinning from ear to ear. "Why do you answer a question with a question?"

He laughed and heaved himself to his feet to go in search of a book—two books, in fact, and he needed several minutes to find what he wanted in each of them. At last he laid them aside and folded his hands over his paunch.

"I don't know. Nobody ever found out—which is very unusual in the Republic! It was three months after the Michiel case, but I agree that that isn't very long, so there might be a connection. Old Marco Erizzo died and there was speculation that Gradenigo would replace him as a procurator of San Marco, but he just resigned from the Council of Ten and went into seclusion." He pulled a face. "I knew his wife's brother quite well, and he said even she couldn't get an answer out of him!"

So had there been a miscarriage of justice? Had the Three convicted the wrong man? Had that burden of guilt provoked a deathbed confession?

"If I can't even answer your small one," Celsi grumbled, "what's the big one?"

I drew a very deep breath. "I need to know on what evidence the Council of Ten convicted Zorzi Michiel of patricide."

The old gossip muttered, "I don't think it ever . . ." He clambered off his chair again to retrieve yet another book from the shelves, peering at the spines to find the right one. Then he laid it over one on the desk, where the light was better. After a moment he returned to his chair, shaking his head.

"Thought so. What I heard . . . just hearsay, of course. It always is with the Ten. What I heard was that the Three just informed the Ten that they all agreed the boy was guilty, but he had fled abroad."

No outsider was supposed to know even that much about the innermost workings of the government.

"The Three, then," I said. "I need to know on what evidence the inquisitors convicted Zorzi Michiel of patricide."

Celsi waggled his dewlaps at me. "Such a shame! I told you yesterday: if you'd asked me just a week ago, dear boy, I could have appealed to old Giovanni Gradenigo, but he's gone now. Agostino Foscari would have told me, but he went last year and his memory wasn't all that it should be by then anyway. That only leaves the other black, Tommaso Pesaro, and he's hopeless, tight as a coffin lid in a warm climate."

So I said it. "There are files."

Sier Carlo leaned back in his chair and gazed very hard at me. "Your master is supposed to have safer ways than that of learning things. Safer in this life, anyway. We mundane mortals have to resort to such dealings, but he talks with the angels."

"He still needs ordinary information to know what to ask for."

"What of yourself, lad? Too many patricians disapprove of one of us running around after a leech. You, especially, should not take this risk, Alfeo."

"Risk?" I said angrily. "Last night he slit my ribs. If he'd had a clear stroke at me, he'd have put the blade in my lung and I'd have bubbled to death in a few minutes. Even yet I may die of wound fever or lockjaw. Women are being murdered every day, almost, and you talk of risk, *clarissimo?*"

Still he hesitated, chewing his lip. Finally he nodded. "Very well. It will cost you a fortune."

"How much?"

"At least two hundred ducats, maybe more. Only *Circospetto* has access to such files and he does not come cheap."

I squirmed, because I had tangled with the Ten's chief

secretary before. Although I had survived so far, he and I have no liking for each other. His relations with the Maestro were even worse, and we had never before tried to corrupt him.

"Sciara takes bribes?"

"They all do. He's cheap compared to the Grand Chancellor."

"How do I go about it?"

"Midnight," Celsi said, almost whispering. "It must be midnight or soon after. Calle Spadaria in San Zulian. About five doors in from the *campo*, you'll see a door with a grille in it but no knocker, no name or number. You knock two slow and three fast. Hold your light so your face is visible. If no one answers, you are refused. And take a sizable down payment with you."

"I'll be there," I said. "Thank you."

"Be careful, lad," he said wistfully. "I'd hate not to have your cheerful smile around here any more."

19

As Giorgio expertly slid the boat up to the loggia of Ca' Barbolano, I broke the news that we'd be going out again, close to midnight. Boatmen for public hire are foul-mouthed hyenas and the privately employed ones are often not much better, but Giorgio never argues or complains.

"Far?"

"Near San Zulian. You decide where to let me off." San Zulian parish is just north of the Piazza, in an area so congested that there is little water access and the *campo* itself is almost nonexistent. Raffaino Sciara, chief secretary to the Council of Ten, would naturally want to live close to the Doges' Palace, where he spends most of his waking hours. At two hundred ducats a handshake, he could afford to.

I carried the bow lantern upstairs while Giorgio stacked the oar and cushions in the *androne* under a barrage of Luigi's aimless chatter. The Maestro had gone to bed, no doubt with a raging headache, but he had left a prophecy whose writing and syntax were both much better than average. The meaning was as cryptic as ever.

Why hazard in far lands when all you need lies close?
Why seek distant enemies when death is near at hand?
Be not so proud as to spurn help at your feet,
Nor too humble to seek salvation from on high.

I fetched the book of prophecies and selected a quill to transcribe this one. As always, it was ambiguous, haunting the borderlands of meaning, but the first line looked like a hint that Zorzi Michiel had returned from exile, or wanted to. The second could be a reference to bounty hunters or the Ten's assassins seeking him out wherever he tried to hide—the risk of discovery in Venice might be no greater. The third and fourth lines, I decided, would have to wait upon events.

This was Sunday, and the sixth commandment is definitely my favorite, but I couldn't settle to a book with my visit to *Circospetto* hanging over me, so I decided to catch up on my cleaning duties. I fetched a rag, the broom, and the feather duster.

That night I cleaned half the wall of books and the alchemy bench. I do not lift out the books—that takes me a couple of days when the Maestro decides it needs doing—so the bookshelves are little problem. But all the mortars, pestles, beakers, funnels, alembics, and other vessels have to be polished, all the reagent bottles wiped and their shelves also, so by the time I had come around to the door, it was too late to go any further.

Meanwhile I was worrying over Celsi's instructions to take a cash deposit with me. Having no experience in such matters, I should have asked him how much would be appropriate. Knowing better than to try and waken Nostradamus after a foreseeing, I decided to err on the high side, for to offer too little would get me and my proposal spurned. Fifty ducats would be ample, I decided, roughly a year's wages for a married journeyman artisan. I raided the secret cache for eighteen gold sequins, which I weighed carefully, then placed in a money pouch that I hung around my neck, inside my shirt. I also took some small change to buy off muggers if they were too many to fight. I entered the total in the ledger as expenses.

Back in my room to collect my sword and cloak, I decided I had just enough time to try a fast tarot reading. Of course urgency and apprehension make the worst possible state of mind to obtain a clear augury, so I should not have been surprised that the results seemed very mixed at first glance. Some cards made sense, others did not. I tucked them away in my memory and the deck under my pillow, then went to tell Giorgio it was time to go.

The night was quiet in San Remo, the sounds of Carnival far away and muffled. Even the Grand Canal was still when we reached it, reflecting the stars. The gibbous moon was close to the rooftops and blurred by haze as we glided through the night, and I sat in lonely silence in the *felze*, still searching for inner calm and understanding.

Tarot is limited in scope because it is restricted to seventy-eight cards, and only thirty-eight have pictures on them. The numbered cards can drop hints, of course, such as the three of swords to represent the state inquisitors, but the more pictures that turn up, the more explicit the reading. Although mine had been all in pictures, I could make very little sense of it.

The first card, representing the subject or the question, had been the knave of coins reversed, and that I could take as reference to my forthcoming efforts to suborn *Circospetto*, probably meaning that he would not be able to obtain the information I needed.

The lowermost card of the cross, for the danger or problem, was trump number eight, Justice, displaying a woman with a sword and scales. Had the card been reversed, I could have hoped that it was telling me that the inquisitors had wrongly convicted Zorzi Michiel. Since it wasn't, I had to take it as a warning that I was on my way to commit a major crime.

But the left-hand card, the helper or path, showed the second-highest trump, Judgment, with the angel blowing the trumpet and the dead rising from their graves. What sort of help was that? Did it mean I must wait until Judgment Day to learn the answers I sought? Again, I'd have preferred to see it reversed to indicate that Zorzi was innocent, or that he was figuratively returning from the dead. Again, the card was obstinately upright.

The right-hand card was from the minor arcana, the jack of swords as the snare to avoid. I have known that card to refer to me, which made no sense in this context, but it can also mean my old foe, Filiberto Vasco, the *vizio*—the king of swords would imply his superior, *Missier Grande*. I had no need of tarot to warn me to beware of Vasco. If he as much as caught me wearing a sword after dark he would turn me in to the night watch.

Which brought me to the most confusing card of the tarot deck. The top card of my spread had been trump number two, the Popess. Violetta's reading had shown the same card reversed as the snare to avoid, and here it had shown up again in mine, upright, showing the objective or solution.

What the Popess was doing in my reading I could not imagine. I knew of only three women involved in the case. Donna Alina Orio ought to be represented by the queen of coins, because she had wealth of her own. Possibly the Popess's religious implications might be stretched to indicate her daughter, Sister Lucretzia. It could not apply at all, so far as I could see, to Dom's wife, Isabetta Scorozini. If one of the murdered courtesans was intended, I could not see a connection yet.

I was still baffled about the tarot when Giorgio delivered me to watersteps on the Rio di San Zulian. I was no closer to understanding the Maestro's quatrain, either.

"If I'm not back in an hour go without me," I told him with the best attempt at cheer I could manage. "I'll be home in the morning."

"Give her my love, too," he said, which was a surprisingly suggestive remark from him.

As I disembarked, I heard the clock in the Piazza chime midnight. I set off toward the church like a ghost, for my boots made little sound on the stones and I had brought a half-lantern, rather than a torch, so its glow lit the pavement below me and not my face. Carnival is a bad time to wander the streets alone, for the riotous gangs of revelers can be dangerous. Almost every window was dark and I met no one except a quartet of merrymakers, fortunately all too drunk and aroused even to notice me. They went staggering by, sniggering and arguing, with the men blatantly pawing their companions, obviously prostitutes.

I turned south along the Calle Spadaria, walking slowly so I could scan the doorways. Celsi had not said right or left.

"Arghrraw!"

My rapier flashed into my hand, for the sound had been close and—yes!—two golden eyes shone in front of me, on the edge of my puddle of lamplight.

"Arghrraw . . ." it said again, more softly.

Find one rabid cat and of course you must expect many more, for they will bite one another. The city might be infested with them, although I had not heard anyone mention such a problem. I backed up a step.

The eyes advanced. *"Arghrraw!"*

"Now look here, Felix," I said sternly, having visions of needle teeth sunk in my ankle . . . But my mind must still have been grappling with the tarot and the quatrain because then I heard an inner voice that sounded much like the Maestro's: *"Be not so proud as to spurn help at your feet."*

A cat had led me to Alessa when she was ready to talk. A

cat had found me refuge when the mob was after me. I backed up three steps.

"*Arghrraw . . . Arghrraw . . .*" The cat followed, softer still, but more urgent.

A door opened not ten feet ahead of me. Although the light escaping from the entrance was in truth very faint, it seemed to flood the alley. It was not even bright enough to illuminate the man emerging, but I knew his voice.

"I will tell them. Good night to you, *lustrissimo*."

"And to you, *capitano*," Sciara replied.

By that time I had closed my lantern and was backed into a doorway, trying to make myself as flat as paint. If the departing visitor turned in my direction he would be certain to see me, even in the dark *calle*, for it was so narrow I would be within arm's length of him. He would hear my heart thundering like a charge of heavy cavalry.

No. Saints be praised, *vizio* Filiberto Vasco went the other way, toward the Piazza and the Doges' Palace. His boots tapped off into the night, the puddle of light from his lantern danced around his feet, and Raffaino Sciara closed his door.

I stood where I was until I stopped shaking, which took several minutes. My tarot had warned me of the jack of swords, the quatrain had told me to accept help at my feet. Had the cat not delayed me, I would have rapped on that door while Vasco was standing on the other side of it, and I had no imaginable reason to be calling on Raffaino Sciara even in broad daylight, let alone at midnight. Had I been betrayed? Had Celsi reported what I planned? Or his servant? I assured myself that there were a dozen reasons why *Missier Grande* might have sent his lackey to ask Sciara something or tell Sciara something, and none of them need have anything to do with me.

For a third time cats had helped me—except that it must obviously be the same cat and more than just a cat. It might be a demon from hell, but I was going to give it the benefit of the doubt from now on. I opened my lantern and saw the cat sitting in the middle of the *calle*, watching me and licking a paw.

"Thanks, Felix."

"*Arghrraw . . .*" It stood up and paraded southward, tail high, until it stood in front of the door with the grille, *Circospetto*'s door, the door that *vizio* Vasco had just left.

A *cat* was telling me that it was safe to proceed and I was crazy.

No, I must trust my new helper, and Felix was now standing waiting for me, staring inquiringly as if wondering why I was taking so long. I walked over to it and bunched my knuckles to make the signal I had been told.

Knock! Knock! Rap—rap—rap.

I turned the half-lantern so my face would be visible.

I had to wait, but I had expected that little ploy.

"What do you want?" asked a whisper.

I could whisper too. "Information."

"This is a new departure for you, *sier* Alfeo."

It was Sciara. Even a whisper can be recognized. Any other time I would have given him a smart-alecky response but not tonight. Tonight I felt I had sunk too low to amuse anyone, even myself.

"Desperate times require desperate measures, *lustrissimo*. Are you going to let me in?"

The door opened a few inches in well-oiled silence. I pushed it wider and stepped into darkness beyond.

"Lock it!"

I turned the big key. Then I encountered a heavy curtain, and beyond that a very dimly lit corridor with another curtain, and finally a room. It was barely large enough to hold the table in the center, flanked by two chairs and bearing a lantern, but at last there was light enough for us to see each other. Another door at the far side presumably led to either Sciara's house or a back exit.

He looked even more like the Grim Reaper than usual, for I had never seen him except in his secretary's blue robe, whereas tonight he wore a black hat and cloak and his skull-like face seemed almost to float in the air. He did not sit or invite me to.

"Who taught you that knock, Alfeo?"

"No names, *lustrissimo*. You can help the one who sent me and no one else can."

The death's-head showed its teeth. "He is too mean to pay for what he wants you to buy."

"Not this time. Women are dying."

"He cares?"

"We both care and so should you."

Sciara was enjoying baiting me too much to stop yet. "If I knew anything that would help Their Excellencies catch the killer, *clarissimo*, do you think I would not have shared it with them?"

"Information can mean different things to different people. Are these word games part of the process or are you keeping me here until Vasco can return with the *sbirri*? You will have to explain my presence in your house, you know."

Sciara drummed thin fingers on the table. "Tell me what you want."

"To see the evidence that the Three used to find Zorzi Michiel guilty of patricide eight years ago."

His total lack of reaction was admirable. I might as well have asked if it was raining. Venetian magistrates, several hundred of them, are noblemen elected by the Grand Council and their terms of office are limited, all except the doge's. The clerks, guards, secretaries, ducal equerries, and all the rest who make the government work, are drawn from the citizen-by-birth class, and are employed for life, or in some cases until they reach sixty. Sciara has been *Circospetto* for as long as I can remember and knows everything. He could probably recite by rote the records I wanted to see, although I should not have believed him.

He pouted. "That file may be eight years old, but it has been attracting much attention of late. For me to remove it even briefly would be extremely dangerous."

"So now we're bargaining. Name your price." Yes, I was an impudent young puppy, but I was a *clarissimo* and he was only a *lustrissimo*. We nobles have our rights and arrogance is one of them. Humility would shell no cockles with Raffaino Sciara. His eyes shrank as if they were withdrawing into his head.

"You come here tomorrow night, a half hour later. If I do not answer, you go away and try again the next night. It may be several days before I manage to obtain the material you want to see, understand?"

I nodded, my mouth dry.

"When I do," he said, "you will look at the papers while I watch. You write nothing and take away nothing."

"Agreed."

"Five hundred ducats."

"Absurd! Two hundred."

He smiled. "Five hundred and not a *soldo* less. Fifty of that now."

He had me by the throat and we both knew it. He did not trust me any more than I trusted him and he must be enjoying watching me squirm.

I reached inside my doublet. "You'll have to settle for eighteen sequins now, it's all I brought." I was four lire short.

The tip of his tongue showed for a moment, snakelike. He had not expected me to have such lucre on me and had been looking forward to kicking my young butt out into the alley. He probably wished he had asked for more.

"Nonrefundable," he said.

"No."

"Then we have no agreement. Just looking for those files will be dangerous for me."

Job himself could not have bettered my sigh. "Nonrefundable, then," I agreed. I spread eighteen little disks on the table.

"Tomorrow at half an hour past midnight. Four knocks."

I nodded and turned on my heel without a word. I had made my debut in major corruption. I might make a politician yet.

There was no sign of my supernatural feline helper out in the *calle*. Feeling soiled and with a sour taste in my mouth, I hurried back through the dark to the watersteps where Giorgio was waiting. If I had just thrown away fifty ducats, Nostradamus would skin me.

20

Nostradamus can always surprise me. Next morning he hobbled into the atelier on his canes, obviously still in pain, and by the time he had settled into his chair, I was there with his willow bark potion. I should properly have slunk quietly away and given him an hour to sheath his fangs, but I was anxious to head off to Palazzo Michiel. Besides, I wanted to get the ordeal over with.

"Good morning, master."

He grunted, which was better than snarling.

"Concerning my visit to *Circospetto* . . ." I broke the news about the five hundred ducats and the forty-nine already gone. Since the wages due to me for the entire seven years of my apprenticeship will only be seventeen ducats, I expected to be torn into little pieces and fed to the fish of the canal.

He grunted again. "Good. You made the correct decision."

Rejecting the temptation to sink to the floor in a dramatic swoon, I said, "Thank you, master."

"Had he asked for only the two hundred you mentioned, I would have forbidden you to go back there. We have done Sciara down so often that he might have forgone that much just for the spite of seeing me exiled and you sent to the galleys. But I doubt if even he will pass up five hundred."

"Um . . ." I said, baffled by this backward thinking. "Yes, master."

Of course Nostradamus would collect from Violetta, but that would mean that his final reward for catching Honeycat would shrink by the same amount. This could be ominous. Had he given up hope of earning his fee?

"And I need counseling on a matter of cats, master."

He looked up at me with an expression that would flake paint off a Tintoretto. "Cats?"

I explained about cats: cats that force me to detour and so lead me to find Alessa in a weak moment, cats that direct me to a refuge when the mob is after me, and cats that delay me so that *vizio* Filiberto Vasco doesn't catch me red-handed trying to bribe *Circospetto*. One cat, or three? Not a cat in the normal sense at all, of course, so what? As I spoke he frowned and tugged at his goatee. Afterward he stared across at the wall of books for a while, scanning it as if he were mentally scanning through their contents, book by book. Perhaps he was.

"You been summoning without telling me?"

"No, master."

"Curious," he murmured. "I had not thought of . . . Well, I advise you to be very careful. I have exposed you to much strange lore in a very short time. It may not have seemed short to you, but when you compress the wisdom of centuries into just a few years, it can take on a life of its own. I may have been reckless. You may have opened channels to unexpected realms. *Three times but never four?*"

I scrabbled hastily in the back rooms of my memory. "In the *Iliad*, Patroclus tried three times to scale the walls of Troy and fell back, but when he tried again, Apollo struck him down. Diomedes, too. He attacked the god three times, and each time Apollo brushed him aside, but on his fourth attempt the god roared at him to warn him off. And Achilles—"

Violetta would have been proud of my classical scholarship. Even the Maestro grudgingly nodded approval.

"Yes, yes, Homer knew it, but it is older than that. I was thinking of the Hebrew tradition, to forgive a sinner three times but never four. Three times this apparition has helped you, you think. Now it has gained your confidence so that next time it may entrap you."

"Or it may be truly benevolent?"

"It may be," he said sourly, "but be careful! If there is a fourth time—Heaven forbid!—the stakes will be very high. Let me see that wound of yours."

I suspected when Giorgio delivered me to the Riva degli Schiavoni that I would be too early for donna Alina Orio, so on reaching Palazzo Michiel, I asked for Jacopo. Admitted, I sat on the same bench as I had two days before and studied the same pictures. The solution to Gentile Michiel's death hid somewhere in this building certainly, and I was more convinced than ever that the courtesans' deaths were related also; I just did not know why I thought that.

I was not alone in that belief, obviously, else why did so many people want the Maestro to investigate an eight-year-old murder that the Council of Ten had declared solved? Donna Alina Orio Michiel did. Violetta did, if indirectly. It seemed highly likely that Giovanni Gradenigo had, just before he died. And the Council of Ten did not.

No long wait this time—Jacopo appeared in short order, trotting down the great staircase and striding forward to meet me with a smile of greeting. He was even more magnificently garbed than before, his britches and doublet a concerto of cream and purple brocade, and he had somehow contrived to have his silken hose and his ruff both in the same shade of cream, instead of white. Moreover the ruff was huge, with innumerable points around the edge like a sunburst, but that helped to disguise the top-heavy effect of his overlarge chest and shoulders. His bonnet matched his waist-length cape of silver and blue, and the buttons on his doublet were chunks of amethyst. He was an eye-popping vision of excess and I was tormented by jealousy.

If I could trust anyone in the Michiel household, it should be Jacopo. He could have been no more than eleven or twelve when his father died and he was also in the clear for the courtesan murders, because if I tried to tackle him the way I had tackled the fake friar at San Zanipolo, I would bounce right off.

We bowed and greeted.

He made no move to lead me anywhere. "You bring a contract? The old witch will be delighted. She has been on pins and needles since you left, worried that Nostradamus will turn her down."

"The price may startle her."

"Bah!" he said in exactly the tone the Maestro uses. "She has more money than she can count, nothing to spend it on, and not much time left to try. You'll have to be patient, though. The daily reconstruction is still underway. Skilled craftsmen are at work. Is there anything I can tell you or any way I can entertain you until she considers herself presentable?"

I had very few questions to ask Jacopo, but I might as well put them now. I doubted that his half-brothers would let me within hailing distance of themselves or their staff until the matriarch had blessed my quest, perhaps not even then.

"What do you know about the knife that was used to kill your father?"

He eyed me warily. "How much do you know about it already?"

"I heard that it was a family possession."

He grinned, which seemed an odd reaction. "True. It had been a prized family treasure for centuries and then became an infamous one. Come along and I'll show you."

He went upstairs at a fast trot, which I had to match, but fortunately there were only a few servants around to frown at such impropriety. We crossed the wide *salone* to a glass case standing against the opposite wall. Amid a collection of ancient books, Roman lamps, Greek jars, some antique coins, and a few Turkish curiosities, there was only one weapon, a dagger. It had an S curve to it, with an animal head for a pommel. The grip was made of bone and the scabbard of silver. The blade was not visible, but would be very little longer than my hand, while the hilt would fit comfortably in a man's fist.

"It's called a *khanjar*," my guide said cheerfully. "Syrian. Made of damascene steel. It was collected in 1204 at the sack of Constantinople by one of their"—his smile faltered—"*my* ancestors. Unfortunately he collected it between his ribs. Fortunately his son was there also and was able to salvage the dagger, if not save the situation."

"He saved the family honor, though. He must have killed the killer or he couldn't have brought back the sheath."

Jacopo nodded. "Never thought of that."

Or perhaps the dagger had been routinely looted from a corpse and its story had been embellished over four centuries. I could not but admire the deadly little horror—an assassin's dream, small enough to be easily concealed and quite long enough to kill a man. "This cabinet is kept locked?"

"It is now. It wasn't back then, when our father was stabbed. I used to play with the *khanjar* when I was small and it was still just as sharp as it must have been in Constantinople. In fact . . ." Jacopo hesitated. "I was the one who noticed that it was missing after the murder and opened my big mouth in front of witnesses. Apparently the *shirri* had not thought to ask anyone if we could identify the weapon."

"And how did the scabbard find its way back this time?"

He stared at me blankly. "I don't know. I suppose it was left behind in the Basilica. The killer wouldn't want to be caught wearing it, now would he? Not with blood on it."

I wondered who had been crass enough to put the dagger back on display, but I wasn't crass enough to ask.

Jacopo started to stroll. "Let's go and see if the painters and decorators have completed today's masterpiece."

I went with him. "If Zorzi has come back to Venice, he must have found somewhere safe to hide. Who would help him? Who would give him shelter?"

"One of his harlots, I suppose. You'll be an old man before you finish questioning all of those maenads."

"He had quite a reputation, but I was thinking of family. Bernardo?"

"No."

"Why not?"

"Good riddance, in his view. Why start the tongues wagging all over again? Why queer the Council of Ten? I know the Ten now are not the same men as eight years ago, but they're all part of the inner circle. You go nowhere in politics in Venice if the First Ones don't like you."

"Domenico?"

"Never!" he said, even more firmly. "He has the means, I agree. He comes and goes a lot, to and from the mainland. He has a lot of contacts there. Even the Ten may not be able to keep track of Domenico, not completely. And Dom sometimes took Zorzi's side in the quarrels, but that was years ago, when Gentile was alive. He's the last one to want him back now."

It's always helpful to have a witness who likes to gossip.

"Money?" I said.

"Definitely money," Jacopo agreed. "If Zorzi came back and was pardoned, he would own one third of the *fraterna*."

Which was a reminder that the two Michiel brothers had benefitted not only from their father's death but because their brother had been disqualified from sharing in the windfall. Jacopo, being illegitimate, would not be a partner.

"Their mother? Could she be hiding Zorzi?"

Jacopo frowned. "She couldn't help directly. She almost never goes out of the house—Communion at Christmas and Easter, that's about all. That's the way proper ladies live, in her view. She might provide money. She would do that. You think that's why she's hiring Nostradamus—because Zorzi wants to have his name cleared so he can come back?"

"Or has come back."

We reached the end of the *salone* and climbed a few steps to a corridor. The Michiel palace was a warren, assembled from more than one building, and in total it was considerably larger than Ca' Barbolano. My guide continued at the same ambling pace.

"Zorzi's not in this house, if that's what you're thinking," he said. "I'd know if anyone knew. I'm part family and part servant. There's nowhere and nobody could hide him from me." He sounded proud of that, but I'd marked him as a busybody within moments of first meeting him.

"And don't be surprised," he added, "if the lady has company. Bernardo is spitting musket balls about this Nostradamus idea of hers. He'll want to nip you in the bud."

Interesting! Suspicion stirred. "What bothers him most about it?" I asked. "Just renewed scandal? Or the fee?" Or was it that he feared whatever truth Nostradamus might uncover?

For a moment I thought that I was not going to receive an answer, then my companion said quietly, "The Council of Ten."

"They've been asking questions?" I knew from Sciara that the file had been receiving attention lately, but this confirmation of the Ten's renewed interest made the floor quake under my feet.

"They've asked *Bernardo* questions—unofficially so far. A *fante* dropped in not long after you left on Saturday. We had a family conference about it yesterday. They even let me sit in."

"Is that unusual?"

"The rule is that I'm not family when I want to be and vice versa."

"It's worrisome news. Do you know what sort of questions?"

Again there was a pause before he spoke. "He didn't ask about you, *clarissimo*. I know because Domenico asked Bernardo that. The Ten just wanted to know if we'd heard rumors that Zorzi had slipped back into the city, when we last heard from him, and so on."

"Did you all get your stories straight, then?"

Jacopo laughed. "We had a screaming, rip-roaring row, the best fight we've had since Gentile died and Zorzi left. Accusations of greed, duplicity, and senile dementia volleyed back and forth. Bernardo roared, Domenico sneered, Lucretzia sobbed, Fedele preached hellfire and Christian charity, sometimes in the same breath. Even Isabetta said a few sharp words. I just sat there like a cherub and enjoyed it all thoroughly. At the end, when they had all realized that they were going nowhere, I said that, as my conscience was quite clear and I had no guilty secrets to hide, I intended to answer all your questions fully and honestly. Then they all had to agree that they would do the same."

We had reached a door I knew. Jacopo halted.

"Do you suppose that one of them is a murderer and will lie to you?" he asked.

"That's for my master to decide," I said, although I knew that Jacopo himself had been lying to me like an Ottoman camel trader.

He reached for the handle. "Brace yourself for Venus In Splendor."

21

I could see no change in donna Alina since my previous visit. The face paint was no thicker, the impressive strings of pearls were the same, and if the black gown and shawl were not, then they were identical copies. Nor did she deserve Jacopo's slurs about her age. In her fifties she could reasonably look forward to another decade or so to spend the money he mentioned so bitterly. This time she was alone, reading a book. I knew it was a stage prop because she was not holding it at arm's length as she had held the letter she read to me the last time, and she made no effort to mark her place before closing it and handing it to Jacopo to shelve.

I bowed, was permitted to kiss her fingers, offered a chair. As before, she left her flunky standing. I admired her Paris Bordone portrait again; I still liked the bronze cherub better than the ebony desk.

Alina wasted no time on small talk. "So your master will do as I ask?"

"He is willing to try, madonna."

"How generous of him."

"He accepts no fees unless he succeeds, so he must be selective in the cases he accepts." I offered the contract.

She ignored it. "How much?"

"Two hundred ducats if he can prove that your son Zorzi did not stab your husband."

"And what else does it say?"

"He needs information, so he requires that all members of your household answer certain questions that he has instructed me to ask."

She hissed and then sucked in her hollow cheeks. "Absurd! You will write it all down and require everyone to sign what you have written. Then the blackmail will start."

"No blackmail, madonna. I will write nothing. I don't need to. 'Near Milan, twelfth January. My most beloved lady mother, it was with deepest sorrow that I added to your burdens by fleeing from the Republic, knowing that my actions will be taken as evidence of guilt and bring calumny upon you and everyone I hold dear. I was warned just in time that the Chiefs of the Ten had ordered my arrest. For reasons known to you—' "

"Impressive! Can you remember every word of a conversation also?"

"Most of them, madonna. You: 'Why is a messenger boy claiming to be a patrician?' Me: 'I am a patrician, madonna, my birth is listed in the Golden Book. I carried only a letter of introduction and—' "

"Jacopo, read me that contract."

Jacopo took the paper from me—with his left hand—and read it out. Once he inserted a mistake to see if I would correct him, which I did. I had been waiting for him to try that old trick. When he had done, donna Alina rose from her chair and strode over to the black escritoire. While Jacopo fussed around producing pen, ink, wax, and sand, she held up the second copy of the contract at arm's length and read it through to make sure it said the same things.

"I will not accept this nonsense about the *bocca di leone*," she said. "I am hiring your master, he should report to me alone."

"If his search is unavailing, then of course his regrets come to you alone, madonna. But the law is clear that any citizen having evidence bearing on a major crime has a duty to report it to the proper authority, which in the case of murder is the Council of Ten. The Lion's Mouth letter box for the Ten is in the palace, of course, but there are many other drops around the city, and if we choose ours carefully and time the drop, we can be sure it will not be read for several hours. This gives us ample time to report to you."

She pouted, which added five years to her face and ten to her neck. "Who pays the cook eats first. Nostradamus will send his report to me and if it is acceptable, then I shall see that a copy goes to the Ten."

Having had the same argument with clients before, I just shrugged. "If you insist." The Maestro had never had a client turn out to be guilty of a major crime, but he has explained to me that all his contracts include standard wording that they are subject to the laws of Venice just in case this ever happens. Thus he cannot be sued for breach of contract if he turns his client in, although I don't see why a headless corpse would care to argue.

"Then you must say so," donna Alina announced. "Write it in, Jacopo, both copies."

Jacopo wrote left-handed, of course; the trait sinister often runs in families. When he had amended both copies, she signed and sealed them—right-handed—and returned to her favored seat.

"What else do you need to know, *sier* Alfeo?" She pursed her lips tightly and narrowed her eyes.

"I understand that you were the only one to see the murderer?"

"I did not really *see* him. It was very dark after the brightness. The Basilica is not an especially large church, you understand, considering its importance, but it must be the most beautiful in the entire world. The whole of the inside, all the domes and the walls and arches, are decorated with gold mosaic displaying the history of the city, and Our Lord with the saints and apostles, his Holy Mother, a most incredible sight."

I have seen the inside of the Basilica several times. What she was saying was not very relevant to her husband's death, but she was talking so I let her ramble on.

"And the Christmas Mass is most special, you know, held just before midnight by an ancient special dispensation from the Pope, with the most beautiful music, and all the senior officers of the Republic come in procession, together with men from the great *scuole*, the friars, and priests. Truly, it was the most memorable experience of my entire life. And the church was very dim until four men, standing at the corners of a cross, lighted threads, like fine fuses, that spread the light out to hundreds of candles—one thousand five hundred candles, Gentile told me, and some dozens of very large, twelve-pound candles, and they all seemed to light by themselves, all at once, and the entire Basilica blazed up like the sun to greet the day of Our Lord's birth!"

I sighed in wonder.

She sighed in nostalgia. "And then, oh horrors! The glorious Mass came to an end, as everything must come to an end. We had just gone out into the atrium, and it was so dark out there, but I had found Gentile and taken his arm, and suddenly someone pushed me roughly, and I cried out in complaint and clung tighter to my husband, but he made a strange noise . . . more like surprise than pain, really. He fell, dragging me down with him. And I realized that he was bleeding . . . So, no, I didn't really see the murderer. Except that he did not seem very tall." End of recitation.

"Thank you, madonna."

"What else?"

"The reasons known to you why Zorzi could not prove his innocence."

The letter she had shown me previously had been invented by Domenico and his wife and meant nothing, but the forgers had avoided mentioning the explanation Zorzi had given his mother for failing to clear his name, perhaps because they had not known exactly what that was. What he had said might or might not be whatever she was going to tell me after she stopped glaring at me like a Barbary corsair.

"Jacopo, go and wait outside."

The family by-blow's face froze, but he spun on his heel and marched to the door. I expected him to slam it behind him, but he managed to close it quietly. Silence. I waited.

Finally: "*Sier* Alfeo, I do not deny that at times my late husband was very autocratic. He had strict standards, even by the standards of the Venetian patriarchy."

I nodded understandingly.

"Nor do I deny that my son was a sinner, but he was a man of spirit also and knew that he had two half-sisters and a half-brother born out of wedlock. He regarded Gentile's reprimands as sheer hypocrisy." She paused, as if realizing that she was avoiding the issue. "Zorzi frequented courtesans, yes. But at the time of Gentile's death, he was enamored of a woman of noble birth."

Even after so long, telling me this was a strain for her. Her hands were knotted into fists and her cheeks blotched red under the paint. I helped her along.

"You are saying, madonna, that on the night your husband died, your son was clasped to the bosom of a married lady?"

She nodded. "That was why he could not defend himself from the charge of murder."

Zorzi had an alibi? I was tempted to laugh aloud. Even a

notorious libertine could have delusions of honor, apparently, but this might be the easiest two hundred ducats the Maestro had ever earned.

"If you, in strictest confidence, were to tell me the name of—"

"I do not know her name."

I must have looked disbelieving, because she continued grimly.

"I know only that she was young and married to an older man. Zorzi told exaggerated fairy tales of his debauchery with courtesans just to annoy his father, but he was very discreet about the others. Other one, I mean. That was a true love affair!"

"Did you tell the inquisitors about her?"

"No. They asked me about the murder itself, because I was there, and I told them everything I knew. They never asked me where my sons were at the time, why should they?"

"Did they not question you again after he fled?"

"No. By then they had convinced themselves of his guilt."

"You are certain that your son refused to tell the inquisitors the name of the witness who could give him an alibi? It was not that he did name her and she contradicted his story out of fear of her husband's wrath?"

"No. I begged him to tell them, but he insisted he never would."

That was the end of that path. Was she lying to me? Had Zorzi lied to her? Had the boy's mistress lied to the Three? I was no nearer knowing why some maniac was going around murdering courtesans.

"Still more questions, *messer* Zeno? I find this conversation wearying and unnecessary. I engaged Maestro Nostradamus to clear my son's name, not to inflict you and your eternal questioning upon myself."

"Just one more, madonna, undoubtedly a painful one for you. When did you last see Zorzi?"

She sniffed as if I had committed a social gaffe. "The day of my husband's funeral. We had no sooner returned to the house than he changed out of mourning and appeared in his usual finery. No long months of mourning for him, he said; he had paid his respects, and anything more would be hypocrisy."

"Did he hint that he was heading to the mainland?"

"No. No, he certainly did not. He told me he had found the archangel of all courtesans, Venus in the flesh, and he was going off to, um, visit with her and see if she was as good as her reputation." Donna Alina's face hardened. "It must have been she who warned him that the Ten were going to arrest him."

"I think not, madonna. I have spoken to the woman, and she claims that she was expecting him but he never arrived."

"Indeed?" She raised her painted brows, corrugating her forehead. "And what is the name of this paramount beauty?"

"That I may not reveal. I am much indebted to you for your help." I rose to take my leave. "My master gave me some questions to put to both *sier* Bernardo and *sier* Domenico; also some for a few senior servants. I may tell them that you wish them to cooperate?"

She pulled a face. "Let Jacopo back in."

I went to the door and opened it slowly in case he had his ear to the keyhole and needed to skedaddle, but he was leaning against the wall on the far side of the corridor, arms folded and eyes hot with anger. I winked and stepped aside.

He marched in and bowed excessively low. "How may I serve, madonna?"

"Stop sulking," she said. "It's childish. Escort *sier* Alfeo around and tell everyone that he asks questions with my permission. If anyone refuses to answer, report them to me. Now go away, both of you. I am upset and need to lie down."

"Frail as the Walls of Troy," Jacopo remarked after the door had been safely closed and we were walking the corridor together.

"She is a tough lady," I agreed.

"Where to, *sier* inquisitor?"

"*Sier* Bernardo is inspecting meat at this time of day?"

"Yes, but in a dignified, aristocratic way."

"Is *sier* Domenico available?"

"He told me he would be in the library all morning. This way, then."

Our path returned us to the big *salone* where the murder weapon was preserved in its glass mausoleum. In the window overlooking the *riva* and the shipping basin sat the plump little lady I had seen with donna Alina on Friday. At first I thought she was alone, the epitome of the sequestered Venetian nobleman's wife dying of boredom as the world went by without her; but then I saw she had a child with her and was pointing out the sights. I knew who she was.

"Pray present me to donna Isabetta," I asked my guide.

"Signora Isabetta," he snapped, but he changed course.

Isabetta acknowledged me with a careful lack of expression, but she did invite me to be seated, which was both gratifying and unexpected. The child, aged about five, huddled close to her mother, alarmed by a stranger.

"Maria, dear," Isabetta whispered, "you go with Jacopo and find Nurse. Thank you, Jacopo." Mousey she might be, but she had no hesitation about giving him orders. She watched the two of them depart, and then waited for me to speak, all bland and respectful, eyes demurely downcast. The huge *salone* was hardly a private space, but her behavior in meeting alone with a man would not meet with her mother-in-law's approval. I wondered if she had planned this.

"I am sorry to interrupt you, madonna."

She nodded agreement to my feet.

"Do you mind answering a few brief questions?"

"What do you wish to know, *messer?*"

"You married *sier* Domenico before his father's death?"

Another nod.

"So you knew Zorzi. What sort of a man was he?"

"An icicle in a furnace." She spoke softly, guardedly.

"You refer to his lifespan or his character?"

She did not return my smile, perhaps did not even see it. She was a very tightly controlled lady. "The latter. First, of course, he was the handsomest boy in Venice and possibly in all Christendom, truly beautiful. He knew it. Men stared at him in the streets. He was witty, talented, and cultured. He dressed like a peacock and danced like a butterfly."

"The furnace?"

"The furnace was the way he looked at women. The moment I met him, his eyes were telling me that he had been waiting for me all his life, that I was indeed fortunate beyond all women, and if we could just slip away from all these other people he would demonstrate what men were for. He was still making the same offer the last time I saw him." She hardly moved a muscle while whispering all this to me. An onlooker at a distance would not have known we were conversing at all.

"And the icicle?"

"Was what I saw when I looked into his eyes."

I bowed my head in praise. "You are a wise and observant lady. Did he kill his father?"

"That is up to you to discover, is it not? She signed your contract?"

"She did."

A tiny hint of a smile came and went, leaving a hint of contempt behind. "I knew she would. She has been obsessed with her lost son ever since he fled."

"You bring Zorzi to life for me. Will you give me the benefit of your judgment of donna Alina?"

"No."

Wise, observant, *and* careful. "Then was Zorzi capable of murdering his father?"

"Only if it was necessary."

"Necessary for what?"

"For his own happiness. What else mattered?"

"Did you know that he was having an affair with a married woman?"

"Lots of them. You refer to that story that he could not explain his whereabouts without betraying a lover? Zorzi . . ." She paused, frowning very slightly. "It is hard to talk of such a libertine having any sort of honor, but he did have some standards. He was no puffball. He kept himself extremely fit—so he would never disappoint a friend, he said. And he resisted any sort of authority. I often wondered if he might have run away to protect a woman, just as a temporary measure. His mother might have put him up to it—going into hiding until they catch the real killer. If that were the case he would have had to be innocent, of course."

"Then the Ten declared him guilty and gave up looking?"

"It's possible."

"Yes it is. So he was innocent?"

"I doubt if Zorzi remained innocent much beyond his twelfth birthday, but he may not have been guilty of patricide."

"And his mother may know where he is? Quite apart from the letters you and your husband provide for her?"

"I doubt it, now. If he stayed in any one place for long, the bounty hunters would have caught him. She really believes the letters."

I was inclined to believe that, but not ready to check it off as certain. Alina was a cunning and manipulative old woman, and I strongly suspected that Isabetta Scorozini detested her.

"I understand that you had a family conference yesterday?"

Isabetta's face resumed its waxen inscrutability. "I will not betray confidences, *messer*. Nothing that was discussed yesterday can have any possible bearing on what happened in the Basilica eight years ago."

While I was working out the politest way of contradicting that statement, I saw Jacopo striding toward us like a war galley preparing to ram. The chance of learning anything from Isabetta had just ended, so I rose and thanked her and spoke my farewells.

"Did you know that Zorzi was having an affair with a married woman?"

Jacopo gave me the answer I expected from the family snoop: "Of course I did." He did not look at me as he said it.

"Even then you knew, or you have learned since?"

"Even then. More than one of them. He didn't care what they were, as long as they were female—servants, whores, or senators' granddaughters."

"But apparently he was with a *lady* on the night your father died. You don't happen to know her name, do you?"

"No."

By then I trusted very little of what Jacopo Fauro told me, but that time he was probably telling the truth. I had trouble imagining the libertine Zorzi bragging of his conquests to a much younger half-brother. That seemed out of character. He boasted to anger his father, not to impress the cook's bastard.

22

The Michiel library was not impressive as a book collection but as a room it was spectacular—large and bright and gloriously decorated. There we found Domenico with three artisan-class men, all standing around the central table, studying building plans. He looked up as we entered.

He beamed. "I did not think I should escape for long. Greetings to you, *clarissimo*!"

I responded. I thought for an instant that he was going to embrace me. If he thought of it he changed his mind quickly. We bowed.

"Jacopo," he said, "you have a good eye for style. See if you can figure out why this chapel extension looks off balance. Let us take a breath of air, *sier* Alfeo." He escorted me to a glass door leading to a small balcony overlooking the canal, thereby cutting out Jacopo much more graciously than his mother had. With the glass door closed, we were alone and could not be overheard.

Domenico wore well-cut gentleman's clothes in sober, somber gray. With his keen, aquiline features and easy charm he seemed all ready to sell me the palazzo of my dreams or relieve me of my current rat-infested hovel, whichever I wanted.

"So Nostradamus thinks he can find the person who killed my father, does he?"

"He is willing to try, *clarissimo*."

He leaned back against the parapet and rested his elbows on it, studying me with that odd smile displaying lower teeth.

"Then I had better start by pleading my own innocence and saving you having to ask. On the night in question, I attended San Zaccaria with my wife and her widowed sister, who was living with us at the time and has since died. The priest could testify that I was there, but the church was very full, so his evidence was not quite as convincing as it would normally have been. My companions later swore that I never went out, but of course they would say that, wouldn't they? I was wearing my black robes, the church was dark, and we sat near the door." He shrugged. "I did not slip out and murder my father, but if you want to assume that I was secretly glad when the Ten fixed on someone else as the murderer, then I couldn't deny it under oath. Does that help?"

"It helps a lot," I said. "When did you last see your brother?"

"Zorzi? Right after the funeral. I met him as he was leaving the house, decked up like a peacock."

"Do you know where he was going?"

"I can guess why, but I don't know where, or to whom."

"Did he say . . . What was his mood?"

"He was scared out of his wits," Domenico said brutally.

"He was?" That was not what donna Alina had told me.

"He was hiding it, but I knew him well enough to tell. Remember that he was a skilled actor and liar."

"Was he?" It must be a family trait.

"He could never have scored so well with women otherwise. Mostly he bought harlots, but he also collected amateurs."

Jacopo had told me that Domenico had taken Zorzi's side

in the family quarrels. Perhaps he had, but now I suspected
that he hated his youngest brother. If he hadn't hated him
back then, he hated him now. Because he had been jealous of
the young hedonist? Because Zorzi was a killer? Because the
possibility of Zorzi returning was a threat to his share of the
family *fraterna*?

"Do you know what was scaring him?"

"The Council of Ten, of course. Zorzi was a bad boy, a
prodigal, a rakehell. He had gotten away with it until then
because of his name, but murder changed the rules."

"Do you know who tipped him off that the Ten were
about to arrest him?"

"The Ten, of course."

I must have looked surprised, because Domenico laughed.

"It was the crime of the century, *sier* Alfeo! A patrician
murdered in the Basilica itself! It shook the entire Republic.
The Ten were under enormous pressure to find the killer, so
look at it from their point of view. Zorzi had motive, because
his father was threatening to disinherit him—which he did
every Tuesday and Friday, but this time he had sounded more
serious. Zorzi had no alibi. He claimed he was defending the
name of a noble lady, but who would believe a public outrage
like him? No, it was simplest for the Ten just to drop him a
hint that *Missier Grande* was coming to get him and Zorzi
would solve their problem all by himself. He ran away so he
must be guilty. Simple."

And I thought I was a cynic! "Was he guilty?"

"I think he was," Domenico said sadly. "Somebody killed
our father, and he seemed then, and still seems, the most logical culprit. If so, he deserved the headsman's ax. If he wasn't
guilty of murder he deserved banishment anyhow, and that's
what he got."

"You told me on Saturday that you thought some bounty
hunter had turned in his head by now."

He sighed. "I still think so." He paused for a while, pensive, staring down at a potted plant beside the wall. "It's hard for me to think of Zorzi doing anything so horrible, but even then I couldn't think of anyone else who would do so and I haven't since. I certainly think you're wasting your time trying to find evidence that the Ten couldn't find eight years ago."

"My master owns my time, and he's the one who's wasting it." The noon bell began to sound, notes floating out across the city signaling time to down tools and eat the midday meal. Domenico straightened up and took his elbows off the parapet, tall and hook-nosed like his Orio mother, not broad and beefy like the Michiel strain. His move implied impatience. My time was up.

"If Zorzi has come back," I asked, "who is sheltering him?"

He rolled his eyes, mockery in his smile. "Oh that would have to be me, wouldn't it? I scuttle back and forth to the mainland all the time, and up the Brenta River. I own property on the mainland, which I have probably riddled with secret chambers just for this purpose." Again the curious smirk. "I know, you're only doing your job and I shouldn't sneer. I have no idea. Why should he come back and risk his neck? Why should he be going around murdering fallen women? Why should anyone in his right mind help him in that game—because he must have help, his face is too well-known. That's what you're really after, isn't it? Zorzi is only a blind. You really suspect that someone related to him has taken to strangling his old playmates."

I felt a little nettled that he could see through me so easily, although it was obvious enough. "If that were true, who would be the most likely killer this time?"

"Jacopo," Domenico said firmly, reaching for the door handle. "He's not up to Zorzi's standards as a satyr, but he sows enough wild oats to feed the Cossack cavalry. Can't think why he'd be murdering the lovelies, though."

He ushered me back into the library. The artisans had gone but Jacopo was still poring over the drawings. He looked up cheerfully.

"I sent the men for their dinner, Dom. Your chapel's too small."

His brother frowned and went around the table to look.

"Make it twice as big," Jacopo said. He cupped a hand on the paper. "This big."

"That would cost eight times as much."

"You can't do style on a shoestring, man!" Jacopo pirouetted, whirling his cape. He was showing off for my benefit, trying to persuade me that in private he was on equal terms with his brothers. "Look—it's the buttons that make this outfit. My tailor used ugly little glass balls. I made him take it back and put these amethysts on. It cost ten times as much, but look at the result."

Domenico stared down at the drawing and then shrugged. "Twice as big it shall be, then. A cathedral of a chapel." He smiled across at me. "He has an incredible eye. He's right every time." So now he was all brotherly love, not mentioning that seconds ago he'd offered up the family by-blow to me as a sacrificial lamb.

I understood that I was not to dine with the family when I was led to the kitchens. There I got to share a bench at the table reserved for senior servants: Bernardo and Domenico's respective valets, two *popier* gondoliers who row at the rear, and Jacopo himself. I could guess from the others' reactions—or lack of reaction, rather—that Jacopo always ate there. As an apprentice I would not have minded, but Domenico had given me my title, so this put-down was a calculated insult to me, and perhaps to his mother for imposing me on the family.

The lesser servants, sitting at the other table, were all women except for two junior *de mezo* boatmen, who would row at the bow, a young page or footman, and a Moorish slave. Such distinctions matter as much at that social level as they do in kings' palaces. I recognized the maidservant, Agnesina, who had been mending clothes in donna Alina's company on Saturday, but apparently signora Isabetta ate with the gentry.

The brighter side of this snub was that I had intended to question the servants anyway and now I had a chance to do so in a relaxed atmosphere. It did not take me long to learn that none of them had been employed there for more than a couple of years. That was not truly surprising, because the rich are constantly complaining about the difficulty of holding onto servants, but it was a setback to investigating the murder of Gentile Michiel. As for the courtesan inquiry, I never had any intention of asking the staff who in the house might be creeping out at night to strangle or stab four women. There would be an uproar, a mass flight, and the news would be all over the city in an hour.

I settled down to making the best of my lesson in humility and the reminder of how the other half eats. My pride suffered less than my stomach.

Sier Bernardo had returned from his duties in time for dinner and condescended to receive me afterward in his office, which was a small but lavish room containing an oversized desk and very few books. He sat behind the desk. I was left on my feet and so was Jacopo, who stood just behind me so I couldn't watch him. His inclusion this time was a surprise.

"My duties for the Republic are weighty and consume much of my time," the inspector of meats declared in his sonorous orator's voice. "The matter you are investigating was settled, so far as I am concerned—so far as anyone in Venice except my dear mother is concerned—many years ago, and its resurrection now can serve no purpose. Moreover, I have an important visitor due in a few minutes. What is it that you want to know?"

"Where you were on the night your father was murdered."

He scowled at me under bushy black brows. "I was here, in my residence, at home, and in bed. I had been suffering for several days from a recurrent excess of phlegm and green bile, a cause more of discomfort than danger, I admit, but disabling in spite of its lack of morbidity. The physicians had bled me, so I was in no state to go anywhere at all."

As an alibi that was not perfect, but good enough for now. The inquisitors would surely have questioned all the servants who might have discovered his absence during the crucial period. I could not, for they had since scattered to the four winds.

"Do you believe that your brother was guilty of patricide?"

"Without a shadow of a doubt."

"Why?"

"Because the Council of Ten so decreed, and I am a loyal servant of the Republic. To call into question the solemn conclusion of the most senior tribunal of our government verges upon perfidy and sedition. Furthermore, young man, if you believe for a moment that the honored magistrates presently comprising that august tribunal would ever contemplate reversing the deliberated conclusions reached by their sublime predecessors, then you have been led into deep folly, and your duty as a scion of one of the ancient and most noble houses of our patriciate is to educate that foreign-born charlatan you work for in our laws and customs rather than let him confound your thinking."

"Your mother does not agree."

He drummed fingers on desk, a gesture in a patrician equivalent to a bull pawing turf. "Holy Writ enjoins each of us to honor his father and his mother, and I tolerate her for that reason. Her experience of the world has been greatly limited and you must remember that persons of her sex lack the natural logic and judgmental ability that the Good Lord grants to men. As an elderly, but loyal, daughter of *la Serenissima*, who has borne many children and endured much suffering through the misdeeds of the youngest of them, she deserves her family's respect, which I freely grant her. I tolerate the whimsies of her old age with patience, but I cannot let affection mislead me into sharing her delusions."

The moment he paused for breath, I asked, "Do you think your brother is still alive?"

Jacopo wandered over to stare out the window, standing with his back to us as if our conversation was of no interest whatsoever.

Bernardo growled. "If you ask do I hope that he is still alive, then of course I must answer in the affirmative. I pray daily that he has found happiness through sincere repentance and the grace of God, as I have found it in my heart to forgive him. I am encouraged to believe that he flourishes by letters my mother has received from him, two of which, so I am informed, have been shown to you."

"I have seen letters purporting to be from him. *Sier* Domenico admitted to me that they were forgeries."

Bernardo smiled into his beard. "Have you not yet realized that of course he has to say that we believe them to be forgeries? We should have a duty otherwise to turn them over to the Ten."

That did not explain a Venetian watermark on a letter written from Savoy.

"*Sier* Domenico told me he thinks *sier* Zorzi is dead."

Sigh, another patient smile. "Same answer."

"You believe, then, that your brother is still alive?"

"Zeno, I have neither seen, nor spoken with, my brother Zorzi for eight years. What I believe and what *sier* Domenico believes are equally irrelevant and immaterial. As indeed, I regret to say, is this whole conversation. I ask and hope that you and your principal will be gracious to my mother and considerate of her feelings, for if you abuse her trust in you, I shall see that the full weight of the Republic descends upon you."

"Where does Jacopo get all his money?"

Dropping his pretense that he was ignoring us, Jacopo spun around.

"We pay him to wait upon donna Alina," Bernardo growled. "As she ages, her ability to retain servants has deteriorated markedly. She is moody and intractable."

In the background, Jacopo rolled his eyes at an epic understatement.

"You pay him enough to spend ten ducats for amethyst buttons on a single doublet?" Even if the lady had the disposition of a badger, she could not be worth that much.

Bernardo scowled, eyes glittering. "She has recently indulged him by letting him collect some of her rents, and I am of a mind to have my bookkeepers review her ledgers to see how much of that money may have inadvertently gone astray, but I do not see how that can possibly concern you. Now, if you have no further questions—"

I flashed my best mountebank-apprentice smile. "Oh, but I do! Two of them. I should prefer to put them to you in private, though."

Furiously red to the tips of his ears, Jacopo marched across to the door and this time he did slam it behind him.

"I am informed," I said, "that the Ten sent a *fante* to ask you some questions just after I left on Saturday. Will you tell me briefly what they wanted to know?"

I expected the big man to refuse. He swelled even larger, but then he shrugged. "Questions much like yours. Had I heard from Zorzi? Did I know where he was? I told them I had assumed for years that his head had been turned in for the bounty money so the Ten should know the answers better than I did."

"*Had* assumed? You don't now?"

"What are you after?"

"I'm curious to know why the Ten feel the need to ask. That was all they wanted—to rehash the old inquiry?"

"They asked much the same rubbish you've been asking—where I was when Father was murdered. Where Domenico was."

I raised an eyebrow. Mine might not be as bushy as his, but they are trained to be expressive. "So the Council doesn't trust its own records? Or it thinks the case needs revisiting? How interesting! Thank you. The second question. You had a family meeting yesterday. Why was your mother not present?"

Bernardo reared up on his feet. "This is intolerable! I have been more than patient with you and shall not stand for any more of this insolence. Get out! Remove your impudent, upstart San Barnaba carcase before I have it thrown out."

I bowed, backed to the door, and bowed again as if he were the doge himself. I thought I knew who had killed his father and so did he. It had not been Zorzi.

23

The moment I closed the door behind me, Jacopo grabbed my shoulder in a crushing grip, spun me around, and slammed me back against the wall. I had not been mistaken in estimating his strength. His eyes blazed; his face was scarlet with fury. He thrust it close to mine.

"Bernardo is a lying turd!" he roared. "Alina pays me nothing and I do not wait on her! She hates me because I'm living evidence of her husband's lechery. She treats me like mud, as you saw, and wouldn't give me a stale crust if I were starving. My money comes from a share in the family fortune."

I had hold of my dagger by then, and silently raised it so the point was in the gap between our two noses. Realizing that I could have put it elsewhere and still could, he released me and backed off.

"I understood that only sons born in wedlock could share in a *fraterna*," I said quietly. Was I actually going to hear a true story in the Palazzo Michiel?

"It's only a very small share compared to theirs. They voted me in. There's nothing to stop them doing that."

"Why should they? You said they were planning to throw you out last December."

Jacopo pouted like a sulky child. "I said that because by then you'd spotted that I was one of Gentile's by-blows. We try . . . My brothers prefer to keep our relationship a secret. Officially I'm just Jacopo Fauro, Domenico's secretary."

That excuse made no sense, but by then he must have been hopelessly entangled in the conflicting falsehoods he had told me.

"Why should they be so generous? Just brotherly love?"

He turned and started walking, forcing me to follow if I wanted to hear his reply.

"You heard Domenico ask my advice. I help him! I have an eye for design. When he hears of a property that may be available, I go and make the first inspection. He almost always accepts my judgment now. I help conduct buyers around. He needs someone he can trust not to accept bribes."

I thought I wouldn't trust Jacopo to put a *soldo* in the poor box for me. He stayed quiet until we were descending the great staircase.

"Dom likes me to dress up," he said. "It impresses the customers."

"And girls?"

"No. I wear rags when I go prowling. They charge too much if I dress fancy." He said that seriously. It might even be true.

When we reached the outer door he opened it for me and closed it without another word. It was a fine winter afternoon and I enjoyed my walk home across the city.

I found the Maestro in his favorite chair by the fireplace, opposite a lady dressed in the style and quality that indicate the wife of a successful merchant or member of a learned profession—doctor, apothecary, lawyer. At first glance I assumed we had a new client, probably wanting a horoscope or other foretelling. To my astonishment, I realized that she was Violetta, woman of infinite variety. She was smiling and he seemed to be in a fairly good mood, although it is always hard to tell with him.

"You look disgustingly smug, apprentice," he said. "You have discovered who is murdering courtesans?"

"No," I admitted. "I know why they are being killed, though. And I know that Zorzi Michiel did not kill his father."

Nostradamus cautiously eased himself farther back in his chair. "Then you had better tell us that before madonna Violetta leaves. Bring a chair."

I fetched one of the pair that stand beside the armillary sphere. Normally it is the Maestro who reveals the solution to the mystery, so I was eager to get my chance this time, especially with my darling present.

"Gentile Michiel was killed with a *khanjar* dagger, which they still keep on display, and which was freely available to anyone in the house. Contrariwise, any outsider would have had much trouble getting hold of it, and no servant would have been admitted to the Basilica that night. In short, that weapon trumpeted to the heavens that the killer was a member of the family.

"Jacopo was only a child then. Bernardo and Domenico had fair but not unassailable alibis. Zorzi refused to give one. I don't know about Friar Fedele, but he has renounced the world and the flesh, so what motive could he possibly have? The same goes for the daughter, Sister Lucretzia.

"But donna Alina was frantic that her favorite child was about to be dispossessed. She lived a very secluded life, kept in purdah by a tyrannical, puritanical husband, so—unlike her sons—had no opportunity to go out and buy some nondescript, anonymous weapon. Ergo, she was the one who took the dagger. She need prepare no alibi, because she was entitled to be present. She is right-handed. No man, tall or otherwise, pushed her aside—she made that up. She carried the sheathed dagger in her left hand, perhaps hidden in her sleeve or a muff. In the crowded darkness, she drew it with her right, threw herself at her husband, and stabbed him in the back. They fell together and she screamed that she had been pushed."

The Maestro did not seem surprised, but I never expect him to. "Why did the Council of Ten not see this?" he murmured. "Are you really so much smarter than they are?"

"On average, yes," I admitted. "I expect they were hampered at first because the idea of a lady, a noblewoman, committing such a crime is almost unthinkable. Gentile's sons were unlikely enough, but his wife defied belief. No doubt the inquisitors would have worked their way around to the idea if they had been given time, but at first they did not even think to ask if any of the family recognized the weapon. Eventually young Jacopo blurted out in front of witnesses that the *khanjar* was missing from its display case."

"Who told you that?"

"He did. But even before that happened, donna Alina's children must have known who was guilty. The lady is undoubtedly crazy by most standards, but her sons decided to protect her, which tells you what sort of a husband she must have had. Domenico himself told me, 'Run from hounds and they will chase you.' Zorzi was chosen to be the goat. I expect he was bribed with a substantial pension, enough to buy all the courtesans he can handle, wherever he is. Lechery was his only interest in life and it is available anywhere for a price. He probably dropped a confession in the Lion's Mouth on his way out."

I gave my master a meaningful glance to convey the message that we would find that out when *Circospetto* showed me the Ten's file on the case. So far as I knew Violetta was not aware of my midnight bribery. He might have told her, though, because she was nodding. She was gray-eyed Minerva, the clever one.

"Have you any evidence?" the Maestro asked testily, "or is this all wind?" He would not be happy to have a murderer for a client.

"No witnesses," I admitted. "But Jacopo hinted on Saturday that Alina was even more upset by Zorzi's conviction than she was by the murder. I wouldn't put much stock in anything he says, but Domenico later said much the same. It makes sense if she had known about the murder in advance but the verdict was a surprise. Listen to this: the children had a conference on Sunday. They even included Jacopo, who told me what everyone said except donna Alina, and when I asked Bernardo if she had even been invited, he flew into a rage and threw me out."

My master snorted. "You are jumping to conclusions again. You do not know for a fact that donna Alina was not present?"

"No, but what were they talking about? Not money or politics or even scandal, because they had brought in the two religious, who don't care about those. They included Jacopo, whom the lady treats as a drudge but who probably knows more about her behavior and state of mind than anyone else now. Donna Alina was not invited because she was the agenda!"

Nostradamus pouted and I assumed that he was unable to challenge my logic. I should have known better.

"Maybe donna Alina was the agenda," he growled, "but that doesn't mean she killed her husband. They may have been trying to stop her from hiring me to prove Zorzi's innocence because—as you just told us—that means that another of them must be guilty. That other may not be donna Alina."

Violetta was frowning, too, equally unconvinced. "If the lady really killed her husband, then why has she hired

Doctor Nostradamus to find the 'real' killer? It would be suicide. Is she as demented as that?"

"She may be," I said. "She may be weighed down by guilt and willing to risk anything to see her boy again. She may have put her own guilt completely out of her mind. Or she may have deluded herself into believing that she will never be suspected. People do things like that. She may be playing a huge game of bluff. But she did insist on changing the contract so that the Maestro will report his findings to her before he feeds the lion."

"You mean she believes he will do that even if he finds proof that she is the murderer?"

"Perhaps. She may expect him to try blackmailing her."

"Is Jacopo really Zorzi?" the Maestro asked.

Violetta gasped, but I had been expecting the question.

"He could be," I said. "The Council of Ten has been known to accept a massive fine in return for a secret pardon, even for major crimes. Even if it hasn't done so in this case, it's been eight years. He wears a thick beard and Zorzi was clean-shaven. All the servants who knew Zorzi have gone and the genuine Jacopo, if there ever was one, could have been disposed of with a bag of silver and a ticket to Rome or Milan. The family is very small, with no close relatives on either side. Jacopo obviously has more money than most young men can dream of. Also, according to Bernardo, he's a lecher like Zorzi."

Nostradamus was nodding impatiently. "But?"

"But," I admitted, sorry to topple such an elegant solution, especially when I'd worked it out for myself, "I'm more inclined to believe Jacopo is younger than me than older, porcupine beard or not. And if he is the reprobate returned, he is going around killing off the courtesans who knew him in his first life. I can't see either the Ten or the family standing for that."

My master grunted. "Neither can I."

"Then who is doing the killing?" Violetta asked.

That was the primary question, after all.

"A hired bravo," I said. "Nobles do not do their own strangling or stabbing. They pay other people to do that."

Medea's eyes flashed an angry green. "Who?" she demanded. "Who is paying the killers?"

I thought I knew the answer, but I had even less evidence to go on than I had for Alina being Gentile's murderer. "Motive's been the problem all along, hasn't it? And timing, too—why is this happening now? I think that Zorzi has tired of exile and wants to come back and clear his name. According to the family, he refused to give an alibi for the night of his father's murder because he was romancing a noble lady and would not betray her to her husband. Possibly the lady has died, leaving a signed confession. I don't believe that she even existed. I think Zorzi was with a courtesan as usual.

"As for the motive—Domenico and Bernardo do not want him back because they would have to relinquish his share of the *fraterna*. Alina shouldn't, because if he is acquitted she would become the obvious culprit and if he isn't he'll be beheaded. Someone in that family, possibly more than one person, thinks that Zorzi's chances of clearing his name can be undercut by killing whichever courtesan he was patronizing that night so that she cannot testify on his behalf. He probably had a few current favorites, and they don't know which one they need, so they have hired a professional assassin to hunt down and murder all the most likely."

The Maestro groaned. "A thousand angels hear my prayer! You think that after eight years the Council of Ten will reverse its own verdict on the unsupported word of a harlot? You can buy that sort of testimony for a ducat! I thought you said Zorzi Michiel left a confession before he ran away. He will now pass that off as a joke?"

"I'm not sure about the confession," I admitted. "Donna Alina did tell me that she was not questioned again after her son disappeared, and that sounds as if the Ten had very good evidence that he was guilty."

Nostradamus pulled a face that would have terrified gargoyles. "I doubt very much that anything less than a signed confession from someone else would persuade the Ten to change its conviction of Zorzi Michiel, probably not even that. I think, madonna, that you need not listen to any more of these myths and legends. You may go about your business. Indeed, you will have to hurry to complete it before vespers."

Violetta rose, so I did. She curtseyed to the old rogue and I followed her out. I followed her all the way out to the landing, pulling the door closed behind me.

"So where are you off to?"

She smiled as angels smile. "To see the Popess."

"Who?" I must have jumped like a frog, because she eyed me oddly.

"Sister Lucretzia. That's if I can get in to speak with her. You think you could? You want to try on this gown?"

"The tarot warned you that the Popess was a danger to be avoided!"

Violetta laughed lovingly and blessed me with Helen's dark-eyed smile. "But I think the Popess trump is more likely to be the abbess than the nun. If the old dragon as much as suspects what sort of woman I am, she will have me run out of town." Helen is the loveliest of Violetta's personas, not the smartest.

"Yes, I think the abbess is more likely, and it was the abbess reversed you drew. She could have you arrested, darling!"

"You can kiss me. I'm not painted at the moment."

I did so, of course, and finished quite breathless. I have a heart condition where she is concerned. "You free this evening?"

She shook her head. "Poor Alfeo! No, I told my patron I might be late as it is. Tomorrow at noon?"

"I'll try." I tried to kiss her again, but she declined. "Give all the girls my love." I watched her go down the first flight, then went back to the atelier. I headed for the chair I had used, intending to put it back where it belonged. The Maestro appeared to be deep in thought, but he spoke.

"Leave that. Use it. Now report properly."

"Properly" means every word, or as close as I can remember. I sat down and flexed my memory. First I had to empty it of a question.

"You think Sister Lucretzia can help us? She's probably spent her entire life in Santa Giustina."

"Won't know unless we ask and I can't send you."

"True. Did Violetta tell you that her tarot showed the Popess reversed as a snare to be avoided?"

He scowled. "No."

"And yet last night on my reading the Popess upright showed as the solution."

Nostradamus pretends that tarot is childish and overrated, but I suspect that's because it works better for me than it does for him. Despite his scoffing, he does not ignore my readings when he is stuck with a problem.

"Start your report with that, then."

It takes hours of reporting to cover hours of interviewing. We adjourned for supper and resumed. I was weary and hoarse by the time I got to the point where I was seen off by Jacopo. Then the questions started.

"It was Jacopo who shopped Zorzi? By reporting that the dagger was missing, I mean. Who put him up to that?"

"I didn't ask," I said. "I only know because he volunteered the story. I assumed it was just a spontaneous error. He was only a child."

"I've told you: never assume anything. Someone may have put him up to it. Someone may have put him up to telling you . . ."

A rap on the door knocker stopped him. I went out to see and was startled to find the sinister form of Antonio waiting on the landing. Surprise gave way to terror.

"She's all right?"

His forked beard twisted around a fearsome leer. "She was all right when she promoted me to messenger boy." He handed me a letter.

I thanked him and started to open it. He had already turned to leave.

"No use replying," he said over his shoulder as he started down the stair. "She's gone; her *giovane* was waiting. And if you offer me a *soldo*, I'll break your neck." He looked back again at the first landing. "I got well paid."

"Don't tell me," I said and closed the door. Damn him! I could easily imagine Helen rushing to go out, handing the note to him and throwing her arms around his ugly neck to kiss him when he agreed to see that I got it. I hoped that was all he had meant.

"A letter from my beloved," I said as returned to my place in the atelier. "All it says is, *Was not allowed in, so Popess no help*." I could not help adding, "As predicted, but at least she's safe."

Nostradamus grunted but did not comment on the pros or cons of tarot. "It's time to count out the gold for *Circospetto*."

The night was young yet, but I was happy not to have to talk any more. I fetched the scales and a heavy bag from the secret cache. While the Maestro watched in sullen silence, I counted out one hundred sixty-three sequins and weighed them. I added two ducats and two lira and put the lot in the money pouch. It weighed more than a pound, but it was not bulky.

At that point my master announced that he was going to

bed, which did not surprise me when his hips were obviously still troubling him severely. He spurned my offers of help, though, and hobbled off on his canes. I put the money pouch in a desk drawer and tidied up the pile of books he had left by his chair. I had hours to wait before my appointment with Raffaino Sciara, so I could catch up on my housework.

I took the chair I had been using earlier and carried it back to its place behind the door. At that point I said, "What?" to myself. I may even have spoken it aloud. A moment later I started to laugh. An observer might have thought I had taken leave of my senses. I certainly spoke aloud when I said, "Oh, tarot, I love you!" Then I laughed even harder.

24

The atelier door is opposite the fireplace, and behind the door stand the two chairs. The armillary sphere and various astronomical instruments stand farther along the wall, then comes the cabinet of sky charts, and so on. That brings you to the corner with the window wall, which holds only the big double desk, my seat at the near side, and the Maestro's at the other. I had been able to see Sister Lucretzia from there, but mostly I had concentrated on the Maestro's verbal tussle with Friar Fedele.

An armillary sphere consists of a series of bronze or brass rings, most of which can be moved, all set in an outer horizontal ring, which is fixed atop a pedestal. We use it to calculate the positions of stars and planets at various times of the year. The horizontal ring, which is called the Horizon Ring, unsurprisingly, is wider than the others, like a circular table with a very large round hole cut in it. It is possible to set small objects on it, or balance larger ones, and what I had found on it was a book bound in brown leather.

I had not put it there and the Maestro never would. I knew right away who had, but none of us had seen her do so. She could have laid it on the other chair, but there it would have been more conspicuous and her brother might have noticed it as he was leaving. Now I knew who was represented by the Popess in my tarot, bless her beads and wimple!

I carried my find over to a lamp and riffed through it. A few pages at the end were blank, but the rest was a diary of numerous short entries. I fancy myself as open-minded, but the very first one I read made my jaw drop.

Thursday, 7ᵗʰ.
Chiara Q, dinner and theater, her house. Twice in bed on her back, once on a chair with her straddling him.

I won't quote any more of them. Some were much worse. They all followed the same pattern, a date without month or year, a woman's name, and then a note of the sexual actions and positions employed. In rare cases more than one woman was mentioned, and sometimes men also, although then only by Christian name. Many of the acts mentioned were obscene, some illegal, and at least one carries the death penalty.

The wonder was not that a nun had disposed of the book, but that she would even soil her fingers to throw it in the Grand Canal. Had she stolen it with the deliberate intent of delivering it to the Maestro? I could not imagine her daring to take it home to the convent.

Should I show it to him right away? That would be my normal reaction, but *Circospetto* might be going to show me the Ten's records on the case very shortly, and I might do a better job of understanding them if I had studied the book first. I took it to my desk, gathered lamps, and set to work.

Nowhere was the hero of the saga identified except by the male pronoun. I had never seen Zorzi's writing, but the hand looked nothing like the letters Domenico had forged, which had deceived donna Alina. I fetched out the Orio contract I had just filed and compared her signature with the book. Signatures are not the most reliable samples of handwriting, but the match was close enough to strengthen my suspicions. Since I had seen an identical book in the lady's treasure box, I had to assume that she had written the filth.

I had trouble imagining the most egotistical young toady regaling his mother with his prurient exploits and her paying him for it, but that was the only explanation that came to mind. How big a fortune had she squandered on her son's vice? What must her marriage have been like that she had resorted to such vicarious entertainment?

At first the entries were sporadic, as the hero took up the sport. After a few months' practice he had became a satyr, rarely missing a night, sometimes enjoying two separate women in different places—or possibly he had just become a more creative and convincing liar, although it's a rare man who can deceive his own mother. Besides, this sordid catalogue merely confirmed what Alessa had told me about his habits.

I had no way of proving that the book was genuine, but I soon established that it was at least relevant to our search. A few rare mentions of Saints' days instead of dates led me to a *1 Tuesday* following a *28 Monday*, and the universal calendar from our astrological bookshelf told me that I had found March 1586. As March 1 is New Year's Day in Venice, I marked the place with a piece of paper and went looking for 1587. I rapidly established that the record ran from the summer of 1584 to December 23, 1587. There it stopped, a few hours before Gentile Michiel died. The book was either an incredible hoax or it was extremely germane.

The last record consisted only of the name "Tonina Q" with no details, pornographic or otherwise. December 23 listed Caterina Lotto, who had apparently been an accomplished acrobat, but was doomed to be Honeycat's third victim, in spite of her fearsome guardian, Matteo Surian. That discovery prompted me to go back to the beginning and riff through, listing each woman's name and the date she first appeared. Venice is reputed to have ten thousand courtesans, but at the end Zorzi's catalogue listed only sixty-seven, which seemed a quite modest total for a healthy youngster with unlimited money and minimal morals, over a period longer than Scheherazade's thousand and one nights.

When I had reached the end I worked backward, noting the last time each name appeared. That took me longer, but it confirmed that some names were mentioned only once, others frequently. I did not have time to count the number of times each name appeared, but I could identify his favorites, which included all four of Honeycat's victims: Lucia da Bergamo, Caterina Lotto, Ruosa da Corone, and Marina Bortholuzzi. I also recognized the names of some highly regarded women whom Violetta had mentioned. Alessa appeared many times—she seemed to enjoy gondolas—but there was no mention of Violetta, to my heartfelt relief.

Four single-mentions and three favorites were identified only by Christian names, the favorites being Chiara Q, Lodovica Q, and Tonina Q. Recalling donna Alina's report of Zorzi defending a true love I noted that those might be the amateurs Domenico had mentioned, not courtesans—I could not bring myself to think of them as ladies, not in that company. Most of the seven bore unusual names, perhaps aliases.

Apart from gondolas, the scenery mentioned included chairs, tables, and floors; also haystacks, grass, stables, and a coach, all which must have been on the mainland.

At last we had the courtesan murders unarguably tied to Zorzi Michiel and in the morning we could start sending out warnings to any women Violetta and Alessa had missed. It was time for me to go. I checked that there was no light showing under the Maestro's door and left the book and my notes on his side of the desk. I added a note: *The Popess left this for you on Sunday.*

I hadn't done my dusting.

* * *

Again Giorgio rowed me to San Zulian. Normally I tell him
what I am up to and the fact that I had not explained these
midnight journeys was making him uneasy. Again I walked
the deserted streets by feeble lantern light, for the moon was
clouded over. This time I had only my shadow for company,
not even a cat. Illogically, the fact that now I carried a fortune in gold under my shirt made me more nervous than before, as if thieves might somehow smell it from the shadows.
I was actually happy to see the door with the grille. I was
probably early and risked running into another scoundrel on
a similar mission, but I had no intention of lingering outside any longer than I had to. I rapped the four-knock signal
on the boards. Moments passed until I began to feel faint for
lack of breathing, then a face appeared in the darkness behind the bars and I heard the bolt being drawn.

It was not until we were both in the room with the table
that either of us spoke. As before, Sciara wore black and a
sardonic, cadaverous smirk.

"Did you get it?" I asked, louder than I expected. The
question was superfluous, because he had a coin balance
waiting.

He stood with his fingers on the table, looking across at
me with a fixed, catlike stare. "Of course, or you would not
have been admitted. I warn you, though, that some documents seem to be missing."

"What isn't missing?"

He shook his head. "I cannot say and will not look to see.
First you pay, then I let you examine whatever was in the
folder when I retrieved it. I swear that I have not opened it or
looked inside. There is something in there, but not as much
as there should be. No argument. Pay now or go."

The terms were unconscionable and the moment I

brought out the gold, then that mysterious second door might swing open and *Missier Grande* march in to arrest me. If Sciara was just cheating me and there was nothing of value in the folder, I should have no recourse except to poke my rapier through him, but that would be no solution and little satisfaction. If I refused to trade, more women might die. I reached for the pouch.

"You will understand," he remarked as he began weighing the coins, "that I cannot furnish you with a receipt?"

I pulled out the chair on my side of the table. "Of course we must trust each other. Let there be honor among thieves."

He showed his teeth in a satisfied leer at the balance. "Excellent, one grain over. You are generous." He dropped the coins in a bag and hung it on his belt. He returned my money pouch.

Only then did he pull out his chair and sit down. Reaching under the table, he produced a document folder, a large sheet of heavy paper with its corners folded over to make an envelope, tied up with ribbon. I could see right away from the older creases and dust marks that the package had been originally folded around much thicker contents. It had been plundered, perhaps quite recently.

Sciara held it close to one of the lamps and scanned the writing on the outside. "*Sier* Giovanni . . . That's odd. These usually begin with the original report to the chiefs of the Ten . . . The chiefs' decision . . . a special meeting of the Three . . . Bless my soul, Their Excellencies met on the morning of Christmas Day! I don't recall that ever happening."

"Why don't we just see what's in there?" I demanded, for the contents clearly could not match the length of the index.

"Oh, the impetuosity of youth!" Sciara murmured, but he set to work on the binding.

"Do documents often go missing from such files?"

"Not since *Domine* Spataforta became grand chancellor."

He opened and spread out the cover, exposing about a dozen or so sheets of paper held together by ribbon. I could almost believe he was too embarrassed to meet my eye as he passed them across to me.

I moaned. "Sixty ducats a page? I hardly dare touch such valuable material." Few things taste more bitter than the knowledge that one has been played for a dupe. Sciara must be enjoying himself enormously, remembering past slights. I began at the back, where the earliest documents should be.

The first was a report: *Testimony of His Excellency, NH Giovanni Gradenigo, member of the Council of Three.* Clearly he had made a formal report to his brother inquisitors, and the secretary had written it as if he were any ordinary witness. The man who had summoned me to his deathbed was about to speak to me from the grave.

Gradenigo had been present in the dark and crowded atrium and was apparently quite close when Gentile Michiel was stabbed. His first warning had been a woman's screams, followed by clamor from many throats. He had fought his way through the fleeing, panic-stricken mob, and it sounded as if he had been a large, or at least powerful, man. He found Gentile Michiel writhing on the floor, with donna Alina down there beside him, desperately trying to staunch the flow of blood. Counselor Foscari, the "red" among the Three, arrived moments later. Normally an investigation would work its way up through the chiefs of the Ten to the full Council, and only then to the Three. In this case the state inquisitors had been right on the spot. They had seen the blood firsthand. But its setting within the holy precincts of the Basilica had made this a highly unusual case from the beginning.

Either Pesaro or Foscari asked a question and the clerk had followed normal interrogation style:

Question: The witness was asked if he recognized anyone who was close when the murder was committed.

Answer: "No, there was complete confusion. People had fled in all directions. Donna Orio Michiel may be able to testify to that when she recovers, by God's grace. We must pray that others will come forward."

Then Agostino Foscari took up the story, backing up Gradenigo's version and going on to describe Michiel's death, still down on the floor, waiting for medical help to arrive; not that doctors could have done anything for such a wound.

Then came an exchange that hit me like a bolt of lightning.

Question: The witness was asked if he observed the murder weapon.

Answer: "I did. When we were certain that the victim had been gathered to the Father, and when poor donna Alina Orio had been escorted away, I watched *Missier Grande* remove the dagger from the corpse. He showed it to me and *sier* Giovanni."

Question: The witness was asked to describe the weapon.

Answer: "It's an ordinary straight dagger of *landsknecht* type, made in Germany. You could find a dozen of them for sale in the city. It's probably a century or so old and has recently been sharpened."

For a moment I sat amid the thunder of our case against donna Alina crashing to the ground in ruins. Jacopo Fauro's tale of the sack of Constantinople might be based on truth, but the *khanjar* dagger had absolutely nothing to do with his father's murder. Why had I trusted him to tell the truth even sometimes?

Without looking at Sciara, I forced my mind back to the work. The rest of that document told me nothing new. It ended at the bottom of the next page, in midsentence.

The next sheet was an account of the Michiel family as it

had been at the time. Bernardo was married then, which I had not known, and Domenico had one child by his morganatic spouse, Isabetta Scorozini. Lucretzia and Fedele had already entered the cloister. Zorzi was dismissed with the single word *giovane*.

Then came a brief statement signed by Bernardo Michiel, written in the third person but almost certainly based on interrogation. As a bereaved patrician, he would have been treated with silk gloves. He described his illness on the crucial night, confirming everything he had told me and adding nothing new. The same went for statements by Domenico and donna Alina. Friar Fedele and Sister Lucretzia testified that they had been engaged in worship that Christmas Eve in the company of members of their respective orders. No doubt the inquisitors would have examined witnesses who could support the family members' alibis, but those records were missing, perhaps thrown away as unnecessary once the official verdict was reached.

They all, even Fedele, loyally supported Zorzi, dismissing the recent quarrel with his father as nothing new. Gentile had been threatening to disinherit the boy for years and had never carried through. The men all pointed out that his own record was far from perfect, despite the lofty standards he so hypocritically proclaimed.

There was nothing at all by Zorzi Michiel, the convicted murderer, and that silence screamed of wrongness.

I held out a hand. "May I look at that list of contents, please?"

The death's head smiled. "No. I promised only what was in the folder."

I silently consigned Sciara to Tartarus.

I was left with one last piece of paper. The note on the back explained that it had been deposited in the *bocca di leone* in the church of San Geminiano on December 27. It was brief:

To the noble Council of Ten—

I am a fallen woman, a sinner, but I will not defend a murderer. The man who stabbed Senator Michiel in the Basilica talks in his sleep and last night I heard him say he killed his father. He said so several times quite clearly, weeping. His name is Zorzi Michiel. He has a birthmark in the shape of a cat near his private parts, which is why he is called Honeycat. So may you know him.

I felt cold fingertips run down my back. I looked up quickly and caught the tail end of a smirk. Despite his denials, Sciara had known what I would find in the file. I held the paper up to the lamp, but it was cheap stuff with no watermark.

"The Republic maintains that its tribunals pay no heed to anonymous letters," I said.

He nodded. "That is correct."

"Correct that they say that is what they do, or correct that they do what they say?"

He favored me with one of his rotting-corpse smiles. "In practice, Their Excellencies do have certain stringent procedures for evaluating unsigned submittals. In the case of the Ten, an anonymous letter is examined by the three chiefs and the six ducal counselors sitting together, and only if those nine are unanimous is it brought before the full council, and the council must vote five-sixths in favor of considering it. Even after that, a four-fifths majority is needed before action can be taken."

Would those safeguards have been observed in the most egregious crime Venice had known in centuries? Surely any lead at all would have been followed up. If the inquisitors suddenly and unanimously decided that they should lock up the prime suspect for a few days and nights and post witnesses to listen to his snoring, no one would ask what had given them such brilliant simultaneous brain waves.

"If that paper you are studying is indeed unsigned," Sciara continued, "then most likely it was left in the folder precisely because it was deemed to be worthless."

"You are implying, *lustrissimo*, that anything worthwhile has been removed?"

"Oh no, I did not say that, *sier* Alfeo."

He was very adept at implying without saying. I could never hope to know whether the file had been censored just prior to my seeing it or at some earlier time for some other reason. I handed the papers back in silence and stood up.

Sciara displayed mild surprise. "So soon? You must have a remarkable memory."

"I have better things to do at this time of night," I said. I bowed and turned to the door.

"I am truly sorry your time was wasted, *clarissimo*."

"It was not wasted, *lustrissimo*."

I wanted him to think I had learned more than he knew.

In fact, I had learned more than I knew.

25

The Maestro appeared earlier than usual that morning; I was still sweeping the floor when he came stumping into the atelier, leaning on his staff. The absence of the canes was meant to show that he had recovered. I opened my mouth to congratulate him and he cut me off.

"What's that?" He pointed to the book on his desk.

I told him. He changed direction and went to sit there, instead of in the red chair, and I knew he really must be feeling better. By the time I had put the broom away and returned, he had laid down both the pornography and my notes and was leaning back in his chair, scowling.

"What did you learn from Sciara last night?"

I sat opposite and told him, quoting the documents word for word, or very nearly so. "We have no case left against donna Alina," I concluded. "I should have realized sooner that Jacopo is not merely a liar but an addicted liar. Apparently he never tells the truth if he can fool you with a good yarn. That's an interesting defense, isn't it—if you are known to be perpetually untruthful, you cannot be caught out in a lie?"

The Maestro's scowl did not change. He tapped the book. "And this sewage?"

"The wheel of fortune turns. We can't use the dagger to make a case against the lady, but now we know for certain that someone in the Palazzo Michiel is killing courtesans. It was written by donna Alina, I think. The writing fits her signature, both on your contract and on the statement I saw last night. I glimpsed either that book or an identical one in the casket where she keeps Zorzi's letters. Seems she gave him money and he repaid her with dirty stories. I doubt that he knew she was keeping a record. Sister Lucretzia left it on your armillary sphere when she was here on Sunday. I didn't notice it until last night."

Neither had my master, so he couldn't scold me for being unobservant.

"It is not the sort of uplifting literature I associate with nuns."

"Nor I, master. She had just come from the family reunion. Either someone gave her the book at the house or she stole it. The casket has no lock, just a ward—you spread both hands on the lid and say, 'My dearest treasure.' That's all; easy enough to spot if you know about such things."

"Why?" he demanded, eyes narrow.

"Why did she steal the book? I don't know."

"Why do you think she stole it?"

I had met all these people; he had not. "Assuming Lucretzia was told about the murdered courtesans—and I think they were the subject of the family gathering—she must recognize the book as evidence that someone in Palazzo Michiel is at least involved and likely the actual killer. Whether she intended to destroy the evidence and changed her mind, or knew that Fedele was going to stop in here and try to prevent you from investigating their father's death . . . or perhaps Fedele himself put her up to it. What do you think?"

"I need to see her," he muttered.

I refrained from uttering mocking laughter. "Even Violetta couldn't talk her way into Santa Giustina. Probably

Lucretzia was allowed out to visit her family only because her brother asked. An abbess won't talk back to a priest, but she'd surely set the dogs on people like you and me."

Nostradamus sat and glared at the offending book. "This thing is poison! I don't see why it hasn't provoked more killings already. I ought to have you take it straight to the palace and give it to the chiefs of the Ten."

"I'll take my rowing clothes with me." I wasn't joking, much. The galleys were starting to seem like a real possibility now.

He did not deign to answer. After a while he started tugging at his goatee, which is a sign that he is thinking hard. I quietly opened a drawer and took out Johannes Trithemius's *Steganographia* so I could get started on the numerology homework my master had set me five days ago. The learned abbot of Sponheim instructed us in how to send messages to specific angels, and after about an hour, when I was seriously considering an appeal for help to Gabriel, Nostradamus at last emerged from his reverie.

"*Damnātio!*"

"Master?" I closed the book on a finger.

"Donna Alina seems to have faith in me. She could have given the book to her daughter to deliver to me."

"If she is not the killer . . ." I had not quite rid my mind of that assumption. "Why the nun, though? Surely a nun should hurl such smut into the nearest canal?"

"Because Lucretzia is the only one Alina trusts?"

I gulped and said, "Yes, master," humbly.

"Get me the knight of cups!"

"Er . . . ?"

"Vitale's solution was to be the knight of cups reversed, you said? Get him. Bring him."

Somewhere a shutter opened . . . "Ah! The *cavaliere servente?*" I should have seen that Jacopo might fit the "solution" card in the reading I had made for Violetta, but I hadn't met him when I did it.

"Of course. Bring him and I'll reverse him."

"How far may I turn the screw?"

"All the way to the headsman's ax."

I pursed my lips in a silent whistle. He rarely gives me so much leeway.

"If he won't come, any second-best?"

"No, it must be Jacopo. And I want Vitale here when he arrives."

"Master, Violetta never rises before noon!"

"Then waken her. This is urgent. Tell her to dress like . . . provocatively."

"You're not asking for much," I murmured, but I couldn't have been quiet enough, because he glared at me. He expected me to drag a natural-born citizen away from whatever he was doing as if I were a Council of Ten *sbirro*. And also dictate how Violetta was to dress, which was even more dangerous. Tactics would be important. I marked my place in the thrilling *Steganographia*, selected pen and paper, and wrote a brief note, which I rolled up and tied with a ribbon.

"I think I'll go armed, if you don't mind."

No reply. I set off to fetch my sword. As I stepped out into the *salone*, someone rapped the door knocker.

It was early for visitors. It was even earlier to see Fulgentio Trau active in the world, but from the look of him he had been on night duty, guarding the doge's bedchamber. He was clearly a bearer of bad news. He spoke no greeting, smiled no smile.

"The doctor awake?"

I nodded and stepped aside to let him enter, ushered him into the atelier.

Nostradamus moved as if to rise, for a ducal equerry far outranks him.

Fulgentio raised a hand in forbiddance. "Please stay, Doctor. I bring a very brief message to you and to your apprentice. It is from 'a high official,' but I am forbidden to say whom." He glanced at me to make sure I was also listening. "I am instructed to tell you both that this is your last warning, and you are granted this mercy only because of your many past services to the Republic. You must stop asking questions about the death of Gentile Michiel. You will disregard this warning at your peril, both of you."

Fulgentio shrugged, and muttered, "That's all. Sorry."

As he turned away, the Maestro said, "Wait!"

"Doctor?"

"I would take it as a great favor, *lustrissimo*, if you would deliver a very brief note to the distinguished person who gave you that warning."

Fulgentio smiled sadly but warily. "I will gladly try, of course. But I may not succeed and I doubt very much that it will do any good."

"Understood," the Maestro muttered. "Alfeo?"

I strode across to the desk and readied my pen and inkwell in record time, choosing a sheet of our finest rag paper.

"Two lines should do it," he said. "*I give my sacred word that I have no interest in previous crimes and my only intent is to prevent future murders.* Sign it for me."

I pursed lips in a silent whistle of astonishment. If the old miser was sincere in abandoning the Gentile murder contract, then he was voluntarily giving up a significant fee for the first time in my experience. I went off to the kitchen for a lighted candle. When I returned, I affixed his signet, then handed the letter to Fulgentio.

"And tell them that goes for me, too, with brass buttons," I said.

He gave me a look that said I was walking on a razor's edge. He bowed to the Maestro and headed for the door. As

I let him out of the apartment he said, "For God's sake, make him be careful!" and then trotted off down the stairs.

I went back to the Maestro, who looked as if his fuse had burned down to the touchhole and he was ready to explode.

"Any instructions for today, master?"

"*Aargh!*"

Not promising. "That warning came from the doge himself, I think."

"I don't."

"Oh! Master, have you any idea why the Ten don't want you to investigate this affair?"

He repeated, *"Aargh!"* even louder.

"You are keeping secrets from me." I was hurt. I knew everything he did; what had he seen that I hadn't?

"Some things are too dangerous to know. Just because you are my apprentice, you are not required to break the law. The instructions I gave you a few minutes ago still stand, but if you refuse to obey them, then I am helpless."

"I'll get my sword," I said, and departed.

Violetta had only recently gone to bed. Even little Milana's normally unshakable good cheer faltered when I gave her the message I brought.

"It's not an hour since her patron left, *clarissimo.*"

She only calls me that when I am being completely unreasonable. I apologized, assured her it wasn't my fault, and insisted that the matter was urgent, all of which I had done already. Then I made a quick and cowardly escape, down to where Giorgio was waiting for me. I settled in the *felze.* He already knew where we were bound.

He pushed off. "You look worried."

I adjusted my face to a smile. "I'm just annoyed that I can't see what the Maestro has seen."

"Your whole life must be a misery then."

It would be worse if I finished up chained to an oar. "I think this Honeycat case is about to blow open," I said. "But I don't know who's going to come down in pieces."

"That," the gondolier barked, "is a disgusting expression."

"It's a disgusting case," I said.

The doorman at Palazzo Michiel must have known me by then, but the studied lack of recognition in his expression warned of choppy water ahead. I asked to see Jacopo Fauro.

"I regret to report that I have orders not to admit you, *clarissimo*. I may accept written communications only."

Congratulating myself on my foresight, I produced the scroll I had prepared. It was addressed to Jacopo and said only, *Her dearest treasure is going to the chiefs.* The doorman took it and closed the door on me. Declining to take a seat alongside the half dozen other men waiting for audience—several of whom were smirking at the sight of a sword-bearing sprout being refused admittance—I strolled across the *riva* to stare out at the ships and lighters in the basin. A chilly wind made the morning sunlight dance on the water, but spring would come. I could see Giorgio along at the Molo, chatting with some other gondoliers.

I wondered who would receive the note. The Michiel household had more crosscurrents than the lagoon of Venice itself and Jacopo lurked in the center of it all, a spider in a web of lies. At times he was a flunky, at others a fraternal partner. Sometimes he served donna Alina, sometimes he spied on her for her children. He obviously spied on them for her. Bernardo and Domenico told different stories as the fancy took them. Zorzi had been framed for murder, possibly with his own connivance, but certainly helped along by someone. Now one of the two religious in the family had exploded a mine under it by revealing that odious diary. Mixing metaphors is one way of passing the time.

The door swung open and Domenico Michiel appeared in the opening, red faced and pugnaciously prognathous. *"Zeno!"*

I strolled in his direction and he vanished back into the dimness of the *androne* to await me. I entered and closed the door. Apart from Domenico himself, the big hall was deserted. The real estate trader and I could have a good, no-holds-barred, uninterrupted rowdy-dowdy.

He shook my note under my nose. "What does this mean?"

"It means that you read other people's correspondence, *clarissimo*."

"Fauro is a servant. What do you want of him?"

"He told me he was your business partner."

"Tell that to the Turks. What do you want of him?"

"The truth."

"Go to the ninth circle of hell."

I thought his rage seemed contrived, but if he truly did not know what my note meant, he must have shown it to someone who did and that someone had reacted strongly. I confess I was enjoying myself.

"Then the book must go to the chiefs of the Ten."

"What book?"

I quirked an eyebrow skeptically. "Your lady mother knows what book. Or Jacopo does. Briefly, *clarissimo*, certain evidence that has come into my master's possession shows beyond doubt that someone in this house is connected to a continuing series of murders in this city. The learned doctor wishes to question Jacopo Fauro concerning the matter. If Fauro is unable to allay his suspicions, my master will have no choice but to deliver the documentary evidence to the authorities. Then it is highly likely that *Missier Grande* will show up here within hours."

"For Jacopo?" Domenico's shock was more convincing than his previous anger. Had he expected another name?

"Perhaps for other people also. I repeat, *clarissimo*, that the implications appear damning."

"My mother engaged Nostradamus to learn who murdered our father, on the baseless assumption that it wasn't Zorzi. How can Jacopo possibly know anything that will help? He was only a—"

"My master already knows who murdered your father, *messer*, although he has not yet assembled a legally admissible case." What was one more small lie in that temple of deception? "His first priority is to prevent any more courtesans being murdered."

"You dare to threaten me? You dare accuse my half-brother of being a murderer?"

Why not, when he had one convicted murderer in the family already? "My understanding is that he is a vitally important witness."

"By Heaven, your master has fancy ideas for an upstart foreign leech! If he wants to speak to anyone in this household, let him come himself. We'll see who questions whom." Sweat gleamed on the bridge of his aquiline nose.

I explained about my master's infirmity. For a moment I was afraid that *sier* Domenico would decide to return with me in Jacopo's stead, which was not what the Maestro wanted at all. Nostradamus could hope to browbeat Jacopo, but not his older, richer, patrician half-brother. It was not yet time for Domenico.

I bowed. "I shall inform my master of your decision, *clarissimo*. He will have to make his report to the Ten without your assistance."

My bluff worked.

"Wait! Wait there!" Domenico jabbed a finger toward the bench I had decorated for so long on Saturday, spun on his heel, and disappeared at a very fast walk.

I waited.

And waited.

I was not seriously worried that Ca' Michiel would send word for the *sbirri* to come and relieve them of that intolerable nuisance, Alfeo Zeno. The book was my defense. The Michiels would dance to the Maestro's fiddle as long as he held the book.

The knocker rapped. The footman emerged from his unseen kennel to admit two artisan-class men, who asked to see Domenico and were told to wait outside.

At last Jacopo came trudging down the stairs, alone. He was dressed much more modestly than I had yet seen him and I judged that he was scared. Not terrified, but more worried than angry.

I smiled. "Good morning."

He scowled at me and said nothing.

Nor did he speak as we walked along the *riva*, to the Molo where our boat waited. I put him in the *felze* and sat on the thwart facing him, because I did not trust him within snatching range of my sword or dagger. Still neither of us spoke until Giorgio had rowed us away from the watersteps and started to sing. It's not easy to eavesdrop while singing.

"How did you steal the old cat's diary?" Jacopo asked.

"She hadn't missed it?"

"No. She screamed and spat and threatened to claw Domenico's face off. What's in it to get her so riled?"

"I think you know."

He shook his head. He was recovering his normal insouciant self-confidence already. Some people believe that they can lie their way out of anything.

"I've seen it there in the casket, but never seen it opened. How did you get hold of it?" His eyes narrowed. "Magic?"

"No magic. I can't tell you, but my master may."

"You're not seriously suggesting that I go around murdering whores, are you?" He portrayed the innocence of angels.

"I'm not suggesting anything. Nostradamus does the thinking, I'm just the messenger boy. It might not hurt if you thought back to where you were on the nights they were attacked, though."

He saw the trap right away. "Tell me what nights those were and I'll try." He smirked. Jacopo Fauro thought he was smart and so he was, but he was in for a surprise when he went up against Nostradamus.

26

Jacopo did get a surprise, but not quite in the way I expected. I was surprised, too, although I should have been forewarned by the witless expressions on the faces of the twins, Corrado and Christoforo, who were lurking in the *salone* outside the atelier door.

To start with, Nostradamus was on the wrong side of the fireplace, sitting very upright in one of the green chairs. Secondly, he was socializing in a most atypical manner with the person beside him in the other, but even he cannot avoid being charmed by Violetta when she exerts herself. I had passed on his instructions that she was to wear something provocative and the result had the impact of a Jovian thunderbolt. The square-cut neckline on her gown of crimson and silver silk extended halfway to her bellybutton and the lace bodice under it was a cover in name only. The skirts were as sheer as a dawn mist. She rose and curtseyed to Jacopo when I introduced him. His eyes bulged as if he had a severe case of goiter.

I had my hand on my sword hilt. If she blurted out that they had met before, back when he called himself Zorzi, he might attack her or try to flee. She did not, though, and the moment of danger passed. He bowed to her.

I saw him settled in the red chair and went to the desk to record the match, which ought to be a walkover. The odds were terrible. He had a clear view of Violetta and if he could keep his mind on the Maestro's questions at the same time, then he was not the hot-blooded adolescent he was supposed to be. Violetta was not there just to distract him, although that might be a useful side benefit.

Yes, primarily she had been brought in to identify Zorzi, in case that was Jacopo's real name. With that possibility now disposed of, Nostradamus still had a second string to his bow, which is quite typical of the way his mind works. Violetta was being set up as bait for Honeycat. Did she know? I did not comment, but nor did I bother to hide my anger when I caught the Maestro's eye. He ignored it, waiting while I organized paper and pens. When I dipped my quill, he began.

"I hope you do not object to signorina Violetta's presence here, signor Fauro. She has an interest in this investigation."

Jacopo laughed. "Who could possibly object to the presence of such a goddess? I shall drag out this meeting for as long as I possibly can. And I must say that I am deeply honored to meet a man whose fame has spread all over Europe." He was holding his own so far.

I wrote it all down—not with my normal penmanship, and much abbreviated, but within my powers to turn into an accurate transcription.

"Donna Alina retained me to investigate the death of your honored father, and I was already looking into the death of Lucia da Bergamo for signorina Violetta."

"Poor Lucia was a friend of mine," Violetta explained sadly.

They were overdoing it. The message they wanted to convey was that Violetta was a courtesan, and Jacopo would have to be a babe in arms not to know that just from her dress.

"I regret that I was not familiar with the lady," he said blandly.

"Lucia," said the Maestro, "was one of at least four courtesans recently murdered in the city. It appears that all of
these deaths are related."

"You think Zorzi has returned to Venice and is murdering more people?"

The Maestro stretched his lips in what he thinks of as a
smile. "That would be the implication if I believed that your
brother committed the first murder, but I don't. What exactly
is your position in the Michiel household, signor Fauro?"

"Galley slave."

Violetta grinned encouragingly.

The Maestro said, "Be more explicit."

"Kennel boy, then. I have been page, drudge, and gardener. When my beard grew in, they were all ready to give
me a couple of ducats and throw me out into the world to
seek my fortune, but at the last minute the harridan decided
she needed a *cavaliere servente*. I am much more *servente* than
cavaliere, and there is no romantic aspect to my duties, but I
put up with her, which nobody else can."

"When did that happen?"

"Two weeks before Christmas."

"And your responsibilities?"

He shrugged. "Fetch and carry, write letters, read to her,
cut her toenails, count the ornaments—she is convinced the
servants are stealing from her all the time—shop for her, listen to the same stories a hundred times, dust the tops of the
pictures . . . Very exciting. It wouldn't be so bad if she went
out once in a while, to the theater or dinner parties, but she
never does."

I set aside a sheet, reached for another, and numbered it.
The Maestro paused to make sure I was keeping up.

Then, "You are no relation of hers."

"No, Doctor."

"She pays you well."

"So she should. Galley slaves at least get fresh air and exercise."

"To excess," the Maestro agreed. "Do you recognize this book?" He had been hiding it behind him in the chair.

Leaning back, Jacopo crossed his legs. Then he folded his arms, which is another defensive gesture. If I noticed it, the Maestro surely did. The knife was drawing closer to the quick.

"It looks like donna Alina's diary. She went looking for it this morning and it had disappeared."

"Tell us about that," the Maestro said with another snaky smile. "When Alfeo arrived this morning, his letter was brought to you?"

"No. Last night s*ier* Bernardo decreed that only he or *sier* Domenico would have any dealings with you or your apprentice. This morning he was out, so the letter went to Dom. He came to ask me what it meant—ask both of us, because I was with the hag in her reception room, writing up her rent books. She rushed into her bedroom and looked in the casket where she keeps the book and it wasn't there. She went into screaming convulsions."

"You mean that literally?"

"Literally, she threw a tantrum."

"Hysteria?" the Maestro said sadly.

"I am not familiar with the word."

"Extreme emotional agitation caused by a disorder of the uterus. This is Tuesday. I have good reason to believe that the diary was removed on Sunday. She cannot be a very keen diarist."

Jacopo uncrossed his legs uneasily. "I have never seen her write in it. Her fingers are so swollen now . . . I've never seen inside it. She called it her diary, that's all I know. And if that is what you are holding, then you are in possession of stolen property, Doctor Nostradamus."

"Not necessarily. I was given it as a gift, by Sister Lucretzia."

I almost jumped out of my chair. Why had he revealed that? It was a shocking breach of faith.

Jacopo frowned suspiciously. "I don't believe it! Why would my sister do a thing like that?"

"I don't know why."

"I tried to get into the convent to ask her," Violetta volunteered. "But I was turned away. I wrote a letter, but so far she has not replied." She sighed. "The abbess may have intercepted it, of course."

"She stole it!" Jacopo insisted, still staring at the book. "Her mother would never have given it to her, or even let her look at it."

The Maestro flashed a glance at me to see if I was keeping track of lies. I nodded. "Who else in the Palazzo Michiel keeps a diary?" he demanded.

"I think Bernardo does, just political stuff I think. No one else."

"Do you get much time off, signor Fauro?"

"*Me?*" Jacopo laughed. "If I ever do get an evening to myself, may I call on you, donna Violetta?"

She gave him a smile that promised all the pleasures of the Sultan's harem. "I would love that, but my evenings are mostly spoken for well in advance."

"I am told," the Maestro said quickly, before the conversation could slip away from his control, "that you are a ladies' man."

"Far from it," Jacopo said. "I am not quite a virgin, but kitchen maids are the extent of my experience, and few of them."

The Maestro sighed. "Alfeo? How many have you detected so far?"

"I have lost count, master. According to Domenico, 'He

sows enough wild oats to feed the Cossack cavalry.' Donna Alina's hands look extremely healthy and she moves them naturally. Signor Jacopo says that she never goes out, but she spoke to me of furniture she had seen in friends' houses. He claims ignorance of the book's contents, yet he says it was not suitable for his sister the nun. He says he was a gardener, but he knows enough of the Greek Classics to refer to the maenads. He told me he is a partner in the family business, but he eats in the kitchen and the rest of the family call him a servant. I don't know if anything he ever says is true."

"Jacopo," the Maestro said, demoting him to servant status, "this book contains the names of many courtesans, including all four who were murdered in the last month."

The cords in Jacopo's neck tightened. "They were not murdered by me!"

That was certainly true of the last victim, Marina Bortholuzzi, because the killer I had tackled on the grass of the Campo San Zanipolo had not been Jacopo Michiel.

"You dress like an Ascension Day parade," Nostradamus said contemptuously. "Are you suggesting that donna Alina Orio showers gold on you just for reading to her and cutting her toenails?"

Jacopo seemed to swell, making me think of a young bull being tormented by a scrawny old rooster.

"Yes! *Yes!* I'm the only one who cares for her at all. Her own children keep her locked away and ignore her. I'm all she has, and I think she likes to make believe that I'm Zorzi come back to her. I'm about the age he was when it happened. What if she is deluded? It's her own money and if she wants to spend it on me so I can dress up like a young nobleman, what crime is that? Did you drag me here just to accuse me of dressing well?"

The Maestro ignored the outburst. "The first time Alfeo called at Palazzo Michiel to speak with *sier* Bernardo, he was kept waiting more than two hours. When he was shown the door, you were waiting outside for him. How did you know who he was and that Bernardo was not going to receive him?"

Jacopo unfolded his arms, spread his palms. "One of the footmen pointed him out to me. That was Alfeo Zeno, he said, helper to the great clairvoyant Nostradamus . . ."

"So you went and told donna Alina?"

"I was on my way to her already. Yes, I told her. I remarked that it seemed very strange that *sier* Bernardo would snub him so."

"You did not think to ask Bernardo why?"

"Rugs do not question feet."

"But then?" Nostradamus said. "Then, after Alfeo had been received by donna Alina, and you were showing him out, you said . . . Alfeo?"

"He told me," I said, "and I quote, 'Your mention of the Honeycat name was tactfully done. We were all terrified that you would tell the old bag about the murdered courtesans and make her convulse.'"

Jacopo had twisted around to look at me. He turned back to snap at the Maestro. "That was last week! You expect me to remember the exact words we were speaking?"

"Alfeo does, and I recall him telling them to me, because they made little sense then and less now. Either you are lying about the footman or you were conspiring with Bernardo and possibly Domenico. Which was it?"

"I don't remember trivia," Jacopo said sulkily. "I'm not your precious Alfeo."

"No. I think you are getting very tangled. Try telling the truth for a little while."

"I did tell you the truth. I just tidied it up a little in order to be tactful. If you want the raw facts, I was helping Domenico when Bernardo received your letter and came to show it to him. They agreed that you were an interfering busybody charlatan, that you were probably hoping to blackmail us, and that your gutter-feeding *barnabotto* messenger boy was a disgrace to his ancestry and did not deserve an answer. And they ordered me to have nothing to do with him, either."

Nostradamus beamed. "Splendid! See how refreshing it is? Keep it up. So you went and told donna Alina?"

"Of course. She's been driven crazy by a lifetime in captivity. She told me to intercept him outside. It made her day."

"What changed in December?"

"December?"

"Why did donna Alina suddenly decide she needed a *cavaliere servente* two weeks before Christmas? She had lived eight years a widow without one?"

Jacopo shrugged his heavy shoulders. "Yes. I don't know. She took pity on me, maybe. I told you they were going to throw me out at the end of the month."

"You don't know? Her decision saved you at the very edge of the precipice and you didn't make it your business to find out why? You snoop and sneak and eavesdrop. You spy and pry and lie. What changed in December?"

"Nothing I know of except I got a job."

"Who killed Gentile?"

"Zorzi."

"Rubbish! He would never have used a family heirloom as a weapon. According to what you told Alfeo, it was you who informed the Ten that the *khanjar* dagger was missing—not the Ten directly, perhaps, but you blabbed it out in front of witnesses. What witnesses? Why were you present? Who put you up to it?"

"Oh, this is ridiculous!" Jacopo said. "I don't remember. I was twelve years old and had just lost my father. The family was being brutal because he was no longer around to protect me. The servants were sneering that I would be sent away. I'm told that I told someone, but I don't remember doing so. I was only a kid."

"You knew that someone in the family had killed your father with that dagger. Obviously it was his wife, because she was never allowed out and had to use the only weapon she could find. Zorzi fled into exile to protect her."

Silence.

"Why don't you answer?"

"You didn't ask a question. If she killed him, why has she hired you to prove that Zorzi didn't?"

"I can explain that, but I won't. First, do you know what an accomplice is, Jacopo? Or what a conspiracy is?"

"I'm not a lawyer."

"Nor am I. But someone in that house is showering you with money so you can bull your way around the flophouses of Venice, hunting for certain women. Their names come out of this book. Once you have found them, they die. Once might be coincidence. Four times means you are as guilty as the killer. You are an accomplice both before and after the fact. Your head will roll on the Piazzetta. Where were you last Saturday night?"

"In a flophouse. With *two* girls and Zaneto, our chief boatman. The bed was quite crowded at times."

I assumed that the truth had just changed again, but keeping up with the recording was taking too much of my attention to leave me time for analyzing.

"The women are kitchen maids by day, I suppose," Nostradamus said acidly. "You arranged an alibi for each one of the murders, I am sure. Don't waste your breath denying it. Possibly everyone in the family does, because the actual murders are committed by a hired killer. Do you know his name?"

Jacopo stood up. "You are pigheaded stupid, old man."

"Are they all in it, or just one of them?"

Silence.

"You see, Jacopo," the Maestro said, "nobody wants Zorzi back. Domenico and Bernardo would have to share the *fraterna*; their mother would get beheaded for murder, and you would be out of a job. That's why the women are dying—because Zorzi was with one of them that night and she can give him an alibi. Without that he dare not return."

This was very much what I had suggested the previous day and been mocked for. Jacopo was not the only one spinning yarns.

"You asked why donna Alina hired me to expose the real killer. Because to clear Zorzi's name, I must find the woman who can give him an alibi. Remember that Alina insisted that my contract be changed—you yourself wrote in the change. She wants to be the first one I inform of that woman's identity. Then the witness will be exterminated before the Ten's *shirri* can get to her. Understand?"

Jacopo folded his arms, but he towered over the Maestro and Violetta in their chairs, and I dropped my pen, bracing myself to leap to their defense if necessary.

"This is sewage, pure sewage!" he said. "You are crazy. How can you possibly find a particular whore, not just on the morning after but eight years after?"

"I have found her. The last companion named in this book," the Maestro continued, "is 'Tonina Q.' Zorzi spent the night before the murder with Tonina, but she is mentioned many times before that, and I have established that he did, in fact, visit her the following night also. That fact was not recorded in the book, doubtless because of the tragic event that occurred then. Tonina was married and not a courtesan, but her first name really was Tonina, Tonina Civran."

"It's not as glamorous as 'Violetta Vitale,'" Violetta said.

I realized my jaw had fallen open, and closed it. Fortunately she was looking down at her hands, not at me. "I was very young and very poor, so I was married off to a man very old and very rich. Then I met Zorzi, who showed me what I lacked. We were so in love . . . I simply cannot describe the difference he made to my life. It was spring after winter, it was daybreak. After his father's murder, he insisted I must not come forward to testify, but I was terrified that he might be accused of the killing. I went to my husband and told him what had happened. I said that I would have to report this to the Ten. He ordered me out of his house—but by then Zorzi had already fled to the mainland. After that I needed to earn a living, and I knew only one way I could do it." She gave Jacopo a wistful smile.

He made a skeptical noise, which I was hard put not to echo. "And just how did Doctor Nostradamus find you?"

"I found him. I live next door in Number Ninety-six. Alfeo and I are friends. When my friend Lucia was murdered, I asked the doctor to hunt down the killer for me, and that murder turned out to be related to Gentile Michiel's. Venice is not so enormous that such things cannot happen." Smile again, sadder than before.

I did not believe a word. She had never been Tonina Civran. The Maestro had put her up to this; it was worse than merely using her as bait. It was human sacrifice.

"So she will clear your brother's name," the Maestro said. "Alfeo, when will you have the report ready for the Ten?"

"Not long, master," I said, not knowing what answer he wanted.

"Good. Go and tell your mistress, Jacopo, that I shall send Alfeo over with my report this evening. If she wants to catch the next *traghetto* across to Mestre first, that is her privilege, but I shall claim my fee."

Jacopo took a step closer, young and big and angry. I gathered my feet under me, ready to leap if he made a hostile move.

"You're a wrinkled old fraud," he told the Maestro. "That Basilica was swarming with priests and nuns. I have two other siblings who could have taken that dagger, and at least one of them was in the Basilica that night." He turned and strode over to the door.

"Wait! Jacopo, do you know the meaning of the word 'entailed'?"

He turned, glowering. "Tell me."

"It refers to property that can only change hands by inheritance. Donna Alina inherited her wealth when her brothers died in the plague. No matter what she may have promised you, those lands and buildings must pass to her own children when she dies. Any documents she may have given you regarding them are worthless."

He did not change color, for anger had already made him pale, but the blow hurt. "What do you know of it? You're lying!"

"No, I am not the one who is lying. Ask your brothers if you don't believe me. Jacopo, you are very naive compared to them. They let your mother squander wealth on you, but they can put a stop to that whenever they want, and they can drop you like an anchor whenever they want. You still have time to go to the chiefs of the Ten and tell them what you have done. Alfeo will go with you and deliver the book as evidence. I am sure Their Excellencies will be merciful if you go now, before they send the *sbirri* for you."

Jacopo spun around and threw the door open. I sprang up and followed him out. The twins were still there, still hoping for a glimpse of Violetta when she left, and a long, lingering stare would be even nicer.

I told them, "Tell your father we need . . . Never mind." Giorgio was already hurrying along the hall. I bowed to our departing guest. He had been entertaining, if not enlightening. "Giorgio will see you home, *lustrissimo*. Hopefully we shall meet again this evening." I opened the front door.

"Don't count on being let in," he said.

"Signor Fauro?" Violetta called, emerging from the atelier.

"You won't mind if the doctor's boatman drops me off at my door?" Awkward on her pillar shoes, she reached for his arm, and of course he offered it. She rewarded him with a smile that made the twins sigh audibly and almost made me choke.

I wanted to hurl him down the stairs rather than let her touch him. I wanted to scream at her to be careful, because she had been chained to the rock like Andromeda, fodder for the monster.

27

I went down one flight to the balcony and watched to be sure that Violetta disembarked safely at Number 96. Only then did I return to the atelier. The Maestro was making a painful progress back to his favorite chair and I was too furious to offer him a steadying arm.

"Was there any truth at all in any of that?" I demanded. "Violetta was never Tonina Civran. She cannot clear Zorzi's name. You scoffed when I suggested that the courtesans were being murdered to stop one of them giving him an alibi."

"Offhand"—he sighed, easing back into comfort—"no. I mean I cannot think of any significant facts being correctly included in our conversation, except Sister Lucretzia's participation in transporting the diary. You notice that Fauro did not correct his story about the dagger? Of course he was very young at the time and may not remember events correctly, so that falsehood may not have been deliberate."

"You are staking Violetta out as bait!"

He nodded sadly. "The only alternative I could see was to enlist demonic help, and that would be especially dangerous in this case. A dark spirit powerful enough to block a major sin like murder would put up enormous resistance."

"She'll get murdered!"

He chuckled softly. "You think you are the only brave person in the world? She knows the risk and agreed without a moment's hesitation. She will be well guarded. We have baited our hook and must wait to see who bites."

"But if the Michiel killer is using hired brawn, then he'll be all you catch, not the real culprit."

"But he will tell all his little secrets to the Ten."

I winced. "Did you believe Jacopo when he said that either Fedele or Lucretzia was in the Basilica that night?"

"On balance, I am inclined to doubt that either of them had the seniority to get into such an august ceremony as the doge's Christmas Mass." Nostradamus scratched his beard. "I know Zorzi wasn't there, which is what matters."

"How do you know that?"

"Because the Ten would not be making such a fuss now if they were certain they had condemned the right man. The present Council of Ten is covering up for its predecessors and trying to protect its reputation."

I slumped down in my chair and gathered up my papers. "And the Orio estate? Is it entailed as you call it?"

"I have no evidence, but I should be astonished if what I told him is incorrect. Patrician families keep family wealth where it belongs—in the family. Donna Alina had five brothers. That the plague would carry off everyone but she would have seemed so unlikely at the time their wills were drawn up that the prospect would not have been considered. The lawyers would have tacked on some standard paragraph giving her a life interest."

That sounded very weak to me, evidence of how desperate he was.

"You really believe that Jacopo will go home and report

to the murderer—whether knowingly or unwittingly—that Zorzi Michiel was with Violetta Vitale on the night Gentile was murdered? And that the murderer will dare act on that information?"

Nostradamus sighed. "There is an alternative. Jacopo deceives himself too, remember. He lives in a fantasy world of his own making. I hope that he will now see how dangerous his own position has become and go to the chiefs to confess. Pity him. He was reared in a palace, even if he did have to eat in the kitchen. If his father had lived he would probably have been provided with an apprenticeship, but apparently nobody else cared. Then, suddenly, he is offered more money than he has ever seen in his life just to dress up like the rich playboy noble he has always dreamt of being and haunt brothels. Do you wonder he succumbed? Or that he shuts his mind to what is happening as he tracks down the victims? Poor devil!"

Put that way, yes. If the Maestro had correctly analyzed Jacopo's role in these crimes, then he was going to be yet another victim of whoever had murdered Gentile Michiel.

"It must be time for dinner," he said. "Afterward you will write out our interview with him in fair and prepare a report for the chiefs of the Ten. I dare not withhold that diary from them any longer."

My master had his priorities, but I had mine. I gobbled my dinner and made all speed for Violetta. The fastest route was by way of the roof, of course, but if the security at Number 96 was as tight as it should be, I might have to spend more time explaining myself than I would save. I ran downstairs instead.

I found Antonio outside the door of Violetta's suite, supervising a carpenter who was installing three massive bolts. She was on the inside, supervising both men. She was also clad in a loose house gown, being long overdue for her day's helping of sleep.

She flashed me a smile. "I've decided to stop you sneaking in on me at ungodly hours in the morning."

I blew her a kiss and went around the corner to the kitchen door. My key worked, but the door would not open. Then I heard bolts being drawn; I was admitted. We completed the kiss in proper form, ignoring Milana's smiles in the background.

"This is madness!" I said when we paused for breath. "If you must be bait, at least come and stay with us next door, where you will be safe. We have an excellent guest bedroom."

She touched the tip of her tongue to the end of my nose. "Oh, and wouldn't you like that!" She was dark-eyed Helen, ready to tease me to distraction.

"Wouldn't you?"

"For a day or so, I suppose. Not enough variety for longer."

"Vixen!" I kissed her again.

She broke free. "I am safer here, my darling, because I have more protectors. Antonio has brought in extra guards—all good men he knows and trusts. We'll have guards on duty by night *and* day. Now we have bolts on both doors, as you can see, and it would take a cannon to break through these doors. I even canceled all my engagements for the next three evenings!"

I sighed and nodded; tried to kiss her again and was balked when she laid fingers on my lips.

"But," she added coquettishly, "I will be lonely all by myself. I could use an extra bodyguard."

"I know a good man!"

She smiled at me under her lashes. "So do I. Don't forget to bring your longsword, soldier."

I took all afternoon to transcribe the Maestro's interview with Jacopo, because I was on tenterhooks and my mind kept wandering. I wondered how similar my report might be to the one our champion liar would deliver when he returned to the Palazzo Michiel. Would the killer, whichever of them it was, swallow the bait, or recognize the trap the Maestro had set? Had word already gone out to the hired assassin that another deadly task awaited him?

It was only when winter dusk was falling that I reached the end and passed the final sheet across the desk to the Maestro, who had been ostensibly reading Paracelsus's *Archidoxa* all afternoon, but had done much more frowning and beard tugging than page turning. He had followed my progress, page by page without comment. Now he scanned the ending and nodded.

"Not bad," he conceded effusively. "It will suffice."

Praise indeed! I had expected a dozen corrections at least.

"Now my report to the Council of Ten," he said. "File copy first."

He dictated a brief account of Violetta's plea that he track down her friend's killer, his discovery that there were other victims, and his efforts to prevent more killings. The name "Honeycat" had directed him to the Palazzo Michiel, and from there had come the enclosed book, believed to have been sent to him by donna Alina Orio . . . and so on. After this, not even an abbess rampant would keep the Ten away from Sister Lucretzia.

"Read it back," he said. Then, "It will do. Make a fine copy of both."

He was rarely so uncritical and I began to suspect that the Council of Ten was never going to see my handiwork. Nevertheless, I did as I was told. Then I wrapped up the damning book, my report, and the accompanying letter. I sealed the package with wax.

"I'd better go," I said.

"Later," he added, glancing at the windows. "After we have eaten."

"The Ten will be meeting by then." The three chiefs of

the Ten, who set its agenda, are appointed for a month at a time and must not leave the palace during their term, but the entire council meets in the evenings, although not every day. After it adjourns, the three state inquisitors retire to their own chamber to conduct their own sinister business.

The Maestro dismissed my objection with a shrug. "There is still time. I have been considering my latest fore-seeing, the one about hazarding in far lands and death being near at hand. You did not spurn help at your feet . . . You have seen no more of the mysterious cat?"

"No, master." I sat down, but I know him too well. I could tell that he was procrastinating, hoping against hope that his trap would be sprung before he was forced to turn over that damning evidence to the Council of Ten. Once that happened, a blanket of secrecy would fall over the case and we might never learn what happened.

"Are we overlooking anything in our respective predictions?" he mused.

That was a command for me to start interpreting. The implication that I was his equal as a seer was mere flattery.

"Your first quatrain predicted the fourth murder very well. The second . . . The first two lines—*hazarding in far lands* and *death near at hand*—suggest that Zorzi has returned to Venice or plans to. *Not spurning help at your feet* suggests my phantasmal cat. Explain *Salvation from on high* to me, master."

He pulled a face. "I can't. The other three lines work out, so keep it in mind. And your two tarot readings. Revisit those for me."

"The reading for Violetta has turned out quite well," I said with touching modesty. "I mean the queen of coins facing the problem of Death reversed could hardly be plainer. You just reversed the knight of cups by sending Jacopo home to bait your trap, which will turn out to be the solution if it works." Or sheer disaster if it didn't, but I might as well claim credit for giving him the idea.

"And the Popess reversed?"

"Violetta would say that it meant the abbess of Santa Giustina who refused to admit her."

I thought that even Nostradamus would have trouble interpreting that as a significant prophecy, but he managed it. "The warning may have restrained her from revealing too much. If the abbess had guessed that she was a prostitute, she would have reported her to the censors. And Fortitude as the helper? Your Violetta is a brave woman to participate in our little stratagem."

"My deck names that card Strength."

"Well, even if we don't count it, four out of five is still remarkable. Very few tarot workers could equal that. Now your own reading?"

Hmph! "Not so good," I admitted. "The Popess as the solution fits, because Sister Lucretzia brought us the book. The snare was the *vizio*, all right, but I hardly need tarot to warn me of Filiberto Vasco; and it was your quatrain and the phantasmal cat that saved me from him. Nothing else helps at all. The problem was identified as Justice. I suppose that means that Zorzi was innocent, or justice for killing the four women; it's apt but not helpful. The helper was Judgment, which tells me nothing."

The Maestro stroked his beard and frowned at me. "The subject or question was the knave of coins reversed?"

"That's a good indication of *Circospetto* taking bribes."

"Then why was he reversed?"

This had been bothering me also. "I don't know. He got his money and gave up virtually nothing." All we had learned for five hundred ducats was that the murder weapon was not the *khanjar* dagger Jacopo had said it was.

Nostradamus tugged his goatee for a moment, which meant that he was seriously thinking, not just wasting time until Honeycat dramatically burst in on us to confess.

"Suppose Sciara cheated? Suppose it was he who removed the rest of the documents, just to score off us?"

"Possible," I admitted. "Likely, even."

"Then perhaps he told you more than he intended? Outsmarted himself? The rest of the material would have taken you all night to read and might not have been of value. Because you were not distracted by that, you may have picked up something vital in what you did get to see."

"You're saying I missed something in what he did show me?"

He sighed. "I don't know. That's up to you. I could entrance you and see what I might squeeze out of your memory that you have overlooked."

"No!" I said automatically. I hate it when he puts me into a recall trance, because I cannot remember afterward what I said or what he asked, and I always suspect him of prying into my private thoughts.

"Then you do it!" he snapped. "You ought to be able to put yourself into an introspective trance by now. You must practice more."

Again he glanced at the window to see how the day was fading. There was fog moving in. "Go and find out if Mama has supper ready."

"Yes, master." He expresses interest in food about once a decade. "You are expecting visitors."

"It is possible," he agreed sourly, annoyed that I had seen through him. "Not necessarily Honeycat, but I kicked the hive very hard. Somebody ought to react."

As I reached the atelier door, our door knocker summoned me and I looked back. "Nicely timed, master."

With a smirk of satisfaction, he began levering himself upright. "Pass me my staff."

I saw him headed for the red chair before I went out to the *salone*. I had never approached the front door with greater apprehension. Who was out there? A bravo with drawn sword? *Missier Grande* come to arrest us? Jacopo repentant? One of the Michiel brothers breathing fire? The mysterious Sister Lucretzia returning?

28

I was wrong on all counts. The doge himself would have surprised me less. Beetling over me like a dormant volcano stood Matteo Surian, once Matteo the Butcher. I suppose I gaped at him. He was decked out in his Sunday best, clothes far grander than he would ever have worn in his respectable days as a tradesman, and I could tell at a glance that last week's sodden wreck was now dried out. As an effort of will, that was remarkable. His eyes were no longer bloody pits, but they held a cold, implacable ferocity I recalled from his fighting days on the bridges. At the sight of me he beamed with relief. It was a fair guess that he had never in his life entered a palace like Ca' Barbolano except by the tradesmen's entrance, and mine was the face he had come looking for.

"*Sier* Alfeo!"

"Matteo! You are welcome! Come in, come in! What brings you here?"

With a leer of triumph he opened one of his huge fists to reveal a tightly folded piece of paper. "I found the note!"

"That's wonderful! Excellent! Come and show it to my master." The *shirri* had hunted for that paper, so now we were harboring even more evidence that should be delivered at once to the chiefs of the Ten.

Fortunately the *salone* was dark, for its grandeur might have scared him away. On the other hand, he was so excited and pleased with himself that he might not have noticed. He did not look around him as I ushered him into the atelier, just went striding over to the only person present. The Maestro had settled in his chair and now looked up with astonishment at the giant looming over him, offering his find.

Nostradamus accepted it and ordered him to a chair, joking that his old neck couldn't bend at that angle any more—he can put people at ease when he wants to bother. Meanwhile I was lighting more lamps.

"So where did you find this, Matteo?" the Maestro asked, carefully unfolding the paper.

The big man shifted uneasily in the green chair, which was hard put to contain his bulk. "It all her furniture, see? She brung it when she moved in. And I knowed she had a place she kept money." He colored. "Didn't mind. I got plenty off her." Meaning Caterina had been cheating her doorman. Most pimps would have beaten her raw for trying that.

"So you went looking for a secret hiding place?" the Maestro asked.

"Press a latch and top lifted up."

"And you found money. How many other papers?"

"No papers . . . Stuff . . ."

"It's yours, Matteo. Caterina would have wanted you to have it. I just want to know what else she saw as precious enough to keep there."

Relieved, Matteo mumbled about some jewels he'd never seen before, but only one paper. The Maestro read it in silence with me looking over his shoulder.

My vessel of love, my fountain of joy—
 Yes, it is your Honeycat who has returned! Tell no one yet,

sweetest of cherubs, not until the pardon has been issued. But the Ten agree that I am innocent and was wrongly condemned. No one else knows, so I must be very careful, but the thought of seeing you again drives me mad. All these years, yours was the laughter that haunted my dreams. I must kiss the roses and roam in the forest again, discarding all caution. What are you doing in this awful San Samuele? I will call on you tonight at sunset and sweep you away to better things again. Be ready then.

I went back to the desk and returned with the Orio contract. Again I watched over the Maestro's shoulder as he compared the two documents. The writing on the note exactly matched that in the contract change written in by Jacopo.

"Matteo," Nostradamus said, "this is all the evidence the Ten will need. We know who wrote this!"

The big man's smile exposed a fearsome set of teeth—not complete, but sized to fit a horse. "They'll have his head, then? The sod who killed her?"

"The ax will fall! But this must go to the Ten right away." His face froze hard as granite. "Let Alfeo take it."

"Matteo," I said quickly, because if those two started arguing I might die of old age before either gave way, "could you recognize the killer's voice if you heard it again?"

He hesitated. "Might. He spoke hoarselike."

"Good. Master, why don't I show that note to Alessa? Those terms of endearment do not come from the book. She can tell us whether they were expressions used by the original Honeycat."

He grunted. "Wouldn't hurt to know, I suppose."

"And I think Antonio might welcome another helper tonight."

I could not expect a man of Matteo's age to leap from roof to roof, or one of his girth to balance on the ledge, so we went around by the land route. This gave me time to explain how we had set a trap for the killer. Then I had to convince our new helper that he must not rip Caterina's killer into cutlets if he did show up.

There were no girls on display in the entrance parlor yet, only two guards I did not know. They regarded me with suspicion and Matteo with alarm. Then one of them recognized him from olden days and the chilly atmosphere thawed. I demanded Antonio, who was fetched. I explained my new helper.

Antonio was not enthusiastic.

"Matteo saw the fake friar!" I protested. "He may be able to recognize the man's voice."

Still the bouncer scowled. "We only have his word for it that there was a fake friar."

I thought there would be sudden murder done then, but the other men intervened, supporting Matteo. I excused myself and went upstairs to see Alessa, being admitted to the *piano nobile* by Luigi and Giulio. Number 96 was certainly the best-guarded brothel in town that night.

Alessa was entertaining guests—some of her own employees, judging by the female chatter I could hear from the corridor. She peered out to inspect me, looking imperially displeased.

I produced the note but gave her no hints, asking only, "Does this look genuine?"

She read it and pulled a face. "The handwriting is nothing like."

"No. How about the words?"

"Trash. And Zorzi would have written it in Greek hexameters." Alessa was a great deal smarter than Caterina.

"I love you," I said, taking the note back.

"Not tonight, thank you." She shut the door on me.

Downstairs, I found that a compromise had been reached. Matteo would be allowed to share in the guarding, but only downstairs. There he could listen for the fake Honeycat's voice. He seemed content with that and it suited me also, because the chiefs of the Ten would want to speak with him, and now I knew where he was.

"It looks good," I told the Maestro. "Next door, that is. It's garrisoned like a fortress, and anyway I can't believe that Honeycat, real or fake, is going to be stupid enough to try a frontal assault."

"Neither can I," he admitted cheerfully. "But I think he'll do something. Now we'll need a covering letter to the chiefs explaining where we got that note. And when, too."

The writing did not take me long, but I had to unwrap the package and reseal it. Time was running out if I wanted to deliver this to the chiefs before the entire Council met, which I very much did. It would be a peace offering, a letter of surrender. The Lord alone knew what the Ten might decide to do to me if it heard I had been back to Palazzo Michiel after Fulgentio delivered his warning.

"I'll tell Giorgio," I said, rising.

"Later. Tell Mama we need to eat as soon as she's ready."

"I can eat when I get back."

He chuckled. "And exactly when will that be? August? Go tell her."

I sighed, "Yes, master," and did so. He just could not bring himself to give up yet.

Mama said *Bisato Anguilla Sull'ara* ready in five minutes. Nostradamus would need that long just to get into the dining room, so I went back and told him supper was ready.

I got one mouthful before the door knocker sounded.

29

I looked to the Maestro for instructions.

He was smirking like a mummified monkey: surely this time someone had taken his bait? "Get it. Use your discretion."

My discretion said my wisest move would be to retrace the steps of Marco Polo on a fast camel, but I headed out obediently. This time the visitors were a lesser surprise than Matteo—Bernardo and Domenico Michiel, grim and imposing in their black patrician robes and tippets. I hauled the door wide and bowed low.

"*Messere!* You honor my master's house."

Evidently they agreed with that, because they strode in past me without a word. I led them to the atelier and its two green chairs.

"My master will be here directly, *messere* . . . Lamps . . ." I lit a dozen candles in the chandelier, using a long taper, not the Word, and by then the Maestro was hobbling in through the doorway, tapping the floor with his staff. I presented him to the noble guests. As soon as he was seated, I headed to my place at the desk, where the package still lay in its wrapping.

He beamed without showing his teeth. "How may I serve you, *messere?*"

Domenico spoke first, which surprised me. "You claim to have in your possession a book belonging to our mother. Will you please let us see this book?"

The Maestro leaned back to consider this request. "My apprentice has spent the entire afternoon preparing an account of this volume for the benefit of the noble Council of Ten, explaining how we obtained it. Had you arrived only a few minutes later, *messere*, he would have been on his way to the palace with it. You may, if you wish, accompany him to assure yourselves that I am telling the truth. Otherwise I am willing to *show* you the book, or a page or two of it at least, but you will first agree that it is in my custody and you have no claim to remove it. You must guarantee that there will be no unseemly squabbles or attempts to appropriate it."

Bernardo swelled like a bullfrog but got no further than, "*Doctor . . .*" before Domenico laid a hand on his arm to silence him.

"We shall be happy to abide by those terms, *lustrissimo.*"

Nostradamus nodded to me. I broke the seals, unwrapped the parcel again, and produced the offensive diary. I took it across to them. Again it was Domenico who took charge, accepting the book with his left hand and then opening it so that his brother could see also.

It was at once obvious that they had been warned what to expect. After one glance Bernardo averted his face. Domenico tried several pages at random before slapping it shut and handing it back to me. Had Jacopo described the contents for them, or had they cross-examined their mother? I took the book over to the desk.

"The illustrious lords and I shall need no record of our discussion," the Maestro told me. "You may go and finish what you were doing."

I departed, but without umbrage, because I knew what

he really meant me to do in the dining room. The spyhole there provides an excellent view of the atelier. Domenico (tall) and Bernardo (wide) had their backs to me, but I could watch my master's face and hear everything being said.

". . . understand your concern," the Maestro was saying, "and it does you both credit, but filial duty must sometimes come second to our obligations to the Republic."

"Never fear that we understand that completely," Bernardo proclaimed, "but the laws of Venice recognize that there are persons whose responsibility is lessened, persons whom circumstance or the Good Lord in His wisdom have tasked so hard that they cannot now be judged by quite the same standards as we more fortunate folk. Donna Alina was quite unhinged by the tragedy of our father's death, an infamous and sacrilegious outrage committed before her very eyes, and followed so suddenly by the Ten's condemnation of her son and his flight. I confess that she suffered a breakdown that prostrated her for many months, and indeed one may argue with some justification that she has never recovered her former peace of mind, nor thrown off the sorrows that haunt her."

"Both you and she have my deepest sympathy," Nostradamus retorted, "but you admitted a moment ago that the book is in her handwriting. I have attested that it contains the names of four recent murder victims, a connection that cannot be passed off as sheer happenstance. Furthermore, and most importantly, the book appears to have been written prior to your father's death and the ordeal you describe."

Bernardo tried again. "I will not contest those statements, *lustrissimo*. And I will go so far as to admit that our mother was acting oddly even then. Our father kept the fact concealed from us and I blame myself, as the eldest child, for not comprehending soon enough the difficulties that beset their marriage. It was only after his tragic passing that we appreciated the situation. In the space of ten years, she had borne five children who lived, and she may have had miscarriages also."

The Michiels had come a long way in the last three or four days. From outright denial that there was smoke, they were now offering a fire of diminished responsibility.

"There may well be extenuating circumstances," Nostradamus said, "but that is for the Council to determine, not me. The salient fact is that the book is evidence in a series of murders and I have an absolute duty to turn it over to the Council. With deepest regret I must decline your request."

Domenico took over. He was, I had decided, by far the smarter of the two. Bernardo was all thunder and no lightning.

"You are not suggesting, I hope, that our lady mother has been going around strangling and stabbing people? She almost never leaves the house, and then only to go to church, accompanied always by servants or family. She couldn't even find the Rialto on her own."

"No, *messer*. I agree that blades and silken cords are not ladies' weapons. Poison often is. The bravo is."

"And just how would our dear mother go about finding and then hiring an assassin?"

"She would use an accomplice," Nostradamus said with a hint of impatience. "And you know to whom I refer."

"Jacopo," Domenico said sharply, "is the second reason we came to see you, Doctor. To warn you, in effect. Jacopo Fauro is completely incapable of separating truth from fiction, even concerning inconsequential trivia. He's a pleasant enough lad and quite useful at times. We are fond of him or he would have been sent packing years ago, but he has this infuriating lack of veracity. Nothing he told you can be trusted."

Nostradamus nodded, solemn and sincere. "I am greatly relieved to hear this, *clarissimo*. I was seriously concerned by some of what I was hearing. For example, he told Alfeo that your honored father was stabbed with the same *khanjar* dagger you keep in a display case."

"Oh, saints preserve us!" Bernardo exclaimed. "You think we would keep it around to remind us if that were true? That is an utter falsehood, quite typical."

"And he has given us several accounts of what his duties are—not that those are any of my business directly," the Maestro added quickly. "But it might shorten this discussion if I had a better idea of what is likely and unlikely. He is your business partner, *sier* Domenico?"

"No, he is not my business partner! Far from it. Not even my messenger boy. He does have a remarkable eye for style and proportions, and I ask his opinion on those quite often, but no more than that. We tried to put his talent to work by apprenticing him to a builder and later to an artist; and several other people, too, but none of them could tolerate him for long. He spouts more fables than Aesop! If I were to let him near anyone I was doing business with, the *Quarantia* would be convicting me of fraud in no time."

The Maestro nodded understandingly. Knowing him as I do, I could tell that he was enjoying himself hugely. "It is a great shame. As you say, the boy has charm and talents. You keep a diary, *sier* Bernardo?"

There was a perceptible pause before the man addressed replied, "No. What did my miscreant half-brother tell you about that?"

"Nothing at all, which I found interesting. No diary? You, *sier* Domenico?"

"Not I, either."

Bernardo cleared his throat. "I do keep a notebook of my political dealings, *lustrissimo*." He was on his best behavior, much more gracious than he had ever been to me. "A sort of ledger, really. You must understand that politics is largely concerned with mutual back scratching. At every meeting of the Grand Council I cast my vote to oblige *sier* Piero on one issue and *sier* Polo on another. Someday they will return the favor. If the matter is really important, I may persuade my brother to accompany me and cast his vote also. I need to keep track. What on earth has that to do with the present topic?"

"Everything. It has cost four women their lives."

"I think you had better explain that accusation," Bernardo said coldly.

"Last September, were you not summoned to the bedside of the late Agostino Foscari? It might have been you, *sier* Domenico, but I judge the family politician to be a more likely choice." He received a nod from Bernardo. "And did not Foscari, right there on his deathbed, break his ancient oath of office by divulging to you a secret he had guarded for the last eight years of his life? Thus he eased a great burden on his conscience and laid one on yours. Was his confessor present, by the way? He probably instigated this repentance."

Pause. "Who told you this bizarre story?"

The Maestro stretched his lips in a wicked grin. "Mostly your mother, although she was not aware that she was doing so. She mentioned to Alfeo that the Council of Ten did not interview her again after Zorzi fled into voluntary exile. That is extraordinary! If the Ten had wanted to know where he had gone, surely his mother would have been the first person to ask? Granted she is of patrician stock and they would treat her more gently than they would a woman of the lower classes, she still should have been questioned."

The brothers exchanged glances and Domenico said, "Keep talking."

"The timing of events requires that some specific incident triggered the recent murders, but there is no point in continuing this conversation if I am mistaken. Well, did Agostino Foscari send for you when he was dying, *sier* Bernardo?"

"He . . . Yes he did." It would have been easier to pull Bernardo's ribs out than information.

"And did you pass on the secret he told you to any other members of your family? Back in September, I mean?"

"That is irrelevant," Domenico said. "Surely?"

"No." The Maestro was making little effort now to hide his pleasure at taunting the two patricians. "Foscari was an inquisitor when your father was murdered, of course. Another of the Three was *messer* Giovanni Gradenigo, who departed this world only last week. Nearing his end he sent for me, which was a strange choice, because we had never met. Alfeo went in my stead but did not arrive in time to learn what the dying man had wanted to tell me. He did learn that Gradenigo had become upset upon being informed of the death of the courtesan Caterina Lotto. At first I suspected he may have known her personally. It seems that this was not his style, but she had been one of Zorzi's associates, so it is more likely that Gradenigo met her when the Three interrogated her at the time of Gentile's death."

"You are building castles in the clouds!" Bernardo said. "Zorzi 'associated,' as you call it, with half the harlots of Venice."

"But," the Maestro persisted, "two others were dead by then and Gradenigo had been informed of them also; that is a reasonable hypothesis, at least. There is no point in continuing this conversation if I am wrong, so I must ask you outright, *sier* Bernardo, did Agostino Foscari tell you that one such woman reported overhearing your brother confess to the crime of patricide?"

"Yes."

Surprise! I had expected Bernardo to refuse to answer. Either he could see that the Maestro would then ask how many more women must die before he would face facts, or else he was being especially forthcoming in order to distance himself from the fork-tongued Jacopo. For me, the eavesdropper, it was teeth-clenching time. If the Maestro's question were quoted to the Ten, they must suspect that he had bribed an official to reveal state secrets. If they suspected, they would investigate.

"Did he name this informant?"

Bernardo growled. "No. Doctor, is it possible that eventually, in the fulness of time, we may come to an explanation of this windstorm?"

"I hope so, *messer*. Foscari died in September. Let us move on to the curious events of December. Your mother keeps her confidential papers in a warded box. To open it one must know both the words and gestures of a minor spell. You, *sier* Bernardo, keep your 'political ledger' as you call it, in a similar box?"

Bernardo mumbled something I could not hear.

The Maestro did. "I thought so. Those caskets may seem secure to the uninformed, but in reality they are not. Any reasonably skilled practitioner of the dark arts could override the minor spell with a stronger. They cannot long withstand even a gifted busybody like your Jacopo Fauro. He must have broken your mother's code, perhaps years ago. At some time he overheard your words. At another, perhaps, he witnessed your actions. Last December he opened your casket in your absence and read through your diary. He learned Foscari's secret—and sold it to your mother!"

Domenico laughed. "*Lustrissimo*, you certainly have managed some high-class snooping of your own, but a lot of what you are spouting is mere speculation. If you are trying to befuddle us into telling you this supposed dark secret that the dying Foscari supposedly imparted to my brother, then you are wasting your time and ours."

"I already know the secret, *clarissimo*." The Maestro put his fingertips together, five on five, as he does when he plans to deliver a lecture. "The truth is that Zorzi Michiel never fled into voluntary exile. He never left Venice."

"Who told you this?" Bernardo growled. "And by asking that, I am not conceding that what you say has any merit."

"No? I told you earlier—your mother told me. Her favorite son vanished without saying farewell or dropping her a note. He did not warn either of you that he was going, or you would have started comforting her with forged letters right away, instead of weeks or months later. The Ten never questioned her as to where he might have gone. They announced his guilt rather than reveal how he had died. Do I have it right?"

The silence was answer enough.

This was the secret too dangerous for me to know.

It explained why the Ten was so determined to stop any reopening of the Gentile Michiel case, and it totally changed the range of possible motives for the courtesan murders.

"Revenge," the Maestro said softly, as if he had overheard my thought. "Eight years ago your brother was denounced as a patricide in an anonymous letter. A woman gave false witness and now someone is going around killing anyone who might be that perjurer. Four women dead, at least three of them innocent." He waited, but neither of his listeners spoke.

Why hadn't I seen this? He had guessed because his quatrain had prophesied *blind vengeance*.

"I do not know who that spiteful snitch was and I have been trying to convince the Ten that I have no interest in anything connected with the death of Gentile Michiel. That secret is safe with me. But the current murders must be stopped. That is what matters.

"Tonight, *messere*, this case has come to a head. An additional piece of evidence has come into my possession. One of the murdered courtesans, Caterina Lotto, was deceived by a note that purported to come from your late brother. The *shirri* hunted for it, but it was not found until today and then it was brought to me. Obviously it should have gone directly to the Ten and I must turn it in right away. I will also testify that the handwriting is that of your half-brother, Jacopo Fauro."

Both brothers started to speak, and it was the orator's voice than won out.

"No, Doctor," Bernardo boomed. "Understand that we were in no wise cognizant of these deaths! We were not aware that prostitutes were being murdered until last Saturday, when your apprentice came around asking questions about Zorzi, followed not long after by a messenger from the Council of Ten. Jacopo knew, because he consorts with servants and lowlifes, which we most certainly do not. He took great pleasure in enlightening us. I was deeply shocked and distressed. I convened a meeting of the family on Sunday, including Fedele and Lucretzia, and even signora Isabetta."

"Jacopo?"

"We called him in a couple of times."

"Not your mother?"

"Our mother was feeling indisposed that morning. I had a long discourse with her later. At the meeting I suggested that we all demonstrate that we could not have been involved. Jacopo went and fetched a diary of his own, and we looked up the dates, so far as we knew them. We were not certain when the first woman died, but Jacopo had alibis for the three we did know about."

The Maestro had been shaking his head all through this. "I did not say that any of you committed these crimes in person. But Jacopo locates the victims, starting with the information in that old journal your mother kept of Zorzi's escapades. Jacopo baits the traps, as he did by writing the note I mentioned. He may even hire and pay off the bravo who does the actual dirty work, but just because there is no literal blood on his hands makes him no less guilty in the eyes of the law." He chuckled. "Did you happen to notice when he started keeping this convenient diary?"

Domenico sighed. "I did. When do you think?"

"Around the middle of last December?"

"Yes."

"Jacopo Fauro," Bernardo declaimed, "is a compulsive liar.

But why should he murder people to avenge a half-brother he can scarcely remember, a man eight years older than himself?"

"For money, *clarissimo*," the Maestro said. "Just as the bravo does. And who has both a motive of vengeance and all the money required to finance this hellish conspiracy?"

Right at that moment someone started beating a thunderous tattoo on the door knocker. We had another visitor.

30

I could have outstripped a bat between the dining room and the door, but even before I arrived the caller began hammering again. I had given up trying to guess who might call on us next, but I was fairly certain that *Missier Grande* would be more subtle than whoever this was. As soon as I clattered the lock, the racket stopped. The visitor pushed on the door and burst through.

"Where is he?" she shouted. "Where are they? My husband? *Sier* Bernardo?"

Signora Isabetta's head was bare, which is an unthinkable breach of custom and her graying hair was bedraggled. She was gasping for breath, wore a bloody contusion on her left temple, and was not dressed for outdoors. I could hear old Luigi downstairs arguing fiercely with a woman, but of course no lady would leave the house without a companion. Ignoring Isabetta, I strode over to the balustrade and peered down the stairwell. I waved to the watchman to let him know all was well and he waved back. I returned to the *salone*.

Already Giorgio and Mama had emerged from the kitchen at the far end, anxious to discover what all the ruckus was about. Isabetta, no longer in the slightest bit mousey, had

tried the door to the right, discovering the Maestro's bedroom, all dark. As I headed for the atelier, she shot past me
and barged right in. Do not doubt that I followed. The men
were all on their feet by then, even the Maestro, clutching his
staff with both hands, leaning on it for support.

"She's gone!" Isabetta shouted, "She's gone!" She kept repeating it, trying to be understood over the brothers's cries of
alarm and the Maestro's efforts to issue medical instructions.
Domenico grabbed his wife to calm her. I grabbed a chair
and put it behind her knees. Between us we sat her down. I
headed for the cupboard where we keep the medical supplies.

It was Bernardo's cannon voice that prevailed. He bellowed for silence and got it.

"Donna Alina?" he demanded. "She hit you?"

Isabetta just nodded, suddenly gasping for air. Her husband was kneeling at her side, chafing her hand; the doctor
had only a few feet more to go. I put his black bag where he
could reach it, brought another chair for him, and then went
back to the cupboard to fetch brandy.

"Just superficial, I think. Pass me that candle. Head
wounds often bleed to excess." Nostradamus was trying to
calm the patient and everyone else as well. He peered carefully at her eyes.

"What happened, dear lady?" Bernardo demanded. "Re-
lax. Take your time."

"Went in . . . to put her to bed . . . room dark . . . didn't
expect . . . behind the door . . . clubbed me with the
cherub . . . wearing black . . ."

At that point a new voice suddenly interrupted, screaming
at the top of my lungs: *"Did Jacopo tell her about Violetta?"*

If you have ever been out on a very dark night during a
thunderstorm, you understand how a sudden flash will illuminate the entire world—not just the hands that a moment
before you had not been able to see in front of your face, but

even distant mountains. That was how it felt. Suddenly it was very clear that we had made a horrible mistake.

Everyone was staring at me in astonishment. Apprentices do *not* yell like that in the company of their betters. But they all knew what I meant.

Bernardo boomed, "No, we established right at the beginning that Jacopo had just come in. He was brought straight to us, not our mother."

But Isabetta was nodding yes.

He scowled. "And after we had spoken with him, I gave him strict orders that he was not to see her. I forbade it categorically. I warned Agnesina to keep him away from her."

Agnesina was Alina's elderly ladies' maid and I could not imagine her herding Jacopo around even if she were armed with a musket.

"He had been to see her first?" Domenico asked, and again his wife nodded—to the annoyance of Nostradamus, who was trying to examine her head wound. "We should have known he would have gone directly to her. Obviously he went to her first, then went out the stairway and came in again by the front door before reporting to us."

"Where is Jacopo now?" That was me, almost shouting in Isabetta's ear. The others continued to ignore my disrespect.

"If he has any sense," Bernardo said, "he's halfway to Florence already. I told him that our patience was exhausted; that he was to leave our house before noon tomorrow. And I warned him that the only way he could be sure of keeping his head on his shoulders was to get both of them out of Venice with utmost dispatch, and furthermore that it was our intention to cooperate in fullest measure with the authorities."

"Of course he would have gone to her first," Domenico muttered reproachfully. "Why didn't I see that? We should have known he was lying when he denied it."

"No bravo?" The Maestro very rarely loses his air of Jovian

calm, but he was close to shouting too, now. *"You mean she does her own killing?"*

Of course that was what they meant. They could no longer deny it. And that was our terrible mistake. I was an idiot not to have realized it days ago. I had tackled Honeycat on the Campo San Zanipolo and toppled him like a skittle. I should have known that there was something far wrong. A professional killer, a bravo, would have planted his knife in my lungs instead of trying to saw through my ribs. I had been contesting with a *woman*, and a woman more than twice my age.

The room was frozen. Four men and one woman were waiting for someone else to speak, and somehow everyone seemed to be watching everyone else. The Maestro recovered first.

"Donna Alina killed those four women *with her own hands?*"

Bernardo hung his head. "She denies it. We do have a secret entrance . . . She has been known to go out alone at night. This morning we ordered the locks on that door changed and we arranged that she would be closely watched."

"Then Jacopo came home and told her about Violetta?" I said. "Oh, *Gesù!*" The guards in Number 96 were looking out for a man, not a woman. I bellowed orders to lock up behind me and bolted out the door to the *salone.*

I very nearly bowled over old Agnesina, Isabetta's companion that evening, who had just tottered in, puffing from her climb. Howling for Luigi, I bounded down four flights of stairs and set to work unlocking the door he had just finished locking. He squawked with annoyance as he came waddling along the *androne.*

"Lock up behind me!" I ordered.

I hauled the door open and dashed out to the loggia, where the lamp had been lit, although the fog was swallowing most of its light. Only the usual three gondolas were tethered there: the Maestro's and the two belonging to the Marcianas—*sier* Alvise does not own one and cadges rides on the rare occasions he does go out. I had expected to find two Michiel boats there also, but probably their boatmen had tied up amid the seven or eight craft outside Number 96 so they would have company while they waited. The all-male gathering in the loggia there was laughing uproariously at some witticism. The only traffic on the Rio San Remo at the moment was a single boat about three houses away in the opposite direction, emerging from the fog. It was coming toward me and the red light on its prow showed that it was *Missier Grande*'s boat.

I had to make a decision instantly. I could not believe that our fearsome chief of police was simply taking a short-cut to somewhere else on an unrelated matter. No, he was coming to Ca' Barbolano, and I did not have time to reach Number 96 without his seeing me. Then I might not reach Violetta to warn her that Honeycat was female and was coming for her.

Leaping back, I cannoned into Luigi, and had to grab him to save him from taking a tumble. He swore at me anyway.

I took him by the front of his smock and shook him. "Listen! Lock this door *quickly*. Then run to the back of the house and pretend you're even deafer than you really are, understand?"

I had never given him orders like that before, or even spoken with such urgency. Alarmed, he nodded and drooled into his beard.

Even the Council of Ten would not force an entry into a nobleman's house, but Luigi would have to open the door eventually. All I had done was gain a little time.

I raced back up the stairs, all four flights, probably faster than I had come down, shouting ahead not to lock me out. I expected all the Marcianas to come pouring out of the mezzanine suites and *sier* Alvise and his wife out of the *piano nobile* to see what the fuss was about, but they didn't. Only Giorgio's face appeared over the balustrade at the top, peering down.

I reached the top, told him, "Lock up!" and cornered sharply toward the atelier. There was an argument of some sort going on in there, but it stopped at my sudden return. The Michiels would be even less pleased to hear my news than the Maestro. I gasped it out in one long burst:

"*Missier Grande* is on his way here and Luigi will delay him a few moments and your boatmen have tied up next door and if they have any sense they'll stay there."

Then I was gone.

My fastest way to 96 was through my bedroom and across the *calle*, but if I tried that tonight I might be skewered by some over-eager guard. The carpenter might have put bolts on the trapdoor.

I streaked along the *salone*, all the way to the far end, and out the back door, scooping the key to the garden gate off its hook on my way by. I did not linger to find my sword, for it was not weapons the bouncers at 96 lacked, it was information. Down the stairs I ran. The fog was letting in just enough twilight to let me cross the courtyard without cracking my shins on something or falling into the well.

Out in the *calle* I turned to the right and sped up again. Faint glimmers from windows provided only a fitful, patchy light, but I know that warren so well that I could run it blindfolded. There are seven turns between the Ca' Barbolano gate and the land door to Number 96.

Left . . .

Of course Alina would be wearing black; she probably did not own a garment that wasn't black. She could embroider, so she could sew. She could make a Carnival costume, or a friar's habit, *or a nun's*. Violetta had tried to see Sister Lucretzia and had then sent her a note. I had a sudden nightmare of her sitting alone in her apartment—she who never sat alone in her apartment—receiving word that there was a nun downstairs asking for her. Could even Alina be crazy enough to try to enter a brothel dressed as a nun? Was that what had caused all the laughter I had heard?

Left . . .

I wished I had a transcript of the family gathering last Sunday. Like the Council of Ten eight years ago, like even the Maestro and me now, the Michiels had recoiled from believing that a woman could commit such deeds herself. The Michiels had closed ranks in the name of family solidarity, all except Sister Lucretzia. Today that decision had been reversed and the senior brothers had driven Jacopo out into the wilderness.

Right . . .

Where was Jacopo now? In a cell in the palace? Escorting donna Alina? I wished I had brought my sword.

Left . . .

I raced along the straight to the T junction where I had first met my mysterious cat helper. I swung left around the corner and a lantern was uncovered right in my face, dazzling me. I stopped dead.

"Well, well!" said Filiberto Vasco. "We have a rat in our trap."

31

A man behind me laughed and more lanterns were uncovered. I had run straight into the oldest, simplest trap in
the world—*Missier Grande* comes to the front door after
staking out his *vizio* to watch the back. For a moment I just
stood there and gasped for breath, too mad at my own folly
to say a word.

And this was not just bad luck. Ca' Barbolano had been
the target, not Number 96. The *vizio* had put his *sbirri*, four of
them, to block the way to the *campo*. They were armed with
matchlock pistols—private citizens may not own firearms.
He himself had taken up position in the other arm of the T,
the way to 96, to prevent any breakout in that direction. Or
perhaps to stay clear of the fighting, if any. If he had been lying in wait for fugitives from the direction of the brothel, he
would have put his men around the corner I had just turned.

"Where is the book, Alfeo?" he said. "Hand it over, there's
a good boy."

"The Maestro has it," I said. "Look, we've identified the
murderer, the one who's been killing—"

"I've warned you before not to meddle in matters that do
not concern you. Give us the book."

"I don't have it!" I yelled. "The killer is heading for Number Ninety-six, may even be there already, and I must go and—"

"The only place you are going tonight is jail, boy." Vasco is no older than I am. Furthermore, he is only citizen class, so he should treat me with the respect due a patrician, but he was very sure of himself this time. The law arrives and some-one flees: what could be clearer evidence of guilt? *Run from hounds and they will chase you.* He had me cold at last. "I won't ask you again."

"*I do not have the book!* Look, just take me along to the brothel door and let me pass in the warning and then I'll take you back to Ca' Barbolano and give you the damned book, and the name of the murderer, and evidence to prove who killed Caterina Lotto."

I could see Vasco's smirk, because his face was illuminated by the lanterns of the *sbirri* behind me. Also by twilight, for, while he had a tall building on his right, there was a courtyard to his left, and the wall of that was barely more than head height.

He sighed with deep regret. "It seems we're going to have to search you. Take off your clothes now, Alfeo, or I'll have the lads strip you."

Seek salvation from on high.

I looked up. The cat was lying on top of the courtyard wall, watching me with golden eyes. *If there is a fourth time,* the Maestro had said, *the stakes will be very high.* Violetta was in mortal danger; for me the stakes could not be higher. This time I would not wait for Felix to volunteer. I would ask for help if it damned me.

"Look out!" I yelled, and jumped back.

Of course Vasco looked *up*, and the cat came down on his face.

"Rabies!" I screamed. "Get it off him! Oh, please don't let it bite him! Rabies, rabies!"

Alas, I was not at all sure that the *shirri* could hear me over the racket coming from Vasco as his face and hands were shredded. Nothing is feared more than rabies, so it seemed unlikely that any of his men would dare go close enough to help him. Unable to endure the terrible sight, I dodged past him and sprinted for Number 96.

Right . . . As I turned the corner, I heard a pistol go off behind me like thunder. I hoped that the shot had been intended for me and not to put Vasco out of his misery, but firearms kick so much that he would not have been in much danger, even at point-blank range.

Then a quick *Left* . . .

As I raced along the final straight to the watersteps, I could see gondolas going past the watersteps at the end of the *calle*. It felt like hours since I had noticed *Missier Grande*'s boat approaching, but in fact it had been only minutes. Now the convocation of boatmen was leaving the neighborhood like a flock of pigeons. When I stepped through the land door into the loggia, only four of them remained, hanging onto columns so they could lean out and watch what was happening next door, at Ca' Barbolano.

Unobserved, I went on, into the brothel. There it seemed that the news had not yet arrived. Matteo loomed enormous on a stool between two young hostesses wearing what could only loosely be described as clothes. From the somber expressions on all their faces, I guessed that he was telling them about Caterina's murder. The women jumped to their feet to greet me with enormous fake smiles. Matteo looked hard at me, taking in my alarm.

There was another guard present, leaning against the wall at the bottom of the stairs, and him I did not know. He was armed.

"Has a woman come in?" I shouted.

"Who's asking?"

I started to explain, and was drowned out as Matteo and the two women both started to tell him who I was.

"The killer is a woman!" I yelled. *"Has a woman come in?"* I moved closer.

The guard whipped out his sword.

"Yes." Matteo came in on his left and punched him once on the side of the head.

Once was plenty and I dodged him as he fell. Then I went up the stairs as if shot from a mortar, three steps at a time, hearing the pounding of boots as Matteo followed. I was relieved to see that Luigi was one of the two men guarding the door to the *piano nobile*, but they both drew their swords.

This time I did not shout. "The killer is a woman! A woman's in there?"

Luigi nodded and reached for his keys. "A widow lady. Arrived just a few minutes ago. Sent in a note. Violetta said to let her come up, it was all right."

"It is not all right!" I said, pushing past him and leading the way to Violetta's door. I moved gently, though, for Venetian terrazzo floors tend to bounce slightly and might alert the intruder that a Crusader army was on the way.

Luigi turned his key very quietly in the lock. The door did not move.

"It's bolted!"

Matteo slapped us both aside with a two-armed gesture, clearing a path. He backed up to the wall behind, then hit the door like a war galley ramming. The door shuddered, as well it might. He backed up again, and slammed it again, and that time I think he would have gone through a brick wall. Nine two-inch screws ripped out of seasoned timber and the door flew open. He stumbled through with Luigi and me right on his heels.

Hearing a stream of oaths, curses, and abuse from Violetta's *salotto*, we ran that way. And there they were, Violetta and donna Alina, down on the floor, both screaming, wrestling for possession of the *khanjar* dagger. Alina was on top and the dagger was hovering over Violetta's face, but Violetta was holding it away from her. Fortunately I did not have my sword with me, or I would have killed the madwoman on the spot. Instead I grabbed her by the forearms, heaved her off her intended victim, slammed her right wrist against the edge of a table to make her drop the knife, and then threw her into a chair.

Then I turned to comfort Violetta, but she wanted no aid from me.

"Bitch!" she yelled. "She-devil! Who is she?" Spewing abuse, she scrambled to her feet and went for Alina with fingernails drawn. "Hell cat! Madwoman! I'll rip her face off . . ."

I grabbed her and discovered that the tarot had meant Violetta, not Matteo, when it predicted a need for strength. Fortunately, if embarrassingly for me, Luigi came to help and between us we pulled her away.

"Hippolyta!" I shouted. "Calm down!"

I had uncovered a new Violetta persona. Between us, Luigi and I forced the Queen of the Amazons into a chair, where she continued to simmer, still snarling and spitting.

Meanwhile Matteo was standing over Alina to make sure she stayed where she was. She was screaming with fury and pain. "You broke my arm! I'll see you hang for this! Animals! Do you have any idea who I am?" And so on. She was dressed in black, yes, but in the weeds of a respectable widow, not a nun's habit.

Luigi chuckled. "Loud, aren't they?"

Already the room was filling up—girls, guards, customers, madams. There had been a scuffle in a brothel and it must not be allowed to become any more than that. I caught Violetta as she tried to spring out of her chair again; I persuaded her to sit down and accept a glass of wine that happened to be handy. Then I found the dagger and its scabbard and took possession of them. A sheet of paper on the table looked to be in Alina's handwriting but signed as being from Sister Lucretzia, so I appropriated that and the envelope also.

By then Antonio had appeared and was ordering everyone out. The belligerents had fallen silent, except for sobs of pain from Alina.

"I know this woman," I announced loudly. "And her sons happen to be visiting Nostradamus in Ca' Barbolano at this moment. The doctor there can attend to her arm. *Missier Grande* is there also. Let's get her out of here."

"And what about me?" Medea yelled, green eyes blazing.

"You hurt?"

"No, but no thanks to you and your crazy charlatan wizard!"

"All thanks to you," I said. "I'll come back with those as soon as I can. Antonio, can you nail up that door for the night? Matteo, bring the woman."

Medea melted into Helen. "You're just going to leave me?"

"For now." I risked bending to kiss her cheek and didn't lose my eyeballs, as I would have done a moment ago. "I'll be back as soon as I can unless they throw me in jail."

I retrieved donna Alina's hat and veil from the floor and dropped them on her head any-old-how. "Your sons are waiting, madonna."

32

Antonio led us down to the loggia—me and a grinning Matteo shepherding donna Alina. She had refused to let him carry her, but she had fallen silent and was trembling violently, close to shock.

There were still only four boatmen there and I recognized all of them as Michiel employees. A quick peek out between the pillars confirmed that *Missier Grande*'s boat was still tied up outside Ca' Barbolano.

I recalled some names from my experience of servant fare in the Michiel kitchen. "Zaneto, isn't it? Alfeo Zeno."

He scowled at me and my companions. "I remember you. What do you want?" He could not possibly recognize donna Alina under her veil in that light and I did not want to reveal who she was.

"This lady is a real lady, not a worker here. She fell and injured her arm. A doctor lives in that house where your masters are visiting. Would you be so kind as to ferry us to the watergate?"

"There are other visitors there, *messer*."

"*Missier Grande*, yes. But I need to talk with him also."

Left with no further argument, he helped us load our

patient aboard, which was hard to do without jostling her injured arm.

"Business as usual now?" Antonio asked.

I hesitated only a moment. Vasco had wanted me to give him the book, so *Missier Grande* had come for the book, so the chiefs of the Ten had sent him for the book, and if the chiefs knew about the book, then they had Jacopo Fauro under lock and key.

"Business as usual," I agreed.

Our voyage took only moments, but that was long enough for me to work out the timing. Had Jacopo been arrested, he would have been left to meditate on his sins for a while before he was questioned, and even then, being Jacopo, he would very likely have tried to lie his way out of the mess. The chiefs must have learned of the book from him and their very fast response indicated that he had almost certainly turned himself in, confessing everything, fast and furious. The Maestro had predicted that the Ten would be lenient on him if he did that, a prophecy I hoped would prove to be one of his good ones.

A couple of *shirri* eyed us suspiciously as we disembarked in the Barbolano loggia, prepared to prevent our entry.

"I am *sier* Alfeo Zeno and I live here. This lady is in need of medical attention and I have some evidence to hand over to *Missier Grande*."

They accepted that, but one of them escorted us upstairs.

Three more *shirri* were standing near the atelier door and moved aside to let us in. Bernardo and Domenico were still in the green chairs. Isabetta sat in the red one and Nostradamus at the desk, she wearing a bandage around her head and he a puckish grin. *Missier Grande* stood in the center with the package under his arm. He seemed to be still asking questions, as if he had not been there long. Everyone looked around when we entered. Then the brothers recognized our veiled companion and leaped to their feet in alarm.

"The lady claims she has a broken wrist or arm," I said. "I haven't examined it." I nodded respectfully to *Missier Grande.* "She was attempting to kill the courtesan Violetta Vitale with this dagger, which I recognize as coming from Palazzo Michiel. This is the note she used to gain admission, written by herself and signed with her daughter's name."

By then Bernardo and Domenico were helping their mother over to the examination couch.

Gasparo Quazza, *Missier Grande,* is a large and inscrutable man, whose very impassivity is intimidating. One glimpse of his red and blue cloak can disperse a riot faster than gunfire. No one could like him, but I respect him and he has always played fair with me. Once, very early in my apprenticeship with the Maestro, I did him a great favor by rescuing his infant daughter. That would not stop him from hoisting me on the strappado if the Ten so ordered, but they haven't done so yet.

"And the accused's name, *sier* Alfeo?"

"Donna Alina Orio, these noble lords' mother. May I assist my master while he attends to her injury?"

I fetched splints, scissors, and bandages from the medical cupboard. Quazza began questioning Matteo to get his side of the story. *Missier Grande* is not an inquisitor. He merely carries out the orders of the Ten and might have been told little about the Michiel case. He had been sent to fetch the book and no more. He could not ignore dramatic accusations of attempted murder, but he certainly would not arrest a noblewoman on his own initiative, nor me either, unless I had blood on my hands.

Looking alien and scared, Agnesina was huddled behind the door, in what I now thought of as Sister Lucretzia's chair. Isabetta remained hunched in the red chair, looking old and haggard, with a bandage around her head. Seeing that Nostradamus no longer needed my assistance I moved out of the way of Domenico and Bernardo, who were anxious to crowd in and fuss. I went to Isabetta and dropped to one knee. She looked at me with distaste.

"How do you feel?"

"Sick. I hate brandy."

"If that's all, you were probably very lucky." Her pupils were the same size and she did not seem sleepy; both good signs.

"When you held your family council of war on Sunday, why was donna Alina not invited?" I began with a question about Alina because Isabetta obviously did not want to talk with me and I knew that there was no great affection between the two ladies in Palazzo Michiel.

Sure enough, she wrestled her headache aside long enough to say, "She was indisposed."

"What sort of indisposed?"

"She had taken a fall."

"Nasty bruises?" I said. "The previous night I threw her to the ground in Campo San Zanipolo and fell on top of her. How did she dispose of the blood stains on her habit?"

Missier Grande was well within earshot and had stopped his whispered interrogation of Matteo. Isabetta showed no signs of being aware of him, but I noticed that she was speaking louder.

"I suspect she burned it in her fireplace, piece by piece. I noticed an odd smell in her room that afternoon."

"What was decided at Sunday's meeting, anyway?"

"Nothing!"

"You decided nothing, or you decided to do nothing?"

She pouted and for a moment I thought the spring had dried up. Then she said, "All we could agree on was that Fedele would visit Nostradamus and explain the folly of his ways."

Agreed maybe, but I suspected that Isabetta and Lucretzia had been two dissenting voices, if they had been allowed to speak at all. The point was immaterial now. I dearly wanted to find out how Bernardo had described Zorzi's death to the family, but I dare not ask that near our silent listener.

"One thing bothers me still," I said. "I didn't see the feet of the fake friar who stabbed Marina Bortholuzzi, but the one who killed Caterina Lotto had bare feet. To walk city streets without shoes requires either courage, stupidity, or years of practice."

Silence. I tried again.

"Jacopo always made sure he had an alibi, and Alina could slip down that secret staircase by herself, but how did she travel across the city? Did she dare hire a gondola? Friars carry no money and own none. It would be a long walk to San Zanipolo or Cannaregio for her, even with shoes on. I mean, when does a Venetian lady ever go for long walks?"

Isabetta eyed me like dog droppings on a doorstep, but again she couldn't resist the opportunity to tattle on the woman who had ruled her life for so many years.

"Oh, you'd be surprised. I know of one very respectable lady who used to slip out at night and prowl the city disguised as a friar. She started doing this during Carnival once, she said, but she enjoyed a wander in the moonlight so much that she began doing it quite regularly. Eventually her sons found out and tried to stop her. She went on a hunger strike until they relented. There was no danger, she said. No one would try to rape a graybeard friar and everyone knew that it would be no use trying to rob one. They gave her back her friar's robe and tried following her. They discovered that wandering was all she did: no secret liaisons, no dens of vice. So from then on they turned a blind eye."

"I am very grateful to you for that little story, madonna. Have you any thoughts on how Sister Lucretzia came to leave that incriminating book here?"

"I prefer not to speculate on that."

"Quite understandable. What puzzles me is, who could

have known what the diary contained, other than the person who wrote it? A resident who had lived in the house for many years would have more time to, er, explore the owner's bedchamber, shall we say, than servants who come and go so often. Jacopo is the obvious culprit, but a woman would have had easier access to the donna's bedchamber than he would."

Isabetta nodded. "This is true, *sier* Alfeo."

"And poor Alina, on Sunday, resting her bruises. Had she perhaps taken a spoonful of laudanum that day to ease the pain?"

The lady came very close to smiling. "Two spoonfuls."

"And you checked to see that she was resting comfortably. And when Fedele said that he would visit Nostradamus and try to scare him into abandoning his investigation, you took Sister Lucretzia aside and suggested . . . ?"

"Nothing at all! What will they do with her, do you think, *sier* Alfeo?"

"Donna Alina? The woman is deranged. A convent, I expect. It may look like a jail cell but it will be called a nun's cell. I don't think anything more than that. As for Jacopo . . . I think he has gone to the Ten and confessed. If so, I hope he may have saved his life." I also hoped that he was telling the inquisitors everything imaginable. They would rather send a strong young man like him to the galleys than to jail, and in that case they would not want to wreck his shoulders on the strappado.

Isabetta nodded. "That's about what I was thinking."

Then she uttered a cry that was almost a scream and I leaped to my feet.

Vizio Filiberto Vasco was standing in the doorway. He was mobile, although leaning on a *sbirro*'s shoulder, but he was a terrifying sight, his clothing soaked in blood and his face ripped to a wasteland of blood, hair, and raw meat. His eyes seemed to have escaped damage, for they burned black and white in that horrible gory mask. They were staring at me.

Missier Grande muttered an oath and strode over to him. The *sbirri* reported in low voices. I heard my name several times and saw other faces glance in my direction. One of the men pulled over a chair for the victim.

Another *sbirro* was holding a honey-colored cat by the tail. It had been almost blown apart by a firearm at close range, so that only its backbone still held its two halves together, and both were badly burned. It was, needless to say, very dead. It stank up the room.

Missier Grande beckoned me and I went across to them.

"Is this yours?" He pointed at the dead cat.

"Emphatically not, *capitano*. I have seen it around this area before, though, or another like it. Last Friday a cat blocked my way at just about the place we met it tonight. It was behaving so oddly that I knew right away it was rabid, so I retreated and went by another route."

"You did not report this to the priest, or a *sbirro*?"

"No doubt I should have done, but it happened very late at night, and I assumed that the animal would be dead by morning." I could not resist asking Vasco, "Did it bite you?"

He raised bloody hands as if he wanted to leap up and strangle me, but a *sbirro*'s grip on his shoulder restrained him.

"Witch!" he said. "You set your familiar on me! Witchcraft!" His lips were so torn that his speech was badly distorted.

"Not I," I told *Missier Grande*. "I saw something out of the corner of my eye and looked up. I shouted a warning and jumped back. I regret that he did not react fast enough."

Some of his own men were nodding.

"I charge him with witchcraft!" Vasco mumbled.

I sighed. "There was no witchcraft. I was running to Number Ninety-six because I had a very urgent message to deliver—that a woman might seek to commit a murder there. As it happened, I did arrive there just in time to prevent that dreadful crime. But on my way there, your *vizio* stopped me and demanded a book. I assured him that I had no book with me, and if he would just accompany me to the door of Ninety-six, so I could deliver my warning, then I would gladly come back here with him and give him the book I thought he wanted. And then . . . What was it were we talking about after that, just before the cat attacked you?"

Vasco did not answer. His men began to grin, because that had been when Vasco threatened to strip my clothes off in public. Dark alley or not, he had no authority to make such an obscene threat to any resident of Venice, whether nobleman or lowly beggar.

Missier Grande raised his eyebrows at the silence.

I have never reminded him of the debt he owes me and I never will. I have never seen him waver in his duty because of it—except maybe then. Or perhaps he was merely acknowledging all the priceless information I had just extracted from Isabetta Scorozini for him. Whatever the reason, that night he gave me the benefit of any doubt he may have had.

He pointed at the reeking cat. "See that gets burned," he said. "We must get the *vizio* to a surgeon for stitching."

"I do pray that it didn't bite him," I murmured. Rabies is always fatal, and it can take months for the symptoms to show.

Ignoring my good wishes, *Missier Grande* glanced around the company. "Their Excellencies may wish to question some of you tomorrow regarding these events, but now I bid you all a good evening."

33

So our guests departed. Giorgio took Matteo Surian back to San Samuele, and the Michiels left in their own boats.

I had not realized how hungry I was. Fussing and scolding, Mama Angeli had removed our uneaten *Bisato Anguilla Sull'ara* and produced piping hot *Canestrelli alla Griglia*. The Maestro, in an astonishingly good mood, raided his hoard of favorite wines for a bottle from a vineyard I had never heard of. Although impatient to return to 96 and comfort Violetta, I sat down without complaint and set to work.

"A most interesting case," he remarked between scallops.

I thought we had been very lucky to avoid disaster. "You may have trouble collecting a fee from Violetta. Her contract specified that you would catch a *man*."

He puckered his cheeks in satisfaction. "Jacopo was just as guilty, and the Caterina note condemns him as an accomplice."

I conceded the point with a nod. "But you have no hope of seeing any lucre from the Michiels."

He took a sip of wine and smacked his lips. "They will not want to face a lawsuit."

The gall of the man! Bill the brothers for proving that their mother had murdered their father?

"You gave the Ten your sacred oath that you had no interest in Zorzi's death."

He scowled. "So I did. A letter of sympathy, then, and hope that they feel like acknowledging my assistance with a suitable honorarium."

"Yes, master." I was more interested in eating than talking. The sooner I could leave the better.

"Of course the case is not quite closed. You still have to tie up a few loose ends."

"*Me?*"

"Yes, you." Nostradamus waved a fork vaguely. "Every adept develops his own particular style to some extent, his personal talents. I am detecting hints—as I should be by this time—that you are finding your own skills, your particular strengths. For example, after you almost caught Honeycat in the Campo San Zanipolo, you were quite insistent that the root of the mystery lay in Palazzo Michiel. That suggests a burgeoning intuition."

I swallowed. "Um . . . Maybe. Matteo had told me that the fake friar didn't smell like a friar, and the one I tackled certainly didn't. When I grabbed donna Alina tonight, I . . . I was reminded that she uses rose water. I think the whole palazzo has a scent of rose water, and that smell was what I was detecting—without realizing, of course."

My master banged his fist on the table. "You don't need to explain *everything*, you know!"

"Sorry."

"Remember that in future! But your tarot, now. What did *Circospetto* let slip so that the knave of coins was reversed? Certainly Sciara alerted us to the fact that Jacopo had been lying about the dagger, but we would have discovered that soon enough without him. By the way, who first misled us about the *khanjar* dagger?"

"Jacopo."

"No, he just encouraged your misapprehension. Think about it. What was the cat that sought you out so often, and what were its motives? Does it relate to XX of the major arcana?"

I probably blinked like an owl. Trump XX is Judgment, of course, the card my tarot reading had used to represent my helper. The cat had helped me several times and died for its pains, but that was the only resemblance I could see to the trump.

"What had a cat to do with angels blowing trumpets and the dead crawling out of their coffins?" I demanded.

The Maestro did not answer. "Are you starting to channel spirit help?"

"Not that I am aware of, master."

He smiled. "I'm sure you will, once you have meditated on these matters enough and attained the necessary trance state. Clearly the final answers are up to you this time."

I swallowed my last scallop and emptied my glass in barbaric indifference to the vintage. I pushed my chair back. "Then, if you will excuse me, master, I will start my meditation at once." I left at a run, before he could forbid me, but I thought I heard him chuckle as I went out the door.

After locked myself securely in my room, I headed for the central window. Number 96 would be back to normal now, so I need not fear feckless sword-wielding guards. Violetta had canceled her engagements, meaning I could have her all to myself for the whole night, perhaps several nights. And she should be especially grateful. The warrior's reward! Bliss! I opened the casement.

"*Arghrraw . . . ?*"

The cat was sitting on the window ledge, licking a paw.

Everyone knows that cats have nine lives. I reluctantly set aside my lustful ambitions. It was pay-off time.

"The cathouse is on the other side of the *calle*," I said.

"All right, Felix. I am grateful for all your help. What do you want from me?" Other than my immortal soul, perhaps.

The cat leapt silently down and stalked across to the door, where it turned its golden stare on me again. *"Arghrraw . . ."*

"You want to lead me somewhere?"

"Arghrraw . . ."

I retrieved my cloak from the wardrobe.

A dense winter fog had come in with the tide, so thick now that a golden halo glowed around my sputtering torch. Again I let myself out through the courtyard gate. Well muffled in my cloak, I followed the cat around the bends of the *calle* until we came to the T where we had first met, and where it had rescued me from Vasco that evening. Without hesitation it turned right, toward the *campo*, tail stiffly upright.

We met no one. With sounds muffled by the bone-freezing fog, the city seemed deserted. Canals lay flat as smoked mirrors, without a ripple. We headed generally westward, along deserted *calli* and across the empty Campo San Polo. I soon knew that we were heading to either the Palazzo Gradenigo or Santa Maria Gloriosa dei Frari. The latter was the one. In the middle of the Campo dei Frari, my guide jumped up on the gossip bench at the wellhead and turned to look at me.

"Too early?" I sat there also and opened the edge of my cloak invitingly. With fastidious paws the cat climbed up on my lap and lay down. Its fur was cold to the touch, which made me shiver, so I refrained from trying to stroke it. I made a covering for it, leaving its head free. It purred.

"Is there anything I should know?" I asked softly.

It curled up tighter and went to sleep. Count that a negative.

Perhaps I had been brought there to meditate in the dank and salty night. I needed no trance, though. The Maestro had identified the questions for me and the bones of the tragedy were visible now, like a rocky headland emerging from the fog. The last pieces came into view—the Judgment trump, and all those assorted pieces of paper I had seen in the last few days. Without meaning to, I had collected handwriting samples for just about everyone in the Michiel family.

Although it felt much longer, I probably sat there no more than fifteen minutes before I saw another torch approaching. The bearer was darkly anonymous, with his cowl raised. He had bare feet.

I rose, cradling the cat in one arm, raising my torch with the other.

"Bless me, Father, for I have sinned."

He stopped where he was, some paces back. "Who's that?"

"Alfeo Zeno."

"You have a good priest in San Remo. Take your burdens to him."

"These burdens concern you also, Brother Fedele."

"Good reason why I should not hear your confession."

"All the more reason why you should, as you were the cause of some of my troubles."

The friar sniffed. "You are insolent. Include that in your next confession."

"You may assign me a penance for it if you wish. I assure you that I have sought you out on a matter of grave urgency. I also bring sad news of your mother."

He shrugged and turned. "Come, then."

I followed him back the way he had come, and in a moment we came to magnificent doors of the great church. We paused there to stub out our torches and put them in the barrel, but then he noticed the cat.

"You can't bring that animal in here."

"This animal is evidence, Brother. It is possessed by a spirit, whether demon or not I cannot tell. And you may assign me a penance if I am deceiving you."

He stared at me for a long moment, as if assessing my sanity or lack of, but in the end he led me inside. Billows of fog swirled in with us. The great sculpted cavern was as cold and deserted as the world outside, lit by a few faint candles at the far end that seemed no brighter than fluttering stars. Its austere and awesome beauty was invisible, but the very stillness seemed holy; I could *hear* the silence as if it were built into the stone.

Fedele did not go to the confessionals, but to a candle stall near the door, where a single flame burned. There were two stools there, so we took one each. This time the cat refused my lap in favor of the floor, where it sat erect, staring at the friar, who ignored it.

"Never mind this nonsense about confession, my son. Tell me what troubles you." Fedele did smell like a real friar.

I drew a deep breath. "Father, I subverted an official of the Republic. I gave him money to break his oath of office. He let me see a confidential document."

Silence. Fedele's stare was as stony as the cat's.

"The trouble began long ago," I said. "But it lay dormant until last September, when the doctors advised *sier* Agostino Foscari that the time had come to send for a priest. You told us you were not that priest. Even so, I do not expect you to comment when I report what I believe the dying man said. He recalled the murder of your father and how that dastardly, sacrilegious act appalled the whole city and profaned the Basilica, the jeweled heart of the city, the embodiment of its dedication to San Marco.

"In their determination to find and punish the culprit, the Council of Ten broke its own rules and met in the morning, and the morning of Christmas Day at that. It then, I believe, did something that is legal but much criticized—it delegated to the Council of Three not just some of its powers but *all* of them in this case. Inquisitors Foscari, Gradenigo, and Pesaro were given free rein to find the perpetrator and bring him to justice as soon as possible.

"For several days they made no progress, while the Republic seethed with righteous fury and cries for vengeance. The Three must have questioned the dead man's youngest son, for he had an evil reputation for debauchery, cause to fear disinheritance by his father, and no witnesses to testify where he had been that night. But how could he have gotten into the Basilica? They would have been reluctant to charge the boy with so heinous a crime in the absence of positive evidence, for they were fair men, even if they might have treated a man of citizen class more sternly. They probably did not seriously consider the victim's widow, a noblewoman of unimpeachable character and breeding. How had she, who never went out unaccompanied, managed to obtain a mercenary soldier's dagger? No, the Three would have been hunting for some outsider, a thwarted business opponent, most likely. But they were baffled.

"Then came a breakthrough. An admitted prostitute accused Zorzi Michiel of confessing while talking in his sleep.

"The Three, armed with all of the Ten's powers, decided to take the anonymous letter seriously. They arrested Zorzi Michiel—in secret, as is customary—and they put him to the Question. They had his wrists bound behind him. They had him raised on the cord and then dropped. The pain is beyond description as the victim's shoulders are—"

"You need not elaborate," the friar snapped. "We have all seen it done in the Piazza. It is a common enough punishment."

"But the criminal usually knows how many hoists he must endure, and three or four are usual. In interrogations the witness knows only that the torment will continue until he can stand no more, and on, beyond even that. He may be repeatedly dropped. He may have weights tied to his feet.

His hands and face turn an incredible red. His joints are wrenched apart, his ligaments torn. The strain—"

"*Stop!*"

"If you wish. As you know, Brother, the pain is so terrible that a man who does not confess on the cord cannot be hanged. Zorzi did not confess. He died. Possibly his heart stopped, or his rib cage collapsed. It can happen. It did happen."

Pause. Then the friar whispered, "How do you know this?"

"Because it explains what followed. The state inquisitors faced a new problem. They still had no culprit and now they had a dead man to explain. What could they do next? Torture the boy's mother?

"They committed perjury. They disposed of the body and announced that they had found proof of Zorzi's guilt but he had escaped. Nothing too unexpected there, not in the Venetian system of justice. Case closed. But they made no effort to find out where he might have gone—they did not even question his mother about that!"

"Is there much more of this?" Fedele asked wearily.

"I fear there is, Brother. Because Foscari, before he died, perhaps prompted by his confessor, summoned *sier* Bernardo and told him the story of his brother's death. Bernardo went home and wisely told no one. Like a fool, though, he wrote it all in his diary, perhaps thinking that it might clear the family name at some far future date. He told the rest of you last Sunday. The sickness you had all thought cured erupted again; the buried corpse rose from the grave.

"Unfortunately, by then Jacopo had already read the diary. And he had told your mother that Zorzi had been betrayed by a whore. Your mother was the only person on earth who knew for a fact that Zorzi Michiel had not stabbed his father. All these years she had believed him safe and sound somewhere on the mainland. She determined to be revenged on the perjurer, whoever she might be."

"Alfeo, Alfeo! You are saying that my mother, donna Alina Orio, not only killed her husband but has now set out to kill all the fallen women in Venice?"

"Not all, only those your brother was patronizing in the weeks leading up to Gentile's death—any woman who might have lain with him *after* that sad event and betrayed his confession. She had a list of possible culprits because Zorzi recounted all his exploits to her, and she kept a record of them. I cannot explain her motives for doing so, but perhaps you have met such a sin before."

"You have any evidence to support this ridiculous allegation?"

"We did have. We had the diary your mother kept of her youngest son's fornication. Now the Council of Ten has that record. Both names and handwriting match. Your mother's crimes were proven beyond doubt this evening, Brother. She attempted to murder another courtesan, who would have been the fifth she had slain. Fortunately she was caught in time. She is presently at home in the custody of your brothers."

Fedele bent his head and prayed.

The cat watched him.

An aged man with a cane entered the church, put a coin in the box for a candle from the rack beside us, and then headed off toward the altar. He seemed not to have noticed our little group, not even the cat.

Shivering as the cold sank through to my bones, I waited until Fedele had completed his prayer and was ready for more.

"Now it is obvious why your mother hired Nostradamus. The diary named the courtesans but not the 'amateurs'—as your brother Domenico called them, the adulterous married women that Zorzi seduced. She hoped he would identify some of them for her to hunt down.

"Last Wednesday, you were summoned to the deathbed of Giovanni Gradenigo. He did not know that the friar who arrived at his bedside had once been Timoteo Michiel, any more than you had realized that your own father's death would play a part in his confession.

"Of course Gradenigo told you much the same story as Foscari had told his confessor, except that he went further, because one of Zorzi's women at that time was not a courtesan but a highborn lover, an adulteress by the name of Tonina. That is a rare name, and in this case it referred to donna Tonina Bembo Gradenigo, wife of Marino Gradenigo, Giovanni's son. After the Council of Ten proclaimed Zorzi Michiel's guilt and flight, she went to her father-in-law and admitted that Zorzi had been with her when Gentile was stabbed. Zorzi was innocent, she said, and must be pardoned and recalled. But Zorzi was beyond recall, alas.

"Gradenigo concluded that he had tortured an innocent man to death and blackened a noble family's name. Racked by guilt, he swore his daughter-in-law to secrecy. He abandoned politics and devoted the rest of his life to good works."

Pause. Then Fedele said harshly, "This is unbelievable!"

"There is an alternative," I admitted, "but it is even worse. Zorzi had truthfully said he could not produce an alibi without betraying a lady. Perhaps he was just posturing and believed that he could always tattle if he had to—until he learned, too late, that his lover was the daughter-in-law of one of the state inquisitors, one of the men interrogating him. Had he not known that? Did they break him on the cord so that he blurted out Tonina's name, but Gradenigo and his partners refused to accept the alibi and just kept on torturing him?"

After a moment Fedele mumbled, "Gradenigo was an honorable man."

That was the only answer I would ever get. It seemed that Zorzi had withstood the torment and taken his secret to the grave. Despite his debauchery, he had been no weakling.

"But you have no proof of any of this flummery," the friar said harshly.

"No, Brother? When Gradenigo was dying you blocked his dying wish to speak with Nostradamus. When you came calling on Sunday and the Maestro speculated that the murder weapon had been available in Palazzo Michiel, you encouraged him to think so. You did not actually tell a lie, although you knew very well that his guess was wrong. You did not want the case reopened, although by then you knew that Zorzi had been unjustly condemned. You were hiding something."

"I did not wish my family to suffer more," the friar muttered.

He was still twisting the truth.

"That too, no doubt," I said. "But now I have seen the anonymous letter, and last Thursday you wrote a note to me, if you remember." Of course one could not hang a man on a mere handwriting resemblance and I had compared them in memory only, but Fedele did not know this.

He sighed. "Many laws still define a cleric as a person who can read and write, Alfeo. Not a day passes but some illiterate person asks me to write a letter for him."

"Brother, you are still doing it! Do you honestly expect me to believe that you wrote out a virtual death warrant for your own brother without insisting that the true author's name be included?"

Fedele was silent, staring blindly along the great nave toward the faint candles on the main altar beyond the choir and screen.

"You composed that note!" I insisted. "Why, why? What motive could you possibly have had to bring a false accusation against your own brother in full knowledge of the horrors that might result?"

How could a man of God have lived with that guilt all these years? And for the last week he had lived with the awful knowledge of *how* Zorzi had died, and the certainty that he had sent his brother to the most terrible of deaths.

"Motive?" He lowered his gaze to the cat, but I did not think he was seeing the cat. He was seeing the past. "Motive . . . ? The human soul is a noisome pit, Alfeo. Priests know that better than anyone. I have had to listen to confessions even worse than my own. In that note I lied about who I was and what evidence I had, but I honestly believed Zorzi to be guilty. He was a fiend from hell!

"I took my vows at fifteen. I thought I could resist the temptations of the flesh. Zorzi was two years younger than I, and even then he laughed at me and said I would regret my decision. He was right, so right! I was wrong. The fires burned up far hotter than I had dreamed they would.

"Zorzi mocked me for it. At sixteen he was promiscuous. At nineteen he was a rake, a compulsive fornicator, and proud of it. He would brag of his sins to me, tell me he was taking my share also. Our father was a moral, upright man. Yes, he strayed sometimes, but we all do that. He supported the church and gave alms generously. He had tried to bring up his children to be good Christians and he succeeded with all but one of them. I adored my father!"

His mother adored Zorzi.

Timoteo swore an oath of chastity; Zorzi was a lecher.

Timoteo swore a vow of poverty; Zorzi wallowed in his mother's wealth.

Fedele swore absolute obedience; Zorzi did anything he wanted.

"Why did you denounce him?" I demanded.

"Because he killed our father!"

"He told you that?"

The priest raised his pain-racked eyes to mine. "Yes. No. Not quite. He swore he had a very good alibi, because he had been in bed with two harlots at the time, one for him and one for me. He was *laughing* at me! Yes, he did tell me he was guilty, but not in words. With smiles, gestures, hints . . . I knew and he knew I knew. I thought the end justified the means and so I brought him to justice. He fled into exile, we thought, and that seemed an absurdly lenient sentence, far less than he deserved. *I did not know about Tonina Gradenigo!*

"For eight years I felt no guilt. Then, not a week ago, I learned that I had been wrong! wrong! wrong! I betrayed my brother and I betrayed my mother, who had needed my help for so long. I had blamed her, not my father, for everything." He shook his head and started to gather himself, as if to rise and stalk away, back into his lonely, private hell.

"Zorzi died proclaiming his innocence and protecting his mistress, you think?" I said.

"Isn't that what you have been telling me?"

"No. He may have been protecting your mother. Can you not see the pattern, Brother?"

Fedele slumped back on the stool and stared at me. "Pattern?"

"Alina has been murdering women with Jacopo's help. Jacopo did the dirty work beforehand, the legwork. He found the victims and made all the preparations, even writing the notes that would lure the fallen women to their deaths. But when the time came, he would always arrange a good alibi, and she wielded the knife or the silken cord. That was how she had worked with Zorzi, Brother. She was repeating the pattern. Who do you think gave her the dagger eight years ago? Who put her up to it? Who suggested she save her poor baby from his daddy's wrath?"

"Zorzi was guilty all along?" The friar's eyes widened in sudden hope.

"Oh, yes. They were *both* guilty. Your mother you can see tomorrow . . ." It was my turn to stare at the cat, which had barely moved a whisker through all this long conversation. "But Zorzi? Could you forgive him now, Brother? If your brother were truly repentant and trying to make amends and came to ask for your blessing, could you give it?"

Fedele shouted at me, raising echoes in the huge church.

"If God gave you wings, would you fly, Alfeo? Do not ask such sacrilegious questions, such blasphemy! What happens now? You have called me Cain and I have not denied the charge. You will denounce me?"

"I could not. The only evidence that could be produced in court is the note and I ought never have been shown the note. In any case I would not, and neither would my master. In effect, although you lied, what you said was true. Zorzi was an accomplice in your father's death, as guilty as your mother and with far less excuse. But I would never denounce you, because of the cat."

Friar looked down at cat as if he had forgotten it. The cat stared back.

"Oh yes, the cat. Your familiar, I suppose?"

"No, Brother. Please understand that my master's first objective always was to prevent any more murders. He is an avaricious man, but a good Christian in spite of it. I happily do his bidding. Throughout this case, that cat has been *helping* me. I first saw it last Friday, when it blocked my way. I thought it must be rabid, so I went by another road, and that turned out to be a very fortunate decision. On Saturday I tried to stop your mother from killing Marina Bortholuzzi and was chased by a mob that thought I was the killer. The cat showed me a refuge. On Sunday it saved me from arrest. Tonight it intervened to save a woman's life. This is no ordinary cat, Brother."

Fedele crossed himself. "It is possessed by a demon!"

"A strangely cooperative, right-thinking demon. A honey-colored cat?"

It was, of course, the last of the tarot predictions. The card showing the helper had been Trump XX, Judgment, the dead rising from their graves. I said, "Do you believe in ghosts, Brother?"

The staring match continued.

"Well? Do you, Brother?"

Fedele whispered, "I suppose . . . Yes."

The cat shot into his lap. He almost fell off the stool, hands raised so as not to touch the animal. He must be even less of a cat person than I had been.

The cat cuddled itself in tidily, curled its tail around, and began to purr, staring up at the friar's anguished face.

I rose. "You can try an exorcism if you want, Brother, but perhaps you should just offer your blessing. He died unconfessed, remember. By the look of him, I think he is ready to give you his forgiveness and accept yours. Then he can be on his way."

At the door I looked back. The friar was embracing the cat and it seemed to be licking his tears.

ACKNOWLEDGMENTS

In the course of writing these stories about a parallel historical Venice, I have collected a personal library of over forty books, and borrowed many others from libraries. To acknowledge all of them would be tiresome and also unfair, because I have improved certain facts and made some accidental mistakes also.

For this story, though, I should acknowledge my debt to three books in particular. First, *The War of the Fists: Popular Culture and Public Violence in Late Renaissance Venice*, by Robert C. Davis, Oxford University Press, 1994. Matteo the Butcher is my invention, and I have changed the dates slightly, but otherwise I have followed Davis's account of a unique and astonishing custom in a city that has always been unique and astonishing. The Ponte dei Pugni is still there in San Barnaba parish, although nowadays it has parapets to keep people from falling off.

A book I have borrowed much from is *Coryat's Crudities* (1611). (I have the Scolar Press facsimile edition of 1905.) Thomas Coryat journeyed from London to Venice and back in 1605, mostly on foot, and thus invented the "Grand Tour." On his return he wrote what may fairly be called the first travel book since Pausanias's *Description of Greece* in the second century AD. Coryat includes vivid descriptions of much of the Venice of his day—although some of his observations are clearly wrong (he describes the nude statue of Mars in the Doges' Palace as representing the goddess Minerva). It is thanks to him that I know that the Campo San Zanipolo was not yet paved.

Another valuable eyewitness, an exact contemporary of my imaginary events, was Fynes Moryson, another Englishman. Moryson visited Venice in 1593, 1596, and 1597. I have a collection of extracts from his records published as *Shakespeare's Europe: A survey of the condition of Europe at the end of the 16ᵗʰ century*, edited by Charles Hughes, published 1903, reissued 1967 by Benjamin Blom, Inc., New York. I used Moryson's eyewitness description of the doge's procession to San Maria Formosa and the Christmas Mass in the Basilica. I have had a private tour of that church, which included sitting in darkness until those glorious, incredible golden mosaics appeared, gradually being illuminated. It is an experience one could never forget. Nowadays the trick is done with electric lights, of course, so I was fascinated to discover that it was done with candles back in Alfeo's day. But the Venetians have been managing the tourist trade since before the Crusades.

GLOSSARY

altana a rooftop platform

androne a ground-floor hall used for business in a merchant's palace

atelier a studio or workshop

barnabotti (**sing:** *barnabotto*) impoverished nobles, named for the parish of San Barnaba

Basilica of San Marco the great church alongside the Doges' Palace; burial place of St. Mark and center of the city

broglio the area of the Piazzetta just outside the palace where the nobles meet and intrigue; by extension the political intrigue itself

ca' (short for *casa*) a palace

calle an alley

campo an open space in front of a parish church

casa a noble house, meaning either the palace or the family itself *cavaliere servente* a married woman's male attendant (and possibly gigolo)

Circospetto popular nickname for the chief secretary to the Council of Ten

clarissimo "most illustrious," form of address for a nobleman

Constantinople the capital of the Ottoman (Turkish) Empire, now Istanbul

cortigiana onesta a courtesan trained in art, music, literature, etc.

Council of Ten the intelligence and security arm of the government, made up of the doge, his six counselors, and ten elected noblemen

doge ("duke" in Venetian dialect) the head of state, elected for life

ducat a silver coin, equal to 8 lira or 160 *soldi*, and roughly a week's wages for a married journeyman laborer with children (unmarried men were paid less)

fante (pl: *fanti*) a minion of the Ten

felze a canopy on a gondola (no longer used)

fondamenta a footpath alongside a canal

fraterna under Venetian law, brothers held family property in common unless they agreed otherwise; a joint-stock company in modern terms

giovane (pl: *giovani*) a youth or young man (note: *Giovanni* = John)

Great Council the noblemen of Venice in assembly, the ultimate authority in the state

khave coffee (a recent innovation)

lira (pl: lire) a coin equal to 20 *soldi*

lustrissimo "most illustrious," honorific given to wealthy or notable citizens

magazzen a tavern that does not sell food and stays open around the clock

marangona the great bell in the campanile San Marco, which marked the main divisions of the day

messer (pl: *messere*) my lord

Missier Grande the chief of police, who carries out the orders of the Ten

Molo the waterfront of the Piazzetta, on the Grand Canal

padrino (pl: *padrini*) literally a "godfather"; in the War of Fists, a leader and also umpire

Piazza the city square in front of the Basilica of San Marco

Piazzetta an extension of the Piazza, flanking the palace

riva a broad quay or street flanking water; literally a "shore"

salone a reception hall

salotto a living room

sbirro (pl: *sbirri*) a police constable

scuola (pl: *scuole*) a charitable confraternity open to both citizens and nobles

sequin a gold coin equal to 440 *soldi* (22 lire)

Serenissima, la the Republic of Venice

Signori di Notte young aristocrats elected to run the local *sbirri*

soldo (pl: *soldi*) see DUCAT

Ten see COUNCIL OF TEN

Three the state inquisitors, a subcommittee of the Council of Ten

traghetto a permanent mooring station for public-hire gondolas; also the association of gondoliers that owns it and ferries that dock at the station

Veneziano the language of Venice

vizio *Missier Grande*'s deputy

Dave Duncan is the author of more than forty books of fantasy and science fiction. He and Janet, his wife of more years than they care to admit, have three children and four grandchildren. They live in Victoria, British Columbia, the only city in Canada with a bearable climate. You can find him at www.daveduncan.com.